Fall back in love with the rich, deeply moving novels
of *New York Times* bestselling author
MARIAH STEWART

"She excels at creating emotionally complex novels that are
sure to touch your heart."

—*Romantic Times*

"Someone to watch and savor for a long time."

—*The Philadelphia Inquirer*

"One of the most talented writers of mainstream contemporary fiction. . . ."

—*Affaire de Coeur*

"Stewart's storylines flow like melted chocolate."

—America Online Writers Club Romance Group

A DIFFERENT LIGHT

"Warm, compassionate, and fulfilling. Great reading."

—*Romantic Times*

"This is an absolutely delicious book to curl up with . . .
scrumptious . . . delightful."

—*The Philadelphia Inquirer*

PRICELESS

"The very talented Ms. Stewart is rapidly building an enviable reputation for providing readers with outstanding stories and characters that are exciting, distinctive, and highly entertaining. *Priceless* continues to expand on this truly winning storytelling tradition."

—*Romantic Times* (4½ stars)

"Flowing dialogue, wonderfully well-rounded and realistic characters, and beautifully descriptive passages fill the pages of *Priceless.* . . . Not to be missed."

—RomCom

"In the style of Nora Roberts, Stewart weaves a powerful romance with suspense for a very compelling read."

—*Under the Covers Reviews*

MOON DANCE

"Enchanting . . . a story filled with surprises!"

—*The Philadelphia Inquirer*

"An enjoyable tale . . . packed with emotion."

—*Literary Times*

"Exciting . . . a joy."

—*Romantic Times* (4½ stars)

"Stewart hits a home run out of the ball park . . . a delightful contemporary romance."

—The Romance Reader

WONDERFUL YOU

"Compares favorably with the best of Barbara Delinsky and Belva Plain."

—Amazon.com

"*Wonderful You* is delightful—romance, laughter, suspense! Totally charming and enchanting."

—*The Philadelphia Inquirer*

MARIAH STEWART

A
Different Light

POCKET BOOKS

NEW YORK   LONDON   TORONTO   SYDNEY

Pocket Books
A Division of Simon & Schuster, Inc.
1230 Avenue of the Americas
New York, NY 10020

This book is a work of fiction. Names, characters, places, and incidents either are products of the author's imagination or are used fictitiously. Any resemblance to actual events or locales or persons, living or dead, is entirely coincidental.

This Pocket Books paperback edition January 2010

POCKET and colophon are registered trademarks of Simon & Schuster, Inc.

For information about special discounts for bulk purchases, please contact Simon & Schuster Special Sales at 1-866-506-1949 or business@simonandschuster.com.

The Simon & Schuster Speakers Bureau can bring authors to your live event. For more information or to book an event contact the Simon & Schuster Speakers Bureau at 1-866-248-3049 or visit our website at www.simonspeakers.com.

Cover design by Melody Cassen
Photo of woman © Veer

Designed by Peng Olaguera / ISPN

Manufactured in the United States of America

10 9 8 7 6 5 4 3 2 1

ISBN 978-1-4391-5510-3
ISBN 978-1-4391-6660-4 (ebook)

To Lauren, with best wishes
for your happily ever after

A
Different Light

1

The first light of day filtered into the room through lace curtains that fluttered in the dawn breeze, a remnant of the storm that passed through in the early morning hours. The soft scent of roses wafted upward, their branches sagging against the brick and stucco house like tired old ladies hunched together on a park bench.

Athena Moran opened her eyes and stared miserably toward the window through which the pale rays of sunlight had begun to dance. Last night's forecast for rain to last throughout the morning had raised her hopes that the inclement weather could perhaps even last the entire day. No such luck, apparently. She kicked off the thin blanket and went to the window to look up through the trees. The blue May sky was unblemished and the sun sparkled. It would be a perfect late spring day.

Damn.

Athen sat on the edge of the bed, running her fingers through the cascade of straight black hair that flowed down her back, and sighed. With the passing of the storm, her only excuse to avoid the annual Woodside Heights Memorial Day picnic had passed with it.

"Mommy! Look! The rain stopped!" Nine-year-old Callie danced into the room and pulled the curtains all the way back. A splash of gold spilled gleefully across the green carpet, mocking Athen with its cheerfulness.

"So it has." For Callie's sake, Athen forced a smile. Her daughter had eagerly looked forward to this day for the same reason she had dreaded it.

"So what time?" Callie skipped back across the hall to her room. "The picnic starts at eleven. What time can we leave?"

"Well." Athen debated the merits of going early and leaving early, or going late and possibly missing some of the people she most wanted to avoid.

Like, oh, maybe her father's mistress.

"Can we go right at eleven?" Callie pleaded.

"We have a few other things to do today, Callie," Athen hedged, trying to buy a little time before making a commitment.

"What other things?" Callie poked her head back into the room, half in and half out of a Hannah Montana T-shirt.

"Well, we have to go see your grandfather."

"We can do that on our way to the park. We can have breakfast right now and then go see Grandpa. Then we can go right to the picnic."

Pleased with the agenda, Callie ran off to finish dressing.

"It's only a picnic," Athen muttered under her breath as she grabbed her robe from the foot of the bed and headed to the bathroom. "I've gotten through worse days than this over the past couple of years."

She turned on the hot water and watched the shower stall steam, repeating, as if a mantra, "It's only a picnic."

The annual Memorial Day picnic sponsored by the Woodside Heights city fathers at Enid Woods Memorial

Park gathered together all past and present city employees and their families for a day of fun and games. As daughter of a former, much-loved city councilman, Athen had attended every year for as long as she could remember. As the wife of a city police officer, she had served willingly on various committees over the past twelve years.

Her father's stroke three years ago had been devastating. Paralyzed and deprived of speech, Ari Stavros was confined to a wheelchair at Woodside Manor, a small private nursing home on the grounds of an old mansion. It was never easy for Athen to sit and chat with her father's old cronies, especially on the one day each year when stories of him in his prime abounded. His old friends always made a special effort to share their favorite recollections with her, as if they needed to remind her of how witty he had been, how devoted to the city, in particular to the Greek community he had served for so long.

And then, there was *that woman*, the one her father never discussed with her even before his stroke took away his ability to speak.

If in the past facing her father's cohorts had been difficult, this year would be endlessly more painful. This year she would attend as the widow of the town's only police officer killed in the line of duty in over twenty-two years.

John Moran had been an enormously popular figure in the Woodside Heights Police Department. Street smart and well educated, handsome and affable, he'd been dubbed "Lucky" by the local press for his daring in the face of the dangers that increased steadily as the drug traffic began to flow from New York City, a mere twenty-five miles away. The new bypass off the interstate made it easy for the runners to slip into this small northern New Jersey city, make their connections, then zip back onto the highway toward

New York or Washington. Often, John Moran would be waiting for them when they hit the city limits. He'd made more drug-related arrests than anyone else on the force and, more than once, had been heralded for his bravery.

One night in January, on the corner of Marshall and Oak, John's luck ran out. A carefully planned drug bust had been aborted when a small child stepped out of a corner market directly between the undercover officers and the dealer. John had leaped from behind a Dumpster to pull the boy out of the way at the exact moment the dealer pulled his gun and fired. The child dashed away from the scene with no more than a scratch on his elbow and had run home to tell the tale while John Moran lay face down on the concrete, blood seeping from a hole in the back of his head.

The city had afforded Johnny a hero's funeral, with representatives from just about every law enforcement department in the state of New Jersey attending. The press had a field day with the story, and for days, Athen could not leave her house without being photographed. The slain officer's widow had been pure marble, blinking back tears that never fell in public, even when her sobbing daughter had clung to her waist as John's body had been lowered into the ground. Photographs of a dry-eyed, stony-faced Athena Moran, stoically comforting her in-laws and gently consoling her husband's partner, were picked up by the national wires and appeared in almost every major newspaper across the country.

For all her stalwart façade, those closest to Athen had been worried, knowing John's death had rocked her to her very soul. The once-dancing gray eyes were mirrors now only to the void within her, the dazzling smile only a memory. Her fiery beauty seemed to evaporate, leaving her face drawn and tired, a telltale sign that the tears that were held back in public had been wept in solitude every night for the past five months.

Athen had cut her ties to all but those most inti-mate of friends, had gone nowhere she hadn't needed to go. Her life revolved around her daughter and her fa-ther. Messages from worried friends left on her answer-ing machine went unanswered; those left with Callie were never returned. In her heart she knew there was a life to be lived, decisions to be made about her future and her daughter's, but she was unable to face them. She tried to convince herself that time alone would heal her, as if one day she would wake up and be whole again. She recog-nized self-deception for what it was, but was powerless to move beyond the spot where she stood.

Until that cold January day, even Athen's social life had revolved around John. Her one night out every other Monday had been with the wives of his fellow officers—dinner, gossip, support. Since John's death she'd only gone one time. It hadn't taken long for her to figure out that she was a reminder of what could happen to any one of them. Her shattered life was a whisper that their lives could be destroyed just as easily as hers had been. She'd read their minds in an instant: *There but for the grace of God . . .*

She went home early that night, and had lain awake for hours cursing John for having left her and taking her life with him. She never went back to the group, and none of her former friends ever called to ask her why, nor had anyone made an effort to urge her to come back.

Stepping from the shower and reaching for a towel to dry her hair, Athen tried to calm herself. Were it not for Callie, she'd skip today's event without a second thought. But she knew that her daughter, eager to see the girls and boys she'd known since birth, had been counting the days. Separated by neighborhoods and different schools, Callie always looked forward to Memorial Day and the chance to renew old friendships, play games, and swim in the lake. Athen silently prayed that Callie would not feel set apart from the other children as she herself now felt from their mothers.

Athen pulled a short pale yellow cotton knit dress over her head, and cinched it at the waist with a wide green belt. She sat on the edge of the bed and tied the multicolored leather thongs of her sandals around her slim ankles. She reached for a straw hat and tied the ribbons under her chin slightly to one side, and stepped back to look critically at herself in the mirror for the first time in months.

She looked pale, almost haggard, and woefully old-fashioned. She took off the hat and went into the bathroom and turned the light back on. She wound her hair up into a soft twist and secured it with a wide clip. Better, but not great. On a whim, she snapped a piece of dried baby's breath from the wreath that hung on the bathroom door and tucked the sprig into her hair. She rummaged through a basket of makeup that sat unused for months and found blush, a pale lilac eye shadow, and mascara. When she finished, she stepped back to take a look.

Passable, but just barely.

The merry widow I'm not, she told herself, *but I'll be damned if Callie's going to that picnic with a woman who could pass as her grandmother.* She added a little more blush and some lipstick. The extra color was an improvement. She snapped off the light and ran downstairs where Callie waited impatiently.

ATHEN PARKED AT THE FAR end of the lot where her car would be shaded by the century-old trees. Though not quite eleven, the morning temperature had already risen into the eighties, the humidity rising along with it.

"Mom, look! Grandpa's on the patio." Callie took off toward the back of the white-columned Georgian mansion, running up the grassy slope, all legs in white shorts and sneakers. She waved a greeting to Lilly, the nurse's aide, a large woman of gentle touch and gentle humor, and came to rest on the bricks at the feet of the old man in the wheelchair.

Only six when her grandfather suffered the first stroke, Callie had few memories of him as the strong giant of a man he once had been. As Athen neared the place where her father sat silent and imprisoned, her heart ached to see how the once-broad shoulders that had carried her as a child were now so small and slumped, the hands that had lifted her into the air now lifeless and pale.

"Pateras," she addressed him formally, with respect, in Greek. "I've a letter from Demitri."

She kissed the top of his head and pulled a chair closer, taking the thin white pages from the neatly addressed envelope. She read aloud the letter from her father's brother, first in Greek, then in English, and couldn't help but wonder how much he understood. She chatted, first a one-sided conversation with him, then a few words with Lilly. Falling silent, she watched Callie feed the ducks that gathered at the edge of the pond.

Lilly left them, and Athen confided the day's fears and anxieties to her father in a tearful whisper. She told him how the emptiness inside her seemed to widen rather than diminish as time passed; how her life had no meaning, no direction, except for her daughter.

"Did you feel like that when Mama died?" she asked softly. "I don't remember what it was like for you then, only what it was like for me. I was so little, but I remember you kept going, kept working and going to meetings. How did you have the strength to go back into the world once she'd left it?"

There would be no response, she knew, nor any recognition that he had heard or understood. The dark brown eyes—so like Callie's—flickered briefly. If there'd been a message there, its meaning was lost to her. The man who had been both mother and father to her since she was five years old seemed no longer to exist. Her guardian, her champion, who had so carefully and lovingly sheltered her from the world's dangers, could shelter her no more.

She watched a black speckled caterpillar inch across the bricks and waited for the enormous lump in her throat to dissolve. Moments later, Lilly appeared to announce lunch, and Athen kissed her father good-bye, promising to return tomorrow to bring him all the news from his old friends.

Callie greeted her mother's beckoning call with a loud "Yahoo!" as she dashed from the pond to the parking lot.

Athen's stomach churned as she pulled out of the drive, knowing this would be a very long afternoon. The fact that Diana Bennett was the first person she saw upon arriving at the park was a sign that the day was going to be every bit as bad as she thought it would be.

"Hey, Ms. Bennett. Hi!" Callie called out merrily and jumped out of the car.

"Is that you, Callie? Good Lord, you've grown another two—make that three—inches since the last time I saw you." Diana smiled. "I've missed seeing you out at the academy. Aren't you taking riding lessons anymore?"

"Mom said maybe I can start again in the fall. I hope so." Callie's sadness at having suspended her riding lessons over the past few months was evident. She brightened when she told Diana, "We just came from seeing Grandpa."

"Oh, can it, Callie," Athen muttered under her breath as she prepared to exit the driver's side.

"How is he this morning?" Diana's face tensed slightly.

"He's okay. The same." Callie's attention was diverted by the appearance of one of her old friends. "Hey, Mom, there's Julie. Hey, Julie! Wait up!"

Callie sprinted across the asphalt, turning back once to wave. "See ya, Ms. Bennett . . ."

"See you, Callie." Diana turned to Athen with obvious caution. "Hello, Athen."

Ari Stavros's mistress faced his daughter across the back of the car.

"How are you holding up these days?" Diana asked with what appeared to be genuine concern.

"I'm fine." Athen opened the trunk and made a point of checking the contents of Callie's beach bag: the carefully folded swimsuit, the towel, the sunscreen.

"I'm sure this is difficult for you. To be here, I mean, after John . . ." Diana began hesitantly.

"I'm fine." Athen slammed the trunk with more vigor than was necessary. How could Diana possibly know how hard things were for her?

"Look, if you need a refuge, if things get tough, I'll be here. If you need to escape . . ."

"I'm fine, Diana. Really," Athen insisted, averting her eyes to the left as another car pulled in to park next to her. Relieved to see an old friend behind the wheel, she turned her back stiffly on Diana as she greeted the newcomers. When she turned back, Diana was gone.

The day passed in a haze of handshakes and hugs, much as Athen had known it would, and she'd survived. Late in the afternoon, she sat alone on the small rise overlooking the playing field where the children's games were being set up. Searching the gathering crowd, she found her daughter in the midst of a group of young girls pairing off for the sack race, bending down to tie their legs together much as she herself had done so long ago. Unconsciously, her tongue sought out her front tooth, capped since that Memorial Day when she was twelve, when Angie Gillespie's foot, tied to Nancy Simpson's, collided with Athen's face as they fell in heap at the finish line.

Lost in reverie, she did not hear the approaching footsteps until it was too late.

"Oh, my, would you just look at that bunch?" Diana Bennett sat down beside Athen on the grass and nodded to the group of men gathered not fifty feet away, set off slightly apart from those flocked around the picnic tables. "Our fearless leaders. Defenders of the city. Dan Rossi's sitting on that beach chair like Caesar at a field maneuver, surrounded by all his little generals. The man who would be king."

Athen smiled wanly as the feeling of being trapped washed over her. She had no desire to engage in conversation, personal or political, with this woman. She turned her attention to the white-haired man in the dark glasses and the Mets cap.

Dante Rossi, the mayor of Woodside Heights and its undisputed political kingpin, was seated in a folding chair no doubt provided by a devoted employee to spare the boss the discomfort of perching on the edge of backless picnic benches with the peons all afternoon. His closest advisers stood around him in a cluster like the palace guard.

"And look at Harlan Justis—that's City Solicitor Justis." Diana pointed discreetly at the tall thin man who was lifting a tiny infant from the backpack with which a young mother struggled. "That son of a gun is playing the crowd. Now check out Rossi, watching Justis. See his face? 'Someone had better remind old Harlan that no one's a candidate until I say he's a candidate.'" Diana effectively mimicked the mayor's gruff tone.

"Candidate for what?" Athen asked, curious in spite of herself.

"Mayor, of course."

"What do you mean? Rossi's been mayor forever."

"It only seems like forever." Diana laughed. "But actually it's been a little less than eight years. Look at those meatheads. Circling like sharks around a capsized boat. Just waiting for Rossi to give one of them the nod for the big chair."

"But Rossi's still mayor."

"He won't be, after November." Diana leaned back on one elbow, a bemused expression on her face.

"Is he retiring?"

"Sort of. Forced retirement. City charter says four consecutive terms max. This is Rossi's fourth term."

"Oh." Athen slanted a glance in Diana's direction.

It was as close as she had ever been to the woman with whom her father had kept company for so many years. Athen didn't know for certain how many. Ari had never discussed Diana with his daughter. It had been John who'd mentioned his father-in-law's relationship with the young woman as if Athen had known about it. She had not.

Athen had been shocked when she learned that her father was seeing a woman who was only ten years older than Athen herself. Secretly, she hadn't been certain that what she'd felt wasn't jealousy as much as shock, but she'd never been sure if she was jealous because her father had found someone else to fill his hours, or if she was offended because it was part of his life he would not share with his daughter.

"What a sorry group," Diana went on. "They all want it so badly they salivate every time they get within ten feet of that office, bending over backward to please Rossi in any way they can."

"Why?" Athen studied the woman's face surreptitiously.

Diana had those Angelina Jolie lips that were so in vogue, and crystal blue eyes, long dark lashes, a peaches-and-cream complexion. Her short blond hair curled around her face in ringlets. She was very pretty, Athen conceded, though the very opposite of her mother, who had been olive skinned, with hair and eyes as dark as night.

"Because whoever he picks to run will win."

"But won't there be an election?"

Despite her best efforts, Athen couldn't help but compare the two women. Melina Stavros had been a tiny doll of a woman, small boned and fragile as a butterfly, chained to her home by the heavy braces she wore on both legs. Diana was soft and rounded. An athlete all her life, she excelled at tennis and riding, and played softball on the city's team. Athen had watched her play once, when the police department had challenged the City Hall team. It seemed at the time that everyone's eyes had been on Diana, the pretty young pitcher who stood boldly on the mound and struck out more than her fair share of batters.

"Elections mean nothing in this city, Athen," Diana explained. "It's a one-party town. Dan Rossi *is* the party. He'll choose his own successor."

"You mean whoever he picks will win? Automatically?"

And Diana is so contemporary. She wears makeup and has a career as a CPA. Mama was a page from an old-fashioned novel, old country in her ways and in her dress, beautiful in her simplicity.

"Oh, there'll be an election. But Rossi could run Lassie in this city and the party faithful would vote for the dog." Diana grinned. "And each one of those little mutts over there wants to be Rossi's dog. If he has a favorite, though, he hasn't let on."

"Why doesn't Rossi just name a successor and be done with it?"

If Melina had been candlelight, Diana is sunlight on an open field.

"What? And put a premature end to all this butt kissing?" Diana laughed out loud. "My guess is that Rossi doesn't want to give it up, pure and simple. He loves it all too much. He loves the power."

"But he'll still be head of the party, right?"

"It's not the same." Diana shook her head. "My gut tells me if Rossi could find a way to hold on to it all, he would."

"What could he do if the charter says four consecutive terms?"

"Good grief, Athen, didn't you learn anything about politics from your father?" Diana chided good-naturedly, blue eyes twinkling.

"No." Athen was hoping that her father would not be mentioned, and was uncomfortable now that he had been. "I've never been particularly interested in politics."

"That's what brought us together, Ari and me, you know? I was just starting out in the finance office; Ari was already on the City Council." Diana stopped, realizing that Athen had deliberately turned her face from her. "But you don't really want to hear about that, do you?"

"Not really." Even to herself, Athen sounded childish.

"Why? Are you afraid I have something of him that you don't? And even if I do, what would that take from you?" Diana spoke quietly, but there was anger beneath the soft tone. "This you need to know: I have loved that man for seventeen years. That's right, since you started college. I've stayed in the background and never intruded into your life. Not when Ari had the stroke. Not when John died and I wanted to comfort you, because I know how much you've lost."

"You've no idea what I've lost, Diana."

"You think that all these years I've been merely an easy diversion for a lonely widower, don't you? You can only think of one reason why your father would want to be with me, right?" Tears swelled in Diana's eyes but they did not fall.

Embarrassed, Athen sat in silence.

"How old are you now, Athen? Thirty-five?" Diana stood. "Don't you think maybe it's time you grew up and accepted your father as a man who has a life that doesn't revolve around you? Can't you grant him that small measure of independence? And if he's found happiness with someone who isn't your mother, can he not be forgiven for that?"

Stung and surprised by the outburst, Athen watched with flushed cheeks as Diana stalked off in the direction of the parking lot.

❧ 2 ❧

Athen remained on the spot, wrapped in embarrassment at having caused such an impassioned and unexpected outburst. While not wanting to know the details of her father's affair, she had no desire to intentionally hurt Diana. And Diana had been right. Athen assumed that her relationship with Ari had been strictly fun and games, that he wasn't proud of the fact and so had never involved Diana in any way with his family. Ari had attended his daughter's wedding unescorted, and had spent every holiday, every birthday with Athen and John, though, she now recalled, he had always departed immediately after dinner.

Diana's quiet declaration of love had left her disconcerted. Had Ari returned that love? For the first time Athen wondered if her failure to offer her father the option of bringing a guest to share Christmas or Thanksgiving or birthday celebrations had hurt him. Had he been reluctant to ask Athen to share him with Diana, or had he been unwilling to share Diana?

The children's games concluded and Callie jubilantly ran to her, proudly showing off the medals she'd won for swimming and for the pie-eating contest.

"Let me guess," Athen said wryly. "Blueberry, right?"

"How'd you know?" Callie asked.

Athen laughed and pointed to the front of Callie's shirt.

"Oops." Callie giggled and rubbed the purple stains.

"It's okay, honey. It'll probably come out in the wash, and if not, then you have a new shirt to garden in." Athen glanced at her watch. "Hey, it's getting late. Why don't you start gathering up your things, and we'll . . ."

"Aw, Mom, it's not that late," protested Callie.

"It will be by the time you find everything and we get out of here. Go. Find your things. Meet me at the car in fifteen minutes."

Athen stood and brushed off the grass clinging to the backs of her bare legs. She looked over at the picnic grove and saw that Dan Rossi was on his feet, preparing to leave. She should go pay her respects, she told herself. He and her dad had served together on the City Council for many years, and whenever Dan saw Athen, he never neglected to remind her that the two men had been great friends. He'd been a great source of support to her not only after her father's stroke, but after John's death as well.

She caught his eye from thirty feet away, and a broad smile of recognition spread across his face. The old man abruptly ended the conversation in which he'd been engaged. Beaming broadly, his arms opened to enfold her.

"Athen, sweetheart." He embraced her warmly. "What a joy to see you. You are well? And Callie? And your blessed father? You must tell me how he is doing. Not a day passes that I don't think about him. Come and walk with me a bit and we'll talk. I haven't seen you since, well, since that terrible day when John . . . God rest his soul." Rossi shook his head sadly. "You're getting your checks on time? The worker's compensation, the pension . . . ?"

"Yes, everything's been on time, Dan. Everyone's been very helpful."

"God help them if they're not," he told her. "We take care of our own, that's a fact. You need anything—I mean anything—you call me directly, you hear? Not Mary Fran, you call me. Though, of course, soon enough Mary Fran won't be there. You remember Mary Fran Ellison?"

"Sure."

"My right hand. Best assistant anyone ever had. Gonna be next to impossible to replace her."

"Is she retiring?" Mary Fran must be close to seventy, Athen recalled.

"Back surgery. Had a car accident last year, let them operate on her back. Worse now than she was before, can't sit for more than an hour at a time. Anyone ever wants to operate on your back, Athen, you tell them to go to hell, hear?" They were nearing the parking lot, and Dan waved to a departing fireman and his young family. "What are you doing with yourself these days, Athen? Did I hear you went back to teaching?"

"I went back as a substitute last month. I thought maybe I'd go back to teaching full-time when Callie started middle school. I quit when she was born because I wanted to stay home with her, after having lost my own mother when I was so little." *Why am I babbling?* she asked herself, a flush settling on her cheeks.

"Ah, but that was a tragedy, her dying so young. If I've said it once, I've said it a million times: Melina Stavros was the most beautiful woman I've ever known. We all mourned her, Athen. Just as we all mourned your John. As fine a man as ever wore the uniform, no question about that. Ah, and your father . . . well, it breaks my heart to even think about it." Rossi pulled a white linen handkerchief from his pants pocket and wiped at his eyes. "So . . . you're thinking about maybe going back to the classroom, eh?"

"I'm not sure when. When I'm ready." She glanced away.

"Well, I'm a great believer myself in the importance of timing, you know. Always have been. Just don't put it off too long, hear? Not enough time in our lives that we should waste a bit of it." He waved to a passing group, calling after them, "Good to see you. Glad you could make it."

They walked toward the spot where Athen parked her car. Callie was nowhere to be seen.

"So what do you do with your time?" he asked directly.

"Not a whole lot."

"That's not good, Athen. Not good at all. You're young, you've a whole lifetime ahead of you."

"It's just so hard. . . ."

"I know it is. Didn't I lose my own Madeline two years ago? Don't I know how hard it is to go on? But you have to. My best advice to you is to find something meaningful to do with your time. Find a job that matters to you. After Maddie died, the only thing that kept me going was the job."

"I couldn't handle teaching full-time right now. I'm at too many loose ends, Dan. It wouldn't be right to inflict someone in my present state of mind on a classroom full of children."

"It doesn't have to be teaching, Athen. I bet there's plenty you could do if you gave it some thought. You gotta find something to fill the hours, honey. Get your life moving forward again." He stopped again to shake a hand or two. "Hey, there, Bob, Susan, glad you joined us. Sue, tell your sister we missed her today.

"Like I was saying, Athen, you should look into finding a little something to keep your mind occupied, you know, until you get your feet back on the ground again. Think about it. Anybody would love to have you on their staff, bright and pretty as you are. Love to have you myself." He stopped in midstride and grabbed her arm. "Now that's an idea. Why not come to work for me?"

"For you? Doing what?"

"Answering my phone, keeping the wolves from the door, keeping my day organized."

"Dan, lately I can't even organize my own days."

He didn't appear to have heard. "The more I think about it, the more I know it's just the thing for both of us. I need to replace Mary Fran, and I can't think of anyone I'd trust more than you."

"Dan, I can't replace Mary Fran. I've never worked in an office. I have no office skills."

"Nothing to it." He dismissed her objections with the wave of a beefy hand. "Just like running a house."

She shook her head. "Thanks, Dan, I appreciate the offer, but no, I don't think so."

"Don't give me an answer now, give it some thought."

"Dan, I can't commit to anything long-term right now."

"Athen, we're not talking long-term." He laughed good-naturedly. "Since I'll be out of a job myself come November, you'll be, too. The new mayor will want his own right hand sitting outside that door, not someone loyal to his predecessor. Long-term employment is definitely not an issue here. But it will get you out of that house for a little while and give you a change of scenery, which I suspect you need."

"Still, I don't . . ."

"Here's my car now." He motioned to the driver of a

dark blue Cadillac inching its way through the crowd. "All I ask is that you give it some honest consideration."

She nodded and held out her hand to him.

"What handshake?" He scoffed. "Give the old man a hug, eh? There you go, now, great to see you. You think about what I said. You give me a call, hear? My love to your dad."

THE WHIRLWIND THAT WAS DAN Rossi disappeared into the back of the waiting Cadillac. The driver hesitated momentarily as the throng jamming the parking lot parted like the Red Sea to permit the vehicle to pass.

"Hey, Mom! Julie and Jessie are going to the ice cream parlor on the way home. Mrs. Myers said I could go if it's all right with you," Callie called from five cars down.

"Okay, Athen?" Liz Myers stuck her head out the window. "We won't be long. We'll drop her off on the way home."

"That's fine. Thank you," Athen called back, motioning Callie to her and scrambling in her bag for her wallet as Callie ran to her with an outstretched hand. Athen handed her a five and reminded her that there'd be change.

"Thanks, Mom." Callie gave her an abbreviated hug and ran off.

The crush of departees descended upon the two-lane exit like ants jockeying for position on an M&M. Athen waited patiently for her turn to pull onto the highway. At the last minute, she changed her directional signal from left to right, and eased onto the road that led back through the park.

The air was cooler with the descent of the sun behind the trees and she opened the windows to let the evening breeze flood the car. She turned on the radio, still set to John's favorite classic rock station, KROC out of New York. Though jazz was more to her preference, she hadn't been able to bring herself to change it. She turned it off abruptly.

She drove absentmindedly for a few minutes, thinking how the day had turned out to be okay after all. Better than okay, she admitted. Except for that little to-do with Diana. She rounded a curve, breaking sharply to avoid the opossum that had stepped from the shoulder onto the asphalt. The animal froze, and Athen could see the sparks from a dozen tiny eyes peering over the mother's back. "Careful, Mama," Athen whispered as she drove around the frightened creature.

She slowed at the end of the road, and realized she'd driven to the back entrance to Woodside Manor. Might as well stop in for a minute, she thought, and say good night to Dad. Wonder what he'd think about Rossi's job offer.

She followed the dirt drive to the front entrance, and headed for the section of the lot closest to the building. For the second time in less than five minutes she slammed on her brakes.

In the first spot nearest the gate sat Diana's little blue sports car.

The motor running, her arm resting on the open window, her chin in her hand, she debated for only a moment before quietly turning the car around and heading for home.

THE FIRST CRACK OF THUNDER rattled through the night silence and the heavens came suddenly to life, a raucous opening act for the rowdy sound and light show about to begin in the skies above Woodside Heights.

Callie stumbled through the dark, fleeing to the safety of her mother's bed.

"It's okay, Callie." Athen patted the left side of the bed in answer to her daughter's unspoken question. "Come on. Climb in."

Callie snuggled in and curled up beside her mother. Athen stroked the back of the child's head, her fingers catching here and there in the wild tangle of curly brown hair.

"I hate when thunder does that," Callie mumbled. "When it sneaks up on you in the night. Like it's waited up there in the sky all day till you go to sleep so it can jump out at you in the dark and scare you half to death."

Callie yawned, and inched closer. "Tell me again why we have thunder. And don't give me that stuff about the trolls bowling."

Athen lay wide-eyed, staring at the ceiling.

"I don't remember," she admitted sheepishly. "I know it has something to do with positives and negatives, but right at this minute I can't seem to recall the details."

"Daddy would know," Callie said quietly.

"Yes, baby," Athen whispered. "Daddy would know."

Athen closed her eyes and tried to return to sleep, but the rain rushed against the windows as if gushing from a giant hose.

She lay awake listening to Callie's breathing until she was certain her daughter was on her way toward peaceful slumber, then eased her legs over the side of the bed. The soles of her feet slid over warm fur. The dog's huge head snapped up quickly to identify the human whose foot dangled just slightly over her neck.

"Go back to sleep, Hannah." Athen leaned over to pat the dog's yellow rump, then walked quietly toward the doorway. Under one foot, a soft rubber object squeaked. Hannah's favorite toy, a small orange hedgehog, lay right inside the door, close by, as always, to Hannah.

Quietly, Athen crossed the hall to Callie's room and closed the windows, proceeding next to the back bedroom. Hesitating only briefly, she turned on the light, averting her eyes from the sudden brightness. She stood in the doorway, surveying the remnants of the only home-improvement project John had ever failed to complete.

The wallpaper table still bisected the room, a sheet of paper cut, but not hung, held flat by a level at one end and a book at the other. The earbuds still dangled from the iPod he'd left on the ladder shelf. He'd finished two walls the day before he died, and had tried to finish a third on what was to be his last morning. Unaware of his fate, he'd risen early and proceeded to work on the new guest room in preparation for a visit from his sister, Meg, the following week. He'd worked steadily through the morning, eager to finish that one wall before he'd have to stop, change into his uniform, and report for the four-to-midnight shift.

Athen had not been there when he left for work that afternoon, having had a number of errands to complete before picking up Callie at the school bus and taking her to the library. She'd run through the afternoon's itinerary a thousand times in her mind since that day. Which of her tasks might she have omitted that would have brought her home in time to say good-bye? The supermarket, where she'd stood in line for ten minutes, her cart filled with who could remember what? The drugstore, where she'd leisurely thumbed through magazines before making a selection from the paperback novels that lined the shelves of one aisle? Had she picked up

Callie at three at school instead of at the bus stop a half hour later, would they have returned from the library before he left the house? Where had she been when he closed the door behind him for the last time?

And had she arrived home in time, would she have known that it would have been good-bye? Would she have kissed him more passionately, some unknown intuition gnawing at her to give him yet one more hug?

She had not said good-bye, had not kissed him.

Before leaving the house, she'd stood in the doorway watching his meticulous measuring of the wallpaper. He looked up from his work and yanked the earbuds off.

"Looks great," she'd said. "The room will be gorgeous. Certainly suitable for visiting royalty."

"Or at the very least, my sister. Where're you off to?"

"Errands," she'd replied. "Then to pick up Callie for a very quick trip to the library so she can get the one last book she needs to complete her social studies report."

"What's she doing? Something on Native Americans? She talk to Meg?"

"Last week. She also talked Meg into taking photographs of the reservations around Tulsa and mailing them out so she'd have them in time for her report, which is due before Meg's arrival. Callie figures this to be an easy A."

John had chuckled, knowing his sister, who coanchored the evening news at a network affiliate in Tulsa, would gladly give her only niece more information than any nine-year-old would ever be able to assimilate.

"Well, hopefully, Meg won't get carried away and include some of her boyfriend's political speeches on the abuse of the Native Americans at the hands of the U.S. government."

"Clinton has historical documentation to back up . . ."

John frowned and cut her off with a wave of the paste brush.

"I know, I know. I'm aware that everything he said was true. I just didn't need to hear it all night Christmas Eve and all Christmas Day. I'm glad Meg's not bringing him back with her this time."

"Frankly, I'd rather see Callie present the truth in her report."

"Whatever. Anyway, it'll be great to have the old Meg back for a few days instead of the political activist she turns into whenever he's around."

"What makes you think she only turns it on for Clinton's sake?"

"Because I know my sister. Changes her commitments every time she changes men. Been doing it all her adult life."

"Well, since she isn't seeing him anymore, it really doesn't matter."

Athen watched him climb the ladder and press the paper onto the wall, expertly smoothing it out with the long flat brush and eliminating tiny ripples with his fingers, pushing it firmly into place with his hands.

"What do you think? Think the room will be done by next weekend?" He stepped back to admire his work.

"I think so. It looks wonderful. The furniture will look great in here, don't you think?" She shifted her weight from one foot to the other, visualizing for the hundredth time the way the room would look once it was completed.

"I do." He nodded as he replaced the earbuds.

The pale butter yellow paper dotted with white roses would be the perfect backdrop for the bedroom set stored in the attic. They'd brought the furniture from her father's house before it was sold two years ago, after Ari suffered his second stroke and Athen had to face the fact that he would never leave Woodside Manor. The 1930s walnut bed, two dressers, and two bedside tables had been polished and readied to be moved downstairs.

"Do you need me to pick up anything for you?" A glance at her watch told her she needed to leave if all her errands were to be accomplished in time to meet the school bus.

John stood on the ladder, looking down at her, singing along with the song playing on the iPod.

"You say something?"

"I asked if you wanted me to pick up anything for you while I'm out."

"We're running dangerously low on Doritos."

"Message received." She turned to go.

"Hey, Thena," he called to her as she reached the top of the steps.

She went back to the room and stuck her head through the doorway.

"Wait up for me tonight," he said.

"What's in it for me?"

John smirked.

"Well, then." She smiled up at him and blew him a kiss. "I guess I'll see you when you get home."

John put the headset back on and resumed singing, his voice following her through the hall and down the stairwell.

"Damn you, John Moran. Damn you for dying." Standing alone in the room where she had last seen him alive, she spoke aloud to the apparition. "Damn you . . ."

The wind blew up again suddenly, sending a cold chill of rain into the room. Athen closed the window as the thunder began to roll with renewed vigor, the sky beyond the trees now bright as midday, the lightning now a frenzied dance across the sky. She turned the light off, unable to bear another second in the room. She leaned against the wall in the hallway, wiping her face with the hem of her nightshirt.

A brilliant flash illuminated the entire house. A deafening crash like nothing she'd ever heard split the night, and was followed by the terrible tearing of wood. The house seemed to shake to the foundation, as if sitting upon an earthquake's fault.

"Mommy!" Callie screamed in terror.

"I'm right here, baby." Athen went quickly to the bedroom and collided with Callie in the doorway. "Lightning struck something very nearby. I think it might have hit one of the trees in the backyard."

Callie clung to her in fright. Hannah howled as sirens screamed above the storm.

"Come on, Callie. Let's take a look."

Athen turned on the hall light as they hurried into Callie's room. They pulled aside the curtains at the window overlooking the backyard and gazed down in horror. A tree had fallen, flattening most of the garage.

"Daddy's tree!" Callie cried. "Oh, Mommy, it's Daddy's tree!"

Callie buried her head in her mother's chest and wailed. The magnolia that John had planted the day they moved into the house twelve years ago lay split right down the middle.

Lights flickering in the homes of their neighbors announced that most of the street had been awakened by the crash. The few who had slept through it were surely now being roused by the sound of the police cruiser as it rounded the corner at the end of the street.

"You okay, honey?" Athen caressed the trembling child. "You want to get your robe on and come downstairs with me? I think the worst of the storm is over now."

"Why are the police here?" Callie tugged on her robe and followed her mother into the room across hall.

"I guess they want to make sure no one was hurt and that no wires were brought down." Athen pulled on sweat-pants and a sweatshirt just as the doorbell rang. Hannah, barking and growling, flew down the steps.

"Hey, Fred, come on in." Athen opened the door and greeted the officer.

Fred Keller quickly stepped inside the entry as the lightning from the passing storm flashed in the distance.

"Are you guys all right?" the short stocky officer asked.

"We're fine." She nodded. "But it looks like we lost one of our trees."

"Any wires down?"

"I don't know."

"We'll take a run out back and have a look. You got any lights out there?"

"On the back porch. I'll turn them on for you."

Fred went back out the front door, where he was joined by three other officers who were already heading up the driveway.

Athen and Callie turned on the back porch lights and peered out the door. John's magnolia had been split cleanly in two, one half smashing the garage, the other huge section demolishing their neighbor's fence.

Athen went out on the back porch and surveyed the damage wordlessly. Callie wrapped her arms around her mother's waist and cried.

"Daddy's tree is gone, and it smashed his garden, too."

She pointed across the lawn to John's prized perennial beds, covered now by the huge tree trunk.

Damn, cursed Athen silently. The tree would have to be removed, the garage rebuilt, the Sullivans' fence replaced.

"Daddy would know what to do," Callie lamented.

"And so do I, pumpkin," Athen assured her.

When he finished cursing, John would have called their insurance agent. And that would be Athen's first move, first thing in the morning.

❧ 3 ❧

The sound of the slamming car door at the end of the drive announced the arrival of the insurance adjuster, right on time. Athen peered out the window as the young woman started toward the front door, and was there to open it before the bell was rung.

"Mrs. Moran?" The adjuster handed her a business card as she introduced herself. "I'm Susan Watson. Mr. Fisher, your agent, called this morning and asked that I come out first thing."

"Yes, he told me to expect you. Thanks for being so prompt. I guess you're pretty busy today, after that wild storm." Athen ushered her into the house.

"We insure a lot of homes in Woodside Heights, so yeah, we're jammed." Susan followed Athen into the kitchen. "Would you mind if I called my office before we go outside? We're supposed to call in as soon as we get to each stop."

"I don't mind." Athen waited by the back door while Susan keyed her phone and reported in.

"Let's take a look at that garage." Susan tucked her cell phone back into her bag when she finished her call. She trailed behind Athen through the back door and into the yard, where steamy fingers of mist rose like smoke from the wet grass that was warming in the sun.

"Boy oh boy." Susan whistled, looking at the remains of the garage, the front section of which lay in a heap on the ground. "Please tell me that your car's not in there."

"It wasn't. I was lucky."

"I'll need a list of the contents of the garage with as much information as possible. Brands if you know them, receipts if you have any. List where and when you purchased things and, if you remember, how much you paid. We'll do the best we can for you, but the more information you give us, the more accurate your settlement will be. I'll have a contractor out by tomorrow morning to appraise the garage."

"I appreciate that you came out so quickly. Fortunately, my husband kept very detailed records, so I should be able to find receipts for most of the larger items."

Susan walked to the base of the tree and took a camera from the large satchel-like purse that hung over her shoulder and began to photograph the damage. "We won't pay to replace the tree, but we'll pay to remove it and whatever damage it's caused. I might as well go over and talk to your neighbor while I'm here."

The adjuster started across the yard in the direction of the next property. She paused and looked over her shoulder.

"It's a shame about the tree, Mrs. Moran. Must have been a beauty. It's going to be hard to replace it."

Harder than you know, Athen thought sadly.

༺༺ ༺༺

A WEEK LATER, ATHEN STOOD at the kitchen window, watching the contractor's men clear away the debris. First they cut the remains of the tree into large chunks. A pang shot through her when the chain saw made the first cut. Who knew it could hurt to see a tree cut up? When they finished, the stump was ground out. Nothing remained but a pile of sawdust where the tree once stood. It was almost as if it had never existed.

In her mind's eye she could see the sapling John had proudly planted. Dripping with sweat from his effort, he had walked back to the porch where she waited, hands on her hips, wondering why, with so much unpacking to do, he had chosen moving day to plant a tree.

"My grandmother always said the land's not yours until you plant something on it," he'd told her solemnly.

She'd smiled at his Irish sentimentality and pulled his wet face to hers to kiss him. She still remembered the taste of sweat and grime, and she remembered how he'd laughed and wiped away the smudge he'd left on her chin with his fingers.

From the rubble, one of the laborers lifted her prized bicycle and tossed its twisted frame onto the Dumpster. John bought it for her five years ago when she'd become serious about her biking. She hadn't ridden since that last sixty-mile race, back in the beginning of November, before the weather turned cold, before her life had been turned upside down, before the things that used to matter lost their meaning. She had declined invitations from members of her bike club all through spring. She simply lacked the energy to join them.

Her attention drifted back to the here and now, where the contractor's assistant was removing debris from the garage.

"Hey!" she yelled when she saw what was in his hands." Don't throw those out!"

The startled young man looked over his shoulder as she flew off the porch.

"The insurance company will pay for new ones," he told her.

"We don't want new ones. We want these. They're not damaged."

"Where do you want them?"

"I'll take them." She held out her arms and he passed her the assortment of garden implements. "Are there any more undamaged?"

He disappeared into the shell of the garage and brought out a hoe, a short-handled shovel, a smashed bucket from which poked the shiny green handles of a transplanting trowel, and a long, thin dandelion digger.

"You find any more of this stuff, you bring it to me, okay?"

"Sure."

She carried John's gardening tools onto the porch and inspected them, surprising herself with the delight she felt at having found them all intact. She couldn't wait to show Callie.

Athen spread the tools on the wooden deck like newly found treasure. John had been passionate about his gardens, devoting hours to plot plans and soil improvement, nurturing the new plants he brought home from Ms. Evelyn's little nursery up on the hill. Every January, he would eagerly await the arrival of the newest nursery and seed catalogs. Then he and Callie would sit for hours, poring over the offerings until they made their selections, carefully planning what they'd plant and where. When the weather warmed, he and Callie would set out for Ms. Evelyn's nursery to make their purchases. Athen rarely accompanied them, having little interest in gardening beyond the dishes she could create with the fresh produce, and the spectacular bouquets that would fill the house later in the summer. From May through October, their yard would be ablaze with color from every angle, and passersby would ring the doorbell to express their admiration.

Athen stared down at the tools of John's leisure hours, the solid hardwood handles tipped in dark green enamel. They were imported from England and made to last a lifetime; she'd ordered them from one of his catalogs seven years ago as a special surprise. She'd first found the catalog on the kitchen counter, open to the page upon which the tools were displayed. Several days later, the catalog—open to the same page—had been left on the dining room table. The following week, when she found it in the living room, open on a table next to John's favorite chair, she'd taken the hint and ordered the lot of it for his birthday. He'd been more pleased with his garden tools than with any gift she'd ever given him.

She'd give them to Callie as soon as she arrived home from school. It had been Callie who'd worked by his side—digging, planting, and weeding. She would be thrilled to have these precious reminders of her father and the special times they'd shared.

At noon Athen went into the house and poked through the day's mail. She straightened the kitchen for what seemed like the fifth time. She looked around for some small task with which to occupy herself. Laundry? Done on Saturday; there weren't enough clothes in the hamper to justify the effort. She'd paid the household bills on Thursday, shopped for groceries on Friday.

She sat at the kitchen table and looked out the window

at the view, so stark with the absence of the tree, and wondered what to do with the rest of the day. With the rest of her life. When the tears began, she made no effort to wipe them away.

How had she spent the hours before he had left her? She could not remember the days being so long. She still had the same errands to run, the same number of meals to cook, the same house to clean, the same activities with Callie. Since John's passing, her life seemed to be nothing but huge chunks of time waiting to be filled.

Even the leisure activities of her old life were no longer of any consequence. Biking tired her. Her painting required too much concentration. The Greek Community Center, where for years she had tutored older residents as well as the recent arrivals in English, was an unwelcome reminder of happier times.

When Callie was little, Athen's world had been defined by the needs of her child. She had loved those days, before Callie had started school, when the weather was the only restriction on how they spent the hours. Looking back now, time seemed to have passed in little more than the blink of an eye. How much faster would the years ahead pass, years filled with nothing but watching Callie grow up? Had John so filled her life that there was nothing of her that he had not taken with him?

When John had twenty-five years in the force, they'd planned on buying a house in the country where they'd live out their days. They'd find an old farm where John could have his own nursery, stocked with plants he'd grown in his own greenhouse, just like Ms. Evelyn. Athen would keep the books for John's nursery business and entertain their grandchildren when they came to spend their summers.

Funny how she had never counted on this.

A police officer's wife should know what can happen, she chided herself. *We all think it could happen only to someone else, that someday we might be called upon to consol. We never want to believe that we might be the one to be consoled.*

Athen rose and poured a glass of water, the silence closing in on her. Callie had two more weeks of school, then day camp for the summer, then school would begin and the new year would follow, then yet another and another. She forced the image of an endless succession of empty days from her mind.

Maybe next year . . .

"Maybe next year what?" Angry with herself, she slammed the glass on the counter, splashing water onto the tiled floor. "Maybe next year what?"

Nothing is going to magically appear and make things better. There will be no sign to point the way to the rest of my life. This is the rest of my life. I will not move from this spot unless I take the first step. And there will never be a better time to take that step than now.

"So what's it going to be?" She stood in the center of the kitchen. "Big girl who wants to see what else life has in store or poor pitiful me who will sit on the sidelines, watching the world go by, for the next, oh, thirty or forty years?"

She inhaled deeply, let the air out in a long, hushed whoosh.

"I'm thinking big girl."

Tired of feeling pathetic, tired of feeling like a victim, tired of facing every day with a knot in her chest, of feeling sorry for herself, Athen reached for the phone. Afraid she'd change her mind if she gave herself time to second-guess her decision, she lifted the receiver and punched in the number she'd known by heart since she was a child.

"Good morning," she told the unfamiliar voice that answered the main switchboard. "This is Athena Moran. I'd like to speak with Mayor Rossi, please."

ATHEN'S TRANSITION FROM HER SELF-IMPOSED hibernation to the demands of her new status as a working mother had gone much more smoothly than she had dared hope. Callie, rather than accusing her mother of abandoning her as Athen feared, barely raised her eyes from the newest addition to the Twilight saga to pronounce the news as "cool."

Meg, John's sister, had been delighted with Athen's news.

"I can't wait to call Mom and Dad and give them the good news. It's about time you joined the living again," she'd happily told Athen.

Athen's first-day jitters had been unwarranted. The entire staff at City Hall seemed to comprise old friends of hers from high school, old friends of her father's, and parents of old friends. Everyone greeted her with the warmest of welcomes. If anyone had been disappointed to have been passed over for the job on Athen's behalf, no one let on.

Mayor Rossi himself had been all business as he succinctly explained what he expected of his new right hand.

"Read the paper," he instructed.

"Read the paper?" she repeated.

"The newspaper. The *Woodside Herald*. Tells you just about everything you'll need to know for the day. Who's bickering with whom. What cars are out of commission because some bozo ran his city wheels into a fence. Which group of activists or malcontents will most likely be knocking on my door that day."

He leaned back in his huge black leather chair and lit a cigar.

"It'll all be right there, the whole day spread out in front of you. The most important thing you'll do for me is read the paper and circle the articles I'll need to read. Leave it on my desk.

"Next, you go to the city's website. You check for emails and you print them out. I'll want to see them so we can talk about how you're going to respond. You'll put those in a file and leave them on my desk with the newspaper."

"How about your personal email?"

"I don't do that. I just get what comes through the city's website." He waved a hand as if he couldn't be bothered. "Anyone has something to say to me, they can call me or they can go to the website. Oh, and that reminds me." He snapped his fingers. "I want you to keep an eye on the *Herald*'s website as well. Watch for comments that people post after articles about the city. Oh, and editorials. Letters to the editor in the hard copy of the paper, follow-up comments from the website. Those pages need to be checked, too. You'll print out anything relevant."

"Why don't you just read the articles online?"

"I like the feel of the paper. I don't like the computer. I need anything done on the computer, you'll do it for me."

"All right."

"I get in at nine sharp, come hell or high water. Unless there's an emergency, I never schedule a meeting before ten thirty and until that hour I only make phone calls, I never take them. Anyone calls before ten thirty, you take a message and bring it in to me, unless they're returning a call from me. You don't discuss anything—not who calls or who walks through that door—with anyone. Not anyone—except me. And you will tell me everything you hear and everything you see. Period."

She stared blankly at him from across the desk.

"Any questions?" He tapped the ash from the end of the cigar.

"Not so far." She smoothed the skirt of her new gray linen suit, purchased in anticipation of her first day and selected by Callie the previous weekend ("You have to buy it, Mommy, it matches your eyes").

"You'll start at eight. Gives you enough time to scan the paper, the website, and get my coffee ready. I take it black. The cups are on the middle shelf of the armoire behind you. I expect the coffee and the paper on my desk at nine. I have meetings with Council every day at three p.m. Starting today you will sit in on the meeting to listen and observe. You will not speak or voice an opinion unless I ask you for one. You will take notes that you will type up and print out for me. No other hard copies." He paused. "I didn't ask if you know how to type."

"Well, sure."

"Edie—you know Edie, right? She can type any letters that you don't have time to do. God knows she has only about an hour and a half's worth of her own work to do on any given day, but that's why she's support staff. She's supposed to support you as well as me. Which reminds me. You'll keep my personal files locked. I have the only key. Ask for it when you need it and return it as soon as you're done. It's not that I don't trust you, Athen." He softened slightly. "If I didn't trust you, you wouldn't be sitting in that chair. I'm more afraid someone would lift the key from your desk, maybe even have a copy made, who knows? Confidential stuff, a lot of what goes on inside this room. Can't take too many chances, you know? And also, you're going to . . ."

The buzz of the intercom interrupted whatever he was about to say.

"What is it, Edie?" He lifted the receiver. "Okay, sure. Put him on. Jimmy, thanks for getting right back to me. Yes, of course I did . . ."

Athen used the interruption to covertly survey Rossi's office. If she hadn't known better, she'd have sworn she was in the paneled library of an English lord's manor house. The carpet was a huge red, black, and cream oriental. The paintings were landscapes done in muted oils. Crimson drapes narrowly striped in black—custom-made, from all appearances—hung from four large windows, effectively blocking out any view of the city beyond the room. The desk had a mahogany top large enough to play billiards on. The left side of the room featured black leather furniture: oversized sofa, love seat, and two deep chairs. At the center of the grouping was a large round mahogany coffee table. She twisted slightly in her seat to inspect the tall armoire that dominated the wall behind her. It, too, was mahogany, nine feet tall and nearly as wide. It was obvious that no expense had been spared in His Honor's honor.

"Okay, then, are we straight here?" Dan turned his attention back to Athen as he hung up the phone. Without waiting for an answer, he nodded and said, "Good. Let's get started."

He raised himself from the chair and walked around the desk, gallantly offering his hand to assist Athen from her seat, much as an old-world *patron* might do. He guided her to the door with one hand on her back and walked her to her desk.

"Edie here will give you a hand with things." He nodded at the diminutive silver-haired mouse of a woman who appeared to have been waiting all morning for the moment when Rossi's door opened. "Show Athen where the coffeepot is, the ladies' room, the supply closet, whatever you think she needs to know. Introduce her to anyone she doesn't already know."

He turned to Athen. "I have a meeting with the city's union reps in twenty minutes. Should run through lunch. I'll be back in time for my three o'clock. I'll expect you to have coffee ready."

He strolled to the elevator, punched the down button, and was immediately rewarded with opening doors. He stepped inside and was gone.

"Well," Athen said uncertainly. She turned to Edie, trying hard not to focus on the purple, red, and black scarf that rode in an untidy heap around the neck of the older woman's lavender knit dress. "Well, then."

He'd left her no work. No letters. No filing. No instructions. She looked at Edie expectantly, hoping she might make some suggestions. When she did not, Athen sat at her desk outside Rossi's door and booted up her computer, musing that more than once during her conversation with her new boss, she'd felt her eyebrows rise. Coming from anyone other than Dan, his expectation that she keep his coffeepot filled might have been seen as somewhat chauvinistic. But even if he hadn't been the mayor, or many years older than she, the fact that he was an old friend of her father's guaranteed she'd be deferential. Besides, he was of another generation. And it wasn't a big deal. Dan was just a little old-fashioned in his expectations.

More like a feudal lord, she mused. But she had been raised in an old-fashioned home, where old-world customs and traditions had been honored, none more so than respect for one's elders. She'd been around men like Dan Rossi all her life. Her family was full of them.

"Edie, how do I set up my password on my computer?" Athen frowned.

"No point in starting with that right now." Edie glanced at her watch. "It's almost eleven fifteen. I go to lunch at eleven thirty. Be glad to help you when I get back. Of course, by then you'll probably want lunch."

"No, no, that'll be fine," Athen assured her. "Twelve-thirty will be fine."

"Well, it may not be right at twelve thirty. I have a little shopping to do," Edie explained unapologetically. "But as soon as I get back."

"Sure. That'll be fine." Athen smiled wanly as Edie returned to her desk on the other side of the hallway, just beyond the elevator.

Athen sighed, and began to search the desk drawers, looking for the manual. After ten unsuccessful minutes, she closed the bottom drawer and sighed again.

"I'm going for lunch now, Athen," Edie called from the elevator. "Can I bring you anything?"

"No, that's okay. Thanks."

"See you later."

"Right. Later." Athen wiggled the fingers of one hand in Edie's direction as the elevator doors closed. "I'll be right here when you get back. Right here, just me and the newspaper . . ."

❈ 4 ❧

The Fourth of July holiday fell during Athen's second full week of work. She was surprised at how much she looked forward to a weekday that did not begin with the insistent whine of the 6:00 a.m. alarm. Callie, however, not wanting to miss a minute of the festivities of the day, dragged her mother's reluctant body downstairs for breakfast at six thirty, reminding Athen that the early worm got the best viewing spot on the street. To that end, they'd set out for the center of town around eight, Athen on foot, Callie on her bike.

"'I . . . love a parade,'" Callie sang gaily as she marched in time to the beat of the drums as the high school band passed before them

This year, as every year, the folks in Woodside Heights were treated to an Independence Day spectacle guaranteed to be "the best ever." The lineup included a string band from Philadelphia, bagpipers from Virginia, Revolutionary War–style drum and bugle corps from Connecticut, and, of course, the Woodside Heights High School marching band. The parade proceeded for a full twenty-five minutes, the local children filling in at the end on bicycles patriotically decorated with red, white, and blue crepe paper.

Athen kept in step with the crowd as it followed the

parade to the park where speeches would be given by the city fathers, and everyone would join in the Pledge of Allegiance and National Anthem, after which the children's activities—races and a softball game—would continue throughout the afternoon. The long, hot day would end with a fireworks display over Woodside Park.

"Hey, Mom, watch my bike, okay?" Callie rolled the bike toward Athen, who barely caught it as it careened toward the ground. "This is my race."

Athen steered the bike to the line forming along the track and joined the other parents who gathered to watch their offspring in the footraces that were about to begin. Two dozen or so young girls, ages ten to twelve, lined up. Athen craned her neck to locate Callie, whose recent birthday qualified her for the race. Always competitive, Callie was performing the warm-up exercises John had taught her.

The runners were called to the line and a balloon was popped to start the race. Callie's churning legs carried her quickly to the finish line seconds before anyone else. She won handily.

"Yay, Callie!" Athen happily applauded.

"Your daughter, I'm guessing?" a deep voice from behind her commented.

"Yes," Athen replied and tried to catch Callie's eye in the crowd.

"She's a good runner. She has good form."

"Thank you, yes, she's quite an athlete." Athen turned to acknowledge the compliment.

That his eyes exactly matched his shirt had been her first thought. Both were the same crisp blue of an October sky. Athen flushed scarlet when she realized those blue eyes were staring intently into her own.

"Well, I can't think of a better outlet for kids." He pulled off his maroon baseball cap. One hand tried unsuccessfully to tame the unruly black curls that spilled in sweaty ringlets across his forehead. "Boy, it's a hot one, isn't it? Must be close to ninety already."

"Yes." The red tinge crept all the way to her earlobes.

The boys were lining up for their race, and Athen pretended an interest she did not feel to excuse herself from further conversation with the stranger. He was standing too close, and she found his proximity disconcerting. She moved slightly toward the track as a means of putting some distance between them.

The boys' race was over in a flash, the winner jumping into the air with a hoot. From behind her came a loud whistle. She wondered if it had been the stranger, but she did not turn around. Maybe he'd gotten the message. Maybe he was gone.

"One more race and we can move out of this hot sun." He hadn't gone anywhere. She had not moved far enough.

Athen nodded without comment as the top three to finish from the girls' and boys' races lined up for the final competition.

"I'll bet your daughter gives them all a run for their money."

Again Athen offered no response. She found herself hoping the race would be over quickly so that she could leave. He was making her uncomfortable, but she wasn't sure why.

"Want me to hold on to that bike so your hands are free?" he offered. "You might want to get ready to applaud. Your girl could take it all right here."

"No, thank you, I'm fine," she mumbled, trying to ignore the fact that he now stood close enough for her to smell the faintest hint of his aftershave. Close enough for her to notice, when she lowered her eyes toward the ground in an effort to divert her gaze from his handsome face, that his long, muscular legs were tan below his white shorts.

The balloon popped and the runners passed by in a dusty pack. Callie came in a very close second to the boy who had won the previous race.

Callie walked slowly in a direct line to her mother, her hands on her hips, her expression sheer disappointment.

"You really did well, sweetie." Athen reached out to offer consolation.

"Not well enough," grumbled Callie.

"Hey, Callie, great race," the boy who won called out to her, but when he approached, Callie bent down in a pretense of retying her sneaker and barely acknowledged him. He backed away, a look of dismay on his face.

"Come on, Callie, we'll get a cold drink and then maybe some lunch." Athen patted her on the shoulder, glancing behind her as they walked away. The stranger had disappeared.

As she wheeled the bike across the field, Athen found herself unconsciously sorting through the throng of people filling the park. She was not, she emphatically denied at the suggestion of a small voice inside her, looking for a last glimpse of a maroon baseball cap that topped a shock of black curls.

SHE THOUGHT OF HIM THE next morning as she was going through her closet, looking for something to wear to work. She pulled a blue knit dress from its hanger and slid it over her head. She closed the buttons down the front, and thought about a blue shirt that matched blue eyes that perfectly matched the color of her dress. She slammed the closet door with a loud bang, hoping to scare the image away.

She had neither time nor inclination to dwell on strange men, she reminded herself. She'd been widowed less than a year. She had a child to raise and a job to do. She was a single mother with responsibilities. She banished the intruder from her thoughts and turned her attention to the task of getting Callie to the camp bus on time, and getting herself to the office by eight.

All in all, working wasn't so bad. Her job gave her a reason to get up in the morning, a reason to get dressed in something other than shorts and a T-shirt. It gave her a purpose she vaguely suspected she lacked.

The work itself wasn't much of a challenge, particularly for a woman whose last full-time working experience had been teaching sixth grade in an inner-city school. As Dan had instructed, she read through the paper first thing every morning (after starting the coffee, of course), circling those items she thought would interest her boss in red ink. Next, she logged on to the internet and printed out any emails that had been sent to the mayor via the city's website. She checked the paper's online edition for comments that followed editorials that related to the city's business, and letters to the editor. By the end of the second week, she'd become proficient at determining which items (other than the obvious "Trash Truck Injures Five") contained information Dan would need to begin his day.

Filing never took more than ten minutes, since Rossi preferred to communicate many of his thoughts by telephone, rarely following up in letter form, and almost never by email, unless Athen wrote it for him. Even then, he seemed almost reluctant to put his thoughts in writing. Most of Athen's typing consisted of memorandums to the staff or notes she took at the daily conferences with the council members.

The three o'clock meeting became the highlight of her day. The routine never changed, nor was anyone ever late. The four members of Council and the city solicitor filed in and always took the same seats. Rossi sat on the black leather chair facing the room. Jim Wolmar, the council president, took the chair to Rossi's left. Angelo Giamboni shared the long sofa with George Konstantos, who'd been appointed by Rossi to fill the vacancy on Council following Ari's stroke three years earlier, and Riley Fallon, the lone African-American councilman. Harlan Justis, the solicitor, sat facing Wolmar and Rossi from the love seat. The seating arrangement never varied, nor did the level of participation.

All discussions seemed to consist of a dialogue between Rossi and Wolmar. The occasional request for a legal opinion would elicit a brief and mostly vague response from Justis. Giamboni, the first cousin of Rossi's deceased wife, never spoke unless he was directly addressed, but he always nodded in unconscious agreement every time Dan opened his mouth. Konstantos, well into his seventies, appeared to sleep through most of the meetings. Fallon would, on occasion, make an attempt to offer a carefully worded opinion or present another point of view when an issue might be particularly thorny, but since no one ever responded, it didn't seem to matter. Except, Athen suspected, maybe to Fallon, who could at least go back to his district and say he had made an attempt to sway Council to a decision more favorable to their interests.

It had not taken Athen long to discover two important facts about the city's governing body. One was that the interests of the minorities—the Greeks, the African-Americans, the Hispanics—were of no consequence as far as Council was concerned. The second was that Council met only for the sake of appearance, because the only power in the city rested solely in Dan Rossi's hands. But, she rationalized, it could be worse.

From what she could see, Dan Rossi possessed an un-equaled devotion to the city of Woodside Heights and to its citizens. The man had almost wept to her in private when the city's second-largest employer, a packaging plant, had closed its doors, putting almost eighty people out of work. He seemed genuinely outraged at the rise in crime, the rise in drug trafficking, and the rise in poverty, and the effects of all three on his city. He'd taken Athen under his wing, explaining ever so patiently the inner workings of the city government, the nuances of political parlance.

"Ah, you're a natural for public service, Athen." He'd beamed at her one afternoon when the council meeting had ended and the others had left the room. "I could tell just by looking at you that you understood the ramifications on the city's finances of Fallon's proposal. We'd have to raise everyone's taxes to do what he wants, and you were spot on. This isn't the time to raise taxes. Nope, the apple certainly didn't fall far from the tree. Ari'd sure be proud of his little girl."

Dan would frequently ask her opinion on matters relevant to the running of the city, though more often than not he'd somehow manage to change her opinion by pointing out where she lacked the relevant facts. Once he explained things to her, she could see his point, could see how she had been misled by the media or his detractors, who only sought to push their own agenda. More and more as the weeks progressed, Dan spent increasing amounts of time with her, rehashing meetings, reiterating who said what and what they really meant. He had become her political father figure and her mentor.

"Pateras," she would tell her father, "it's an exciting thing to be involved in the working of a city, but, of course, you know that. I only wish I'd learned more from you. Dan says you had a better understanding of how the city runs, of how things get done, than anyone he's ever known. That you'd be the next mayor if you hadn't become ill. He said you'd have lots to say about the problems the city is having and that he wished he could hear your thoughts right now."

Had Athen been less focused on the fact that her father could not witness her political awakening firsthand, she might have noticed the dark cloud that passed over Ari's face every time she mentioned Dan Rossi's name.

❧ 5 ❧

"Callie," Athen called from the back door. "Are you almost ready?"

"Are you kidding? I've been ready all week." Callie raced to the driveway and tossed a shovel into the backseat. "I thought Saturday would never come."

Guess she's ready, Athen mused as she got into the driver's side.

"Do you remember how to get there?" Callie got into the passenger seat and buckled her seat belt.

"Sort of. You can let me know if I make any wrong turns."

No wrong turns and twenty minutes later, Athen pulled onto the small grassy spot that served as the parking lot for Ms. Evelyn Wallace's nursery. No upscale garden center, Ms. Evelyn's was a true nursery. There was no storefront. Sales were conducted at the old-fashioned cash register inside the door of a slightly dilapidated greenhouse. There were no rows of shiny brass flowerpots, no manicured displays of hothouse plants, no fancy garden furniture.

Ms. Evelyn grew perennials in the fields surrounding her tidy bungalow up on a hill overlooking the city, where the ancestors of the city's African-American community had found refuge after their harrowing journey along the Underground Railroad. Ms. Evelyn herself planted every one of the seeds that grew in her greenhouse, tended the seedlings, and set them out into the fields with the help of her two daughters, now grown, and her sixteen-year-old grandson, Lamar. She grew her plants for the sheer love of growing things, for the delight in the eyes of her customers when they found that species unheard of by the high school kids who worked for the big chain nurseries. Ms. Evelyn loved her plants and she loved her customers who appreciated them. She had adored John Moran.

"Lord, Callie Moran, I'd given up on you this year. Goodness, child, let me look at you. I haven't seen you since the day they laid your daddy to rest, God rest his precious soul." Spry and ageless in denim overalls, Ms. Evelyn wiped a teary eye on the sleeve of her white shirt. "And you there, Athen." She greeted Athen with a warm smile. "I thought maybe you'd gone to one of those fancy boutique places this year."

"Never!" Callie protested. "Daddy always said, 'Nobody has better plants than Ms. Evelyn.'"

"And your daddy knew his flowers, that's for sure." Ms. Evelyn patted Callie on the back with obvious fondness. "You planning on keeping that garden going by yourself?"

"I want to, but, see, we lost a lot of Dad's perennials." Callie told Ms. Evelyn about the tree falling and the resulting empty spaces in the garden.

"Well, now, it's August, Callie, you know my field's all but picked clean by the Fourth of July," she chided, then added gently, "But I do have a few things out back in my private garden that I'd be happy to share with you. You run on back and take a look. Did you remember to bring your shovel? Good. There's some peach-colored foxglove that I know you'll like, honey, and some of that dark pink old-fashioned geranium that your daddy was so fond of. You remember the name for that?"

"Cranesbill," recited Callie proudly as she pulled her garden gloves from a back pocket and armed herself with her shovel. *"Sanguineum."*

"Aren't you something, Callie Moran." Ms. Evelyn's eyes danced as she called after the girl who was now running merrily up the hill. "And make sure to take some delphinium—there's blue, white, and some rose-colored, too, that did real well this year."

"Ms. Evelyn, we don't want to dig up your garden," Athen protested. "We can come back in the spring and . . ."

"Nonsense, honey. It'll give me great pleasure to share with you and help rebuild John's garden. Now you go along with Callie. I see she's got her shovel. Did you only bring the one?"

Athen nodded. She'd forgotten that the routine at Ms. Evelyn's was strictly dig your own.

"Now, you just go on over to that box of tools and help yourself to whatever you need. There should be a shovel there that will work for you."

"Thanks, Ms. Evelyn." Athen peered into the box that was filled with all manner of foreign-looking implements and selected a short-handled shovel that had a long narrow blade, the only thing in the box that looked vaguely familiar.

"Now be sure not to miss the rose achillea, and my goodness, there must be a dozen varieties of aquilegia . . . oh, and liatris . . ." Ms. Evelyn called after Athen as she trudged up the hill in the direction Callie had previously scampered. "And the rose campion is thick as thieves up there. You be sure to dig up a nice clump of that. Stuff self-seeds like nobody's business."

Athen waved and continued her climb, reciting the names of the plants Ms. Evelyn had tossed at her so casually. Aquilegia, something campion. Achillea. Weren't there any common varieties here, like black-eyed Susans or geraniums or pansies?

"Callie, those look half dead." Athen looked over the stash of brown-stemmed, dried clusters Callie had set aside.

"They're perennials, Mom," Callie explained without looking up from her efforts.

"They're the ones that die back after they bloom and come back again next year?" Athen tried to recall the terms bandied about by John and Callie as they poured over seed catalogs. Perennials. Biennials. Annuals. Half-hardy something or others.

"Very good, Mom." Callie grinned as she dislodged a clump of something from the ground and carried it to a clear spot.

"Ms. Evelyn said we needed to dig up some, er, rose something. Actually, she said two rose somethings."

"Rose campion and achillea." Callie nodded without looking up. "Got 'em."

"Okay, then. What should I do?" The parent had the feeling she'd just become the child.

"Dig up some of that gypsophilia." Callie motioned with her head to an area on Athen's right.

"Ah . . . which one is that?"

"Baby's breath, Mom. The white stuff like you get in bouquets from the florist?" Callie was clearly relishing her position of superiority. "Mom, don't you know anything about flowers?"

"Apparently not."

Athen was still struggling with the first plant, silently cursing her lack of technique in dealing with the dried, hard earth when Callie ran off to the greenhouse in search of some flats on which to transport their new garden.

"Damn." Athen inspected splintered fingernails as she brushed dirt from her hands onto her jeans, which were making her legs feel like tightly encased sausages as the temperature rose along with the humidity.

"You know, you're making this a lot harder than it needs to be." An amused voice seemed to float from the edge of the garden.

She looked up, annoyed. The source of the voice leaned casually against the trunk of a tree. Through the sun's glare she could distinguish only white shorts, a white shirt, and white tennis shoes. She held her hand over her eyes to block the blinding intensity of the sun's harsh light.

"How long have you been standing there?" Even without the baseball cap, and with dark glasses covering a good portion of his face, Athen would have known him anywhere.

"Long enough to know this is not something you do very often. If at all."

"How can you tell?"

"No gloves. Real gardeners wear gloves when they're going to be digging." He walked toward her through the rows of plants. "And hats if they're out in the hot sun. At the very least, they'd tie up their hair, if they had as much as you do."

She became suddenly conscious that her own hair, hanging straight down her back, weighed about seven tons and was white-hot.

"Here, let me help." He picked up Callie's discarded shovel. "Would you like me to dig that up for you?"

"That's not really necessary, I can . . ."

"Don't be silly." He smiled and a buzz went off somewhere in her head. "You look all digged out for today. What's your pleasure?"

"Ah . . ." She sought to remember the names Callie and Ms. Evelyn had bandied about, names that had meant absolutely nothing to her. "Ah . . . maybe some, ah, aquilegia."

"Sure. That's one of my favorites, too. Always makes me think of the house I grew up in. My mother always had tons of dark blue and pink columbine along a walk in the backyard."

Columbine? Aquilegia is columbine? Who knew?

"Now, did you want the caerulea, the canadensis, the red star? She certainly has a variety here, doesn't she?" He bent to inspect the leafy fronds as Athen buried her face in her hands and fought the urge to scream.

"Ah . . . the red star would be fine." *Never order anything you can't pronounce*, she reminded herself.

"I always liked the caerulea myself. Did you know that it's the state flower of Colorado?" He looked back at her as he began to dig.

"Ah, no. No, I didn't know that."

She tried to act casual, as if strange men always appeared out of nowhere to do things for her like dig up plants she'd never heard of, flowers she couldn't identify on a dare.

"Mom, Ms. Evelyn sent you a Pepsi—it's diet, like you like." Callie handed Athen the cold can and eyed the stranger suspiciously. "Who's that?"

"Just someone who likes to dig." Athen tilted the can back and swallowed gratefully, then pulled her hair to one side and placed the ice-cold can against her neck. It felt wonderful.

Callie began to pile the plants she'd dug onto the heavy plastic flats.

"Hey, it's the runner." The stranger plunked a large clump of dirt and dried leaves onto a flat. "That was a good race you ran a few weeks back."

"Not good enough to beat that geeky little butthead Timmy Forbes," Callie replied.

The stranger laughed out loud.

"Oh, Callie, that's an awful expression." Athen cringed.

"Well, he is." She picked up one of the flats and headed to the car, calling over her shoulder to her mother, "I'm ready to go whenever you are."

Athen stood up and brushed herself off. Not that it helped. Her jeans needed more than brushing, she noted with some embarrassment. The knees were caked with dirt and she saw lines of grime on her arms where the sweat had streaked downward. It had been a long time since she'd been this dirty.

"Let me get that for you." Smiling, the dark-haired man leaned over and effortlessly picked up two flats. He had deep dimples on each side of his mouth. She wished she hadn't noticed. "Lead the way."

While he loaded the flats into the back of her car, Athen sought out Ms. Evelyn in the greenhouse to negotiate payment for the plants. Her unexpected helper went back up the hill to give Callie a hand with the remaining flats. Athen noticed a young boy walking toward Callie as she started back to the car. He looked as if he wanted to stop and talk, but Callie barely acknowledged him.

The man in the white shorts placed the last flat into the trunk of her car. Athen watched from the greenhouse as he looked around, then shrugged, and after calling to the boy, got into a dark SUV.

I didn't even thank him, Athen thought as he drove off.

"Who was your friend?" Athen casually asked Callie on the way home.

"What friend?"

"The boy who was speaking to you at Ms. Evelyn's."

"Oh. You mean Timmy Forbes." Callie scowled. "He goes to my school."

"Timmy Forbes?" Athen recalled Callie's previous description of the boy, and her face went white. "That man, the one who was helping me dig, was he . . ."

"Mr. Forbes." Callie nodded. "I heard Timmy call him 'Dad' when they were leaving."

Athen grimaced. The helpful blue-eyed man with the great legs and a fondness for digging was the geeky little butthead's father.

❄❄❄❄

QUENTIN FORBES LOADED THE LAST of his plants into the back of the Explorer and slammed the door.

"Let's go, Tim," he called to his son, who was wandering down the hill, kicking a stone.

Quentin slid behind the wheel and turned the key in the ignition. Tim got into the passenger seat and strapped himself in.

"Want to stop for pizza on the way home?" Quentin asked.

"No thanks." Tim shook his head and looked out the side window.

"How 'bout a burger, then?"

"Not unless you want one."

"I can always eat a burger." Quentin put the car in reverse and waved to Ms. Evelyn as he headed for the road. "So, do you think Grandma will like the plants you picked out for her birthday?"

"I guess." Tim shrugged.

Quentin turned on the radio and racked his brain, trying to think of something else to say. His son was obviously bothered by something but he wasn't sure how to get him to open up. Just one more reason to resent his wife for taking off and leaving them the way she did. Not that Cynthia would have been more tuned in to Timmy than Quentin was, he reminded himself. Cynthia had never been tuned in to anyone but Cynthia.

"The girl who was at Ms. Evelyn's," Quentin said. "Is she a friend of yours from school?"

Tim snorted. "I wouldn't call her that."

"What would you call her?"

"A snotty little brat."

"I trust you have good reason for that," Quentin said cautiously. He didn't like to hear his son speak like that about anyone. On the other hand, he remembered what the girl had called Tim, and wondered what was at the bottom of the mutual animosity.

"She just isn't very nice, that's all."

"What's her name?"

"Callie Moran."

"She's an awfully pretty kid. What's your problem with her?"

"What's her problem with me?" Tim retorted. "She hasn't said anything nice to me since I moved here."

"She can't be the only kid in your class."

"She's the most popular. She's the smartest girl in the whole fifth grade, and she's the best athlete." He paused to reflect, then amended that to, "Well, the best after me."

"Maybe she doesn't like being the best after anyone. Sounds to me like she's used to being the best at everything."

"Yeah, well, too bad for her." Tim folded his arms over his chest and stared straight ahead.

They rode in silence for a few minutes, then Timmy said, "All the teachers treat her like she's something special 'cause her father was a cop who got killed."

"What?" Quentin thought of the girl's mother. "When?"

"Some guy shot him when he was trying to arrest him or something." Tim shrugged.

"Wow. That's terrible." Quentin thought of how Timmy was dealing with the fact that his mother had left him to pursue her career. How much worse would it be to have a parent taken from you the way Callie Moran had? "I'll bet it's been really hard for her."

Tim declined to comment.

Quentin thought this might be a moment he could use to get his son to open up to how he felt about his mother leaving.

"It's hard to lose a parent, Tim, under any circumstances."

"Well, at least her father didn't run away from her and go to France to take pictures for a stupid magazine."

"Tim, you know your mother will be back to see you sometime this fall."

"Big deal. I'll bet she doesn't even come." He kicked the bottom of the dash.

"She said she would."

"She says a lot of things." Timmy's bottom lip began to quiver. "And she lies a lot."

Quentin wished he could assure his son that his mother would, in fact, be back to see him in a few months as she'd promised. But they both knew that she did, in fact, lie when it suited her, and one thing Quentin had vowed when she left was to never lie to Timmy. Instead, he tried to shift the conversation from those dangerous waters and back to Callie Moran.

"I'm sure Callie would love to be able to say that maybe she'd see her dad again sometime," Quentin said softly. "Anytime."

"Yeah, I guess."

Quentin silently cursed his ex-wife. For months after she left, he'd kept their home in St. Louis, thinking that maybe his son would be better off in familiar surroundings. Tim went to the same school he'd always gone to, played for the same sports teams, hung out with the same kids. But as time went on, it became apparent that there was no point in trying to pretend that nothing had changed in Tim's life except for the fact that his mother was gone. Nothing was the same, and Quentin had some hard decisions to make. In the end, he'd decided to move east, to the New Jersey town where his mother now made her life with her new husband. If nothing else, Tim would have extended family members. He'd have time to spend with Quentin's mother, and he'd get to know his stepgrandfather and his stepaunt.

Tim had seemed so happy there when they visited over Christmas vacation that Quentin hadn't hesitated to accept when his stepfather offered him their gatehouse as temporary living quarters. They returned to St. Louis only long enough for Quentin to list the house with a Realtor and pack their belongings. The Forbes guys were back in New Jersey by March, and neither of them had looked back. St. Louis held few good memories. Quentin had hoped that the change would be good for Tim, and in some ways it had been. The boy loved his grandmother and his new grandfather, both of whom doted on him. There were stables with horses to ride and meadows to ride through, streams to follow into the woods, and new challenges on the playing fields to be met.

But Quentin had noticed that Tim kept to himself much of the time and didn't seem to have made any friends. At first he told himself that it was because they'd moved in the middle of the school year. Now, he wasn't so sure.

"So what's it going to be, sport?" Quentin came to a stop at a red light. "Burgers? Or no burgers?"

"I don't care."

"How about burgers on the way to the beach?"

Tim's head spun halfway around to face his father.

"The beach is cool. I'd be up for that."

"In that case, it's back to the house to pick up our stuff." Quentin turned left when the light turned green.

"It's nice of Grandma to let us use her beach house." Tim smiled for the first time since he got into the car. "It's such a cool place. I love the ocean."

"Me too."

"If we'd stayed in St. Louis, I'd probably never get to see the ocean."

"We'd have come for visits," Quentin reminded him.

"It wouldn't be the same as being able to go any time we want."

"No, it wouldn't be."

Ten minutes later, they were driving through the gates of Quentin's mother's home.

"Dad, it's okay if Callie Moran doesn't like me," Tim told him before he got out of the car. "You can still like her mom even if Callie doesn't like me."

"What makes you think I like her mom?"

"'Cause you dug up all that stuff for her and carried it down to her car." Timmy grinned, his parting shot before jumping out of the car. "Besides, her mom's hot."

Out of the mouths of babes, Quentin thought as he followed his son into the house. Callie Moran's mom was, indeed, hot.

❦ 6 ❦

It was an obviously depressed Dan Rossi who stepped off the elevator on a sultry Monday morning in late August.

"Can I get something for you, Dan?" a concerned Athen asked. "Some coffee? Maybe something cold? Or some aspirin?"

"Aspirin and cold drinks won't help, Athen, but thank you."

"Is there anything I can do? Anything I can help you with?"

"I appreciate that. But this is something I have to deal with myself." He made a gallant effort to smile.

She tiptoed out of the office, wondering at the cause of his troubles. She all but knocked over Edie, who'd obviously been lurking outside the door.

"Find out what's ailing him?" Edie nodded in the direction of the door.

Athen shook her head.

"If you ask me, it's that damned city charter," Edie volunteered.

Athen sat down at her desk and looked for a copy of the email she'd typed yesterday, the one Rossi had her send to Wolmar right at the close of the day. Maybe there was a clue in it. He'd seemed agitated at the time he'd dictated it to her.

"Yup, that'd be my guess. It's that damned charter, all right," Edie repeated.

Athen did her best to ignore her. Maybe Edie the chatterbox would see she was busy and go away.

Maybe little people from Mars would land on the roof and turn them all into marshmallows.

"You know that part that says you can only serve four consecutive terms?" Edie droned on. "A mistake, if you ask me, putting something like that in there. Now poor Dan has to give up the office." She tsk-tsked. "A finer man never sat in that chair, and that's the God's honest truth." She lowered her voice and added, "Everyone's waiting for Dan to name his successor, and it's going to have to be soon, too. The Labor Day rally is next week already."

"So?"

"So that's when he has to announce who gets the nod

to run. Not that an election means anything in this city. Don't get me wrong," Edie hastened to add, "I'm a faithful member of the party. Always have been, always will be. And I'm loyal to Dan. God knows I'll be just as loyal to whoever it is that Dan picks. It just seems to me to be a waste of money, though, going to the expense of a campaign when everyone knows who's going to win." She paused, then added, "Once we know who's running, of course. That's the beauty of having a one-party town."

"I thought there was more than one political party in Woodside Heights." Athen frowned.

"Well, technically, there is, but only one party has won an election in this city for over a hundred years." Edie smiled. "It takes the drama out of the election when you know who's going to win, but that's okay with me. Who needs the agita?"

The elevator doors slid open noiselessly.

"Oh my, would you look at Himself," Edie whispered as Jim Wolmar strode toward them, a jovial smile plastered on his face.

"Good morning, ladies." He nodded cheerfully, smoothing his tie and shooting the cuffs of the pale ivory shirt under the handsome gray Italian silk suit jacket. "Dan's expecting me, Athen. Don't get up. I can show myself in."

Something about Wolmar had bothered Athen since day one. It could have been the fact that he always wore the same self-satisfied expression. Maybe it was the overly solicitous manner in which he always agreed with Dan, always nodding vigorously, proclaiming, "Absolutely, Dan. Without question," as if Dan's words had been Jim's very thoughts. It could be the way he looked. Tall and trim with a full head of perfectly groomed silver hair, Wolmar might be handsome if he lost that lifeless plastic gaze. He always reminded Athen of an older version of Barbie's friend, Ken.

It was generally believed that Wolmar was Rossi's protégé, that Dan had been priming him to take over the office someday. Apparently, Jim believed that day was now near. Contrasting Dan's mood to Jim's lively steps, it seemed only one of them was happy about it.

Jim was still wearing that same sappy smile when he emerged from Dan's office ten minutes later. The smile seemed to slide to one side of his face somewhat when he approached the opening door of the elevator as Harlan Justis was stepping out. The two men greeted each other warily, like opponents who were sizing each other up for the first time. Athen caught Wolmar trying to steal a peek through the closing elevator doors as Justis entered the confines of Rossi's office.

Harlan Justis looked exactly the way a solicitor of a small city should look. He was well-spoken, well dressed, and well manicured. He was also apparently certain that when the dust settled, he, not Wolmar, would be Rossi's choice to succeed him.

Justis, too, stayed behind closed doors for about ten minutes before emerging with a hopeful look about him. Until Jack Sheldon, the front-runner from the third ward, stepped out of the elevator, smiled, and walked confidently into the mayor's office.

And so it went till noon, resuming again at two. Prospective candidates in, prospective candidates out.

The usual Council meeting was subdued, lasting less than an hour before Dan stood to indicate the session had concluded. As an apparent afterthought, he added that he'd come to no final decision on "that other matter." Wolmar and Justis both seemed inclined to linger for as long as possible, as if waiting to see if Rossi had words of encouragement for either of them. Both were disappointed when it became clear there'd be no further discussion that day.

Athen was in the process of gathering up the used coffee cups when Dan closed the office door.

"Can you sit and talk with me for a few, Athen?" He slumped into his chair.

"Of course."

He motioned to a chair close to him, and she sat.

"I have a terrible dilemma, Athen, a terrible decision to make." He shook his head as if the weight of the world rested upon it.

"The election?" she ventured quietly.

"Yes, of course, the election. How insightful of you to pick right up on that. I have to choose the right candidate, and my heart's burning over it. There is no clear choice here, you see. Jim is a good man, but he's never developed a true feel for the people. Harlan's years away from being the man he needs to be to lead this city. Ah, and the worst of it, Athen, is that in my heart I know I haven't finished the job. There's so much more I'd wanted to do for all those good people out there." He gestured vaguely in the direction of the windows that fronted on the town square.

He turned his head from her, as if to shield her from his display of emotion.

"And the saddest part is that I know all the good things I'd planned will go undone."

"Well, surely your successor . . . Jim, Harlan, whoever . . . will follow your agenda."

"Ah, Athen, you're so naïve." He smiled kindly, as a

father might at his child. "Everyone has their own priorities. No, I'm afraid that Dan Rossi's plans for a better Woodside Heights will leave this office with him."

"But, Dan," she reminded him, "you'll still be head of the party, you'll still be able to influence how things are done."

He shrugged, cavalierly waving his right hand. "There will be other appointees to Council, Athen. Whoever is elected will force a retirement here, challenge a position there, until he has his own people in place. It breaks my heart to say it aloud, but there's not a man among them who won't use this office for his own gain. Not one person who won't put his own interests ahead of the city's."

"Maybe you should look around a little more, Dan, maybe there's someone else you hadn't considered."

"Ah, now there's an idea." He smiled quickly, almost, she thought, as if the idea had been his own and perhaps not a new one. "Perhaps someone who's outside the realm of the obvious. Yes, you may have hit upon something, Athen. You've given me something to think about."

"There are a lot of bright people in Woodside Heights. I'm sure you'll find the right one." She glanced at her watch and stood, preparing to leave. There would be open house at Callie's school tonight, and she didn't want to be late. "There's Ted Raspanti in the finance office. Julian Taylor in the solicitor's office. Jeff Keegan, Harold Greenly . . ."

"Yes, yes." He nodded. "But who knows where their loyalties . . . ? Ah, well, I've kept you too long. I'll see you in the morning. And thank you for listening to an old man whose days in public office are running out."

Poor Dan, she thought as she drove home through the late rush hour traffic. *He's so dedicated to this city.* She didn't often agree with Edie, but it did seem a shame that he'd be forced out of office because of some clause in the charter.

She had just enough time to throw together a quick supper, though not enough time to change her clothes, before dragging Callie off to the open house that preceded the first week of school at Woods Academy.

"I haven't had dessert," Callie protested.

"They always have a dessert reception after the welcome speeches and you know it," Athen reminded her. "Now smile and act like you're glad to be here."

"I'm not glad to be here." Callie dragged behind her mother as they entered the large gray stone administration building of the private school Callie had attended for the past three years. Her tuition had been paid in part by John's overtime, the balance in gifts from John's family, particularly his sister, Meg, who believed that nothing was too good for her only niece.

"The only good thing about this place is the athletic program," Callie continued to whine.

"Soccer tryouts are next week," Athen reminded her as she directed Callie into vacant seat toward the back of the auditorium.

"Yeah, but the public school kids get an extra week of summer vacation," Callie whispered none too discreetly. The boy seated in front of her turned, and, recognizing her, smiled shyly.

"Oh, brother." Callie rolled her eyes and slumped into her seat.

"Oh, brother" indeed.

Athen blushed when the father of that "geeky little butthead" Timmy Forbes turned slightly in his seat and flashed a million-watt smile over his shoulder.

She tried to ignore his presence, tried to force herself to listen to every word spoken by Mr. Landers, the new headmaster, as he outlined his programs for the coming year and his hopes for an even better Woods Academy under his leadership.

". . . and I bring with me a firm commitment to the arts . . ."

Where's the boy's mother? she wondered. *She never seems to be around. Seems like a nice enough kid, Callie's assessment of him aside. Seems to like Callie . . . I'll have to ask her just what characterizes a "geeky . . ."*

"Mom, can we leave now?" Callie squirmed next to her.

"No."

". . . and to continue the level of excellence in the classrooms . . ." The headmaster droned on and Athen's mind continued to wander.

It was so nice of him to help at Ms. Evelyn's, digging up all those plants in the hot sun. A mental image of long, strong tanned legs drifted past her mind's eye. She was staring unconsciously at the broad shoulders directly in front of her. She could not help but notice the casual elegance of his tan linen suit, and the way his thick black hair curled over the collar in little apostrophes.

She mentally gave herself a shake. John hadn't even been gone a full year, and here she was, mentally taking stock of the first guy who caught her eye.

Filled with a sense of guilt, she tuned back in to Mr. Landers, resolutely determined to avoid any further contact with this man who seemed to be everywhere.

". . . and I conclude by inviting each of you to join me for some refreshments in the reception room, where I can meet each and every one of you personally." Grateful applause greeted the conclusion of the speech.

"Can we eat now?" Callie stood, poised to make a break for the door.

"I thought you were so hot to trot to leave."

"I was, but Mrs. Keller is here and she always brings chocolate cake."

Out of the corner of one eye Athen could see that Mr. Forbes was turning as if to speak to her.

"All right." She nudged Callie in the back and followed her daughter out into the aisle. They melted into the crowd, which slowly flowed down the hall into the reception area.

She made a point of always being engaged in conversation, of looking beyond him when she'd turn and he appeared to be making an attempt to catch her eye. She ignored him as completely as possible, though not so completely that she failed to notice the number of mothers and female faculty members who flocked around him.

He must be single. *Widowed or divorced?* she couldn't help but wonder.

She turned her back on the scene and pretended to be interested in last year's artwork, which still graced the walls.

She was congratulating herself on her successful efforts to remain faithful to John's memory when a voice whispered in her ear, "Are you deliberately avoiding me, or are you merely too nearsighted to have noticed that I've been trying to get your attention for the past fifteen minutes?"

"Oh, were you?" She acted unaware, though she had been very much aware. "I've just been catching up with some people I haven't seen in a while. And it would seem that you've had plenty of attention to contend with." She nodded in the direction of the gaggle he'd left stranded at the dessert table, all but biting her tongue the second the words had slipped out. Now he'd know that she'd noticed.

"Ah, yes, the fifth-grade mothers have taken Timmy and me under their wings, since we're the new boys in town." His eyes twinkled as he added, "You remember my son, Timmy. I think he was once described as a 'geeky . . .'"

"Please," she begged, cringing. "Don't say it."

His laugh was infectious, and in spite of her discomfort, she laughed along with him.

"I'm so sorry for that," she told him. "What an awful thing for Callie to have said. I can't imagine why she'd say that about him. He seems like such a nice boy."

"He beat her in the race." He shrugged. "And she's obviously a competitive little girl who doesn't like to be beaten."

"Well, I apologize for her lack of manners," she told him sincerely, "and for mine. I never even thanked you for giving me a hand with those plants."

He waved her apology aside as unnecessary. "And I apologize for not having introduced myself properly. I'm Quentin Forbes." He offered her his hand and she took it.

"Athen Moran." She tried to gracefully disconnect from the handshake but he didn't seem inclined to let go.

"May I get you something from the dessert table?" he asked, eyes still twinkling as she gently tried to pull her hand from his.

"No, no thank you." She wondered if she should just ask him to let go.

"Tim told me about Callie's father." He finally did drop her hand. "I'm so sorry for your loss."

"Thank you." He'd caught her off guard. She hadn't expected his condolences.

"I'm sure it must have been a terrible time for you."

Athen nodded. "Sometimes it still is."

"Mom, can we please go now?" Having launched a successful raid on the dessert table, Callie was impatient to leave.

"I guess it's time I located Timmy and we headed for home, too." Quentin smiled at Athen gently. "It was a pleasure to see you again. Perhaps we'll bump into each other around town."

Athen nodded. Undoubtedly, they would.

"And maybe you, young lady," he whispered to Callie, "will go a little easier on Timmy."

"Maybe not." Callie smiled sweetly, and he laughed good-naturedly as he strode off in search of his son.

IT WAS THE RIGHT THING to do, keeping Callie in Woods Academy, Athen told herself as the turned out the light and shifted around in bed until she found a comfortable position. *Academically, it's one of the best private schools in the state. The new science lab is amazing, better than some college labs, I heard someone say. And their athletic program is tops. Maybe Callie will be able to get a scholarship in soccer or track for the high school program.*

I never asked him about his wife, about Timmy's mother. The thought broke through. *I wonder where she is. Not dead or he would have said something when he brought up John. He'd have said, "I know how you feel. I lost my wife, too." But he didn't say that. I wonder what he's doing in Woodside Heights. What would bring him here from . . . wherever it is he's come?*

Annoyed that he'd invaded her thoughts yet again, she turned over and tried to think of other things to distract herself. Callie had mentioned that she'd like to try out for the theater group at school. Meg would be coming for a visit soon; she'd called last night.

Athen drifted off to sleep thinking of how good it

would be to have a whole week with Meg. Maybe Dan would give her a few days off . . .

She woke sometime later from a dream that had left her heart pounding. In the dream, she'd been speaking to John in the yard. He'd asked about the new plants in the garden. He didn't seem angry, just confused. His face seemed to fade into Quentin Forbes's. Quentin then faded into John, who soon faded into Quentin, and back again. The dream jolted her awake, leaving her feeling sick to her stomach. She got out of bed quietly and stepped over Hannah, following the familiar path down the hall to the unfinished guest room.

I never loved anyone but you, John, she professed to the emptiness within the four walls. She stood in the darkness, more confused and alone than she had felt since the day he had been laid to rest. *I don't know why he's in my head, but I never loved anyone but you. . . .*

❧ 7 ❧

It was a surprisingly rejuvenated Dan Rossi who flew past Athen's desk at eight forty-five the next morning. She'd been engrossed in the paper and hadn't heard the elevator and had failed to detect his step.

"Dan!" Startled to see him—not only fifteen minutes early but in so obvious a good mood and carrying his own coffee—she all but knocked over her mug.

"Athen, come into my office." He grinned, then added, "You can forget the paper for now. We have other things to discuss."

She followed him into his office, mystified, and sat facing him.

"You're awfully chipper this morning," she ventured.

"And with good reason." His large arms rested on the desk, his beefy fingers toying with the handle of his cup. "Athen, I have found the solution to my dilemma. Took me all night, not a bit of sleep, mind you, but the problem has been resolved. And I have you to thank."

"Me?"

He nodded cheerfully. "You hit the nail right on the head. Look beyond the obvious, you said. Look for someone who can be trusted to lead this city without regard for their own personal gain. Now, that right there eliminates ninety percent of the obvious choices." He chuckled. "Look for someone who is loyal to you, Dan, someone who will carry on your agenda to ensure the taxpayers of Woodside Heights get the best representation for their money—figuratively speaking, of course. Pass the mantle on to someone whose motives are pure, someone with a legacy of commitment to this city and its future."

"I said that?" Athen frowned. "I don't remember saying any of that."

"In so many words, you did. That was what you meant, in any case. And so I was awake all night, pondering and praying. And at precisely five forty-five this morning—I noted the time exactly—the answer came to me, clear as crystal. There is only one person in whose hands I can safely leave this city. Only one person who has the truest interests of the people at heart." Dan was on a roll. "Do you know who that person is, Athen?"

She shook her head, baffled, waiting for his announcement.

"That person, Athen . . ." He paused to lend yet another touch of drama to the moment. ". . . is you."

"Me?" she squeaked. "You can't be serious."

"Serious as a heart attack," he assured her.

"Dan, this is crazy. I don't . . ."

"I know what you're going to say." He held up a hand as if to ward off her protests. "You're going to say you have no experience, but think, Athen. You were raised by a man who devoted his life to this city. Over the past few months, you've had more experience in seeing how this office is run than anyone else, being as close to the scene as you have been."

"Dan, I—I couldn't." She was horrified at the very thought. "I don't want to."

"Of course you could. Haven't I told you a hundred times what a natural you are? And of course you want to. You just don't know it yet."

"Dan, this is crazy talk. People would have to be crazy to vote for me. Who would vote for me?"

"Everyone will vote for you." He nodded confidently.

"I have no credentials. I have no record. Why would anyone want me for mayor?" She stood up and crossed her arms over her chest, hoping to keep her heart from falling out. She paced anxiously.

"It's very simple, Athen. They will vote for you because I will nominate you. I am and will remain the head of the party. You will have my full support. My total support. No one is going to oppose you."

"It costs a lot of money to run for office." She tried a new tactic. "I can't afford a campaign."

"Not to worry." He leaned back and lit a cigar. "The party will cover all expenses. And since mayoral races in this city are pretty much uncontested, the expenses will be relatively low."

"I won't know what to do." Her head was swimming, a thousand jumbled thoughts crashing into each other.

"I will be behind you every minute, Athen, I promise you. You will never go into a meeting or a negotiation for which I have not personally prepared you." His eyes narrowed and he leaned across the desk, his gaze intent. "Believe me, I will guide your every step."

"I appreciate your confidence in me, I really do. But there's no way I can do something like this."

"Don't give me an answer now. I realize this is unexpected and will require a great deal of thought on your part." He smiled gently, once again the kindly mentor. "Take the rest of the day off and think about it, about the advantages. The salary for mayor is ninety thousand dollars a year. I imagine, with Callie in private school and college just a few years down the road, the bump in salary would come in pretty handy."

"But the others—Harlan, Jim . . ." She reminded him of the others who fully expected to get the nod, and who would not be pleased with his choice.

"You let me worry about them." He waved dismissively. "I will explain it all to them in terms they can understand. They'll accept my decision, I assure you."

"Dan, I really don't think I want to do this. I don't think I'd be a very good mayor. I'm not qualified, I don't . . ."

"Athen, do you trust me?" he interrupted her.

"Certainly I trust you, but . . ."

"Then trust me in this. I know exactly what I'm doing." His gaze was confident as he studied her face. "It's only two years out of your life."

"And then what happens?" She asked the question he seemed to be waiting for.

He hesitated momentarily, as if debating between a choice of responses, then smiled that gentle smile.

"Who knows what can happen in two years? Perhaps you'll want to run for reelection. Perhaps Harlan will have matured enough at that point. Perhaps someone else would be a better choice. But that's a decision for another day. Today's decision is in your hands. Take the day off, Athen, give it very serious consideration. Take tomorrow if you need it. But come back before Friday morning and tell me you'll accept."

"What happens on Friday?" she asked as she rose from her chair.

"On Friday I will have to tell Council of my choice. You know that the candidate is always introduced formally at the Labor Day rally. That's next Monday, honey. We're running out of time.

Monday. Less than a week away.

"Go now." He stood up and escorted her to the door. "Think of John, and the sacrifice he made for Woodside Heights. Think of the years of service your father gave this city, of how proud he'd be that you hold the office he himself once thought of running for."

The surprise must have showed on her face because he smiled and said, "You didn't know that your father came very close to running for mayor?"

"No, he never mentioned it. Why did he change his mind?"

"Who knows?" He shrugged. "But think of what it would mean to him if you were to run, and win. And think of the great sacrifice John made in protecting the people of this city. I know you'll make the right decision. And remember, I'll be right behind you every step of the way."

She cleared off her desk as in a daze, gathered her purse, and started off to the elevator.

"You don't look so good, Athen." Edie peered over the top of her glasses as Athen pushed the down button and waited for the car. "You feeling all right?"

Athen shook her head and walked through the doors the second they opened.

"SO, WHAT DO YOU THINK, John?" Athen asked in the empty room. For the past twenty minutes, she'd been sitting in the middle of the floor and talking nonstop, going round and round. What Rossi said. What she said.

What should she do?

Something about Dan's proposal—something she could not put her finger on—nagged at her. A question she couldn't find the words to ask stirred somewhere in the back of her mind, making her uneasy and restless. She stood and walked to the window and looked out across the yard. It was naked now without the magnolia, and barren without the masses of blooms John always planted. It was just one more reminder that he was gone.

Athen sighed. She paced. She could not clear her head.

If John were here, he would tell her to get on her bike and go for a long ride and think it through—and he'd be absolutely right. It was just what she needed. Unfortunately, the last time she saw her bike it had been in pieces, flying through the air toward the Dumpster. But there was nothing stopping her from buying another—maybe one of those cool new Raleigh eight-speeds she'd noticed when she took Callie's bike in for a new wheel the day before the storm.

She glanced at her watch. She still had part of the morning and most of the afternoon ahead of her—plenty of time to run to the bike shop and still have time to try it out. She changed into shorts, T-shirt, and sneakers, then tied her hair into a loose tail. If she found a bike she wanted, she could ride it out to see her father.

She grabbed a half-full package of three-day-old rolls so she could stop and feed the ducks after visiting with Ari, then headed for the car. She'd tell her father everything, and maybe, once she'd laid all her thoughts out rationally, the right decision would come to her.

The trip to the bike store had been quick and painless. The store manager was evidently having a slow day because he offered Athen a truly sweet deal on the bike she had her eye on. Excited and pleased, she bought it, fastened it to the bike rack on her car, and drove home. Then, tossing the stale rolls into the small vinyl bag behind the seat, she rode slowly down the driveway, getting the feel of the new tires. She stopped once to adjust the seat before heading out to Woodside Manor.

Soon she was peddling tentatively through the park. Back in the day when she was in shape, she'd made the ride in under a half hour. Today it took closer to forty minutes. When she arrived at Woodside Manor, she wheeled slowly around the parking lot, making huge circles on her bike. For a few moments, she sensed a piece of her old self returning. She wondered if her father would notice.

Unfortunately, she would have to wait to find out.

Diana's blue car was parked in the first space nearest the path. Was she spending her lunch hours out here now?

Athen sighed. She wasn't about to interrupt them. She pedaled over to the pond and stopped under the tall trees. Standing the bike at the edge of the parking lot, she unhooked the black seat bag and took out the package of rolls. The ducks were all clustered on the opposite shore, so she took the footbridge to the other side of the pond.

As she approached, the birds flocked to her, quacking and running on their webbed feet. Long since accustomed to treats being offered by human hands, they clustered around her without hesitation. After she'd dribbled the last crumbs into the open beak of a small brown duck that waited at her feet, she shoved the empty plastic bag into her pocket.

She glanced at her watch and looked across the pond to the parking lot. The blue car was still there.

"Here, give them some of this." A voice from behind her startled her, causing her to jump.

"Sorry if I scared you." Quentin Forbes held out an open bag of popcorn. "I thought you'd have heard me coming down the incline."

"I guess my mind was wandering" was the best she could manage. She had been right. He *was* everywhere.

"Fickle little buggers, aren't they?" He grinned. "One minute they're at your feet, the next minute they're quacking for someone else. Here, hold out your hands."

He poured popcorn into her outreached hands. A crowd of quackers followed the transfer of food from one to the other until they were both surrounded. They tossed the small white kernels until both the bag and their hands were empty.

"That's all for today, folks. See you next time." He rolled the paper bag into a ball and tossed it easily and accurately into the trash can twenty feet from where they stood.

The ducks ambled back to the water's edge.

"Do you come here often?" she asked to make conversation.

"As often as possible." He nodded solemnly. "The popcorn man hates to disappoint his feathered friends."

She smiled and started to walk up the incline toward the footbridge.

"Hey, Athen," he called. It was the first time he'd called her by name. "Have you had lunch?"

Mesmerized by blue eyes, she shook her head no.

"Join me in the park for a hot dog," he offered casually. "Maybe I'll even throw in a Popsicle for dessert."

Athen glanced over at the parking lot, but Diana's car still had not moved.

"Well, I guess I've some time to kill," she said.

"Ah, now, that's a gracious acceptance to a gracious offer," he noted dryly as he joined her at the top of the incline.

"Oh, I'm sorry. What I meant was, I'm here to visit my father." She blushed when she realized how rude she had sounded. What was it about this man that caused her to blush every time they spoke? "He's at Woodside Manor."

"Is he ill?" he asked.

"He had a stroke three years ago," she explained. "I'm just killing time because . . . well, because he has another visitor right now."

"Another family member beat you to it?"

"I really have no family, at least in this country. My mother died when I was five. I have no sisters, no brothers. My father's visitor is a . . . friend." She couldn't help adding, "Of *his*, not mine."

"So what do you like on your hot dog?"

"Mustard would be fine."

"Mustard? That's all?"

She nodded.

"Some fries? Something to drink?"

"Sure. Thanks. Diet anything would be great."

"You got it."

He took off over the hill to the vendor's stand. A few minutes later, he was back, waving her to join him at one of the wooden picnic tables.

He plunked the paper plate holding her hot dog—mustard only—fries on the side, and a can of Diet Pepsi in front of her. She watched wide-eyed as he assaulted the first of his three hot dogs. Chili, mustard, relish, sauerkraut all glopped from the bun in clumps.

"How can you eat that with all that stuff piled on there?" Her appetite diminished with every bite he took.

"It's the only way to kill the taste of the hot dog." He grinned, wiping mustard from his bottom lip. "You should try it sometime."

"No thanks." She grimaced.

"Let me know if you change your mind."

"I'll be sure to do that." She nodded. "So, what about you? What brings you to the park every day?"

"I spend a few hours in the library." He motioned with his head toward the redbrick building at the other side of the field. "Doing a little research for a book I've been working on over the past few months, checking into some local connections with the Underground Railroad."

"Ah, Ms. Evelyn."

"She's a prime source," he agreed. "Did you know that when she was a teenager she wrote down the stories she heard from the old folks up on the hill? She interviewed her grandmother—she lived to be over a hundred—*her* mother had made her way north with her two sisters. It's all there, in the old woman's own words. Ms. Evelyn wrote down every word just as she'd heard it. A few years back she typed it all up and gave a copy to the library. It's wonderful material."

"You came here just to do research for a book?"

"Not exactly. I sort of stumbled onto that when I got out here."

"From . . . ?"

"St. Louis. That's where my family is from, originally. I grew up there, only left to go to college, but I went back after graduation. Worked there. Married there."

"Where's your wife?" she couldn't help but ask.

"Well, I guess right now she's in Central Europe someplace."

"Don't you know where she is?"

"Cynthia works for *American Perspective* . . ."

"The magazine?" Athen was unavoidably impressed. *American Perspective* was big-time.

He nodded. "She's a photographer. A very good one, I might add. Maybe too good. A year ago they offered her the European desk and she took it."

"And you and Timmy couldn't go?"

"Go where? She lives out of hotels. She goes where the news is. Follows the big events." There was more than a trace of bitterness in his explanation. "That's no life for a child. Even if she had time for him, which she admits she doesn't."

"Doesn't she miss Timmy?"

"If she does, she's doing a fine job of hiding it. She's only been back once, to sign the divorce papers. You can probably imagine how that makes my son feel." He crushed the empty soda can easily with his left hand.

"I'm sorry." She could think of nothing more appropriate to say.

"So was I." He tossed the can at the trash bin and missed.

The conversation had taken a bleak turn. Witnessing

his pain had disturbed her. She leaned back and peered through the trees. She was grateful to find the blue car nowhere to be seen.

"I guess I should get going and see my father before it gets too late."

"I'll walk you to the bridge."

He cleaned up the trash and her empty soda can and tossed them into the garbage.

"Why'd you come to Woodside Heights?" she asked.

"My mother remarried last year and moved here. Her husband lives in town. Tim and I stayed in St. Louis for a while after Cynthia left, but, well, I guess there were too many memories there. I thought it would be a good time for Timmy to get to know my mother and my stepfather a little better."

"What about work?"

"Well, as of next week I'll be working for my stepfather."

"Doing what?"

"Don't know exactly yet. There are several options open," he said vaguely. "What about you? Do you work?"

"I work for the city."

"And in your spare time you're a seasoned gardener," he concluded.

"Oh . . . well. About that . . ." She wondered how to admit she didn't know a hollyhock from a ham hock without making herself look silly.

He laughed, and the light mood returned as quickly as it had earlier fled.

"It's okay, Athen," he whispered. "Your secret is safe with me."

"You knew it all along." She laughed. "How did you know? I thought I'd done a pretty good job covering up my ignorance."

"Well, let's start with the fact that you were using a six-inch trowel designed for transplanting little seedlings to dig up a plant three feet wide." His eyes were merry again, making her smile when they met hers. "And these"—he reached for her hands—"are not the hands of a gardener. No calluses. No chipped nails, other than the ones you got fighting with the gypsophila out at Ms. Evelyn's."

He held her hands for the briefest moment before letting them drop. They walked the rest of the way to the pond in amicable silence.

At their approach to the bridge, the ducks sang out and hurried up the ridge, begging hopefully.

"Nothing this time, pals." He displayed empty hands.

"This has been nice, Quentin, thank you. It was just exactly what I needed today."

"Then I'm glad we ran into each other. I'm happy to have been in the right place at the right time." He paused, then gently touched her elbow. "Listen, Athen, maybe I could call you sometime, maybe we could have dinner . . . ?"

"I don't know . . . if I'm . . ." The words "I'm ready" got stuck in her throat.

"I understand." He nodded. "But we could be friends. I would like to think of myself as your friend."

"I think I'd like that." She started across the bridge, then turned back and asked, "Quentin, if someone you cared about wanted you to do something you weren't sure you wanted to do, but they really insisted, what would you do?"

He thought for a long minute.

"I guess I'd have to ask myself: What's in it for me? And: What's in it for them?"

What's in it for me, she silently repeated. *What's in it for Rossi . . . ?*

She wished she knew.

QUENTIN STOOD ON THE BRIDGE and watched Athen wheel her bike toward Woodside Manor's main building. When she came to a stop at the end of the path that led to the front door, she got off the bike and looked around momentarily before rolling it to a spot near the door. She put the kickstand down and left the bike there, disappearing into the building.

Was she really going to leave that shiny new, pricy little model right there, without a lock, for anyone to walk off with?

Lacking the faith in their fellow man that Athen apparently had, Quentin came back down the path and sat on the back of one of the park benches, where he had a clear view of the front door and the bike. He watched for a few minutes, wondering if it had even occurred to her that the bike might not be there when she came back out. Could she really be that trusting? That naïve?

He thought perhaps she might be.

There was something about her that drew him beyond the obvious, that she was very beautiful. He'd often heard people describe a woman as being "as beautiful on the inside as she was on the outside," but it was an expression he personally had never used. He tried to remember if he'd ever met a woman to whom the expression might apply but couldn't bring one readily to mind. Not in this lifetime, anyway. Cynthia had been beautiful on the outside, but inside she was self-centered and self-absorbed. He'd really believed that once Timmy was born, she'd find that the universe had shifted, and that she was no longer at the center of it. Unfortunately, that never happened. If anything, becoming a mother had only reinforced her conviction that no one's happiness was more important than her own. When Tim was two, she handed him off to Quentin and promptly went back to the job she'd reluctantly left behind when Tim was born, determined to resume her climb to the top of her field. It took several years, but she did in fact become the superstar she'd always believed she should be. Last year, she was offered her dream job. If accepting it meant that her husband and her son would have to fend for themselves, well, they'd just have to buck up. By then the marriage had long since died. The divorce was merely a formality. He'd gotten past the pain she'd caused him, but he'd never forgive her for the pain she'd caused Tim.

It was nice to meet a woman who loved her child and honored her family ties. As far as Quentin was concerned, Cynthia had done neither.

The door of the building opened and Athen came outside. She slipped her sunglasses onto her face and walked the bike to the edge of the parking lot. She hopped on and pedaled down the drive and out onto the road. Quentin watched until she disappeared around a bend in the road before starting back over the bridge and across the field to where he'd left his car.

He'd have to hurry or he'd be late for his meeting with his stepfather to talk about his future employment, and he knew he should be focused on that. But he found himself thinking about Athen's curious question. He couldn't help but wonder who was trying to talk her into something she really didn't want to do, what that something was, and whether or not in the end she'd give in.

❧ 8 ❧

The news hit City Hall like a bombshell. Dan Rossi's choice for mayor was . . . *Athena Moran?*

Disbelief spread throughout the building. The evening newscasters from both the local and the cable stations each called no fewer than three irrefutable sources trying to confirm the unlikely story.

Rossi appeared to relish the frenzy.

Athen stood by his desk almost numbly as he made the formal announcement to Council on Friday afternoon, a moment that appeared to give him particular pleasure, Athen thought at the time. The coldly cordial good wishes expressed by the two most stung by Rossi's choice chilled her. Dan's assurances that both Jim Wolmar and Harlan Justis would come around did little to dispel the feeling that all might not go exactly as Dan had promised.

It wasn't the first time she questioned the wisdom of her decision, and it wouldn't be the last.

Athen regretted having put such distance between herself and Diana, knowing that her father's friend would be a good source of sound advice. Athen wished she had the courage to call and ask what she thought about it all, and what she thought Ari would say.

In the end, she based her decision on the rationale that, for better or for worse, she was taking a positive step forward into her future for the first time in months. And it would be an opportunity to do something of value for someone other than herself, she reasoned. She'd lived her entire life in Woodside Heights, had taught its children. The parents and grandparents of those children had voted her father into office, and had stood by her side when John had fallen. Perhaps, in her capacity as mayor, she could do something of lasting benefit for the community, as her father and her husband had done. Dan had tugged hard on that string of civic responsibility, of her legacy, and she'd found it hard, if not impossible, to come up with a reason not to run for the office. Maybe, as Dan insisted, she had picked up more from her father than she realized.

Dan kept Athen pretty much out of sight and mute up until the night of the rally, when he would introduce her and officially present his choice to the party. Requests for interviews from the media had been declined at Dan's insistence until after Monday, which was fine with Athen.

Athen splurged on a new dress for the occasion, after Callie pointed out that she had nothing suitably formal and yet professional to wear to the rally.

"It's 2009, Mom." Callie scowled at every dress Athen withdrew from her closet. "Women are into power dressing. I saw it on *Oprah*."

Athen rolled her eyes, but allowed Callie to drag her to the mall for something more appropriate.

Callie assured her that she was content to wear a dress that Meg had sent her last spring, a light green sundress with a light sprinkling of floral embroidery across the bodice and a ruffle at the bottom.

"I thought you hated that dress." Athen had been fully prepared to bribe Callie out of her favorite cutoffs and new soccer cleats for the event if it had been necessary, but Callie had volunteered to wear the sundress.

"Mom." Callie grinned. "I'm going to be First Kid. It's okay if I look like a geek for one night."

Athen was barely zipped into her own new dress—a linen sheath in a deep shade of red, not too tight, not too short, not too low-cut—before Rossi's driver rang the doorbell. She called to Callie to go out and tell Mr. Rossi she'd be down in a second.

Last-minute doubts plagued her and she fumbled with her necklace. The garnet and gold piece her mother had worn on her wedding day was perfect with the dress. She wondered at the wisdom of her decision not to cut her hair or, at the very least, to have piled it on top of her head instead of leaving it to hang straight down her back in a thick black waterfall.

"Too late now," she muttered as she fastened the garnet earrings on and stepped back to take a look at herself.

"Mom," Callie shouted up the steps, "Mr. Rossi said we have to leave right now."

The butterflies in her stomach transformed themselves into something more sinister and were now in the process of gnawing painfully at her insides as she ran down the steps. From the moment she'd made her decision she'd had no time for second thoughts. *God*, she prayed fervently as she closed the front door behind her, *I hope I'm doing the right thing*.

The biennial rally was traditionally hosted by the party at the home of one of the more well-to-do contributors. This year's honor went to Hughes Chapman, who, with his new wife in tow, would greet the movers and shakers on the spacious grounds of their sprawling home just inside the city limits. Rossi's driver carefully made the sharp turn into the Chapmans' drive and ceremoniously opened the back door to assist his passengers as they exited.

Athen caught her breath at the sight of the redbrick Georgian mansion and the graceful grounds that spread out in every direction.

"What does Mr. Chapman do?" she whispered to Dan.

"Well, locally, he owns the *Woodside Herald*, but that's not where the money is. Real estate, professional sports teams, you name it. I heard he just bought a cable station, wants to make it a news powerhouse. Doesn't get much involved in politics except through his wallet." Dan shook out the arms of his dinner jacket so that the sleeves hung just so. "Only reason I tolerate that damned rag and its liberal reporters is because he owns it. Turned it over to his daughter last year, I think." He plastered a smile on his face. "Hughes, great to see you again . . ."

"Dan, welcome." Their host offered a warm greeting.

Jovial and round with twinkling eyes, at first glance, Hughes Chapman called to mind jolly old St. Nick without the beard.

"So, this is Athena Moran." He grabbed both of Athen's hands in his and chuckled. "We've heard quite a bit about you over the past week or so. Lydia," he said to the elegantly dressed woman to his left. "Lydia, dear, say hello to Dan Rossi and Athena Moran."

Lydia Chapman's greeting was, Athen felt, oddly cool under the circumstances.

"It's a pleasure to meet you, Mrs. Chapman." Athen tried to smile despite the close scrutiny of the very sophisticated Mrs. Chapman.

"The pleasure is mine, Mrs. Moran." She smiled cordially, yet there was no real warmth in her blue eyes. She turned to the young woman who stood next to her and said, "Brenda, meet Athena Moran. Brenda is my stepdaughter."

Brenda's eyebrows raised slightly as she inspected Athen more carefully than the occasion would seem to have warranted.

"So you're Athena Moran," she said in a low voice.

Brenda had golden blond hair piled atop her head, with errant wisps that floated around her face. She wore an ankle-length white silk dress that made no attempt to hide the many curves of her body. She looked to be around thirty, and was every bit as elegant and sophisticated as her stepmother.

Moved forward by incoming partygoers, Dan caught Athen by the elbow and, following the crowd, steered her and Callie toward the tent that dominated the lawn to the left of the house. Athen turned back once, feeling Brenda Chapman's eyes burning between her shoulder blades.

What, Athen wondered, *is that all about?*

She managed one last peek at Mrs. Chapman. *There's something that seems familiar about her,* she thought, *though I know we've never met.*

"Boy," Callie exclaimed, "you could have one heck of a track here. You could do a quarter-mile with no problem."

Hundreds of people swarmed inside the tent, happy, friendly bees in an undersized hive. A podium had been built at the far end for the occasion. It loomed before Athen's eyes like Mount Everest.

Oh, God, she thought as her head began to swim, *there is no way I can get up there in front of all these people.* The small shred of self-confidence she had recently rediscovered was suddenly AWOL.

"Dan." Panicked, she clutched at his sleeve. "I changed my mind. I can't do this."

Dan chuckled kindly and patted her arm. "It's just a little stage fright, that's all. You'll be fine."

"I won't be fine. You don't understand." Her voice was a wild whisper. "It's not just stage fright. I'm scared to death. I won't remember what to say."

"You just read the speech I gave you in the car and you'll do fine."

He motioned to Harlan to get the show on the road.

Dan wants to get this over with. He thinks I'm about to bolt, she noted grimly. *And he's right.*

"Athen, I want you to stand right here. Come on, Callie, you stay with your mother and keep her calm, that's a good girl." Dan escorted them to a position in the front right section of the happy crowd.

Thunderous applause greeted Dan as he approached the microphone atop the podium.

"Friends," he said, and a wave of cheers washed over him, the crowd assuring him that they were, indeed, his friends. "Thank you, thank you, I appreciate that . . . thank you . . ."

When the crowd was subdued, he began again. "Friends, eight years ago I stood here and accepted your nomination for mayor. It has been the greatest honor of my life to have served you. Nothing I've ever done has given me greater satisfaction than holding this esteemed office. I thank each and every one of you for the support you've given me over the years."

More applause.

"Tonight we meet to officially nominate my successor. Now, some might say that choosing your own successor is a little like choosing your own executioner," he quipped and the crowd laughed. "But not so. Our party offered many fine possible candidates, many good and willing servants to choose from. Now, our city faces serious challenges over the next few years, my friends. We've lost countless jobs as the factories closed and businesses have moved elsewhere. Our streets are lined with the homeless and the north side of town has been described as a battle zone. I searched my heart long and hard, believe me, for the answer to the question: In whose hands would this city be most secure? In seeking the answer, I knew we had to find a fresh approach to government. I recognized that the old ways will not resolve the new problems. And I knew, too, that our next mayor must be someone of unblemished character, someone whose life was nurtured with the very essence of public service. Yes, as I prepared to leave office, I recognized my sacred responsibility to bring before you the best man . . ."

The silence was overwhelming. The best man? Had Rossi changed his mind about Athen Moran? From the corner of her eyes, Athen watched as several of the previously denied members of Council stood a little straighter and fixed their ties, their color a little higher, their eyes bright with the hope that Rossi had finally come to his senses. Dan held every member of the audience firmly in his hands. Heads nodded in agreement as he spoke.

As Diana Bennett had once noted, this crowd would vote for Lassie if Rossi asked them to.

". . . the man most worthy to represent you in City Hall, the best man to continue the job I began eight years ago." He paused thoughtfully, then slowly unveiled his best politician's smile. "Only this time, ladies and gentlemen, I believe the best man for the job . . . is a woman. Good friends, I give you Athena Stavros Moran."

He motioned joyfully to Athen, his signal for her to join him at the podium. She could not move. Neither her legs nor her mouth, nor any muscle in her body, would respond to the commands he was giving her. Finally, still smiling broadly, he stepped down and held out his arm to her.

"Dan, I *can't* . . ." Her terrified whisper was totally ignored, as if he had not heard her. He grabbed her arm and placed it through his and all but dragged her through the beaming crowd, which was now loudly applauding her appearance on the stage beside him.

He let the cheering of the crowd feed upon itself, as if knowing it would incite them to a level of acceptance of anything he had to say. At the appropriate moment, he motioned for their attention. When the din beneath the tent began to diminish slightly, he began to speak again.

"Thirty years ago, I entered public life as a leader of the second ward," he told them solemnly, "a position I am not ashamed to say I battled City Hall to achieve. At the same time, our fellow citizens in the fourth ward led a battle of their own. Our growing number of Greek residents fought to be heard. They selected as their spokesman a young man named Ari Stavros. A man who had come to this country just ten years earlier, seeking a better life for his beloved and the family they hoped to raise here. Sadly, his dream was shattered in the worst possible way. Many of us were there with him, sharing his grief, the day his beautiful wife, Melina, lost the battle she fought so bravely for so long.

"But personal tragedy did not deter this fine man from giving his all to his community. As the years passed, we watched Ari grow in wisdom and in leadership. We applauded his rise to city council, for we all knew he was a man of honor who would serve his city with the utmost devotion. And all through those years, we watched his little girl grow up right here in Woodside Heights."

Oh, Dan, enough. Athen ground her teeth.

"We watched that little girl grow into a lovely young woman, watched her marry one of our own. Sadly, we watched as the devastation of Ari's first stroke took his voice from Council. Then, less than three years later, we watched as yet another cruel blow of fate struck this good family."

For the love of God, Dan.

Athen fought the urge to grab the microphone from him and hit him over the head with it.

"Was there a sadder day in Woodside Heights than the day young John Moran was shot down on the street, the day he sacrificed himself for each and every one of us?" Rossi wiped his eyes with his handkerchief, as many of the onlookers had been doing for the past five minutes.

Callie squirmed uncomfortably and finally buried her face in Athen's chest.

My poor girl, I'm so sorry, Athen told her wordlessly as she stroked the child's back. *I had no idea he was going to do this, baby, I'm so sorry.*

She kicked Rossi's ankle sharply, hoping he got the message.

"Athena Moran is a woman whose roots are firmly buried in the soil of this city, literally and figuratively." He raised a clenched fist in the air and Athen flinched, exhaling through her teeth. "A woman who understands sacrifice for the common good, understands what it takes to be a dedicated public servant, and she has graciously agreed to offer her service to you. Please lend your support to her as you once did to her father . . . to her husband. To me . . ."

The crowd exploded, nearly lifting the top off the tent as Rossi drew Athen closer to the microphone. Her legs were on the verge of giving out, melting like ice in the 90-degree heat inside the tent, her knees knocking together like crazed bongos.

"Smile pretty," he shouted into her ear, and she tried to force her mouth into some shape that might pass for one. She held on to Callie, gripping the child's hands in hers until Callie yelled, "Mom, you're breaking my fingers!"

"Where's your speech, Athen?" Dan asked through his teeth. "The one I gave you . . ."

Athen fumbled in her purse.

"This is your debut, honey, don't blow it." He was still grinning, continuing to wave to the crowd as he stepped back and pushed her to the center of the podium. Adjusting the microphone to her shorter height, he jabbed her in the back and said, "Go."

She cleared her throat as she unfolded the speech Dan had written for her, praying she could do more than squeak unintelligibly as she had in last night's dream. The prepared speech was long, and as she scanned it she saw references to her father and to John. Out of the corner of her eye she saw her daughter waiting anxiously for her to begin. Athen folded up Dan's speech and hid it in the palm of her hand. She could not subject Callie to any more of the painful reminders of the past, not for Dan, not for anyone. She leaned slightly forward to the microphone and prayed she would not make a fool of herself.

"I would like to thank Mayor Rossi for this opportunity to address you, not only as a citizen of Woodside Heights, but as a hopeful candidate for office. I know that my experience is thin"—it was Rossi's turn to kick her—"but I assure you my convictions run deep. I love this city and I promise you that if I am fortunate enough to have your support, I will continue the fine work begun under Dan's leadership. If I am elected, I will do my best to make you all proud of me."

Out of the corner of her eye she could see a white shadow. Brenda Chapman moved closer to the podium. It was not the woman's stare that momentarily rendered Athen unable to speak, but the stance of the man who accompanied her. Quentin Forbes stood with his arms folded over his chest, his face tight, his eyes locked onto Athen's, clearly mocking her from across the room. There was no smile of recognition, no sign that they had only so recently decided to be friends. Dumbstruck, Athen momentarily forgot where she was and what she was doing. Dan's second kick at the back of her ankle reminded her.

". . . and I . . . I guess that, umm, other than to, umm, thank my daughter for accompanying me, and, umm, thanking Dan for his support, I . . . I've not much else to say except that I'd appreciate your vote come November." Athen backed away from the podium to enthused cheers of encouragement, looking for Quentin in the crowd. She saw only a glimpse of his back as Brenda looped a bare arm through his and led him to the bar at the back of the tent.

Why is he acting like that? she wondered. *Why did he look at me as if I was a stranger? So he's dating Brenda Chapman. That has nothing to do with me. . . .*

". . . and so I ask you to support my nomination of Athena Moran for mayor of our fine city," she heard Rossi say. "All in favor . . ."

The ayes were like thunder, the nays nonexistent. And so Athen's nomination was official. Unless something ridiculous happened—like the residents being taken over by pod people from another planet—Athena Moran most certainly would be the next mayor of Woodside Heights.

She shook hands and accepted kisses on the cheek from what seemed like hundreds of well-wishers as she attempted to make her way toward the bar to get something for her dry throat.

"Well, congratulations, Athen." Diana Bennett stood before her. "I must say this all came as a big surprise. A *very* big surprise, under the circumstances. I wish you well, of course."

"What do you mean, under the circumstances?"

"Suffice it to say that I wish you had talked to me before you let Dan talk you into this." Diana's gaze was level and cool. Almost as cool as Lydia and Brenda Chapman's, but nowhere near as cool as Quentin Forbes's glare.

"What are you talking about?" Athen felt a creeping rush of fear.

"Mom, there's a stable down there, I can see it." Callie tugged at her sleeve. "Can I go down and see if there are horses?"

"They have some beautiful horses, Callie. Would you like me to show you?" Diana offered as she broke eye contact with Athen.

"Can I, Mom?" Callie pleaded.

"Of course." Athen nodded.

"Call me sometime, Athen," Diana said as she walked off with Callie. "We'll have a chat."

Everyone is acting so odd tonight. Diana, Quentin, the Chapmans . . .

She could not keep up with the conversations around her, and at the first opportunity she fled from the tent to the house in search of the ladies' room, where hopefully she'd have a few moments to herself and could think more clearly. She entered the back door and followed the signs that led to a long hall.

Quentin was leaning against an open doorway.

"Well, well, if it isn't the next mayor of Woodside Heights." Judging by his speech, the drink he held was not his first.

"Hello, Quentin," she said cautiously.

"Nice little speech Mr. Rossi gave for you." He emptied the glass. "Nice touch, dragging out your family tree, Athen, or should I say 'Your Honor'? Now there's a joke."

"What's that supposed to mean?"

He smirked.

"What's wrong with you?" She backed away, confused.

"What's wrong with *me*? What's wrong with *you*? is the question."

"What are you talking about? You've been looking at me as if I have some disease since the minute you first saw me in there, Quentin."

"You do have a disease, all right. It's called political ambition. Manifested by letting a pimp like Rossi lead you out here and parade you around, stepping over the bodies of your father and your husband to get you where you want to be."

"That's preposterous. And disgusting."

"Don't bother trying to deny that Rossi handpicked you for the job." He rubbed his chin, as if in deep thought. "Now, what was the line? Oh, yes. *'The best man for the job turned out to be a woman.'* Very catchy, Athen. Was that your line, or did he come up with that on his own?"

"You've been in Woodside Heights how long, Quentin? A couple of months? What the hell do you know about Dan Rossi?"

"I know plenty, Mrs. Soon-To-Be-Mayor. I know he's

as crooked as a poorly hung picture and he's a political pimp. And if you're smart enough to be mayor, I guess you're smart enough to figure out what that makes you."

"*Acriste,*" she sputtered in Greek, questioning his worth as a human being, "How dare you . . ."

"Oh, yeah, go into your little righteous and innocent act. Boy, did I buy into that. Poor little lonely Athen. You really had me fooled. Well, you know the expression, 'Fool me once, shame on you. Fool me twice . . .'"

"I don't know what you're talking about, and I suspect neither do you. Just get out of my way and leave me alone."

She attempted to brush past him, but he grabbed her by the arm.

"Leave you alone? Not a chance." He laughed and put his glass down on the hall table. He reached into his jacket pocket and pulled out a business card, which he snapped onto the tabletop.

Quentin Forbes. The *Woodside Herald.*

"I don't get it," she said coldly.

"Then I'll explain it to you." His eyes were no longer the warm and gentle blue they'd been on past meetings but chips of ice. "I am, as of last Thursday, the reporter on the City Hall beat. I will be in your face every time you turn around. I will be in the front row at every press conference, and I will be the first person outside your door every time there's a crisis or even a hint of one. And every time you screw up, the entire city will know about it by the next morning."

"Why?" she whispered, shaken by his outburst.

"Because there's nothing lower than a man who looks people in the eye and convinces them that he's killing himself on their behalf at the same time he's robbing them blind. Unless it's someone who sells herself to help him to do it."

"Quentin, you don't understand . . ."

"Oh, I understand all too well. I also understand that you're not the woman I thought you were," he muttered. "Though why that bothers me as much as it does . . ."

The ladies' room door opened, and Brenda Chapman flowed into the hallway.

"Have you met Brenda?" He gestured to the blond goddess who approached them. "Brenda's the managing editor at the *Herald*. Yes, I know she's young, but her daddy does own the paper. There are worse ways to get a job," he added pointedly.

He took the arm of a mildly amused Brenda and led her back to the rally, leaving Athen stunned and confused, alone in the great hall.

"I'D SAY SHE'S REALLY GOTTEN under your skin." Brenda set a champagne glass on the breakfast-room table and kicked off her shoes.

Quentin muttered something under his breath and pulled out a chair.

"God, my feet are killing me. I thought this night would never be over." Brenda sat on the cushioned banquette and pulled her legs up under her. "Now, what was that you just said?"

"It doesn't matter."

"Of course it does," she assured him. In the months since Quentin moved east, he and his stepsister had become close friends.

"I just thought she was different, that's all. She just always seemed . . . I don't know. Sweet. Decent."

"So you've said." Brenda sipped her champagne. "What makes you think she's not?"

"Seriously, Brenda?" He made a face. "We both know what a big phony Dan Rossi is."

"Ah, I get it." She nodded. "Guilt by association. He's a phony, she's been hand selected to succeed him, therefore she's a phony, too."

"I'm sorry I brought it up."

"You didn't. I did."

"In that case, I'm sorry you brought it up."

"And I'm sorry your dream girl didn't live up to your expectations." She patted him on the arm.

He shot her a dark look, and she shrugged it off.

"That's what this is all about, right? You're pissed off because Athen Moran isn't living up to your expectations. You're disappointed because now you think she isn't the woman you first thought she was. I get it."

When Quentin didn't respond, Brenda said, "I hope this doesn't influence the way you cover City Hall. I can always assign you to a different beat."

"Are you kidding?" He smirked. "I'm looking forward to this."

"Don't go looking for trouble, Quentin. The *Herald* has a good reputation. I'd like to leave the paper the way I found it."

"I'll be fair. Objective. But I won't let her get away with a thing."

"Does this have anything to do with the fact that Cynthia's father was indicted three years ago for taking bribes and removed from office?"

Quentin shrugged. "Have you ever met an honest politician?"

"Sure. Off the top of my head, I can't think of one,

but I'm sure there are plenty. Just promise me you'll cover her the same way you would cover anyone else."

"Oh, I'll cover her exactly the same way, don't you worry about that." His jaw set. "Like I said, fair and objective. But I'll be watching every move she makes."

"And I'll be watching you, bro, to keep you honest." Brenda gathered up her shoes and her glass.

"I don't need a keeper, Bren."

"Actually, this time, I think you do." She yawned. "It's almost four. We can talk about this again tomorrow, or not, but right now, I'm going to bed."

She patted his shoulder as she headed for the door.

"I'll see you in the morning." Quentin emptied his glass and debated opening another bottle of champagne. Drinking alone wasn't really his style. He left the bottle where it was, in the cooler.

He'd been stunned when he'd first heard that Rossi was going to name Athen as the party's candidate. He'd been sure it had to be a joke, though why anyone would think that was funny . . .

Once it became apparent that she was indeed running for mayor, Quentin felt that the joke was on him. His impression of Dan Rossi was that he was a scoundrel and a crook, though that had yet to be proven. There was no doubt in Quentin's mind that if Rossi had chosen Athen to succeed him, he'd had a damned good reason for doing so.

The question Athen had put to him in the park that day kept coming back to him. "If someone you cared about wanted you to do something you weren't sure you wanted to do, but they really insisted, what would you do?"

Was this what she'd been referring to? That Rossi had asked her to run for the office?

His answer had been questions to her: What's in it for you? What's in it for them?

One way or another, Quentin was going to find out just what Rossi had promised her, and what Rossi was getting in return.

❧ 9 ❧

As Dan had predicted, the election went off without a hitch. What little opposition that might have existed became lost in the votes of confidence for Rossi's protégé. Dan had campaigned vigorously on her behalf, so much so that Athen had rarely had to make one of the dreaded speeches on her own behalf.

Accustomed to arriving at City Hall at eight, she continued to do so even after her election. At Dan's suggestion, she moved Edie up the hall to sit at her old desk and serve as her new assistant. Athen had agreed for Dan's sake, although Edie drove her crazy. She talked too much—to Athen or whoever was closest. Athen was afraid to speak openly in front of her: Edie's idea of a closely guarded secret was only telling the first fifteen people she ran into.

Athen's first call of the day came every morning at nine—from Dan. They discussed whatever was in the newspaper, then they'd go on to the emails from the website and talk about how she might best respond to them. Following that, they'd discuss her agenda: Dan was ever so helpful in guiding Athen through her meetings. As he suggested, at her first Council meeting she thanked all the members of Council for their support and assured them that nothing would change. Since Dan spoke with both Harlan and Jim each day, most of the discussion seemed to take place between those two Council members.

As a matter of fact, each day's meeting seemed to follow the same agenda, except for when Jim or Harlan would occasionally ask her, "Isn't that what you understood Dan to have said, Athen?" She'd nod in agreement and they'd continue on around her.

Soon Athen felt about as useless as Angelo Giamboni—who after the first month or so cut his attendance to two or three meetings a week—or George Konstantos, who after greeting Athen affectionately and inquiring after Ari—in Greek—had continued his practice of sleeping through each meeting, apparently unconcerned about who was speaking, what they were saying, or even who was mayor. Fallon seemed to be the only member of the group who recognized her new position.

Athen chose to take her own notes, having little else to do.

True to his word, Quentin Forbes faced off with her at every press conference. He always sat right in the middle of the front row where Athen could not avoid seeing him. Even if she refused to meet his eyes, she would have to address his questions. She began to dread these open confrontations, when she would step up to the microphone, primed by Dan to discuss the progress of the new budget or the progress of the negotiations with the trash collectors, and he'd throw her a curve.

Quentin would rise to address her. "Mayor Moran, what is your position on the new shelter for the homeless that's been proposed by the Council of Churches?"

"I . . . ah . . . I haven't had time to study that proposal," she'd stumble, unprepared to discuss anything other than what Dan had placed in her agenda for that day. Whenever she suggested that she discuss something other than what he'd given her, Dan would say, "Wait till you get your feet wet," or "Let's just deal with one thing at a time. Right now, this is the priority. There's time enough to get into these other things, after you learn to handle the reins."

"Surely Mr. Rossi has had time to study it." Quentin would look down at his notes, as if unaware that he'd struck a nerve.

"Mr. Rossi no longer holds public office, Mr. Forbes," she would reply as calmly as her clenched jaws would permit.

"Then may I assume that you will in fact read the proposal yourself?" he would ask, his eyes challenging her.

"You may, Mr. Forbes." She would abruptly break eye contact and look about the room for other questions.

And so it went, week after week, sparring back and forth, she alternately cursing the day she met him and the day she was sworn in as mayor.

He had not exaggerated. He was making her every move news of the worst sort, and it seemed to her that he was deliberately slanting his stories to put her in the worst possible light.

"Mayor ignores pleas from city churches for homeless refuge," the headlines would shout, followed by a story that portrayed her as a modern-day Marie Antoinette. "Mayor signs new pact with FOP on first day of negotiations" preceded the article that went into detail on her late husband's police service and made a point of highlighting the clause that increased the pension for retired officers by 6 percent when the firemen only got 4—failing to note, of course, that during the last session of bargaining the firemen had gotten 3 percent and the police had gotten 1 percent. She could not attend a meeting without him being exactly where he'd promised he'd be: in her face.

Athen looked forward to Christmas in a way she never had before. For one thing, Meg would be home for the first time since last spring, her plans for a visit in the fall having been aborted due to her work schedule. For another, Athen would have an entire week off, one whole week to be herself again, to enjoy Meg's company, and to not have to look into Quentin Forbes's mocking eyes.

At the same time, she dreaded the holiday, their first without John. It would be hard for Callie this year, Athen knew, and she wanted to be there when her daughter needed her.

"Anyone here got a tree they need help decorating?" Meg had blown in through the front door. Her plane had been delayed due to bad weather in Chicago, and she'd phoned earlier in the day to tell Athen she'd take a cab from the airport whenever she finally had the good fortune to arrive.

"Aunt Meg!" Callie whooped and flew down the steps, tripping over Meg's luggage and all but knocking the small woman over.

"Whoa, would you look at this girl! You're nearly as tall as I am, Callie." Meg stepped back to take a good look at her niece.

"That's not so tall." Callie grinned.

"Oh, a jokester, eh? Where's the mama-san? There she is . . ."

Athen embraced her sister-in-law, feeling as she always did around Meg, like an Amazon hugging a pygmy.

Meg, barely five two, made up for her size with her boundless energy.

"Your Honor." Meg feigned a curtsy and Athen laughed.

"God, it's good to see you. You look great. I love the new hair." Athen held Meg at arm's length, inspecting the short permed curls that fell around Meg's face, replacing the miles of honey blond hair she'd sported all her life. "It's wonderful, Meg, you look ten years younger."

"Music to my ears. Oh, honey, where'd you get that tree?" Meg stood, hands on her hips, surveying the scrawny little number Athen had dragged home over the weekend.

"I told you it was too small." Callie turned to her mother with an accusatory air. "I told you it was a poor excuse for a tree. Daddy always brought home perfect trees."

Athen exchanged a chagrined look with Meg, then attempted to put her arms around Callie. "It was as perfect as I could find five days before Christmas. And it was the biggest one I could fit on top of my little car. I'm sorry if it falls short of your expectations, Callie."

"Daddy would never have brought home a tree like that," Callie insisted, tears welling up as she shook her mother off.

"It'll be grand when we get the lights and all the decorations on," Meg assured her as she draped her coat over the back of the sofa. "You'll see. It'll be beautiful. We'll make it beautiful."

"Fat chance," grumbled Callie. "And besides, Daddy always puts the lights on."

"And who do you think taught your father to do so masterful a job, hmmm? None other than his little sister, that's who. We can take care of this sucker in no time flat. Athen, lights, please."

Athen produced the lights and ornaments as Meg sorted through the boxes, checking each strand to make sure all the bulbs worked. Soon the little tree had been transformed and they stood back to admire their handiwork.

"Oh, the angel!" Athen poked around to find the box and drew out the angel she'd bought for their first tree. "Callie, it's your job."

"I can't do it this year." Her bottom lip trembled. "There's no one to lift me to the top."

"Oh, but the tree's not so tall. I'll bet a chair would do the trick." Athen dragged in a chair from the dining room. It elevated Callie just enough to reach the top of the tree and gently place the angel on the uppermost branch.

"Wonderful!" Meg clapped her hands.

"See, it's not so bad." Athen nodded at the tree.

"It's not the same, though." Callie fought bravely to blink back tears.

"No, sweetheart, it's not the same," agreed Athen, her heart breaking along with her child's.

"I think I'll go to bed, now," Callie told them quietly. "Good night, Aunt Meg. I'm glad you're here. Good night, Mom."

She kissed them both and headed up the steps stiffly.

"Oh, Athen . . ." Meg shook her head sadly.

"It's very hard for her, Meg. She and John were so close, they did so much together. I knew she'd have an especially hard time with the holiday."

"And you?" Meg asked.

"It's a little easier for me, I guess. I'm an adult. But still . . ." She glanced at the tree. "I can tell you a story about every item on that tree. Those pinecones—John and Callie gathered them in the park and brought them home and sprayed them gold. Callie was five that year. The plaster angels—we made them three years ago in little plastic molds John found in a toy store. The papier-mâché bells—John made them for Callie her first Christmas."

"Stop," begged Meg, and before either of them knew what was happening, they were seated on the floor, leaning against each other, crying their eyes out.

"Oh, God, I hope Callie didn't hear us," Meg sniffed when the storm of tears had begun to subside.

"I should go check on her." Athen stood up.

"Get a tissue and dry your face before you go upstairs," Meg cautioned. "You look ghastly."

"*I* look ghastly!" Athen laughed shakily. "You should see your face. You've got mascara down to your lower lip."

"I must look like a raccoon." Meg helped herself to a tissue and rubbed the skin below her eyes. "Better?"

"Much," Athen replied as she went up the steps to her daughter's room. "I'll be back down as soon as I check in with Callie."

MEG HAD MADE TEA AND it had cooled by the time Athen joined her in the living room.

"Is she okay?" Meg asked.

"She's better, but she's hurting," Athen told her. "I think she feels guilty about celebrating Christmas without her dad. I think she feels like she's betrayed him by having a good time decorating the tree without him."

"I think that's normal," noted Meg. "It's hard for a child to grasp a concept like "Life goes on." The last thing in the world John would have wanted for any of us would have been for our lives to stop when his did. You both have a lot of miles to go, you know, and he would have wanted you to enjoy every mile of the journey."

Athen nodded thoughtfully. *Izoie synehizete*, her father would say. "Life goes on."

"So tell me how it feels to be the duly elected mayor of Woodside Heights. Ha! What a kick." Meg slid her shoes off, pulled her feet under her, and settled onto the sofa for a long chat.

They sat and talked until well past two, switching from tea to a glass of wine to toast Athen's new position and Meg's homecoming.

"So all in all, it's been pretty smooth sailing," Athen told her as she emptied her glass. "Everyone's been pretty nice to me. Dan gives me advice whenever I need it, which is every day. The only real problems I have are with Council and this one damned reporter for the *Herald* who's made it his life's work to make me as miserable and look as foolish as possible."

"Oh?" Meg poured a second glass of wine for herself, offering a refill to Athen, who declined.

"Council generally ignores me and the reporter won't leave me alone." She pulled her feet up under her.

"What do you mean, Council ignores you?" Meg asked curiously. "How can they ignore you? You're the mayor."

"Well, there's only one member of Council who's very . . . *active*, I guess is the best word. He and the so-licitor both talk to Dan every day, so I guess by the time we meet in the afternoon there's not a whole lot left to talk about." As she spoke, she realized how ineffectual she sounded.

"Wait a minute." Meg held up a hand to stop her. "I thought you replaced Dan as mayor."

Athen nodded. "I did."

"So why is he still talking to . . . who's he talking to, anyway?"

"The president of Council, Jim Wolmar, and Harlan Justis, the city solicitor."

"Do they talk to you?"

"Not so much."

"Why not?"

"Well . . ." Athen sought an explanation that would make her look less stupid than she felt at that minute.

"Do you let Rossi tell you what to do?" Meg's tone was accusatory.

"He gives me advice." Athen chose her words carefully.

"And you do what he suggests you do."

"Most of the time," Athen admitted, then nodded slowly, adding, "I guess all of the time."

"Why do you do that? Why do you let him tell you what to do?" Meg pressed.

"Well, I guess because he knows more than I do about what's going on."

"What are you doing to educate yourself? What steps have you taken to become informed on your own?"

"I haven't really had much time to get into things as much as I'd like to." Athen squirmed uncomfortably under Meg's glare. "I've only been in office for two months. Not even two months."

"Well, what do you do when you don't agree with him?"

"Well, I pretty much always agree with him."

"Because he tells you he's right?" Meg stared at Athen in disbelief.

"Pretty much, but he knows what's best for . . ."

"Don't you have your own agenda, things you think are important?"

"Of course I do," Athen defended herself staunchly. "I'll get to them. I mean, I plan to, but other things seem to keep popping up that need to be tended to."

"Things Dan tells you to tend to? Things he thinks are important?"

"Look, Meg, you're not born knowing how to run a city. Dan has years of experience. I have none. I don't think it's so odd that he gives me advice. I'm sure if my dad could, he'd be advising me, too."

"Giving you advice is one thing. Telling you what to do is something else." Meg stared at her. "You do know the difference, don't you?"

"Of course I do. But, Meg, there's so much to learn. I'm trying my best, but there's just so damned much."

"Just let me get this straight." Meg tapped her fingers on the arm of the sofa. "Dan asks you to run for mayor, gets you elected, then tells you what to do, so effectively he's still the mayor."

Athen did not respond.

"Athen," Meg said quietly, "if Dan still wanted to be mayor, why didn't he just run again? . . . Why did he talk you into running?"

"Because he'd already served four consecutive terms." The true meaning of the words became clear as glass as she spoke them aloud. "And that's all the city charter allows."

"So after your term he can run again . . ." Meg spoke the obvious.

"I don't know. Maybe." Athen had never felt so small, so much a fool in her life. "I guess so."

They sat in silence for a very long moment.

"No wonder the press beats up on you," Meg said after a time. "I'd be beating up on you, too, if I covered Woodside Heights."

"I don't think it's as bad as you make it sound." Athen struggled to defend Dan as well as herself. "Dan really knows this city, he loves it. He knows what's best . . ."

"In whose opinion?" Meg challenged her. "Besides his own, I mean."

"I-I guess in everyone's opinion," Athen told her. "He was a great mayor, Meg, he's done more for this city than . . ."

"Like what? Name three major things he's accomplished over the past eight years and I'll get off your back and never bring it up again." Meg crossed her arms over her chest and waited.

Athen thought hard.

"Has he brought new business into the city? More jobs?" Meg asked.

Athen thought of the layoffs announced just two weeks ago at the paper plant, only one of several factories to suffer severe setbacks over the past two years.

"Has he been able to make a dent in the drug problem? Hired new law enforcement officers, encouraged a town watch in the inner-city neighborhoods?"

Athen recalled a conversation she'd had with one of John's classmates from the police academy back around Thanksgiving. He was thinking of quitting the force. Their weapons were outdated, there were not enough men on the streets, and there was indifference at the top to the problems facing the rank and file. He'd expressed the hope that Athen would take a more aggressive approach.

"Has he formulated a plan to rejuvenate the business district? Improve public housing?" Meg's finely honed ability to see clearly to the heart of things was developed through years as an investigative reporter, and later as a news anchor. She quickly sifted through facts and discarded sentimentality.

Athen thought of the recent HUD report that had declared Woodside Heights's public housing "grossly inadequate." Of the boarded-up, abandoned buildings in the northern sections of the city.

"Seems to me that the most significant thing Mr. Rossi has done in eight years is to find a way to serve eight more," Meg noted bluntly.

"Well, I guess it's been obvious to everyone but me." Athen was suddenly sick to her stomach. Dan had needed someone to hold his place in line, and she'd agreed to do it for him. "You must think I'm a total idiot." She covered her face with her hands.

"I know better." Meg rubbed her shoulders. "But I do think Dan Rossi knew exactly what he was doing when he picked you to be his successor."

"Yeah. 'I'll get Athen to run. She's stupid enough . . .'" Her eyes filled with tears.

"Not stupid, babe. Naïve, yes. Trusting, yes. But not stupid, okay?" Meg moved closer and put an arm around Athen. "Look, wasn't he your dad's friend all those years? They worked together on the City Council, right? I'll bet your dad was a big supporter of Rossi's, too."

Athen nodded.

"So he's a trusted family friend, and you've been brought up to show respect and to defer to your elders. Why wouldn't you trust him? You had no reason to suspect him or his motives. Add in the big losses you've had to deal with over the past few years—your dad's stroke, losing John—Rossi came on like a father figure, I'm betting. Took you under his wing, convinced you that you'd be a natural, and, oh, yeah, he'd always be there to advise you, right?"

When Athen nodded, Meg continued, putting it all in perspective. "So, of course, when he approached you, you had no reason to look for an ulterior motive. Why would you?"

"The way he explained it, me running for mayor would be a good thing for the city, something my dad and John would be proud of." Athen began to cry.

"They will be," Meg assured her.

Athen looked up at her. "How could they be? I've allowed myself to be a pawn. Even if Dan only wants to be mayor again so that he can do really good things for the city, I still allowed myself to be used."

"Yes, you did." Meg sat back against the sofa. "But now that you know, what are you going to do about it?"

What was it Quentin had said to her that day in the park? Ask: What's in it for me? What's in it for him?

Everyone had known all along what was in it for Rossi—everyone, apparently, except Athen.

What was in it for her remained to be seen.

🐾 10 🐾

"Now, bring me up-to-date on your life." Athen poured coffee for Meg at breakfast the next morning and tried to ignore the fact that she still felt the sting of Meg's comments from the night before. Meg's ability to cut so cleanly to the heart of the situation left Athen with the unavoidable knowledge that she had some serious questions to ask herself between now and the time her Christmas holiday concluded. "I take it things did not work out with what's-his-name?"

"That son of a bitch." Meg scowled. "Remember I told you I thought he was seeing someone else? Well, guess who? Jenny Scott!"

"Your next-door neighbor?"

"The same. Of course, we're not neighbors anymore. They moved into a neat little town house on the other side of Tulsa together. Can you believe it?" She put her head back and all but screamed, "I hate men!"

"Until the next one comes along." Athen laughed.

"Well, of course. That goes without saying." Meg grinned.

"Where are you off to?" Athen asked Callie, who was pulling on her jacket and hat.

"To Nina's," Callie told her. "We're working on a project at her house."

"School project?" Meg poured cream into her cup.

"Nope. Something special. A surprise." Callie kissed them both and headed for the back door. "See ya."

"Must be a last-minute Christmas present," Athen explained. "Callie's into arts and crafts this year."

"Speaking of last-minute things, I've a few items to pick up myself," Meg said. "Would you have time to drive me into town?"

"I've got some baking to do, and I haven't finished wrapping Callie's presents." Athen frowned. "Why don't you just take the car and run your errands?"

"Good idea. Thanks. I appreciate it." Meg drained her cup. "Listen, Athen, not that I really mind sharing a room with a ten-year-old for a week—God knows I love Callie like she was my own—but don't you think it's time to finish that guest room? I mean, the chances of my beloved brother coming back to hang those last few rolls of paper are not good."

"I know." Athen sighed. "I think about it from time to time, but then I get depressed and I put it off."

"And if you don't mind my saying so, the hall bath—and the hall, for that matter—are ready to be done over.

And maybe it's time for you to get that bunny paper off Callie's walls."

"I wouldn't know where to start." Athen clenched her jaw as she cleaned off the table.

"Start here." Meg tossed her the phone book, then pulled on her jacket. "The Yellow Pages. Under Paint and Paper."

"DAMN MEG, ANYWAY," ATHEN GRUMBLED as she measured flour into a bowl for the first batch of cookies. "She always has a way of making everyone feel like an idiot." *You're nothing more than a figurehead mayor, Athen. How could you be so stupid, Athen? Your daughter isn't a two-year-old anymore, Athen, nix the bunny paper. . . .*

Athen was miffed, and she took it out on the cookie dough. She was well aware of her shortcomings. She didn't need Meg to point them out to her. It took four batches for the snit to pass, but by the time the last tray went into the oven, she was over it.

When Meg failed to return by two, Athen began to wonder just how many stops her sister-in-law had to make. At four thirty, she left a note on the table, telling Meg she'd be back by five, and arranged a plate of cookies for her elderly neighbor. By the time she delivered the goodies to Mrs. Sands and walked back across the street, her car was safely in the driveway.

"Where's Meg?" she asked Callie, who was gleefully raiding the cookie jar.

"She's in the shower," a cookie-crammed mouth told her. "She has a date."

"She has a what?" Athen hung her coat up in the hall closet and stuck her head back into the kitchen.

"A date with a man." Callie grinned. "Someone she went to college with or something. She's real excited."

Athen started dinner, splashing a jar of spaghetti sauce into a pan and spattering the front of her shirt, wondering who Meg's mystery man was. When the hum of the hair dryer ceased, she went upstairs to find out.

Meg was in a frenzy, struggling into a short black velvet dress and cursing at the zipper.

"Here, I'll do it." Athen laughed and lent a hand.

"I hope you don't mind, Athen." Meg leaned over the dresser and attempted to apply eye makeup with shaky hands. "I mean, with me just getting here last night and everything. But I have waited fourteen years for this date and I'd walk through downtown Woodside Heights naked before I'd miss this opportunity."

"Whoa." Athen sat down on the bed and laughed. "Tell me, tell me."

"Well, when I was in college, there was one guy who was so phenomenal, everyone was in love with him. He dated a girl on my floor senior year and we all used to hang out the window when he'd come to pick her up just so we could watch him walk." Meg groaned as a poorly aimed brush slid eye shadow onto her face. "Anyway, who do I see when I walk into Silver's Card Shop this afternoon but Buddy. Tall, dark, and incredibly handsome Buddy. I must say the years have been very good to this man. So, of course, I had to go over and see if it was really him, you know? So we started talking, and he suggested we take a stroll through town to see the Christmas displays, and we ended up having coffee over at Lorenzo's—I didn't even know that place was still there—and the next thing I knew he was asking me if I'd like to go to a cocktail and dinner party with him tonight. Well, he didn't have to ask me twice."

Meg flounced her hair, nervously glancing at the

clock on Callie's desk. "Oh, God, Athen, he'll be here in five minutes. What do you think? How do I look?"

"Gorgeous. He'll fall at your feet," Athen assured her.

"That's close enough for starters. Thank God I had the sense to pack my lucky dress." She grinned. "This little number has never let me down. Oh, shit, where're my shoes? Oh, God, that's the doorbell. . . ."

"Calm down, Meg, I'll get it." Athen headed for the landing.

"Talk about miracles of fate." Meg kept up a nervous patter as Athen took the steps two at a time. "Him coming here from St. Louis, me coming home from Tulsa . . ."

Athen all but froze in midair.

"What does he do?" she asked cautiously.

"Well, he's writing a book on the Underground Railroad, the local connections and that sort of thing, but he's working for his stepfather, too. Athen, will you please get that door?"

Cement feet carried Athen to the front door. Wooden hands opened it. An obviously startled Quentin Forbes stood on the top step.

"I-I think I have the wrong house," he stuttered. "I was looking for number two thirty-five."

"You found it. Please come in so I can close the door, 'Buddy.'" She motioned stiffly for him to enter.

He stepped inside but only enough to push the door closed behind him.

"Meg . . . ?" He cleared his throat awkwardly.

"My sister-in-law."

"Meg . . . ?" He looked at her blankly.

"Moran." She finished for him.

"Oh. I hadn't remembered her last name. Your husband's . . ."

"Sister."

"I see." He was obviously unaccustomed to such discomfort. Athen found herself enjoying it.

"Buddy, hi." Meg sauntered down the steps in her short black dress, looking casually gorgeous, and it was then that Athen realized how frumpy she herself looked. Her white sweatshirt was liberally doused with spaghetti sauce. Her shoeless feet were clad in white wool socks, and her jeans were faded, her hair a rumble, half hanging from a knot at the back of her neck.

"Athen, I guess you've met . . ." Meg began to formally introduce them.

"'Buddy.'" Athen nodded. "Yes, we've met."

"Well," he said, looking not at Meg but at Athen. "I guess we should . . ."

"Yes," she replied. "You certainly should."

Meg looked at her, questioning, her eyes narrowing slightly, not for a second unaware of the strange undercurrent running between the man of her dreams and her sister-in-law.

"Have a good time." Athen fairly pushed them out onto the front steps. Closing the door quietly behind them, she wondered why she had a sudden urge to bang her forehead against the oak panels.

Athen was still wide awake when she heard the car doors slam. Callie, having chided her for being such a grump, convinced Athen to take her foul mood to bed before ten.

She heard them in the hallway for a few minutes, their laughter floating up the stairwell into her room. It took all her self-control not to tiptoe to the top of the stairs to eavesdrop. The front door closed quietly several minutes later. Athen closed her eyes and pulled the covers up when she heard Meg tiptoe into her room.

"Don't you even pretend to be sleeping, Athena Moran. I know you're not." Meg poked her.

"How was the party?" Athen dropped the childish ruse and sat.

"It would have been a hell of a lot more fun—not to mention less awkward—if you had told me ahead of time that you'd had something going with my date." Meg was ready to explode.

"What?" Athen sat up all the way.

"You could have told me that you and Buddy were more than casual acquaintances."

"Now wait just a minute, Meg. How was I supposed to know that your old college chum 'Buddy' was the same man who's been making my life a living hell for the past three months? And for the record, there is nothing between 'Buddy' and me. Except maybe animosity and hostility."

"Athen, I have known enough men in my life to recognize when a man is dead on his face over another woman."

"You are out of your mind." Athen stared blankly at her sister-in-law.

"All he wanted to talk about the entire night was you."

"I can't imagine why."

"Not to mention the fact that there was enough electricity in that little vestibule when I walked downstairs tonight to light half the Christmas trees in Woodside Heights."

"Meg, you have the most incredible imagination of anyone I have ever met." Athen shook her head. "Look, you don't know what this man has done to me. He goes out of his way to publicly humiliate me every chance he gets. He thinks I'm a political slut, he . . ."

". . . is fascinated by you." Meg kicked high heels across the room and made a spot for herself on the bed.

"I'm telling you, all night long, one question after another."

"Like what?" Athen eyed her suspiciously.

"Like everything. Everything from how long you and John had been married, to what kind of a deal you made with that 'scumbag Rossi,' to . . ."

"What?!"

"Those were his exact words." Meg nodded.

"There was no 'deal,' Meg. I did this because . . . because . . ." Athen was suddenly at a loss. "Because at the time I thought it was the right thing to do. Because I thought I could do something good."

"That's exactly what I told him. I told him you were absolutely incapable of anything that even hinted at being underhanded." Meg paused. "Athen, do you still think that was the right decision?"

"I do, and no vague little innuendoes coming from someone who up until six months ago had never set foot in Woodside Heights is going to change my mind."

"Buddy thinks Rossi is long on rhetoric and short on accomplishment," Meg told her. "He also thinks Rossi is into something shady."

"Rumors, no substance. Who knows where he gets his information, anyway? And I don't want to hear another word. I already know what he thinks of me, so let's just can it."

"I just want to say one more thing. I'm really surprised that you have such a closed mind. Buddy has no motivation to go witch-hunting. What possible reason could he have for going after Rossi if there's nothing there?"

"Because he . . . he hates me," Athen sputtered. "I don't know why but he does. And because he's a reporter—reporters are always suspicious of anyone in politics. It's a prerequisite for the job. And because he's trying to impress Brenda Chapman."

"His stepsister? Why would he care about impressing her?"

"What?" Athen paused.

"Brenda is his stepsister."

Athen thought it through. "Then Lydia Chapman . . ."

". . . is his mother." Meg nodded. "She mentioned she'd met you."

"She and her husband hosted the rally the night Rossi nominated me." Athen's face flushed at the memory of the cool reception she'd received from Mrs. Chapman, the amused glances from Brenda, Quentin's insults. "Quentin Forbes is a . . . a geeky little butthead."

Meg hooted. "He's hardly that, Thena. I think he's really concerned that . . ."

"I could care less what he's concerned about." Athen pushed Meg off the bed with her foot. "I am going to sleep now. And hopefully, by the time I wake up tomorrow, I'll have forgiven you for consorting with the enemy and for bringing that man into my home."

"Okay, okay." Meg stooped to pick up her shoes. "But I would think you'd want to know if there was something going on in which you could eventually be implicated."

"There is nothing going on. Nothing. What could be going on?" Athen sat up. "What was he talking about, anyway?"

"He didn't get into specifics."

"Forbes is blowing smoke, Meg. I am not the least bit concerned about his gossip, and neither should you be. Now go to bed, please."

"I'm going." Meg turned for the door. "But, Athen, maybe you should . . ."

"Enough, Meg." Athen turned her face in her pillow, and for the next several hours fitfully battled the mean demons Meg had brought home with her.

THE HOLIDAY PASSED WITHOUT FURTHER reminder of the shadow that Quentin Forbes had cast over her. Athen pondered his insinuations as she, Meg, and Callie were on their way to see her father on Christmas morning. It annoyed her that even on this day Quentin Forbes managed to get—and stay—under her skin.

Unconsciously, she scanned the parking lot for a little blue car, but it was nowhere in sight.

"Come on, you two," she commanded her passengers, who were merrily singing carols. Callie insisted on bringing her new iPod and dock to fill her grandfather's small room with the sounds of the holidays. "Help me, Callie. Meg, you grab that bag."

Athen and Callie struggled with an enormous red poinsettia. Ari had always filled their house with them at Christmas, and each year on the holiday she would bring the biggest one she could find to add a touch of cheer to his room.

She thought he almost smiled at the sight of them, his eyes offering the welcome his voice could not extend, his gaze lingering upon Callie. Athen opened a cardboard box and removed the brass candelabra shaped like a fishing boat that Ari had brought with him from Greece. She placed the candles in their places and lit them, one by one. Her father stared at their lights, and she thought he might be recalling the many Christmases the small boat had seen over the years.

Next Athen delivered gifts to the nurses' station, seeking out the ever-faithful Lilly for a special cash gift for all the extra care she showered on Ari.

"Why, thank you, Mrs. Moran. Thank you for thinking of me." Lilly smiled. As Athen started back to her room, Lilly added, "Just missed Ms. Bennett. Said she wanted to catch the last service over there at the church but she'd be back."

Athen stopped in her tracks.

"She's been here already?"

"Oh, yes. Break of dawn she was here. Brought a special breakfast to share with Mr. Stavros."

"Is she here every day?" Athen heard herself ask.

"Oh, yes, ma'am. Most days twice a day. She sure is devoted to that man, Mrs. Moran."

"Yes." Athen nodded thoughtfully. "It would appear that she is."

Athen walked slowly back to Ari's room, suddenly filled with gratitude that her father had found someone whose devotion and love was so complete that it could survive such tragedy. In the depths of her own sorrow, she had forgotten that such boundless love did indeed exist. She could almost envy Diana, she thought, as she joined the others who were now singing "Away in a Manger" in Ari's room.

TWO DAYS LATER, MEG AND Athen were seated in the living room, enjoying the blaze of a dancing fire in the fireplace, listening to the *Messiah*, and lounging for the first time in months.

"Athen."

She heard Meg, but only barely, having leaned her head back and closed her eyes.

"Athen," Meg persisted. "I want to talk."

"Don't do it, Meg," Athen said without opening her eyes. "Don't even mention his name."

"I don't want to talk about him. I want to talk about you."

"What about me?" Athen yawned.

"About your life."

"What's wrong with my life?"

"Don't you think it's time to get John's toothbrush out of the bathroom?" Meg asked gently.

Silence.

"Athen, you can't spend the rest of your life grieving over John."

"Meg, please . . ."

"No, Athen, I mean it. You're young, you're beautiful, you're bright—though your career path has led me to question that somewhat lately, but we'll let that ride for now. You can't wrap yourself in the past, build a shrine to a dead man."

"What the hell is that supposed to mean?" Athen's head shot up.

"Look at this house, Athen. You haven't touched a thing of John's since the day he died. I'll bet his clothes are still in the closet."

Meg waited, and finally Athen nodded.

"How long are they going to hang there?"

"Meg, you're overstepping the line a bit." The afternoon's peace had evaporated.

"What line? There's no line. We're family, and as far as I can see there's no one else around to tell you what you need to hear."

"You don't know what it's been like."

"Don't I? Johnny was my brother, my best friend, next to you. He was always there for me, Athen, for as long as I can remember. I could scream with rage every time I think about him dying, and I think about him every day."

Meg's voice was controlled and calm. "But my life didn't end with his, and neither should yours."

"That's not quite fair, Meg," Athen told her. "I've come a long way in the past year."

"Athen, you have no social life. You go from work to Callie's school and home and back to work again. You don't even paint anymore. And how long has it been since you tutored down at the community center? I'll bet you haven't even had that new bike out more than five times since you bought it."

"Meg, I'm a single working mother. And with all the meetings I attend, I don't have time for anything else."

"Stop hiding behind your job! Don't you realize that for the past year you've done nothing but hide? You've hidden inside this house, hidden inside your sorrow, hidden from yourself. Now you're hiding behind Dan Rossi, and you can't keep doing that."

Meg held her breath, waiting for Athen to explode.

"Look, Athen, I love you dearly. You're more than a sister, more than a friend. You can't spend the rest of your life with nothing more to look forward to than a trip to the cemetery to put flowers on John's grave." Meg swallowed hard.

Still Athen did not respond.

"Look, there's a brand-new year starting next week. I know it's hard, but, Thena, John's not coming back."

"I know." Athen bit her lip. "I don't even know where to begin."

"Begin by getting this house spruced up. Move the furniture around. Give John's clothes away. I'll help you. You can go into the new year on fresh ground."

"Okay." Athen nodded. "You're right. And next week I'll . . ."

"Forget next week," Meg told her. "Tomorrow. We're going to start tomorrow."

UPON FIRST SEEING HER FATHER'S clothes removed from the dresser and packed into paper bags, Callie had burst into tears. When Athen explained to her that they would be given to people who really needed them, she brightened.

"Oh, you mean like the homeless guys who hang around Schuyler Avenue?" Callie asked. "Cool. Dad would have liked his warm things to keep someone else warm."

"When were you down on Schuyler Avenue?" Athen folded shirts and placed them in a bag.

"Last week when Julie's mom took us to the movies, we had to detour around Third Street. There were all these people hanging out around the big church on the corner, and Julie's mom said they were all homeless." She picked through a pile of sweatshirts. "Can I keep some of these?"

"You may keep all of them if you want." Athen smiled.

"Well, I think I'll just keep a few. I have warm shirts of my own." She thumbed through the pile, selecting several that had been particular favorites of John's. "Maybe I should go through my stuff, too, Mom. There were a lot of little kids with their moms outside that church. It made me feel real sad. Maybe you should clean out your own closet and we could send lots of stuff down. Ms. Evelyn said . . . "

"Where'd you see Ms. Evelyn?" Athen stuck a stack of brand-new wool socks into the bag.

"She was outside the church. I ran over to see her but Julie's mom made me come right back."

"What was Ms. Evelyn doing down there?" White undershirts, still in their wrappings from last fall, followed the socks.

"She does volunteer work there. She cooks at dinner-time. She said the situation is getting out of hand."

"What is getting out of hand?" Meg carried an empty box into the room. "What do you think, Thena? Shoes, belts in here?"

Athen nodded.

"Ms. Evelyn says there are too many people out of work and more mouths to feed at the church than she can deal with." Callie gathered up the shirts she had selected. "I'm going to clean out my dresser. Then we'll have lots of things to take down to the church and Ms. Evelyn will be happy."

"Spoken like a budding social activist." Meg smiled.

"Frankly, I've been concerned about the situation my-self. Here, give me a hand with these suits . . ."

Callie came back in for some plastic bags, and then dragged them, filled, to the bottom of the steps.

"I'm going over to Julie's, Mom," Callie called up the stairwell. "She's going to clean out her closets, too."

"While you finish up that last shelf there"—Meg mo-tioned to the closet—"I'll go downstairs and make us some lunch. We should be just about ready to take this stuff to wherever it is you want it to go."

Athen was sitting cross-legged on the floor, her back against the bed, when Meg came in twenty minutes later.

"Hey, are you deaf? I've been calling you." Meg paused in the doorway. "Honey, are you all right?"

Athen looked up at her with a white tear-stained face, her bottom lip quivering. The pale gray sheet of paper in her hand rustled, her hands were shaking so.

"What is it?" Meg knelt down and gently placed her hand on her shoulder.

Without a word, Athen passed the letter in her hand to a puzzled Meg, who scanned it quickly.

"Oh," she exclaimed with only mild interest. "Where'd you find this?"

"On a shelf at the back of John's closet." Athen stretched her arm for the tissue box. "There's a whole box of them."

"Athen, don't tell me this is bothering you? A letter from John's old girlfriend that was written sixteen years ago?"

Athen nodded.

"Why?"

"Don't you realize John saved every letter she ever wrote to him? I had no idea they were there." Athen blew her nose.

"So what?"

"So don't you know what that means?"

"It means it was a time in his life that was important to him."

"It means more than that." Athen sniffed. "It means he probably never stopped loving her."

"Don't be ridiculous."

"How could he have? I mean, Dallas MacGregor is every man's fantasy. How could I have thought I could step into her place in John's life?"

"You didn't," Meg said bluntly, "nor should you have expected to."

"Thank you, oh, so very much."

"Thena, you had your own place in John's life. The fact that he once loved someone else . . ."

"Not just someone else, Meg. *Dallas MacGregor*. How would you feel, marrying a man who had been love with a woman who looks like that? A huge movie star—a real *star*—for God's sake . . ."

"I'd feel damn flattered." Meg crossed her arms. "And

it's not as if you hadn't known about John's relationship with her. Why, all of a sudden, is it bothering you?"

"I guess because I hadn't realized he'd cared enough to save all these," Athen whispered.

"Look, John and Dallas were together all through college. But he always knew where she was headed. She was always up front that after college she was taking off for California. I don't think he really understood that all she ever wanted was to be a movie star, that she wasn't about to let a little thing like love stand in her way. Two days after graduation, it was '*Adiós*, John. *Buenos días*, L.A.'"

Athen recalled how John had withdrawn that summer, how subdued he'd seemed when she would visit the usually bustling Moran house. He had asked her out for the first time the following Christmas, taking her to a party at his old fraternity house at Rutgers. A huge photograph hanging over the bar in a downstairs room had stopped John cold as he entered the room. BOUND FOR GLORY exclaimed the sign above the photo of Dallas— Dallas with the platinum hair and the perfect face, eyes to die for, not blue, not gray, but true lavender.

"Athen." Meg drew her attention from the long forgotten image. "What difference does any of this make? John loved you, he married you."

"On the rebound, apparently." She glumly reached for another tissue.

"Now why would you say that?" Meg lowered herself to the floor beside Athen. "Athen, we humans are amazingly fortunate. We have the ability to fall in love, to fall out of love, to fall in love again. And again. And even again."

"I never fell out of love with John. And apparently he never stopped loving Dallas."

"Just because she's gorgeous and famous, you think he carried a torch for her for the rest of his life?"

Athen shook her head, unable to share the memory that flashed suddenly, painfully before her eyes. The look on John's face when he came home one night to find Athen waiting up for him, deeply engrossed in *Lucinda's Pride* on the VCR, the movie for which Dallas had received an Academy Award nomination. He had retreated suddenly from the room, and Athen had known at once where he had gone all those times he would almost seem to disappear before her eyes, his face taking on a faraway look as he mentally vanished to some secret room inside himself, a room she'd never been invited to enter.

"Don't make more out of this than what it is," grumbled Meg. "Good grief, I have been in and out of love with so many men in my lifetime. Well, at least, I believed I was in love with each one of them at the time. Then again, sometimes I wonder if I ever loved any of them." She smiled wryly. "But John loved you enough to marry you, produce the world's most remarkable child, and live, as I recall, a pretty damned happy life with you."

"Yes, we were happy."

"Then what is the big freaking deal?" Meg shouted to the ceiling.

"Well, somehow I always thought that John and I were, you know, meant to be together, that somehow we were . . ." She groped for words.

"No, don't tell me. Written in the stars? Destined for each other?" Meg groaned. "Athen, you are the last living soul on the face of this earth—over the age of possibly five—who still believes in fairy tales. I'll bet you even clap your hands when Tinker Bell's light starts to go out."

Athen burst into tears.

"Oh, God, Athen, I'm sorry." Meg's voice softened as she attempted to comfort the weeping heap that was her sister-in-law. "Look, I think you're just overly sensitive right now, what with all John's things being packed up. This can't be easy for you."

"Maybe you're right. You probably are. It has been hard today, looking at all his things. Touching them. Folding them up to give away." Athen took the tissue Meg held out to her, then motioned for Meg to pass the box over. "But you know, I always believed I'd grow up and find the absolute love of my life and live happily ever after."

"Sweetie, I'm sorry you didn't get your happy ending. But you know, your life's far from over. You've a long, long way to go." Meg rubbed Athen's back between her shoulder blades to comfort her. "And who knows, maybe the absolute love of your life is out there somewhere, right now, looking for you. . . ."

❀11❀

"Buddy said to tell you to watch your back." Meg paused to give Athen a hug before heading toward the security check and eventually her waiting plane.

"If you ask me, the only person I need to guard my back against is 'Buddy,'" Athen replied.

Athen was sad when the time came for Meg to depart. Meg was one of those people who always seemed to be able to put things in perspective. While not necessarily a soothing personality, she did have the ability to shake things up. *She has certainly done that,* Athen thought with a smile as she pulled into her driveway.

She and Meg agreed to make a list of their New Year's resolutions and read them to each other on New Year's Eve. At the top of her list, Athen had written, "Be more assertive in my job." If she accomplished nothing else this year, she promised herself, she would do that much.

She vowed to speak up at meetings, express her own opinions, and present some ideas of her own. It was time, she told herself, to cut the umbilical cord that tied her to Dan. Time to assert herself. It had been easier to follow as she had been led, but starting immediately, she would personally read everything—every memo, every proposal, every newspaper article—that came across her desk. She would not wait for Dan to tell her what was important and what to toss out. She was smart enough to figure that out on her own. She would have to educate herself, and quickly. She would start with something elementary.

"Guess all that stuff's like Greek to you, huh, Athen?" Edie placed a cup of coffee before Athen, who was poring over the proposed budget the following morning.

"If it was Greek it would make more sense." Athen peered over the top of her glasses.

At the three o'clock meeting she tried her hand at being more of a presence.

"Jim, I was looking over the budget proposal." She took a deep breath and forced herself to speak before he could begin his one-on-one with Harlan Justis. "And I was wondering why the transportation numbers are so high. How many cars does the city own, anyway?"

Justis and Wolmar exchanged a surprised look.

"Well, the city has a lot of cars, Athen." Wolmar cleared his throat and spoke as if to a six-year-old. "We have police cars and cars for the code inspectors and, of course, all the department heads—and members of Council—have city cars. Why do you ask?"

"It seems like we have a lot of money in the budget for vehicles," she said. "Does anyone have a list of who exactly has these cars?"

"Well, now, I suppose someone in Finance—or is it Personnel, now, Harlan?"

"I think it's Personnel. Could be Finance, though." Harlan nodded, smoothing his handsome silk tie, visibly admiring its rich green and maroon paisley, which was obviously of greater consequence to him than her inquiries.

"In any event, someone has a list. I'm sure you could get one if you really think you need to. Though I don't know why you would." Harlan forced a patience he obviously did not feel before turning to Jim and clearly dismissing her. "So now, Jim, how do you think we should handle the residents of Fifth Street? They're on the rampage again about wanting more officers assigned to that three-block stretch where the drug traffic has increased."

"I already talked to Dan." Jim leaned back in his chair. "He said just to let 'em all shoot it out."

Stung by their curt rebuff of her effort to participate, Athen got up from her seat and walked to her desk. Beyond the handsomely appointed room she could see the area of the city known as the Devil's Passage, an area two blocks north of City Hall, between Fourth Street and the overpass from the superhighway beyond the city limits. Even from this distance she could see the ugly boarded-up houses, the vacant lots, the abandoned warehouses. She recalled how the neighborhood had once looked, and wondered how it had all happened so quickly.

"Why?" she heard herself say aloud.

"Why what?" Harlan looked up from his briefcase, from which he had withdrawn some documents, which were being scrutinized by Wolmar.

"Why just let 'em shoot it out? Why not send more police officers in if that's where they're needed?"

Riley Fallon, the lone African-American on Council, raised his eyebrows and turned to take a long slow look at her.

"Now, Athen." Harlan took on that expression of having been interrupted by an ill-mannered child. "You of all people should understand the risks to a police officer in an area like that."

"What about the risks to the residents?" she asked.

"Well, now, I would think if anyone was that concerned about their safety, they'd move," he said sarcastically. She nodded slowly, fully understanding the not-so-subtle reminder that she was expected to be seen and not heard.

But at the Wednesday morning press conference, when Quentin Forbes questioned the lack of response from the city to the growing concerns of those residents who had complained yet again to the press about the increasing number of incidents involving handguns in the area south of City Hall, Athen had a surprise for him.

"I'm glad you brought that up, Mr. Forbes." She forced herself to smile, not at him exactly, but at the space slightly above his head. "I spoke very recently with Councilman Fallon, who has agreed to look into the formation of a town watch with the residents. He will also meet with Chief Tate in the very near future to arrange a neighborhood meeting to discuss the situation. Councilman Fallon, perhaps you'd like to take the microphone and answer any further questions on this issue?"

She could feel Quentin's eyes on her as she packed up her notes. It gave her great satisfaction to know that just this once he hadn't caught her off guard. She felt the tiniest surge of triumph knowing that for the first time she would leave a public meeting with her head up.

She felt terrific, all but dancing back to her office from the big meeting room at the end of the hall.

"Oh, Athen, Dan's on line one," Edie told her as she walked by.

"Hi, Dan . . . ," was all she had time to say.

"Rule number one," he said softly. "You never discuss anything—anything—at public meetings or press conferences without discussing it first with me. Rule number two, you do not discuss anything with any member of Council without discussing it first with me. Rule number three, you do not make announcements without first discussing them with me. Rule number four . . ."

"Dan," she began, but he cut her off again.

"Rule number four, you do not commit the police department or any other department of the city to any project that you have not discussed with me. Do you understand, Athen?"

"No, Dan." She paused. "I don't understand. I don't understand what's so harmful about agreeing to meet with a group of residents who are tired of being shot at every time they open their front door."

"Athen, honey, I just don't like surprises." His tone was tightly controlled, each word pronounced slowly and carefully. "And what's all this I've been hearing, anyway? Budget figures, city cars, how many and who's got one."

"Dan, I need to be more involved in what's going on around here. I want to know what's going on," she told him. "I'm the mayor of this city."

"Sweetheart, you are doing just fine." He verbally patted her on the head.

"I'm not doing fine, and I don't feel like I'm doing anything worthwhile. I want to feel like I'm doing something around here besides reading the paper and talking to you on the phone." She closed her eyes, trying to imagine the look on his face.

"All right." He chuckled good-naturedly. "You just tell me first, okay? So that I don't have to hear it from someone else, or read it in the paper. Just let me know what it is you want to do, and we'll talk about it. Maybe I can give you some ideas or point you in the right direction."

How had he known so fast? she wondered as she hung up the phone. *Who had called him?*

Harlan Justis had left the meeting the second it began to break up. He must have hit Dan's number on speed dial as he flew down to his second-floor office to report that Athen had made some unscheduled remarks.

She sat down at her desk and sighed, dejected and still smarting somewhat from the dressing down she'd gotten from Dan. *It was worth it, even enduring his patronizing manner,* she thought, as a slow smile creased her lips, *just to see the look on Quentin Forbes's face. . . .*

It took Athen a week to get the information she'd wanted to back up the transportation numbers on the budget.

"Mrs. Moran?" A young woman peeked around the corner into her office. "Sorry to disturb you, but your secretary's not at her desk."

"What a surprise." Athen looked up from her desk. "She's probably at lunch."

Edie was always at lunch. Or on a coffee break. Or in the ladies' room.

"They said—Mrs. Fulton in Personnel, that is—said you wanted to see the file on the city cars."

"Yes, I do." Athen motioned her in. "Thank you, ahh . . ."

"Veronica. Veronica Spicata."

Athen's eyebrows rose slightly in amusement as the young woman crossed the carpet and placed the file on her desk. Veronica's inky black hair was pulled into a sort of twist at the back of her head and lacquered into submission, reaching skyward in the front, teased into a frothy mist that seemed to account for half of her diminutive stature. Long silver earrings dangled half-moons, tinkling like temple bells, almost to her shoulders. A small arm of silver stars marched up each multiply-pierced earlobe and a half dozen silver chains circled her neck to fall into the space between her collarbone and the top of her yellow knit shirt. Tiny feet in black patent leather high heels, shapely legs encased in black stockings, a short black leather skirt—more leg than leather—wrapped around the killer curves of Veronica's hips. Athen's eyes returned to the hair. She hadn't seen anything like it since Annie Wilson back in high school.

Veronica was Amy Winehouse with a North Jersey accent.

"Thank you, Veronica." Athen smiled and opened the file. Veronica continued to stand before her desk, snapping a wad of gum the size of Athen's fist, prompting Athen to inquire, "Was there something else?"

"I, ah, I'm supposed to wait." She shifted her weight somewhat uncomfortably, swaying slightly on the razor-thin high heels.

"Wait for what?"

"For the file." She nodded toward Athen's desk, her silver earrings jingling a tune in time with the movements of her head.

"But I could be reading this for the next two hours," Athen told her.

"I know, but that's what I was told to do."

"Well, why don't we just make a copy?"

"I'm not allowed to do that, Mrs. Moran."

"What is this, some top-secret document?" Athen exploded. "Look, you walk outside that door and you copy this file. And you bring the whole thing back in to me, okay?"

Veronica hesitated, obviously torn.

"Are you going to tell me you don't know how to use that machine?"

"No, Mrs. Moran. It's just that if I get caught copying the file after Mrs. Fulton told me . . ."

"Don't worry, I won't let Mrs. Fulton fire you for insubordination." Athen shook her head in disbelief. "Besides, everyone on this floor takes two-hour lunches. You have at least twenty-five minutes before anyone else arrives on the scene."

Veronica was back in less than ten minutes with the file and copy in tow.

"Let's take a look at what's in this file that Mrs. Fulton doesn't want me to see," Athen murmured.

She scanned the first few pages in silence, then lingered momentarily on the fourth sheet. Veronica was almost to the door on her way back to her office when Athen said, "Veronica, you'll have to help me a bit. Are all these people department heads? Look here, under Code Enforcement there are nine names. How many people are in that department, do you know?"

She turned the file around and slid it across the desk in Veronica's direction.

"Nine," Veronica replied readily, her gum snapping like popguns at an amusement park.

"All nine people have city cars?"

Veronica's lacquered head nodded emphatically. Not one hair moved independently of any other.

"And the Parks Department . . . I can see why they'd have six trucks, but seven city cars? How many . . . ?"

"Seven employees," Veronica told her.

"Seven cars and six trucks for seven people?" she asked incredulously. "Does everyone who works for this city have a city car?"

"I don't," Veronica volunteered.

"Well, how'd they miss you?" Athen mumbled, scanning the list for Personnel. "Four cars for Personnel?"

"Mrs. Fulton, her assistant, and her personal secretary." Veronica's gum snapped again.

"That's three, Veronica. The list says four." Athen turned the paper around to show her. "Here's the list of vehicle numbers. Maybe this is an old list."

"No, ma'am, I typed that list three weeks ago."

"Then who has the other car?"

"Come on, Mrs. Moran, you know." Veronica rolled her eyes skyward.

"If I knew, I wouldn't ask."

"It's Mary Jo's car," Veronica said, as if reminding Athen of something she already knew.

"Who is Mary Jo?"

"You know. Mary Jo Dolan." The name was all but whispered.

"Who is Mary Jo Dolan?" Athen hadn't a clue.

"Mrs. Moran." Veronica leaned forward, pained at having to speak the obvious. "Mr. Rossi's . . . *friend?*"

"Mr. Rossi's . . . friend"?

Athen cleared her throat. "And just what is Miss Dolan's position with the city?"

"Who could know?" Veronica held up her hands and grinned mischievously. "Except for Mr. Rossi."

"Where does she sit?" Athen toyed with her glasses.

"Anyplace she wants," the young woman quipped.

"Veronica, if she has a city car, she must work for the city." Athen was totally out of patience with this exasperating game. "So tell me who she works for, what she does."

"Wow." Veronica's kohl-lined eyes widened slowly. "You really don't know, do you?"

"Perhaps you should enlighten me." Athen probed for information she instinctively knew she wasn't going to like hearing.

"Well, the story is that she supposedly works in the Personnel office, but she's on some kind of leave," Veronica said, leaning closer to Athen's desk to confide in a low voice.

"What kind of leave?"

"Officially, it's written up as some kind of medical leave."

"She's ill, then? She's on a medical disability because she's sick?" Of course, Athen sighed with relief. She had known there had to be a logical explanation. Still, she shouldn't have a car if she was out sick. "How long has she been out sick?"

"Well, I don't know how sick she is. I mean, I see her around town all the time." The implication was left hanging between them.

"But the city's not paying her, right?" Athen paused expectantly.

"She gets paid every other week, just like everyone else." Veronica shrugged, adding, "Mrs. Moran, I'd get killed if anyone knew I was telling you this. I only know because I overheard Mrs. Fulton on the phone to . . ." Veronica paused.

"To . . . ?" Athen pressed her to continue.

"To Mr. Rossi."

"When? Last summer? Last fall? Before the election?" she prompted.

"No. About a week before Christmas."

Athen gestured to her to spill it all.

"Mrs. Fulton was in her office on the speakerphone with Mr. Rossi. The door was open. Everyone was at lunch. I came back early and I guess she didn't hear me come in," Veronica whispered. "I heard Mr. Rossi tell Mrs. Fulton to carry Mary Jo—continue to pay her full salary—and to keep the car in the department for Mary Jo's use until he told her otherwise."

"There must be reports from her doctor in her personnel file." Trying to sort facts from ugly supposition, Athen glanced at Veronica for confirmation.

"There's nothing in the file, Mrs. Moran."

"Well, somebody must be authorizing her checks. Somebody has to sign them."

"Mr. Wolmar signs all the checks," Veronica told her pointedly.

"How long has this woman been on sick leave?"

"Well, since right after I started, about four years ago."

"Four years!"

Athen was stunned. Four years at full salary, with a city car and no medical reports to justify her infirmity?

"Mrs. Moran, Mary Jo is Mr. Rossi's . . . um, his, ah . . ." Veronica visibly struggled to find the least offensive path to the obvious.

"I think I can guess what she is," Athen said dryly.

The full import of the unsavory news made her almost nauseated. With shaking hands, she unceremoniously dumped the copy of the automobile file into her bottom drawer. "Thank you, Veronica. You can go back to your office now."

"But, Mrs. Moran, you won't tell anyone that I told you?"

"Of course not," Athen assured her. "It'll be our secret."

"Thanks, Mrs. Moran." Veronica sighed with genuine relief. "I really need this job. At least until Sal—that's my husband, Salvatore Spicata (don't you just love alliterative names?)—till he finishes college." The sound of tiny bells followed her as she headed for the door, the original file tucked under her arm.

"Veronica," Athen called to her. "How old is Mary Jo?"

"I think she's about three years younger than me, so she'd be about twenty-one."

"Do you know if she's related to the Theresa Dolan who lives on Prospect Avenue?"

"Mary Jo's her daughter. I heard Mrs. Fulton talking about her being sick."

"Mrs. Dolan is sick?"

"She has cancer. They said it's real bad—like, not-going-to-make-it bad."

Athen nodded her thanks and motioned for Veronica to close the door.

She walked to the big window, drew open the curtains, and stared at the world outside. *Somewhere out there a young woman is being paid by the city for work she doesn't do, driving a city-owned car that the city is insuring. She has been collecting a paycheck and driving the car since she was seventeen. And she is Dan Rossi's mistress.*

Athen's stomach turned at the thought. She thought for a moment that she was going to be sick.

What to do with the worms, she wondered, now that the can has been opened?

🌿12🌿

"A then, Hal Brader from Channel Eight is on line three." Edie spoke to her through the intercom.

"Tell him I'm in a meeting," she grumbled. "Then get Dan on the phone."

It was a given that she'd started the day in a state of agitation. She'd barely slept for the past several nights. The Mary Jo Dolan affair nagged at her continuously. She knew she had to do something about it, but what? To ignore it was to condone it, and she could not do that. On the other hand, she had no idea how she could put an end to it. She'd gotten over the fact that Rossi was having an affair with a city worker. She hated that he'd started the relationship when the girl was under age, but she was now over eighteen, and Athen had no way of proving that anything had gone on before Mary Jo had reached the legal age of consent. So as far as the relationship was concerned, there was little she could do. But the fact that this girl was using expensive city property and had been for several years—well, Athen could do something about that. What, how, and when remained to be seen.

That the spring rain had continued for four days without ceasing did little to improve her disposition.

March had indeed come in like a lion, the temperatures holding just above freezing, the wind blustering down sharply from the north. She'd had enough of rain and cold and didn't really care who knew it. To top it off, the city's churches had banded together in a show of solidarity to attempt to force City Council to hand over the keys to several vacant houses for the homeless to use.

"How are you, Athen?" Dan was obviously in a better frame of mind than she was.

"How do you think I am? Every reporter in the city is on my case over this standoff with the United Council of Churches. Dan, why can't we just let these people stay in those houses up on Fourth Street? I don't see any harm in turning those buildings over for a good cause. The city isn't using them, and since the UCC is offering to do the renovations at no cost to the city, I just don't understand . . ."

"You don't have to understand," he snapped abruptly. "You just stay out of it, do you hear me? No comments to the press. No meeting with these self-appointed do-gooders. Hear me? Athen, do you hear me?" he demanded impatiently.

"Yes, of course, I hear you." She bit her lip, taken aback by his outburst. "But I can't continue to avoid this issue and to dodge the reporters."

"Yes, Athen, you can. And you will. Do you understand?"

"No. No, I don't. There are people in my face every time I open my office door. They want answers. Why is the city refusing to talk to these people? Why am I taking so long to review a sixty-page proposal? And I have no rational answer, Dan. I have no explanation for it. The newspapers are crucifying me."

She could still see Quentin Forbes's icy blue eyes as he challenged her two days ago, demanding to know

just when Her Honor would complete her review of the
Council of Churches' request that the city turn over three
old twin houses—confiscated by the city three years
ago for nonpayment of taxes—for use as shelters for the
homeless who, in ever-increasing numbers, lined the
streets of Woodside Heights. That she'd had no answer
had been humiliating, and played into his worst opinion of her. She wasn't sure why it still mattered what he
thought, but it did.

"Let them," he told her coldly. "Let them do whatever
they want. But you are to continue to ignore it. You are
not to get involved in this issue. When asked, you say the
citizens of Woodside Heights are already overburdened
with taxes. You say that the hardworking citizens are having a tough enough time supporting themselves without
having to support a bunch of freeloaders."

"These aren't freeloaders," she snapped. "That's the
point! Not so long ago, most of these people were hardworking taxpayers themselves—people who lost their jobs
when the mills cut back or closed down. I will not insult
them by calling them names and pretending they don't
count."

"Then you say, 'No comment,'" he growled into the
phone. "But you do not meet with them and you do not
get involved. Period."

"But I want to meet with them. I want to help them,
and I don't understand . . ."

"It doesn't matter whether you understand or not.
This is none of your business."

"None of my business? Are you serious?"

It took her a long moment to realize that he had hung
up on her. She quietly replaced the receiver and sat at her
desk, turning a pen over and over in her hands, her cheeks

burning. Rossi had completely disregarded her concerns over the untenable position he was putting her in, he'd ordered her to do something she did not believe in, and then, to top it off, he'd made it clear that she was not to publicly address the issue.

His last words—"This is none of your business"—had stung the most deeply. She was the elected mayor but the most vital concerns of the people who had elected her were none of her business?

Shattered and shamefaced, Athen sat motionless at her desk. She had no one to blame but herself for the way this was playing out. She'd allowed herself to get caught up in this and she was beginning to hate it. She was stuck here for another eighteen months, trapped in this office. Her palms began to sweat and the room grew smaller around her. She went to the window and opened it, letting the cold rain blow in on her. When she'd had enough, she closed the window and brushed the rain from her face.

Why are those three houses so important to Dan that he would risk making her an object of scorn not just to the press, but to the growing number of citizens who appeared to be supporting the idea of a shelter? The city had no use for the properties. Two blocks from City Hall—a block from a series of abandoned warehouses—of what possible value could they be to Rossi?

"Damn it, it *is* my business." The anger grew hotter inside her chest. "And he had no cause to speak to me like that, as if I have no right to an opinion of my own, no right to question his *orders* . . ."

His *orders*. Of course, she had no right to question his orders. He had made that perfectly clear in the beginning, although she hadn't realized it at the time. He would tell her what to do and she would do it. She had forgotten the rules and Dan had put her back in her place. Whether or not she would stay there was another matter.

Athen reminded herself that fate had handed her one trump card. Several times during her conversation with Rossi, the name had almost slipped from her lips. But given only one weapon, she'd have to be very judicious in choosing where, when, and how to use it.

Depending on how Athen played it, that card could prove to be an ace . . . or a joker.

"THAT WAS MR. LOWRY ON the phone, Callie." Athen poked her head into the living room. "Softball practice has been called off again tonight because of the rain."

Callie barely nodded.

"Callie?" Athen poked in a little farther. "What are you watching?"

Athen came into the room and stood behind the chair where her daughter sat, riveted to the television screen.

"Oh . . ." whispered Athen.

"Is that all you can say?" Callie demanded angrily. "People are standing out in the freezing rain because you won't unlock the door so they go inside that house to get warm and dry and all you say is 'Oh'?"

"Callie, it's not that simple."

"It *is* that simple." Callie spun around in her seat, eyes crackling with accusation. "The city owns that house—it said so on the news—and you are the mayor of the city. You can open up that house, Mom. You know it and I know it. I just don't know why you won't."

Callie got up and rushed from the room, yelling over her shoulder, "Sometimes I wish you weren't my mother."

Stung to her very core, Athen lowered herself onto

the chair Callie had vacated. She had never felt so small, so humiliated, as she did at that moment. Nothing Dan had said to belittle her and remind her of her place, nothing the press had said about her, none of Quentin's jabs had dug as deeply into her soul as her daughter's words.

"It's not worth it," she whispered aloud.

She picked up the remote to turn off the TV, but the scene on the screen held her motionless. The United Council of Churches had organized a sit-in, and for the past four days the news had been filled with the stories of the individuals who had kept the vigil in spite of the storm. She leaned forward to study the faces, old and young, men and women, black and white and Hispanic.

"Yes, ma'am." An elderly gentleman was responding to the question posed by the young reporter who was wrapped in a heavy parka. "We will stay here until the city agrees to talk with us. That's all we're asking for. We just want them to listen . . ."

"I hear you," Athen replied aloud to the nameless, weathered face on the screen. "I hear you. . . ."

I HAVE TO TELL HIM, Athen repeated over and over to herself as she drove into her office the next day. She could not stand the way Callie looked at her, as if she'd betrayed her.

I have betrayed her. I've always taught her to do what's right, and here I'm going against everything I know is right and I can't even give her a reason why. It has to stop. We have to talk, Dan and I. And he will have to listen. He has to let me follow my conscience.

She stepped into the elevator, grateful that no reporters awaited her at this earlier-than-usual hour. Callie's anger had gnawed at her all night. Her daughter's words opened the door for her conscience to nag, and her inner voice refused to let her sleep until she accepted that she would have to take the initiative. It was time to cut the strings that tied her hands.

As soon as she got to the office, she would call Dan and tell him. What was the worst he could do, force her out of office? Judging from Dan's reaction yesterday, he might be just as happy to have someone else—Wolmar? Justis?—step in for her. At least Rossi would feel fairly certain that neither of them would actively defy him, and while he might find himself in a fight to get the office back when the term ended, Dan might think it was worth it to get rid of her.

The doors slid open and she fished in her pockets for the key to her door. Raising her eyes as she crossed the lobby, she noticed a slight figure wrapped in a red raincoat just outside her office.

"Ms. Evelyn? Is that you?" she asked.

"Yes, Athen." The woman turned to her.

"What are you doing here?" Athen shook the water from her raincoat as she slipped it off.

"I wanted to speak with you, if you have a moment to spare." The woman looked at her with weary eyes.

"Of course. Please, come in." Athen unlocked the office and gestured for Ms. Evelyn to follow her inside. She hung her coat up and motioned for the woman to hand over her own.

"Why, you're wet clear through!" Athen shook some of the water from Ms. Evelyn's coat and hung it over a chair.

"Well, yes, I suppose I am." Ms. Evelyn appeared neither concerned nor surprised as she looked down on her sopping-wet trousers.

"Here, put this on." Athen handed her a sweater that she kept in the office. "Let me get you some coffee. Sit down, please." She gestured toward the sofa. "I'll just be a minute."

Moments later, Athen placed a mug of steaming coffee on the table in front of her unexpected visitor. "What brings you down here so early on such a terrible morning?" she asked.

"Well, it's the people . . ."

Ah, yes. Athen nodded slowly. Somehow she had known this had been the woman's mission.

"There are just so many of them. Good, hardworking people, just like you and me, on the streets for the first time in their lives. People who have held jobs from the time they were seventeen, eighteen years old, losing those jobs, losing their homes, through no fault of their own." Ms. Evelyn's voice was soft, devoid of anger or accusation. Just the facts. "Jobs moving out of town, banks foreclosing on mortgages, people with no place to go till they can get back on their feet again. It would break your heart as surely as it breaks mine. I'm asking for twenty minutes of your time, Athen, to come down and see for yourself."

The lump in Athen's throat was enormous. She wanted to tell Ms. Evelyn everything: that she wanted to help but she'd been forbidden to intervene, but the words stuck in her throat.

"All we're asking for is a place for folks to stay while they figure out where to go next." Ms. Evelyn's voice was hypnotically gentle. "We need a place where they can get out of the cold and have a warm shower, sleep in a warm bed. The churches will take care of the expenses. It won't cost the city a dime. We've raised the money. We've had beds, food, and clothing donated. But we need a place to shelter these souls. And I knew if I explained it to you, you'd do the right thing."

Ms. Evelyn took a long, slow sip from the mug, wrapping her fingers around it to warm them.

"I knew you'd hear me out, Athen. Now, some folks say I'm wasting my time, that you're just a cog in the wheel, but I tell them that I know you. I knew your daddy, and I knew your John. I know your child. I know that if you could just see for yourself . . ." Ms. Evelyn shook her head. "Well, I know your heart is just too good to let this go on."

The simple words, their sheer sincerity, humbled Athen, who sat in humiliated silence, knowing that entire families had suffered—continued to suffer—because of her inability to defy the command of the man who pulled her strings.

She glanced around the well-appointed room, the office of the mayor of Woodside Heights. *Where was the power?* she asked herself. *Was it in this office, or did it still rest with the man who had once occupied it?*

Perhaps it was time to find out.

"It looks like the rain has stopped." Athen rose and reached for her coat.

She handed Ms. Evelyn her still-wet overcoat, and met the woman's eyes without shame for the first time since she'd arrived.

"Come on, Ms. Evelyn. Let's take a walk. . . ."

EVEN AFTER HAVING SEEN THE news coverage, Athen hadn't expected the crowd to be quite so large. The wet, shivering mass of men, women, and small children extended from the corner of Fourth and Sycamore all the way up the sidewalk past the third of the big twin houses that were at the center of the dispute. Word of her arrival spread quickly, so that by the time she'd gone less than twenty feet a path opened before her.

The anonymous faces from the news reports were suddenly flesh and blood. Patiently expectant eyes followed her as she passed, but no one spoke to her. But she knew they were all carefully watching to see what she would do.

Those huddled closest to the front of the first house parted ranks silently to permit her access to the building. Police guards stood on the porch, arms folded impassively across their chests.

"Good morning, officers." Smiling as she climbed the steps, Athen assumed an air of confidence she did not feel.

"Morning, Mayor." The officer blocking the door returned her greeting pleasantly. Harry Stillman had gone to school with John, and the two had remained friends. The two younger men, however, shuffled uncomfortably, unsure as to what, if any, action they should be prepared to take.

"I'd like to go inside, Harry," Athen told him without breaking stride as she crossed the porch.

"Chief said no one's to go in," the officer said apologetically.

"Harry, I'm the mayor," she whispered. "Chief Tate works for me."

He appeared to mentally debate for a very long moment, then asked, "Do you have the key?"

The key. Of course she had no key. She shook her head, no.

"I can probably get it open for you." He grinned nonchalantly, assuring her that a locked door was no obstacle for the former center of the Woodside Heights football team.

Athen hesitated, thinking through the unexpected dilemma that she faced. Breaking into the building had certain implications. But who would have the key? She tapped a foot in agitation. She couldn't very well call City

Hall and inquire as to its keeper. Besides, she knew Rossi would know within minutes, and then the door would never be opened.

"Go ahead, see if you can force it," she told him determinedly. "Break it down if you have to."

"No problem." He put a shoulder into the door and pushed. And pushed. The door didn't as much as creak.

"Stand back there, Athen." He put his left shoulder down, got a running start, and slammed into the solid door. The lock gave, sending the officer flying into the front hallway.

Cheers and applause erupted from the watchful crowd. The mood turned from skepticism to hope in a heartbeat.

"Harry? Are you all right?" Athen peered anxiously after him through the doorway.

"Piece of cake." He picked himself up off the dusty floor where he'd landed.

"I owe you one," she told him as she stepped into the hallway.

He smiled broadly, his square frame filling the doorway as he returned to his post, where he was cheered loudly by the onlookers outside. "Were you planning on everyone else coming in with you?"

She hadn't really planned on anything, she realized. "Just Ms. Evelyn," she replied.

"I'll get her," he told her.

Ms. Evelyn's eyes glistened with anticipation as she tentatively entered the hall and took a look around. The house had no electricity, heat, or water. The windows on the first floor were boarded up, and years of dust and grime covered everything, yet Ms. Evelyn looked as if she were gazing upon the interior of a palace for the first time.

"Well now," she said with restrained satisfaction. "This would do just fine."

"It's a bit musty." Athen followed the wide hallway straight ahead into what had probably been the dining room.

"A few bright sunny days with the windows open will take care of that," Ms. Evelyn assured her.

The two women walked silently through the rest of the house, room to room. The dampness was everywhere, and with the windows boarded over the house had a cold, claustrophobic atmosphere. Ms. Evelyn appeared not to notice.

And yet it occurred to Athen, the house was actually in pretty good condition. Aside from needing paint, some plaster patching, some minor repairs to the windows, and a good cleaning, there was no structural damage, no evidence of broken pipes or rotting floorboards as she'd anticipated. Why would anyone abandon such a house, permitting the city to confiscate it?

Athen pushed aside a loose board on one of the second-floor bedroom windows. She could barely see City Hall through the fog that was rapidly rolling in. From above she heard the first rumble of thunder as yet another storm front approached.

"Are all of the houses the same?" she asked.

"Identical." Ms. Evelyn nodded.

"What will you do for heat? How will you make the repairs?"

"We have an army of volunteers. And we can apply for grants from the state and from private foundations, and all the churches have funds set up."

"You'll have to get all the properties up to code before the city will permit anyone to move in," Athen thought aloud. She knew in her gut that the code-enforcement officer would be ordered to prevent the buildings from passing inspection. The growing, twisted knot in her stomach reminded her that the real battle had not yet begun.

"You leave all that to me, Athen. You lease these houses to the UCC and you will be amazed at what we can do in His name," Ms. Evelyn told her.

I hope He knows a way around Dan Rossi, Athen thought as she headed down the stairwell and through the still-open front door.

The crowd hushed as she stepped outside. They were waiting, she knew, for some pronouncement from her, but she had no thoughts to share. She thanked Harry for his part in getting her into the house, all the while wondering how she could get out without having to say anything.

Trusting faces watched her eagerly; hopeful eyes followed her as she reached the top step. Words formed and re-formed within her mind, but no sound passed her lips. The tableau before her remained frozen, expectant.

"Mrs. Moran, does your presence here this morning signal a change in the city's position regarding these properties? Have you and the Council of Churches come to an agreement?" A deep voice she knew all too well broke the silence.

Quentin stood no more than six feet from her. She tried not to look at him, wanting to avoid the taunt that only she would see in his eyes. He was too close to her to be ignored, and she was forced to face him there before the crowd. She wanted to respond intelligently, confidently, wanted to impress upon him that this was not the old Athena Moran who stood before him, and that she wanted him to be the first to know.

Before she could open her mouth, the lights from a

TV camera on her right nearly blinded her as a reporter in a heavy parka thrust a microphone into her face and asked, "Mrs. Moran, these people have camped here for the past four days waiting for a word from City Hall. Why today? What brought you here today after almost a week of silence?"

"A friend asked me to come." Athen descended the steps. Massive clouds, gunmetal gray and almost low enough to touch, sped overhead, rumbling ominously. She'd barely make it back to City Hall before the deluge began.

"Are you considering negotiating a lease with the UCC for all three buildings?" The reporter followed her. "If so, when might the buildings be available?"

"I don't know," she replied as the first fat drops of rain began to splash on the sidewalk in front of her. "I wanted to see them for myself before making a final decision."

"Will what you've seen here today influence your decision?" the reporter shouted above the thunder.

Athen nodded and took a step forward. It was only a matter of seconds before the downpour began for real.

"Can you comment on the suitability of these buildings for use as shelters as proposed by the Council of Churches?" The reporter made it clear that storm or no storm, she would get her story.

"I think the homes are highly suitable, easily adaptable." Athen was all but yelling at the top of her voice as the thunder crashed.

"Will you be recommending to City Council that these buildings be made available for that purpose?" The camera crew was preparing to shut down as the final question was asked.

"Yes." Athen pulled her already saturated collar

around her neck and headed into the storm to return to her office.

"But will you have enough votes to get it passed?" Quentin's note of sarcasm stopped her in her tracks.

She turned to meet his eyes, and having no response, she shrugged her shoulders and turned away.

❧ 13 ❧

The sidewalk was washed over with rainwater that sped downhill like a swollen stream. Fifty feet ahead, water at the intersection was cresting the curb, the storm sewers unable to hold even one more drop in the wake of the week's continuous deluge. Bent forward by the fierce wind, Athen tucked in her chin and hoped she'd be able to tell where the sidewalk ended and the street began. City Hall, though only a few blocks away, was barely visible through the relentless wall of water.

She cursed her high heels and she cursed the storm. The wind lashed wildly at her. Her long hair, as wet as if she'd just emerged from the shower, wrapped around her face so she could barely see. Halfway to the corner, a car pulled up next to her.

"Get in," Quentin shouted through the half-lowered window.

"I'd rather walk." She returned the shout without breaking stride. She reached the end of the sidewalk and took a deep breath as she prepared to step into the swirling water.

"Don't be an idiot." He pulled over to the wrong side of the street so that he was a few feet from her. "The street is half washed away up there. It isn't safe to walk. Athen, get in. Let me drive you back."

She paused at the edge of the curb, unable to tell how deep the water was. Looking up ahead, she could see that the next intersection was fully underwater. A small pickup truck was stranded smack in its center.

Reluctantly, she walked to the car. *No need to rush,* she told herself. *I can't get any wetter than I already am.*

"Thank you." She got into the passenger side without looking at him.

"Well, it wouldn't do to have our mayor washed away in a flash flood so soon after becoming a hero." He leaned over and turned on the heat, and adjusted the warm air to flow in her direction.

Athen hunched into the seat, grateful for the warmth. She stared straight ahead at the wipers that slashed uselessly at the windshield. Quentin drove slowly, turning hard to the right in an attempt to avoid the lake that churned in the middle of the intersection. He made a quick right onto a side street.

"City Hall was straight ahead," she told him flatly. "Where are you going?"

"The street is impassable." He calmly pointed out the obvious. "I thought a detour might be in order, unless, of course, you'd rather backstroke down Fourth Street."

He slowed again as torrents of rain rushed wildly down both sides of the street. He took a left and headed up the hill on Ashbridge, but that street, too, was flooding. He turned up Hoffman Boulevard, seeking the highest elevation in the city. If anything, the rain seemed to intensify.

"This is futile." Quentin pulled into a parking lot behind a convenience store and turned off the engine. Obviously, he was not oblivious to her annoyance at being stuck with him in the confines of his car. "I realize you're not happy to be stuck with me. I think we'll have to wait a bit. I'm sorry."

He pulled back the hood of his dark green parka, allowing his dark damp curls to tumble almost to his eyebrows. Small rivers of water ran down his forehead, and he brushed them away with the back of his hand.

Athen continued to stare out the window, choosing not to respond to his apology. She had more on her mind than the storm. The knot in her stomach had spread. Burning fingers of fear and doubt reached her chest as the enormity of the commitment she'd made came into focus.

Quentin turned on the radio, searching for a station that offered something other than static or hip-hop. He cocked an ear, listening closely as he sped up the dial, then backtracked to tune into something that caught his fancy.

"So." He punctuated the one word with a drumroll of sorts on the steering wheel.

"Don't feel that you have to make conversation," she told him. "I know you don't want to. It was very kind of you to offer me a ride, and I appreciate it, but you don't have to pretend to want to talk to me."

"Fine." Rebuffed, he turned up the volume on the radio.

Athen folded her hands on her lap and gazed straight ahead. Maybe she should have taken her chances with the tidal wave at the intersection.

Quentin, too, stared out the front window, watching the buckets of water that poured from the sky onto his car. The storm gave no indication that it would subside any time in the near future. They sat like total strangers sharing a bus seat.

Finally, she couldn't stand it any longer. She had to ask. "Why are you so mean to me?"

She watched his reflection in the window but did not turn to face him.

"I'd hardly call rescuing you from a watery grave being mean," he noted dryly.

"You know what I'm talking about. Every week. Every opportunity. Grilling me. Harassing me."

"Since when is it harassment for a reporter to ask an elected official for a statement on issues that directly relate to the city she serves?" Cramped in the small seat, he shifted his weight slightly to turn toward her.

"When that reporter knows . . ."

"When that reporter knows that the elected official in question is duping the people of the city by permitting someone other than herself to make all the decisions— a someone whose motives are decidedly suspect? When that reporter knows that the elected official in question has no opinions of her own and allows herself to be moved around this city like the queen on a chessboard . . . ?"

"That is not true," she snapped. "I have opinions."

"Give me a break, Athen. You haven't publicly uttered two words that didn't have Rossi's fingerprints on them since Labor Day. Now, I have to admit that was quite a convincing little show you put on this morning. I would have fallen for that act myself if I didn't know that Rossi had carefully orchestrated it."

"You couldn't be farther from the truth." She laughed wryly.

"Come on, Athen, I know the game. You could at

least be honest enough to admit that for whatever devious little reason, Rossi told you to make nice with the UCC. Of course, the fun part—from my standpoint, anyway—is figuring out what comes next. Maybe the strategy is for you to make a big show for the press, then have the buildings fail inspection. 'Well, now, folks, we did our best to help you out, but those old houses just aren't fit for habitation.' Is that the plan?"

Quentin's impression of Dan at his politicking best was annoyingly accurate.

"You are so far off." Athen leaned her right elbow onto the narrow molding below the passenger-side window and tilted her head as she ran her hand through her sopping-wet hair. "You have no idea."

"Then why don't you clue me in?" He leaned back against the car door and said, "If I'm wrong, you tell me what the point was of that little act of yours this morning."

"It wasn't an act."

"Right." He smirked. "Your compassionate concern wasn't an act. Your indignation at having been called on it isn't an act. While we're on the subject, though, I thought having the cop break the door down was a great move. Added just the right touch of drama. Was that part of the script or were you ad-libbing?"

"God, but you're annoying."

She glanced out the window and took several deep breaths to calm herself as she tried to gauge if the rain had let up enough for her make it back to City Hall on foot, but the wind and water continued their savage slashing against the car.

"Well, I have to admit you've piqued my curiosity," he said. "So if I'm off base, now's your big chance to set me straight."

"Rossi doesn't know. At least he didn't. Of course, by now I'm sure he does."

"Rossi didn't know what?"

"Rossi didn't know I was going to Fourth Street."

"What do you take me for?" He laughed. "There's no way in hell you'd make a move like that without him directing you."

"Believe what you want." She shrugged, tired of his ridicule, tired of the effort it took to fight back.

"Convince me."

"Quentin, I'm too weary for games. I shouldn't have said anything. Just forget I said anything at all."

He studied her face for a moment. "You're serious. He didn't know you were coming here."

She continued to stare out the window at the rain.

"It was Ms. Evelyn, wasn't it? You did it for her. Rossi told you to back off, but she asked for your help and you couldn't say no."

She knew she shouldn't trust him. Past history had taught her that. She could not explain even to herself why she didn't keep her mouth shut.

"Bingo," she heard herself say.

Quentin whistled one long, slow, steady note.

"What happens when you tug on Superman's cape?"

"I guess we'll find out." She shrugged. "He'll try to make me back down. Maybe try to make me resign."

"Don't do it. Don't do either." His fingers wound lightly around her left wrist.

"I may not have a choice."

"Of course you have a choice. Listen, stand your ground. If you quit, he'll just appoint another lackey— sorry, but that's how it looks from here. If you back down, the city will be the same as it was before you stepped into that house with Ms. Evelyn an hour ago. Nothing will ever change. Nothing will get better for those people if you let him force you out."

The rude stranger with the icy stare had vanished. In his place sat the man Athen had met the previous summer, a man with warmth in his voice and in his eyes.

"You don't understand how things are." She could not bear the earnestness of his gaze, the warmth of his hand on her arm.

"I understand much more than you realize." He looked directly into her eyes, a small smile on his lips. "The only thing I don't understand is what took you so long."

"Let's just say that it took me longer than it should have to see what was really going on. Once I did, I couldn't *not* do it." She was suddenly very tired and chilled and wished she was home. "I couldn't keep those people out on the street. And between my daughter, and Ms. Evelyn, and my own conscience . . . I had to do something."

"Now what? What comes next?"

"I have no idea." She looked down at her hands to escape the intensity of his gaze, and for a few moments the only sound came from the rain and wind outside the car.

"Why did you turn on me the night of the rally?" she asked without looking up.

"Well, since we're trading truths, I guess the truth is that I was angry."

"Why?"

"I guess because I thought we were starting to become friends, and I just couldn't reconcile the woman I thought I was beginning to know with the woman who was willing to be used as a mouthpiece for a man like Rossi. I couldn't understand why you would agree to such a sham."

"I didn't know it was a sham," she whispered.

"How could you not know?" he demanded.

"I didn't know *sham* was an option."

"Oh, come on, Athen. You expect me to believe you agreed to do this for him out of the goodness of your heart? What did he promise you?"

"Nothing. It wasn't anything like that. Look, I needed to get my life moving again. I needed something to do, and he offered me a job as his assistant. He was an old friend of my dad's. I trusted him. Then everything seemed to happen so quickly."

"Well, that's one hell of a promotion, wouldn't you say, for a woman with no political experience to go from assistant to top banana in, what, four months?" he scoffed. "It's obvious what he got from this little arrangement. What did *you* think you were getting out of it?"

"Something to give some direction to my life, and a chance to do something good for the city. At least, I thought I could do something good." She knew it sounded lame.

"That's all?"

She nodded.

"Didn't it occur to you that you'd have to make some concessions?" Had that familiar note of ridicule crept back into his tone?

"I didn't think of it like that. He told me he'd help me when I needed it. I didn't know it would be like this." Why did he insist on viewing her as the villain rather than the victim?

"So you get something to occupy your time for two years at the taxpayers' expense, and he gets to keep control while he's waiting to get his office back." His ability to reduce the matter to its most basic level was not unlike Meg's, and every bit as infuriating. "Sounds like a damned fine arrangement to me. If you're Dan Rossi, that is."

"You make it sound like some shady backroom deal." What was there about this man that made her feel she needed to defend herself?

"What would you call it?"

"It wasn't like that. It just sort of . . . happened," she said weakly.

He scowled. "That's what a sixteen-year-old tells her mother when she finds out she's pregnant."

"I'm so tired of this," she said wearily. "Is Dan Rossi really so bad?" *Other than the fact that he slept with an underage girl.* Athen swept that thought aside. Now was not the time to drop that bombshell.

"Rossi epitomizes the worst in small-town politicians." The handsome man with the gentle blue eyes who only minutes earlier had seemed to understand the truth of the matter began to fade rapidly before her eyes. In a blink, the master of the cutting remark emerged once again to take his place. "He permitted this city to be robbed of its livelihood, now he holds it hostage while the people get tossed out onto the street. And from where I sit, you're helping him to do it. You may think you took a stand this morning, but I'm betting that when he catches up with you he'll manage to turn this around, and you will let him."

"*Malaka,*" she muttered in Greek to the wailing storm.

"What's that mean?"

"It means 'jerk.'"

"I've been called worse."

"There's a surprise."

"So we both agree that I'm not perfect. I'm not the one who's been running this city into the ground. Woodside Heights has some serious problems and I don't see where they've been addressed. The unemployment and crime issues aside, from what I understand there's a large minority population in this city that has been virtually ignored for the past eight years."

"Excuse me, there are two minority representatives on City Council," she shot back.

"Oh, Christ, Athen, give me a break." He ran his fingers through his hair. "You mean Riley Fallon and George Konstantos? Fallon is so grateful to Rossi for putting him on Council he'd publicly kiss Dan's butt and thank him for the opportunity. And Konstantos is so senile he thinks Bush is still in the White House. That would be Bush forty-one."

"I admit that Rossi has given me more direction than he should. And yes, it's my own fault for letting him do it. I went along with it and did nothing to find out for myself what was going on. It was easier to just drift along."

"And now?"

"Now I don't want to drift anymore."

"Well, then, maybe Dan will have a change of heart and be really happy that you took the initiative this morning."

She didn't answer.

"Sure, I'll bet once you explain to Dan that what you did today really was best for the citizens of Woodside Heights, he'll thank you for opening his eyes. I'll bet you get a big pat on the back for doing the right thing."

She wanted to slap that mocking half smile from his face. The fact that he was right on target made his derision all the more intolerable.

"Well, I see the rain has slowed down, and since you still have to face the music over your little display of independence this morning, I guess I'd better get you back to your office." He shifted in his seat and turned the key in the ignition. "My guess is that Dan is trying to track you down right about now for a little heart-to-heart."

They shared no further conversation, the animosity slipping back around them like a dark cloak. He drove slowly through the water-logged streets. A few minutes later, he turned into the parking lot behind City Hall.

"I wish you luck, Athen. I truly do," Quentin said as he came to a stop.

"Thanks for the ride." She could not look at him.

She started to open the door when she felt his hand on hers.

"Athen . . ."

She turned to him and forced herself to look into his eyes.

"I liked it better when we were friends," he said very softly.

"So did I."

She got out of the car and slammed the door.

ATHEN STEPPED INTO THE ELEVATOR, pondering her situation. The smart thing to do would be to go back into the office and call Dan instead of waiting for him to call her. She'd explain to him about Ms. Evelyn coming here. How could she refuse such a small request of an old friend? Maybe Dan just hadn't had an opportunity to go through the houses with the idea of turning them into a shelter in mind. Maybe she could get him to walk through with her. Maybe Ms. Evelyn would join them, and he could see it through her eyes, as Athen had, and he'd realize what a good thing it would be. Once he saw for himself, wouldn't he have to come around?

Buoyed by this shred of optimism, she stepped through the opening doors, surprised to find Edie at her desk during the lunch hour. The secretary gestured to Athen's office, her expression curiously smug.

Puzzled, Athen opened the door. She crossed the carpet, unbuttoning her soggy coat, and then she looked up.

Dan Rossi sat behind her desk, in her chair, reading her mail.

"Ah, there you are." He pushed back the chair slightly from the desk. "Just glancing over the agenda. Old habits die hard, I guess. Do forgive me."

He rose and helped her off with her coat. Her instincts told her this was not an act of chivalry on his part, but a means of reminding her whose office this really was. She leaned against the side of the desk, waiting, all of her confidence dissolving in the wake of the chill that went through her.

"Oh, please." He gestured gallantly to her chair. "Do sit."

She walked slowly behind the desk, easing herself into the seat, watching his face.

"So, Athen." He too now sat, directly across from her, his eyes smoldering, his voice taut with control.

She willed herself not to look away.

"What a little newsmaker you turned out to be. You looked wonderful on TV, by the way. The noontime news really did right by you."

When she failed to respond, he tapped softly on the edge of the desk and said in the calmest of tones, "Would you like to tell me what prompted that little stroll down Fourth Street this morning?"

She fought the feeling of being a child caught in a forbidden deed, but the sinkhole inside her grew. She began to sweat.

"I could not refuse to talk to Ms. Evelyn, Dan."

"Of course not. Ms. Evelyn is a pillar of the community, a very popular figure. Talking to her is one thing, showing up at that building—having a city police officer break into the house with the TV cameras running for Christ's sake!—is something entirely different."

His eyes narrowed. The hound cornered the fox. "Especially after I had expressly instructed you to stay out of that situation." He paused meaningfully. "I did, did I not, expressly tell you not to become involved with any of this?"

"Yes, you did."

"You've no idea of the trouble you've caused me, Athen. Now I will have to find a way to undo this mess you've made."

"Dan, I don't understand."

"I believe I told you before that you don't have to understand," he cut her off brusquely. "We'll just treat this as a little delay, that's all."

"Delay?" She was confused. "Delay of what?"

Pointedly ignoring her question, he leaned forward, his eyes boring into hers. "You seem to forget why and how you got to sit at that big desk, young lady. Well, I'm here to remind you. You are there to do exactly what I tell you to do."

She tried to stare him down even while watching the storm within him rise.

"And what I am telling you to do is to call a press conference on Friday and announce that you are still studying the plan. Put off any further announcements until all the hoopla you've stirred up dies down. Then you will announce that the city has declined to release the properties."

"I won't do that."

". . . because they are not up to code . . ."

"Those buildings are in good condition. Granted, they need some updating but . . ."

". . . and are structurally unsound." He sat back, arms crossed over his large chest.

"I cannot do that. I can't renege on this, Dan." Her words were a plea.

"You will do exactly what I tell you do to," he repeated softly.

"Dan, I'll look like an idiot . . . or worse," she protested.

"You play with fire, you get burned." He shrugged nonchalantly. "You had no business making any kind of commitment, particularly one that was in direct defiance of my instructions. You have been a terrible disappointment to me, Athen." He shook his head in feigned sorrow.

Athen thought of the look on Callie's face as she watched the crowd huddled in the rain on the TV screen and of the look in Ms. Evelyn's eyes as she walked through the vacant house that morning. Backing down now would be no less than an act of betrayal. Even Quentin's eyes had held a brief moment of admiration when he realized what she had done. How could she discard the self-respect she'd so recently found?

"I won't," she whispered.

"Are you deliberately refusing to obey me? Answer me, Athen. We both need to know where we stand," he demanded.

"Yes." She was surprised to find it had been easier than she'd thought.

"You know, of course, that I will go around you. I do not need you. You'll have to bring this before Council for a vote. It will be defeated four to zero. The whole city will see you for the idealistic fool we both know you to be. So you see, my dear . . ." He smiled benevolently. ". . . I hold all the cards."

All but one.

Mary Jo Dolan. She wanted to throw the name in his face, but her mouth would not cooperate.

"You have, as they say, bitten off more than you can chew." He rose slowly.

Go on, she told herself. *Say it. You have nothing to lose.*

". . . and I'm afraid you'll find it infinitely more bitter than you can begin to imagine."

He headed for the door.

Ma-ry Jo Do-lan. It echoed inside her head like thunder. She sneezed.

"You catching cold? Must have been that little walk in the rain," he said with amusement. "Do take care of yourself, Athen. We certainly wouldn't want anything to happen to you."

He walked through the door, closing it behind him quietly.

"Mary Jo Dolan," she whispered to the empty room just before she sneezed again.

QUENTIN PARKED CLOSE TO THE back of the building that temporarily housed the *Woodside Herald* and willed the rain to stop. He counted to ten, then made a dash for the door.

It was locked.

Since he was already soaked, he took his time walking around to the side door, which, thankfully, was open. He trudged up the steps to the second floor and, trailing water, went into the coffee room hoping to find a pot already on.

"First break I got all day," he muttered, seeing the dark liquid dripping down from the filter into the pot. He took off his jacket and tossed it onto the back of a chair.

"Well, don't we look dapper." Brenda came into the room looking dry and comfortable. "Or should that be *damper*. As in damper than anyone else around here. Where'd you park, downtown?"

"I parked out back, expecting the door closest to the parking lot to be unlocked. Silly me." He found a cup on the counter and washed it out.

"Sorry. I'll remind the building management people to unlock all the doors at seven." She poured coffee into the mug she held in her hand. "Or I could give you a key."

"A key would be good."

"Maybe you should go home and change out of those wet clothes and come back."

"I leave a sweatshirt and sweatpants in my office for nights when I want to stop at the gym on my way home. I can wear them until this stuff dries off." He looked down at his khakis and his jacket. "I'm wet right down to my skin."

"Suit yourself." Brenda started out of the room, then stopped and turned. "You missed some good TV."

"Oh?" He opened the refrigerator in search of half and half.

"Athen Moran had a cop break down a door of one of those houses on Fourth Street that the UCC wants to use for a shelter." She leaned back against the counter. "She was awesome."

"I was there."

"You were?" Brenda's interest in the story was apparent. "Was she as awesome in person as she was on that tape that the TV stations are showing over and over?"

"Yes. It was pretty cool, watching that door go down." And pretty cool the way Athen strolled in—and later, out—with her head up.

"I'm guessing you're here to write the story that will appear on our website by this afternoon? Maybe ratchet it up a little for tomorrow's print version?"

"That was the idea."

"Good." She nodded. "So what do you suppose happened to change the city's mind about turning over those houses for a shelter?"

"Nothing happened." He shrugged. "And 'the city's' mind-set hasn't changed."

"So what was Athen doing there this morning? What was that all about? Was it all a ruse?" Brenda frowned.

He thought back to the look on Athen's face while she was confessing that she'd gone rogue on Rossi. There'd been no hint of duplicity, just honest emotion. He regretted having given her such a hard time. In retrospect, he had to acknowledge that she'd seemed to believe every word she said. He wished he hadn't been so harsh.

"Athen says she wants to give the properties to the UCC. Says she wants the project to go through."

"'Athen says'? You got her to talk to you?"

"Yes, but some of it's off the record."

She raised an eyebrow and he nodded. "Sorry, but it is."

Whatever Athen thought of him—what had she called him? Something that meant "jerk" in Greek?—he was a man of his word. As much as he'd enjoy scooping every other news outlet, he would never make public the things she'd admitted to him in the confines of his car that morning. Surely she must have understood that or she never would have let her guard down, even for a moment.

"But you can write about her being sincere in wanting to get the project through, right? That's news. That's the only movement out of City Hall since this started."

"Not that it'll make any difference in the long run. She'll never get it through Council, so the whole thing was a circle jerk, as far as I'm concerned."

"You don't think she showed up just to make it look as if it might happen, to maybe get people to go home or to stop bugging City Hall?"

"No, I don't. I think she would like to see the shelter built. I also think she's thumbed her nose at Dan Rossi but good."

"So what do you think will happen next?"

"I think Rossi will find a way to make her pay," Quentin told her. "I think he'll want to hurt her."

"Uh-oh."

"Uh-oh, what?"

"Uh-oh, you're going to do something, aren't you? You're going to try to find a way to help her."

"Don't be silly. What could I do?" He brushed her off. "Even if I wanted to, she wouldn't accept any help from me. She hates me."

Brenda laughed and headed for the door. "You keep telling yourself that, bucko. In the meantime, don't do anything that's going to make the paper look bad or I'm going to have to pull you off the City Hall beat, you hear me? If you can't be objective, you'll compromise the paper, and I can't have that."

"I hear you. I'll keep it objective, I promise." He crossed his heart with the fingers of one hand. "Anything else, boss?"

"Yes. Make sure the story's a good one."

"Don't worry." He took a sip of coffee. "It will be."

❦ 14 ❧

"Can I get you anything else, Mom?" Callie placed a cup of hot tea with honey on Athen's bedside table.

"No thank you, sweetheart." Athen's voice was raspy and several octaves lower than normal. "This is fine. Though you know I don't like you to be around the stove."

"I made it in the microwave like Aunt Meg does. One minute on high," Callie told her proudly. "Is it okay?"

"It's perfect. *Ahhh-choo!* Thanks, sweetie." Athen reached for a tissue and dabbed at her fiery-red nose.

"Boy, you sound awful," Callie noted. "And you don't look too good, either. Your eyes are all kind of weepy and your face is blotchy."

"I get the picture. Thanks for the update." Athen managed a smile.

"I'm going to finish my homework, but if you need anything, just call me, okay?" Eager to be helpful, Callie straightened the blankets for her mother. "And I'll bring your aspirin at ten before I go to bed. That's when you should take them again."

"You're an absolute gem, Callie," Athen told her beaming daughter. "I do not know what I'd ever do without you."

"I love you, Mom," Callie said from the doorway, "and

I'm really, really proud of you. I didn't mean what I said the other night, about wishing you weren't my mother."

"I know, sweetie." Athen smiled, knowing full well that at the time Callie had meant every word. And with good reason, Athen reminded herself.

She sat and sipped at her tea. Hannah plunked her huge canine head on the side of the mattress and whined pathetically, begging to be invited up.

"Oh, all right, Hannah." Athen caved in and patted the other side of the bed. "You can come up for a while."

Gleefully, Hannah sprang onto the bed and over Athen, who barely managed to avoid spilling hot tea on both of them.

"What a lump you are," she told the large wiggling mass of golden fur that had cuddled next to her and happily plunked a big head on her mistress's abdomen. "You don't care that I've gotten myself into the biggest mess of my life and haven't the faintest idea of what to do next, do you, girl?" Hannah's tail thumped on the mattress. "Or that I got caught in a terrible storm and am now as sick as a dog—if you'll pardon the expression." The tail thumped again.

Athen placed the cup on the table next to the bed, slid down the pillow a bit, and closed her eyes, her left hand stroking the dog's head slowly.

"It's all so confusing. I just don't know what to think anymore," she mumbled, mostly to the dog. "I thought Dan was my friend, but he isn't. He was using me, and I trusted him so much I couldn't even see it when people told me to my face. And now he's washed his hands of me because I won't let him use me anymore. *Ahhhh-choo!*" She reached for another tissue. "And Quentin . . . I can't figure him out at all. First he's my friend, then he's not my friend.

Then for just a few minutes today he almost made me believe that he understood, that he believed me. But then that look was in his eyes again. I hate it when he looks at me like that but I don't know why it bothers me so much."

She sneezed again.

The dog moved her head to encourage her mistress to continue the massage but the hand had fallen still as Athen drifted into a blur of fevered sleep.

OVER THE NEXT SEVERAL DAYS, Athen drifted in and out of a heavy, dreamless sleep. She would awaken, drenched in sweat, with no sense of time or place and long-forgotten voices ringing in her ears before once again falling back into the dark void of unconsciousness.

At some point, Dr. Hill had appeared, called in by an anxious Callie. Athen had little recollection of his visit, other than that she was to stay in bed—as if she could have moved if she'd wanted to—until the fever broke and the coughing subsided. He'd left an arsenal of medication that she took when Callie woke her to administer it. Several days passed before she could keep awake for more than an hour at a time, and several more before she was aware enough to realize how sick she'd been.

"Mom." Callie stuck her head into Athen's room. "Mrs. Kelly sent over some homemade soup. Do you want to try to eat some?"

"Sure." Athen tried to sit up slightly. "That was nice of her."

Callie came into the room and pulled the pillows up behind her mother's back and shoulders, just the way Athen had done for her when she had been sick last summer.

"What time is it?" a disoriented Athen asked.

"Around eleven."

"In the a.m or p.m.?" Athen frowned.

Grinning, Callie pulled the shades up to let the sunlight pour into the room.

"Is it Saturday?"

"No, Mom." Callie laughed. "It's Monday."

"Monday!" Athen sank back against the pillows. "Why aren't you in school?"

"Mom, you were really sick. I didn't want to leave you." Callie sat down on the edge of the bed.

"Callie, you can't stay out of school because I have a cold." Athen's protest was punctuated by a deep hacking cough.

"There wasn't anybody else to stay with you in case you got sicker," Callie told her matter-of-factly. "Honest, Mom, it was no big sacrifice."

"Tomorrow you'll go to school." Athen coughed. "But right now, I think some of Mrs. Kelly's soup might be just what I need."

"Coming right up." Callie bounced off the bed and down the steps.

Mrs. Kelly's chicken soup seemed to have restorative powers. Athen had another bowl at dinnertime, and had enough strength to sit up for an hour or two and read a book Meg had given her for Christmas.

She awoke at dawn to find that during the night, Callie had removed the book from her hands and turned off the light. Athen rose on wobbly legs and shuffled into the bathroom, where she faced herself in the mirror for the first time in several days.

"Ugh!" She wrinkled her nose and made a face at her reflection. "You are a mess. And you smell like a goat."

Vowing to take a shower later that day, she stumbled back to bed as her daughter appeared in the doorway.

"How are you today?" Callie asked. "You look better."

"I feel a lot better." Athen smiled. "So much better, I'm happy to say, that you may rejoin your classmates this morning."

"But, Mom," Callie protested, "what will you do for lunch? And you don't even know when you're supposed to take which pills."

"I think I can figure it out. Now go get a piece of paper so I can write a note for you to take to school."

"Aw, Mom." Feigning dejection, Callie went slinking off from the room with her head hanging dramatically low, and they both laughed at her performance.

"You have done remarkably well," Athen told her when Callie came back to force a reluctant Hannah down the steps and out for her morning spin around the backyard.

"Don't say 'for a child your age.'" Callie attempted to coax the huge beast through the doorway.

"I would not insult you by saying that. No one could have taken better care of me. I thank you for all you have done, and I love you for being such a wonderful, resourceful kid. Come here so I can give you a hug." Athen held out her arms.

"Thanks, Mom." Callie hugged her back, then turned her nose up slightly. "No offense, Mom, but you don't smell so good."

"No offense taken." Athen laughed. "I'd already come to that same conclusion. I will take a shower this morning."

"Maybe you should wait until I get home from school, in case you get weak and fall or something."

"I'll be fine," Athen assured her daughter, "but I think you'd better get Hannah outside and then get ready for school so you don't miss the bus."

Callie dressed, made breakfast for herself, called Hannah in from the yard, and brought Athen a plate of toast and butter with marmalade, a cup of tea, and an orange before blasting out the front door for a mad dash to the bus stop.

Hungrier than she'd realized, Athen attacked the breakfast Callie had prepared, downing both pieces of toast and the orange in record time. She placed the tray beside her on the bed and leaned back, sighing deeply, tired simply from eating.

Her thoughts returned to the previous week, and the terrible scene with Dan. It had been like being disowned by a beloved parent.

"Uh-uh," she said aloud. *People who love you do not treat you with such disregard. A loving parent does not tell a child to close her mind.*

Dan had simply washed his hands of her because she was no longer useful to him. It was a loss, but one she could deal with. Being disgraced before the entire community when it became apparent that she was powerless to deliver the buildings to the UCC—now that would be tough.

How would her father react, she wondered, when he found out that she had defied Dan, and in doing so had incurred his wrath? If he could speak, how would he counsel her? Would he chastise her for her actions, or would he be proud of the stand she'd taken? Would he be angered by Dan's treatment of her? She liked to believe that her father would take her part, but there was the nagging thought that she might have created a rift in his long-standing friendship with Dan.

Athen sighed and picked up the book she'd been reading the night before and tried to force herself to focus on the words, hoping to bury her angst in the pages of a good romance. After realizing she'd read the same paragraph at least four times, she stuck a piece of paper between the pages to mark her spot and slapped the covers closed. She sat up and wrapped her arms around her knees, knowing she had to face certain unfortunate but unavoidable issues.

Could Rossi force her to resign? Or would he, as he had threatened, simply render her impotent by instructing Council to ignore her?

She had no means by which to fight, and no stomach for further humiliation at Dan Rossi's hands. But what of Callie, her conscience nagged, and Ms. Evelyn, and the flock of people who'd waited for her in the rain on Fourth Street? She'd made them a promise that she would not be able to keep.

The phone was ringing in the hall, and she managed to get to it by the fourth ring. She leaned back against the wall to steady herself and lifted the receiver.

"Mrs. Moran?" the vaguely familiar voice of a woman inquired tentatively.

"Yes."

"This is Veronica Spicata. From Personnel?"

"Oh, Veronica, of course." Veronica of the Amy Winehouse hair and the Jersey City accent. "How are you?"

"I'm fine." Veronica snapped her gum. "Listen, Mrs. Moran, it's none of my business, but are you really sick?"

"Of course I'm really sick," Athen replied, slightly offended. "I caught a really nasty cold last week."

"Oh, good." Veronica sighed, her relief apparent. "I'm so glad."

"You're glad that I'm sick?" Totally confused, Athen wondered where this call was leading.

"That you really are sick, and that's why you're not here," Veronica explained.

"Why else would I be home?" Athen slid down the wall to seat herself upon the floor.

"Well, I heard that you were sick, then I heard that maybe you weren't sick, and then they started setting up for the press conference in the big council room just now."

"Who is setting up a press conference?" Athen was suddenly all ears.

"That creep Wolmar. It's going to be televised live at noon, someone said, so I just wondered"—Veronica came right to the point—"if you'd been dumped. If you don't mind me saying it, I think you set off a lot of people last week."

"Yes, I suppose I did." Athen avoided a direct response. "I didn't know about the press conference, but I'll certainly tune in. I'm as curious as you are to see what Mr. Wolmar has on his mind today."

"I sort of figured you didn't know." Veronica snapped her gum again. "But I thought maybe you should."

"I appreciate that," Athen told her sincerely, then added, "I should be back in another day or so."

"I'm glad to hear that, Mrs. Moran, because, you know . . ." Veronica paused, then abruptly said, "I, um, have to hang up now."

"Thanks for the heads-up," Athen said to the dial tone.

She remained on the floor for a very long moment, then hung up the receiver and returned to the bedroom to look at the clock. 11:52. The press conference would start in eight minutes. She grabbed a pillow and walked unsteadily down the stairs, Hannah, as ever, at her heels. She went straight to the living room and turned on the TV. Having several minutes to spare, she went into the kitchen. She grabbed another orange, a handful of nap-kins, and a glass of water. She plunked herself on the sofa and wrapped herself in a soft white afghan just as the noontime news began.

". . . bringing you live coverage of the press confer-ence that is scheduled to begin momentarily here at City Hall. It appears that Councilman James Wolmar has called the conference, Mayor Moran being on an indefinite sick leave," the pert little blond reporter noted.

Indefinite sick leave? Athen's jaw dropped

"I'd like to thank you all for attending on such short notice." Wolmar walked to the podium and greeted the throng of reporters who sat before him and smiled benev-olently into the cameras. "I just thought the city's business should continue as usual in spite of Mrs. Moran's absence."

"What is the nature of Mayor Moran's absence, Mr. Wolmar?" an unidentifiable voice asked.

"I believe she has a cold, Miss Sharpless." He smiled at the TV reporter, his offhand manner implying that a mere cold was a pretty shaky excuse for a week's absence. "But, of course, the business of the city goes on, and I just thought you'd appreciate an update on Council's efforts to increase the size of the police department."

Athen sat mesmerized by his performance. He was perfectly at ease in her role, she realized, and he clearly relished every minute. *The bastard.* She scanned the small sea of reporters who were taking their turns asking their questions. How many new officers? Rookies, or will they be taking applications from veterans of other forces? How many of the new officers would be assigned to the down-town area, where the streets were most dangerous?

"Has Mayor Moran recommended the increase in the force?"

She leaned forward to be closer to the screen. She knew that voice.

"Mrs. Moran was not present when the motion came before Council, Mr. Forbes," Jim replied, adding, "and not knowing when we'd see her again, we thought it best to proceed without her."

"Mr. Wolmar, has Council addressed Mayor Moran's recommendations relative to the UCC's request for the buildings on Fourth Street?" Quentin stood in the first row, a small notebook in his hand.

"Mrs. Moran has made no formal recommendation to Council on that issue." Wolmar's sly smile made her stomach turn. "Nor, for that matter, on any other issue since she took office."

"*Bastard,*" Athen muttered.

"Councilman, Mayor Moran gave every indication that the city was willing to work in concert with the UCC . . ." Quentin persisted.

"Mrs. Moran has, regrettably, acted well beyond the scope of her authority. May I remind you, Mr. Forbes, only Council is authorized to dispose of or transfer title of any city-owned property. It would take a majority vote on Council to approve any such motion, a majority, I feel confident in saying, Mrs. Moran will not have, even if she should succeed in having the issue formally presented to Council. And, as I'm sure you know, only a member of Council may introduce an issue for discussion and vote. Since Mrs. Moran has no support on Council, it is highly unlikely this matter will go any further than it already has."

"Why unlikely? It would appear the plans for the shelter have been well received throughout the community," Quentin pressed.

"The issue has no support on Council, Mr. Forbes," Wolmar stated emphatically. He appeared to be done with the matter, but could not resist one final jab. "Mrs. Moran has, unfortunately, needlessly raised the hopes and expectations of the kindhearted and well-intentioned, and she has done so publicly. It could be said that she has, as the expression goes, stepped in it. Yes, Mr. Rand, you had a question?"

Athen's face flushed scarlet with rage, her eyes stinging from the effort to blink back the tears of anger and humiliation. She was not oblivious to the fact that Wolmar had persistently referred to her as *Mrs.* rather than *Mayor* Moran, an intentional slight, she was certain, as if publicly stripping her of her office. Only the reporters had used her title in referring to her.

"What is Council's main objection to the UCC proposal?"

"I think that's a fair question, deserving of a straightforward answer, sir." Jim flashed his best campaign smile.

"Council is, I should tell you, in the process of studying a highly intriguing option for that piece of property. Now, keep in mind that taken as a whole, the city owns several blocks in that area. The proposal we're looking at would increase revenues to the city by adding to its tax base, not drain the city's already limited resources, as Mrs. Moran would like to do."

"Can you give us some further information?"

"I feel—that is, Council feels—it would be premature to make any announcement at this time. But rest assured, ladies and gentlemen, as soon as there is something more concrete to disclose, you will be fully advised."

"Who is behind the other option?"

"Excuse me, Mr. Forbes?" Wolmar visibly bristled, his

brows forming one straight line across his forehead as he leaned forward on the podium and peered down imperiously at the source of the irritation.

"I said, who has proposed the option that you mentioned?" Quentin's eyes narrowed as he studied Wolmar's expression and awaited a response.

"Why, City Council, Mr. Forbes."

"Who specifically made the proposal?" Quentin repeated, only to have Wolmar turn his back on the pretext of giving his attention to the next question.

By this time Athen was on the floor directly in front of the television, fists clenched as tightly as her jaws, cursing alternately in Greek and English as she watched Wolmar slide oh so smoothly into her domain.

The conference was coming to a close, and for just a few seconds the camera lingered on the front row. Quentin Forbes was slowly returning his pen to his pocket, his eyes following Wolmar, his expression deadly. It was the first time she had seen him turn that icy glaze on anyone but herself. That Wolmar was the recipient gave her no small amount of pleasure.

❧ 15 ❧

Athen had intended to go right back upstairs to take a shower after the press conference, but she remained on the sofa to lick the wounds Wolmar had inflicted upon her. How could she show her face at City Hall now that he'd announced her supposed folly to the entire city?

She wondered which sound bite the evening news would dwell on. Would they run and rerun the part where Wolmar had reminded everyone that she, as mayor, had no authority to commit city-owned property, or the part about how she had been irresponsible to the fine folks who'd been duped by her into believing that the long-awaited shelter might in fact become a reality?

And what of tomorrow's papers? She could barely wait to see Quentin's article. He'd have a field day with her, she was certain. Her cheeks flamed as though the fever had returned, and she began to feel extremely sorry for herself. She sat and cried her eyes out until she heard Callie come in through the back door.

"Mom, I'm . . . hey, great, you're downstairs. You must be feeling better. Did you watch TV?" She threw her books on the nearest chair. "Were you crying? Your eyes are all red."

"No, of course not," Athen said, trying to cover, "it's just because of the cold."

"I don't think they were so red this morning." Callie leaned closer for a better look.

"They weren't open so long this morning."

"If you say so."

Callie went into the kitchen for a snack and to let the dog out. She returned with a glass of milk in one hand and an apple in the other.

"Since you're feeling better, do you think I could go over to Nina's for a while? There's a big test tomorrow. Nina said we could study together and she could help me with the stuff I missed while I was out."

"Certainly. Go."

"Will you be okay?"

"I've been fine all day," insisted Athen. "Almost good as new."

"You won't be good as new until you've had a shower and changed that nightshirt," Callie reminded her with a grin. "I think you've had that old yellow nightshirt on since last week."

"No, I have not." Athen laughed.

"Okay, since the weekend. Either way, it's time for a change." Callie grabbed her book bag and leaned over her mother to kiss her on the forehead. "I'm real glad you're feeling better."

"Much better, thank you, sweetie."

"I'll be at Nina's if you need me. Oh, I saw Mrs. Kelly outside when I came home. She said she'd drop off some more soup later."

"Bless Mrs. Kelly." Athen leaned back once more, and listened as the back door opened, Hannah came in from her excursion, and Callie slammed the door on her way out. Hannah frolicked into the living room and attempted to climb onto the sofa with her mistress.

"No way, Lumpasaurus."

Thwarted, Hannah thumped onto the floor alongside the sofa.

After staring mindlessly at the ceiling for a few minutes, Athen picked up the remote control and turned on the TV. Reruns. Talk shows. Ditzy commercials. She turned it off again and thought about the shower she so badly needed. Now would be a good time.

She was almost to the top step when she heard a knock on the door. Hannah flew into the hallway, barking wildly.

The knocking persisted. Athen went back downstairs.

One hand on Hannah's collar and one hand on the doorknob, Athen pulled the door open. On the top step stood not the elderly Mrs. Kelly holding a pot of soup, but the totally unexpected Mr. Forbes, holding a large bouquet of multicolored flowers.

"I, ah, brought you some flowers." He smiled somewhat weakly.

She leaned back against the door, hoping its wooden panels could absorb the shock.

"'Get well' flowers," he continued, holding out the bouquet to her.

"Why?" Flowers from the man who had made crucifying her his life's work?

"May I come in?" he asked, ignoring her question.

"Well, actually, no, Quentin." She was in no frame of mind to spar with him.

He stepped into the small hallway as if he'd not heard her. Wide-eyed, she backed away from him as if he was visibly poxed.

"These should probably go in water." He made a concerted effort to disguise his amusement as he eyed her disheveled appearance. She blushed scarlet as she recalled she was barely dressed and, by her own admission, smelled like a barnyard.

"Thank you, Quentin. I appreciate it." She held her hands out to take the bouquet, hoping he would accept her thanks and then leave. She should have known better.

"Where would I find a vase?" The slightest smile played at the corners of his mouth as he glanced down at her bare feet, half a leg away from her bare knees. One foot instinctively slid atop the other.

"That won't be necessary," she protested as he walked past her, stopping to let Hannah sniff his hand. The dog wagged her tail approvingly.

"Really, Quentin, I can . . ."

"Nonsense. You've been sick. Go sit down. Here? In

the kitchen?" He went into the next room, a large mound of yellow fur sashaying merrily behind him.

"Traitor," Athen grumbled as Hannah's wagging behind disappeared through the doorway.

"What?" he called to her from the kitchen. She heard the water running in the sink.

"Second cupboard from the back door." She threw up her hands and returned to the sofa, painfully aware that she looked like an unmade bed. At least she could hide under the afghan, but there was absolutely nothing she could do about the unkempt web of hair that hung over her shoulders and halfway down her back in thick dark clumps. She fought an urge to pull the blanket over her head.

"Where would you like them?" Quentin returned to the living room with the flowers in a pale green vase.

"Anywhere is fine. How 'bout on the table right here?"

He placed the flowers where she directed. "So," he said.

He seemed uncomfortable, standing as he was in the middle of the living room floor while she lounged like Cleopatra on the sofa.

"Say, those are beautiful paintings." He pointed to a series of small canvases on the wall nearest the door. "The flowers look almost real."

He stepped closer to look. "A.S.M. Did you paint these?"

"Yes."

"They're wonderful. I had no idea that you painted."

"I don't. I mean, I used to, but I haven't in a long time."

"You should start again. They're really good. The shading is exquisite, and the colors are . . ."

"Thank you, Quentin. Now, if you don't mind . . ."

He snapped his fingers. "I almost forgot. I'll be right back."

Dear God, what is he up to now?

She heard him leave the house, only to return in a flash with a brown paper bag.

"I thought it would be nice if we could visit over a cup of coffee." He opened the bag without looking at her. Pulling the small table to a spot midway between them, he placed a cardboard cup in front of her and dumped small white containers of cream onto the table. "How do you like yours?"

"Light with half a sweetener." She stared at him suspiciously as he prepared it to her preference, then opened the second cup and poured in some cream, all the while acting ridiculously nonchalant.

"Okay, Quentin, what gives?" she asked pointedly.

"I just thought I'd stop by and see how you are."

"Since when has it mattered to you how I am?" What, she wondered, was really behind the visit? "And flowers? Don't you think that's a bit much?"

"Actually . . . well, it's the only way I could think of to apologize."

"Apologize?" Her eyebrows climbed halfway up her forehead. Had she heard correctly? "Are you *apologizing*? To *me*?"

"Yes. I've been every bit a . . . What was that Greek word you called me that day in the car?"

"*Malaka?*" Amused in spite of herself, Athen leaned back against the sofa.

"Yes. *Malaka.* A jerk. I have been a jerk."

"Do tell." She tapped her fingers on the side of her coffee container and tried to avoid direct eye contact. He was not, she had to admit, without a certain charm.

"Athen, may I sit down?" he asked.

She gestured toward a chair across the room. He took the one nearest the sofa.

"Rossi's after you, Athen," he declared frankly.

"No!" She feigned surprise, a hand over her heart. "Why, thank you, Quentin, for tipping me off. I'm simply overcome by your concern."

"I mean it, Athen. He had Wolmar call a press conference this morning." He leaned forward as if sharing a secret.

"I saw it," she told him. "Someone called to tell me."

"Who?" he asked.

"A friend in City Hall." She sipped her coffee, grateful to Veronica that she need not be beholden to Quentin for the news.

"I didn't think you had any friends in City Hall," he said bluntly. "Especially after that dog-and-pony show I witnessed this morning."

"So you thought you'd stop over here and be the first to get my reaction." She bit her bottom lip. At least now she knew why he was really here. "Wouldn't that be a nice touch to tomorrow's story?"

"No, Athen, I didn't come for a story." He put his cup down on the table.

"Then why are you here?"

"I wanted to tell you that I'm sorry." His gaze was steady, his voice hypnotically soft and surprisingly sincere. "You told me the truth and I didn't believe you."

"Why would you believe me now?" Sipping from her cup, she attempted to resist the spell cast by his eyes.

"Rossi had Wolmar call that press conference for the express purpose of letting everyone know you are on Rossi's shit list."

"I know that." She jutted her chin out just a bit, refusing to hang her head in his presence.

He swished his coffee round and round in the bottom of its container, but did not take his eyes from her face. "Was it because of what you did last week?"

"It would appear so."

"I'm so sorry," he said gently.

"You're sorry he's trying to push me out?" She remained unconvinced of the purity of his motives, and could not resist playing as hard with him as he once had with her.

"I'm sorry because you don't deserve what they did to you today."

"But I deserved all the crap you've been throwing at me all these months," she snapped indignantly.

"That was different," he replied.

"Oh, of course. Your motives were strictly professional. The journalist's right to know." She drew a sharp breath. "Whereas Wolmar blatantly intended to cut me off at the knees for political reasons. Your motives were pure but his weren't? Is that what you see as the difference?"

"Athen, I never intended to hurt you personally," he protested.

"Yes, you did, Quentin, every bit as much as Jim did. Only he's a hired gun." She paused to cough, and he handed her the water glass that she'd left at the far end of the table. "At least I know why he's after me. I never understood why you were."

They stared each other down for a very long moment.

Finally, he said, "For a long time, I really believed that you were part of it. Now I know better. And, well, I guess it bothered me that you were involved with Rossi."

"Why?" she demanded. "Why would you care?"

"I know how stupid this sounds, and I know I had no right to have any expectations of you, but I wanted you to be the woman I thought you were when I first met you—if that makes any sense at all." He held his hands out in front of him as he sought to explain.

"What was it you thought me to be?" she asked.

"Sweet. Honest. Straightforward. Intelligent. Beautiful." He seemed embarrassed, as if he'd said more than he'd intended.

She rolled her eyes, knowing how she looked at that moment. "You should have stopped at 'intelligent.'"

She stole a sideward glance at his face, seeking a sign of guile. She found none.

"Can you forgive me for thinking you were a . . ."

". . . a political whore?" She squared her shoulders and completed the sentence for him.

He winced at the memory of having called her exactly that. "For all the things I thought you were since you took the job."

"Can you promise never to make a fool out of me again?" she asked pointedly.

"Athen, a reporter doesn't make the news. If you stand up at an open meeting and make statements that indicate you don't have the faintest idea of what's going on, how can I ignore it?" He challenged her sense of fair play.

For the first time it dawned on her that if he had made a fool out of her, it had been because her own actions had made it so easy for him to do so.

"That will not happen again," she vowed firmly.

"Then you have nothing to worry about as far as my paper is concerned." He smiled gently. "I promise to be fair to you if you will be honest with me. And if you will forgive me for . . . well, for everything. Do we have a deal?"

She nodded, understanding that a truce had been called, though uncertain if she'd made a friend or if she'd made a pact with the devil.

"Well." He broke the silence. "Are you going to let Rossi push you out?"

"I don't want to make any statements." She shook her head.

"No, no," he assured her. "Strictly off the record. This is friend to friend now."

"I don't know how to stop him if he wants me out."

"You can refuse to go." Blue eyes studied her intently.

"To what end?"

"If nothing more, to be as big a pain in his butt as he is in everyone else's."

"I don't know if it's worth the humiliation."

"What happens if you resign?" he wondered aloud.

"You saw it this morning."

"Wolmar?" He frowned, then nodded. "I guess that follows."

Quentin's eyes lingered on the photos Callie had placed on the mantel. Callie and John. John in his uniform. Athen holding a newborn Callie, John standing by proudly.

"What?"

"What? Oh, I don't know." He smiled. "I guess in a way, I'm disappointed."

"About what?"

"That you're giving up so easily. That you're giving in to him."

"Why, because you won't have old Athena to kick around anymore?" She tried to make a halfhearted joke.

"Hey, a good reporter doesn't care who he kicks around," he quipped. "Actually, I guess I expected you to fight him."

"Fight a man I can't beat to keep a job I don't want? I don't see any logic in that." She dismissed the possibility with a wave of her hand.

"Would you want it if it was real?" His eyes narrowed.

"You mean if Rossi didn't hold this city in his iron grip and I could do things the way I wanted to?"

"Something like that."

"It's an unlikely scenario."

The slamming of the back door announced Callie's arrival home.

"Mom . . . oh, Mr. Forbes. Hi." She stopped dead in the doorway, as surprised to see him as her mother had been.

"Callie, good to see you." He smiled his best smile.

Callie looked warily the room. "Is Timmy . . . ?"

"Nah." Quentin's eyes danced. "The little geek is riding this afternoon at my mother's."

"Riding?" Callie asked.

"Horseback riding," Quentin explained. "My mother and stepfather have quite a stable. Say, maybe some afternoon you might want to . . ."

"I don't think so," Callie said pointedly, and Quentin laughed good-naturedly.

"Callie, you're being rude," her mother whispered.

"It's okay," Quentin assured her, "but the offer is always open, Callie."

"Thanks anyway, Mr. Forbes." Callie stood looking at them from the doorway.

Quentin took the hint.

"Well, I should be getting back to work." He rose from his seat. "Athen, I'm glad you're feeling better."

"I am, thanks." She debated whether or not to walk him to the door. She recalled suddenly how she was dressed, what she must look like, and decided to stay put.

"I can find my way out." He smiled as if reading her mind.

"Thanks for the flowers." She found herself looking up at him, unable to look away. "And for the apology."

He appeared to be about to say something more, then glanced at Callie, standing like a sentinel at the entrance to the front hallway.

"Well," Quentin said, "I guess I'll be talking to you. Bye, Callie."

"Why was he here?" Callie demanded after he'd closed the door behind him.

"He brought me flowers." Athen tried to appear nonchalant.

"Why?"

"It's customary to bring flowers to friends when they're sick."

"Since when has Mr. Forbes been your friend?" Callie asked suspiciously.

Athen barely heard her, suddenly lost in thought.

"And what did he have to apologize to you for?" Callie pressed.

"For being wrong about something." Athen smiled to herself.

"What was he wrong about?"

"Me." *He was wrong about me and he admitted it. And will wonders never cease . . . the man brought me flowers.*

"Sometimes grown-ups make no sense," Callie muttered as she went to answer the front door, where Mrs. Kelly waited to make her soup delivery.

ATHEN PLANNED TO GO INTO the office the next day, but at dawn she found herself still too weak to get up and get dressed. When she returned to City Hall, she wanted it to be with her head up, and as weak as she still was, she just wasn't ready. She decided to take one more day off.

It's not as if I have piles of work to do when I get back, she thought glumly. *Edie's no doubt taking the mail home to Dan, anyway.*

Around noon she dressed in jeans and a chambray shirt, ate a leisurely lunch, and decided to spend some time with her father.

The day was warm and clear, a perfect spring afternoon. She rolled the car windows down and breathed in the sweetly scented air as she drove through the park. She turned into the parking lot behind Woodside Manor and searched for a spot under the trees. She walked toward the building, and spotted Diana Bennett's car at the end of the first row. Athen glanced at her watch. Diana's lunch hour must be almost over. Athen could wait. She walked to the pond and sat down on the bench to kill some time.

A group of small children gathered on the opposite side of the pond. Laughing with delight, they tossed pieces of bread to the ducks and geese, which swam ever closer to the shore. She thought of the day last summer when she'd stood right in that same spot, and Quentin had appeared with a bag of popcorn. She had liked him that day, she recalled. She'd liked his easy smile and his affability.

She'd thought about him a great deal since his visit the previous afternoon. Once she was able to admit that it had been she who'd set herself up to look like an idiot, she could no longer hold him responsible for the situation she had created. Quentin, while perhaps the most persistent, hadn't been the only newsperson to recognize her blunders.

It's always easier to find someone else to blame than to blame ourselves. Maybe I should be thanking him, she mused, *since it was his harassment that prodded me into wanting to be more informed.*

And just look where that's gotten me, she ruefully reminded herself.

"Athen?" Diana stopped her car parallel to the bench where Athen sat.

"Hey, Diana." Athen waved.

Diana parked the car and walked to the pond on high navy heels that clicked on the asphalt. She wore a navy linen suit with a silk shirt the color of wheat, like her hair. As always, Diana looked like she'd stepped from the pages of a magazine.

"How are you?" Athen asked as Diana approached on the bench.

"How are *you* is the question." Diana removed her sunglasses. "I heard you were very sick."

"I'm better," Athen told her truthfully. "I think I'll be back tomorrow."

"I'm glad to hear it. Your father will be so relieved," Diana told her. "He's been so worried about you. Your health, of course, first and foremost, but everything else that's going on has him very concerned."

"How can you tell?" Athen asked.

"We communicate quite well, your father and I." Diana smiled. "I read the paper with him every afternoon, and we watch the news on TV in the evening. It's not difficult to tell when he's upset, when he's amused. It's all still there in his eyes."

Remarkable, Athen thought. How was it that Diana saw so much that she had not seen?

"I'm glad I decided to come out today," Athen said. "I don't want him to worry about me."

"He's very upset about what Rossi is doing," Diana told her. "Ari'd break his neck if he could."

"That makes me feel so bad, after all the years they were such close friends." It was so depressing to think that she was the cause of her father's ill feelings toward his old companion.

"Who were such close friends?" Diana frowned.

"My dad and Dan." Athen ground the heel of one sneakered foot into the stones at the base of the bench.

"Where did you ever get that idea?" Diana laughed scornfully.

"Why, Dad's known him forever. They served on Council together. They campaigned for each other."

"All true. But whoever told you that they were *friends?*"

"Why, Dan did. But I remember Dan coming to the hospital the night my father had the stroke. He was so kind."

"That SOB just couldn't wait to see if it was really true," Diana growled.

"What do you mean?"

"Athen, your father's stroke was the best thing that ever happened to Dan Rossi," Diana replied bitterly.

"I don't understand."

"Ari worked with Dan for years, but they hated each other. Your father ranked Dan right up there with Mussolini and Vlad the Impaler."

"What?" Athen's eyes widened with shock. "Why?"

"Ari always suspected Dan took kickbacks, but he could never prove it. There's no question your father was on to something right before he had the stroke," Diana related bluntly. "Like I said, Ari's stroke was the best thing that ever happened to Dan. It shut Ari up for good."

"I can't believe this." Athen gasped.

"Oh, it's true enough. The last conversation I had with Ari on the day he had the first stroke was at about nine in the morning. He was railing about something Dan had done, and said he was meeting with him later in the morning and that he was going to put a stop to it."

"Put a stop to what?"

"I haven't the faintest idea. I knew Ari was watching him. I think Dan knew it, too. Whatever it was that set your father off that day must have happened early on."

"He didn't give you any clue?"

"He didn't have a chance. At eleven o'clock I got a call that he'd been rushed to the hospital."

"What did he say, that morning on the phone, do you remember?" Athen prodded.

"Of course. He said, 'I see he's gone too far this time.' Then he said he was going to meet with Dan and that he'd tell me about it over dinner."

"Why didn't you tell me this before? Before I got into this mess with Rossi?" Athen was horrified.

"I don't recall that you asked for my advice," Diana reminded her pointedly.

"Well, that was obviously my first mistake." Athen reached into the bag at her feet and took out her half-empty bottle of water. She opened it and took a drink. "Why would Dan even want me around if he and my dad hated each other so much?"

"You have to be kidding." Diana laughed. "My dear Athen, you were the perfect choice. Widow of the city's own dead hero. Daughter of the city's most popular Council member, and as a bonus, politically naïve to boot. You weren't even aware that your own father wanted to bring Dan down. And who else could have held the line on the Greek vote?"

"Oh, God, I wish I'd known." Athen closed her eyes and tried to imagine how her father must have felt, being forced to watch in silence as his daughter made camp with his enemy. "I'll bet it just about killed Dad to have me so close to Dan for the past six months."

"It was tough for him, I'm not going to lie. But he's kept an eye on you," Diana assured her.

"How?"

"Through me. You must know how proud he is that you finally defied Dan. I think Ari knew all along it was only a matter of time before you caught on."

"How does he know?"

"We watch the noontime news together. Last week, we saw you with Ms. Evelyn on Fourth Street. You should have seen your father's eyes, watching you." Diana smiled. "It was the best therapy he could possibly have."

"How could Dad have known that Dan told me not to go?"

"It was obvious. Dan has been sitting on those prop-erties for three years now. If they weren't important to him somehow, he'd have given them to the UCC himself, if for no other reason than the publicity he'd get, not to mention the votes."

"I wonder what he's got in mind."

"Whatever it is, you can be sure that Dan will profit royally from it," Diana said. "Well, maybe in time you can flush him out."

"What do you mean, in time? I'm out of time," Athen stated flatly.

"Athen, you have over a year left on your term," Diana reminded her.

Athen averted her gaze to the ducks who dove for treats pitched by the children across the pond.

"Has he threatened you?" Diana demanded.

"Not with bodily harm. But he's made it clear that if I stay, I'll be nothing more than his whipping post until the primary."

"Tell me what you plan to do now." Leaning back against the bench, Diana crossed first her arms, then her legs. A shoe slipped off to dangle from the toes of one foot.

"I don't see where I have any option but to go to Ms. Evelyn and tell her I can't help her."

"You mean back down? Let Rossi toss you out like last week's papers?"

"I don't see where I have a choice."

"That's exactly what he wants you to think. Don't let him bully you like that."

"Diana, Wolmar's right. Only Council can direct the title transfer. I acted stupidly."

"Then put the issue on the back burner until you have enough votes in your pocket to win."

"Are you crazy? I have no votes. I've never had any votes. *Dan* has all the votes." How, Athen wondered, could someone so politically astute be so blind to the obvious?

"Not necessarily," Diana replied with a level gaze.

"How do you figure?"

"It takes a majority to pass a motion. Four Council votes, the mayor votes in case of tie, right?"

"There wouldn't be a tie, Diana." Athen fought to control the exasperation welling up within her.

"You concede too quickly," Diana insisted.

"Diana, I wouldn't even have one vote . . ."

"Of course you would. Konstantos is first a Greek. His loyalty is to Ari, and therefore to you," Diana pointed out.

"So that's one vote." Athen held up one finger.

"Athen, it's time you learned to play the game."

"I don't think I want to play the game."

"That's exactly what Dan is counting on. He turns up the heat, you run from the kitchen. Don't give him that satisfaction."

"What would you do?" Athen leaned one elbow on the back of the bench and turned sideways to face Diana.

"I'd play from my strength," Diana said as if stating the obvious.

"I have no strength." Athen laughed ruefully.

"You have one definite ally in Konstantos, and one potential one." Diana held up two fingers.

"Who?"

"Riley Fallon."

"How do you figure? Dan himself appointed Fallon to Council after Bill Saunders died. I can't think of any power on this earth that could turn Riley against Dan."

"Then perhaps you'll have to appeal to an unearthly power."

"You mean pray?"

"Athen, Riley Fallon is engaged to Georgia Davison," Diana said, the emphasis on the woman's last name.

"So?" Athen asked blankly.

"Georgia's father is the Reverend Ralph Davison. Of the AME Church of the Brethren." Diana paused meaningfully.

"Okay, I see the connection with the church, but I can't call Reverend Davison and say, 'I need the vote of your future son-in-law if you want that shelter.'"

"Of course not. You wouldn't be that obvious." Diana smiled. "You would go to Ms. Evelyn—who, of course, is a member of Reverend Davison's church—and you'd tell her how sorry you are, but it looks as if you might not be able to deliver those properties to the UCC after all. You tell her you simply don't have the votes, that you need at least one more and you just can't see how that will happen."

"Assuming that I was interested in doing this, what good would that do?"

"Ms. Evelyn is a highly creative lady," Diana assured her. "She's not likely to sit by idly while her vision of a shelter is in jeopardy. She'll think of something."

"You think she could?"

"There's no doubt in my mind. Think it over, Athen. What have you got to lose?" Diana looked at her watch. "Good grief, I'm late. Go see your dad, Athen, but don't let him suspect for one minute that you'd let Rossi back you down. Give me a call. We'll talk more if you like."

"Thank you, Diana."

Diana flew back to her car, leaving Athen alone to ponder the possibilities.

"PATERAS." ATHEN ENTERED THE COOL room, and her father's anxious eyes followed her. "I'm sorry I haven't been to see you for a while, but I caught a devil of a cold wandering around Fourth Street in the rain last week. I'm much better today.

"Papa, Dan is very angry with me for going there, and for saying I thought the shelter should be permitted, but it was worth it. It was the right thing to do. And maybe, just maybe, between now and next year, I can make something good out of this mess I've gotten into."

She took his hands and held them, looking into his eyes. As Diana had predicted, she saw worry fade away and pride take its place.

"Diana thinks I can do it, Papa. She's helping me to

sort things out." She bit her lip, not bothering to blink back the tears she knew would soon begin to fall. "I wish I'd known her all these years. She is so clever, and so wonderful. I know now why you love her. I'm more sorry than I can tell you for not making it easier for you. Please forgive me. It should never have taken this long for Diana and me to be friends. We both love you so much."

Father and daughter sat silently, both in tears, both in total understanding of one another. It had been a long time since they had been in such accord. Diana had been right. It was all still there in Ari's eyes. Athen had been blind not to have seen for herself.

"And something else, Papa," she told him as she wiped first his wet face and then her own. "If I had known about Dan, how you and he really felt about each other, I never would have gotten into this."

Ari's eyes narrowed at the sound of his old enemy's name.

"Diana told me that there'd been problems between you and Dan, but he never let on. Dan told me you were close friends. I guess he thought if I didn't know the truth, it would serve his purpose better," she thought aloud, still digesting this recent news. "I wish I knew what you know. I wish you could tell me. But maybe, before all this is over, Diana and I can piece it together."

She grinned. "And wouldn't that be something, Ari's girls ganging up on Dan to bring him down."

A look of anxiety crossed her father's face.

"Oh, no, don't worry," she quickly assured him. "We will be very careful, I promise. I may have been very foolish over the past few months, but I promise, I will be very cautious from here on."

She deliberately changed the subject then, bringing him up-to-date on Callie's latest scholastic and athletic accomplishments. Before long she found herself talking about Quentin, how confused she was about him, how a part of her wanted to trust him, and yet at the same time feared the hand offered in friendship might be a ruse to use her, as Dan had.

"On the one hand," she said, "I respect Quentin. He did apologize, and when I pressed, he said very honestly he could not promise to never write an unfavorable story about me again. If he'd been trying to win my trust at any cost, he'd have agreed to write only articles that would cast me in a favorable light, don't you think?"

It could all be so confusing sometimes, she confided, knowing who and what to take chances on.

"In case you are wondering," she told her father as she was leaving, "if Dan wants me out before next year, if he wants the office back, he's going to have to take it from me."

❖ 16 ❖

A then dressed more carefully than usual the next morning, deciding on a crisp black and white linen dress and black high heels that made her appear even taller than she was. She slipped on large gold button earrings and her gold watch. Standing back to inspect her appearance, she tried to put her finger on what, exactly, was wrong with the picture.

"It's the hair," she said aloud, standing in front of her dresser mirror. "I have too much hair. Long and straight may be fine for Callie, but it doesn't do much for me if I want to say I mean business."

She tried wrapping it in a bun, but there was simply too much of it. Never having been much of a hairstylist, she was all thumbs, but eventually decided to braid it and wrap the long braid at the nape of her neck.

"Not perfect, but neater, and certainly more professional. And as Meg would say, image is everything."

She was in the building by eight o'clock, at her desk with coffee she'd prepared by 8:10, long before anyone else would arrive. As she'd suspected, the mail, which should have been piled ceiling high after a week's absence, was nowhere to be seen. Her desk was perfectly clean, and she steamed with every minute that passed until Edie arrived—late, naturally—at nine thirty.

Hearing Edie's banter with Rose at the other end of the hall, Athen went to the door of her office and leaned back against it.

"Good morning, Edie." She forced herself to be pleasant.

"Oh, Athen." Edie was visibly rattled to see her. "What are you . . . I mean, when did you . . . ?"

"Yes, I'm much better, thank you. Nice of you to ask. And yes, it's good to be back." Athen attempted to smile though her jaws were clenched. "Edie, where's the mail?"

"The mail?" Edie repeated nervously.

"My mail, Edie, the mail that comes addressed to this office every day. . . ."

"I—I took the mail home . . . to . . . sort it for you." The woman stammered.

"Then I trust you brought it back." Athen fixed her gaze on Edie's face, which had developed a sudden tic.

"I . . . no . . . I guess I forgot it."

"Then you'll have to go back home and get it." Athen

turned for her office. "I'll just be in here waiting, Edie. It shouldn't take you more than, what, twenty minutes, thirty at the most, to go home and back again?"

Athen closed the door behind her, congratulating herself on her performance. She glanced at her watch. By now Edie would be in Jim Wolmar's office, calling Dan and asking him what to do. And what instructions would he give her? Ignore Athen? Tell her it was stolen? Tell her the truth?

Athen began to pace. She wanted to call Ms. Evelyn, wanted to sit down and talk with her as soon as possible. Of course, Dan would know immediately. Edie would make sure of that the minute Ms. Evelyn arrived and the door closed behind them. It would be better for Athen to go to Ms. Evelyn.

Maybe I should call her now and meet with her tonight. But if she's not there and I have to leave a message, Edie will answer the phone when she calls back and report the call.

"Damn it," Athen muttered, "this is ridiculous. I have an assistant who is working for the enemy, who will without doubt be reporting every move I make from here on, just as she has been doing all along."

Athen sat at her desk and tapped a thoughtful finger on the leather blotter. Maybe it was time Edie got a transfer.

She searched her desk for the interoffice phone list, then scanned the names and circled the number she wanted. As she lifted the receiver, she realized that she was smiling.

"Veronica? This is Athen Moran. Much better, thank you." Athen leaned back in her chair. "Veronica, I want you to clean your desk of all your personal belongings and come up here to my office as soon as possible. Of course you're not being fired. You've just been promoted."

Edie had squawked like a wounded crow when she arrived upstairs—without the mail—to find her things in a box on a chair near the elevator and Veronica happily unpacking her family photos at Edie's old desk. Edie had been even more incensed when Athen told her she'd arranged for her transfer to the Public Works garage, where she'd have a nice desk right next to the storage room. Edie stomped and cursed and ran, no doubt, directly to Dan. Athen wondered how long it would take before the phone rang.

Exactly seven minutes passed before Veronica appeared in the doorway.

"Mr. Rossi's on the phone, Mrs. M., and he doesn't sound happy."

"Good morning, Dan," Athen said evenly, hoping to hang on to the confidence she'd felt since she'd awakened that day.

"You think Edie's the only person I have to rely on?" He skipped the pleasantries and cut to the chase.

"Certainly not," she replied calmly. "But at least I know I'll get my phone calls and my mail."

He laughed. "It won't be that easy to get around me, Athen."

"I don't expect it to be easy, Dan."

"Pack it up, Athen, there's nothing for you in City Hall," he taunted. "Just what do you think you're going to accomplish, besides pissing me off even more than you already have? I'd quit while I was ahead if I were you. There's no place for you to go except down."

She took a deep breath and reached for the trump.

"Mary Jo Dolan."

A long moment passed. "What about her?" he asked cautiously.

"By noon today I want her car keys on my desk." Closing her eyes, she took another deep breath. "And I want her at her desk in Personnel at twelve oh three."

She waited. There was no pretense offered. It was clear he knew exactly which keys to which car she referred.

"Just what do you think you're going to do?"

"I haven't decided. I haven't had time to think about it," she told him with more nonchalance than she felt. She waited for the other shoe to drop, as she knew it eventually would.

"I suggest you think very long and very hard, Athena. You may well be lighting a fire you will be unable to put out." The menace was undisguised.

"By noon, Dan," she repeated coolly. "And certainly the city will expect to be reimbursed for the premiums paid for her vehicle's insurance over the past four years, as well as the mileage."

She mentally patted herself on the back for her clear thinking. "And of course we'll want reimbursement of the wages she was paid beyond the normal six-month short-term disability she was entitled to. I'm assuming she can produce a letter from her doctor confirming the nature of her illness."

Athen twirled a paper clip on the end of a pencil, suddenly feeling a bit jaunty herself.

Dan swore a blue streak. She ignored him.

"And it goes without saying that if she fails to report for work, she will no longer be paid."

He muttered one last obscenity before slamming down the receiver. The gauntlet had hit the ground.

It was then she realized that she was sweating, the palms of both hands as well as her face clammy in the air-conditioned room.

"I did it." She waited for a bolt of lightning to crash through the wall and strike her down. "Oh, my God, I did it."

Rossi had been incensed, enraged. But at exactly noon, Veronica walked into Athen's office, two keys dangling from a chain held between her thumb and index finger, a silly grin on her face.

"Yo, Mrs. M., you're not going to believe who just turned in her car. . . ."

🌿 17 🌿

"A then, it's good to see you up and about and looking fit again. Though your color could be better." Ms. Evelyn squinted at Athen through the bright glare of the early morning sun. "You're still a little pale. And aren't you up early for a Saturday morning? Now, where's that young gal of yours today?"

"She had a girlfriend over to spend the night last night, and I suspect they stayed up quite late," Athen explained, "since they were both out cold when I left the house."

"You be sure to tell her I was asking after her." Ms. Evelyn removed her glasses and wiped them clean on the tail of her red-and-white-striped shirt. "And be sure to tell her in another month I'll have some choice plants from my own fields for her garden. Second-year plants, so they won't be too expensive. There's a bumper crop of some varieties I know John was partial to."

"I'll be sure to bring her back," Athen promised.

"Now, then, what would you be needing today? Too early for perennials, I guess you know that. Unless you're looking for some primrose, or maybe some pansies."

Ms. Evelyn pointed to the flats of gaily colored flowers that sat outside the greenhouse door.

"I believe I do have some flowering bulbs left over from Easter—tulips, daffodils, hyacinths—but other than that . . ." She stopped as if pondering what else she might have to offer.

"Umm . . . maybe some of the gold, ah . . . primroses." Athen hoped the plants she pointed to were, in fact, primroses. "And some of those dark blue and yellow . . ."

"The pansies?" Ms. Evelyn asked and Athen nodded. "They've always been a favorite of mine. You go on, now, and take the ones you want."

Ms. Evelyn waved a friendly greeting to another customer who had turned into the small lot.

"Good morning, Mrs. Stephens," she called as the woman exited her car. "I have those red azaleas you were looking for. Right this way."

Athen poked around the flats, making her selections slowly, all the while anxiously debating within herself as to the best way to approach Ms. Evelyn as Diana had suggested. When Mrs. Stephens had departed, Athen casually made her way to the counter over which an ancient cash register presided.

"I think I'll take four of the primroses, and four of the pansies," she announced.

"Now, when you say four, do you mean four plants, or four flats?"

"Four flats," Athen told her. "Four of each."

Ms. Evelyn nodded and pulled a pencil from her

shirt pocket and began to tally up Athen's purchases on a small piece of paper. "So, now, how are we doing with our shelter?"

"Not very well, I'm afraid—at least, for now." Athen took a deep breath and plunged into the business of politicking. "You know I'm behind it one hundred percent, Ms. Evelyn. Unfortunately, there is very little support for this on Council. I guess you've already heard that. Outside of George Konstantos, upon whose support I know I can rely, I just don't see anyone else coming out on our side."

"Athen, honey, were you not aware that this problem existed when we took our little walk to Fourth Street?" Ms. Evelyn continued writing small numbers in her neat, even hand, but never looked up.

"I suspected there would be some resistance," Athen replied carefully, "but I really thought that when the other members of Council saw how much support there was in the community, they'd come around. Unfortunately, that has not happened." She shook her head sadly. "You may have seen Councilman Wolmar's press conference this week?"

"I certainly did." Ms. Evelyn sniffed indignantly. "And I can tell you that the UCC did not appreciate his comments. Not one bit."

"Then you know where Council stands," Athen ventured.

"I know where Jim Wolmar says it stands." Ms. Evelyn flashed a look of anger.

"Well, right now, I don't see any sense in bringing it before Council, Ms. Evelyn. George Konstantos is perfectly willing to introduce the issue, but since no one else is willing to vote with him . . ." Athen shrugged and lifted her hands in an "I don't know what else we can do" gesture. "Council always votes together, Ms. Evelyn. There's never been a split vote—at least, not since I've been mayor. I've never been called upon to cast a tie-breaking vote. Right now, I just don't see any way to pry one more vote from those three remaining Council members."

"That'll be sixty-four dollars." Ms. Evelyn finished the computation. "Let me put them in a box for you."

The spry little woman disappeared into the greenhouse and emerged with a cardboard box.

"It's a sad day when Woodside Heights can't see fit to take care of the unfortunate in its midst." Ms. Evelyn shook her white-haired head slowly from side to side. "A very sad day, indeed."

"I could not agree with you more, Ms. Evelyn."

Athen held her breath, waiting for Ms. Evelyn to "get creative," as Diana had assured her she would do.

Ms. Evelyn, however, was engrossed in packing Athen's primroses.

"We need another box," Ms. Evelyn muttered, and she returned a second time to the greenhouse.

They carried the boxes of flowers to Athen's car with no further conversation. Athen tried not to panic, tried to stifle the growing urge to grab Mr. Evelyn by the shoulders and yell, "You're supposed to be my secret weapon. Diana said you'd know what to do!"

Before Athen got into her car, Ms. Evelyn offered a hug, but no words of wisdom. Disappointed and depressed, Athen took the long way home.

Her secret weapon appeared to be a dud.

THE HOPED-FOR GAME PLAN NOT having materialized, a downcast Athen poked about the house, looking for something to do.

Remembering the plants still tucked into the trunk of her car, she decided now was as good a time as any to put them in the ground. She changed into jeans and a sweatshirt, pulled up her sleeves, and set about the task of looking through the rebuilt garage for the garden tools.

"Wow," Callie exclaimed as she rounded the side of the house. "Mom! You're digging."

"How very observant of you," Athen replied dryly.

"Where'd the plants come from?"

"Ms. Evelyn's."

"You went to Ms. Evelyn's without me?" Callie protested.

"You were out like a light and I didn't want to wake you, but she did say she'd have some things you'd like in another month or so."

"Oh, boy. What things?"

"I didn't ask. But I'll take you back in a few weeks and you can see for yourself. What are you and Nina up to?"

"We want to go to Carolann's house. Her mom said she'd take us to the movies, then we could go back to her house and have pizza. Is it okay with you?"

"What's the movie?"

"It's the one about the dog on the airplane that gets sent to one airport while his humans go someplace else," Callie told her.

"I guess that's okay." Athen put her trowel down and sat back against the tree. "Do you have any money?"

"My allowance." Callie nodded.

"How will you get there, how will you get home, and when can I expect you?"

"Mrs. McGowan, Mrs. McGowan, and the three of us wanted to sleep over at Nina's." Callie ticked off her responses on her fingers. "Nina's mom said it was okay."

"Stop out here before you leave so I can kiss you good-bye," Athen instructed.

Twenty minutes later, Callie announced she was packed and ready to go, just as Athen finished placing the last primrose in the firm ground.

"Not bad, Mom." Callie raised her face for her good-bye kiss. "Actually, it looks pretty good, for your first flower bed. Dad would have been proud. See you in the morning."

After Callie left, Athen sat on the top step to admire her work. She'd placed the new plantings between the clumps of daffodils that were just coming into bloom. She walked to the end of the flagstone walkway near the street for a different perspective.

"Not bad." She repeated Callie's praise. The colors of the flowers were bright and added a splash of cheeriness to the grass that had yet to green up.

Hands on her hips, she surveyed her little domain. Her eyes followed the walkway to the front of the redbrick Tudor-style house. Elongated arms of forsythia covered with masses of golden blossoms reached upward to the second-floor windows from either side of the front steps.

I should find one of John's shrub books, she told herself, *and figure out how to prune those. This is the second spring they've not been cut back, and they're out of control.*

She strolled up the walk, inhaling deeply as a light breeze bore the scent of magnolia from a neighboring yard. She plopped herself on the steps again, relishing the first sense of contentment she'd felt in . . . how long? When was the last time she'd felt this quiet pleasure in her own company?

Too long, she acknowledged, and she permitted herself the luxury of savoring the minutes of peaceful solitude.

This time last year she had been a lost soul. Granted, her job was now in jeopardy, the most powerful man in the city had it in for her, and she had all but promised a homeless shelter that she could not deliver. But there were other things to consider, things that were more important than Dan Rossi's disposition.

Recently, Athen had returned to the Greek Community Center, and she'd been humbled by the warmth with which she'd been greeted. She had not realized how much she'd been missed, or the value of the service she'd provided. Helping the elderly to fill out medical forms, translating mail, teaching the basics of this foreign English language to those who could read or speak only Greek, she filled a real need. She was grateful to be needed again, grateful to once more find something within herself to give. Returning every Wednesday night had become a priority.

The warming weather, too, had drawn her out of the house, and she could no longer resist the pull of the new bike. She rode early each morning for thirty minutes, and found her enthusiasm for this once-favorite pastime returning. She'd forgotten how much she enjoyed the quiet streets, nearly empty just after dawn, when the fragrance of a new day filled the city. The regular exercise renewed her energy as well as her spirit.

And I've even planted my first garden, she mused. Recalling that John always watered immediately after planting, she went around the side of the house and returned with the hose. She had just finished dousing the newly planted flowers when she recognized the dark SUV that had just parked in front of the house.

"Hi." Quentin walked up the flagstone path.

"Unexpected visits are becoming a habit with you."

"Didn't Callie tell you I called?" he asked. "I told her I might stop by."

"I guess it slipped her mind." Athen wondered if it had been an oversight on the part of her daughter, who was usually reliable when it came to messages.

"Where is the little general?" He peered up the driveway.

"Off with her girlfriends for the night." Athen dried her hands on her pant legs. "What brings you out this way?"

"Timmy had baseball practice this afternoon. I dropped him off at his friend's house over on Falmouth. I thought since I was just a block away, I'd stop in and see if you would be free for dinner." He grinned. "Apparently, you are."

"Ahhh, well . . ." She was suddenly befuddled.

"Look, it's just a casual night out. There's a new Thai restaurant I've been wanting to try. And it's not often I'm footloose and fancy-free on a Saturday night. I guess you get out without Callie about as often as I get out without Timmy."

"Quentin, I don't think it would be a good idea."

"Why not?"

"Well, let's start with the fact that I'll be afraid to open my mouth for fear that anything I say will end up in print."

"This is strictly social, I promise," he assured her. "As a matter of fact, we can agree not to discuss your job, City Hall, anything you feel uncomfortable with."

"You really feel you can stick with that?" she asked skeptically.

"Absolutely." His blue eyes fixed on her without blinking. "Scout's honor."

"Well, I guess we could." She remained unconvinced, but his manner was so sincere. His dimples so deep . . .

"Great. I'll pick you up at— What's a good time? Seven?"

. "At least seven." She held out her hands and arms, which were caked with dirt from her fingers to her elbows. "It will take me at least that long to get cleaned up."

The sun had almost set and the streetlights came on to signal the approach of evening. Standing with her back to the light, she cast a shadow over his face.

"I'll see you then." He smiled and headed for his car.

Athen began to gather up the hose to return it to the backyard, while at the same time watching Quentin return to his car.

No wonder Meg and her college friends hung out the window just to watch him walk by, Athen mused. *He certainly has a great . . . walk.*

✺18✺

Athen stood in front of the bathroom mirror and attempted to apply makeup with trembling hands, questioning the wisdom of having accepted Quentin's casual invitation.

How long has it been since I've had a date? Fourteen years? Fifteen? Whatever possessed me to say yes? What will we talk about? I'm not good at small talk. I haven't had male companionship on a one-on-one basis in eighteen months. Other than my father, of course, or Dan.

Her fingers tiptoed from one hanger to the next in her open closet as she evaluated her wardrobe. *Too matronly. Too dressy. Too casual. Too old. Ugh. Why do I still have this?*

One by one, she rejected everything she owned, then started over again.

She settled on a pair of loden green pants and a pale sage shirt she'd bought on sale but never wore. She frowned at her reflection.

Too . . . plain.

She rummaged through a drawer until she found a paisley scarf, which she tied around her neck. She frowned again. Too nineties.

She gathered her hair with the scarf, and tied it in a big floppy bow at the back of her neck. Better, but still dated.

"I'll bet men don't go through this," she muttered to Hannah. "I'll bet Quentin just got out of the shower and pulled on the first thing he saw."

She studied her reflection in the mirror. The peach-toned blush was soft and okay for the office, but at night it looked too pale. She rummaged through the makeup kit Meg had sent for her birthday and scanned her choices. Maybe the plum would be better. She removed the peach blush and gently stroked on the darker shade. The change was better, fresher. She studied her eyes. *I should have used some shadow. Something darker, but not too dark.*

She contemplated the choices displayed on the little wheel of colored powders. The soft greenish gray shade looked appealing, so she dabbed it across her eyelids, and then, on a whim, she put a little more on the small spongy brush and lined her upper lid as she had seen someone demonstrate on TV.

"It's going to have to do," she said aloud. "But seriously? A makeover is in order."

She slipped into a pair of flats and ran downstairs.

"Come on, Hannah, it's dinnertime." The big yellow

dog ambled into the kitchen and watched Athen pour dry dog food into the hard plastic crater that served as a dinner dish.

Athen glanced anxiously at the clock: 6:45. She found herself tapping nervously on the countertop with her fingers, then stuffed her hands into her pockets to make herself stop. After Hannah inhaled the contents of her bowl, Athen opened the back door and stepped outside with the dog. The air had cooled, so she went back in, raced upstairs and pulled a muted plaid jacket from its hanger. She slipped into it and paused to study her reflection for the hundredth time. The colors of the jacket— eons old—were perfect, but it, too, was dated. She rolled up the sleeves. Better.

She fumbled through her jewelry for a pair of silver earrings that Meg had given her, with their matching ring, for Christmas the year before. She opened the box that still held all three pieces and put on the earrings. In the bottom of the drawer she saw a silver bangle bracelet and she slipped it onto her wrist. Her eyes fell on the ring finger of her left hand, where her plain gold wedding ring still wound its endless circle.

Slowly, she removed the symbol of what she had come to think of as another lifetime. She rolled it around and around in her right hand. So long reluctant to part with it, she now placed it in her jewelry box.

"It's time, John," she whispered. "I'm so sorry, but it's time. . . ."

Ringless after so many years, her finger felt naked. She replaced the thin gold band with the silver ring that matched her earrings just as the doorbell rang. She closed the drawer and ran down the steps.

"Hi!" she greeted Quentin at the door. "Come in."

"You look great." He smiled as if he meant it.

"Thanks." A faint blush crept from her neck to her face. "I just have to let Hannah in."

She all but ran into the kitchen to escape his presence, her heart pounding in her ears. *This is a mistake. Maybe I could tell him I'm sick. I probably will be by the end of the evening if I put food in this stomach.*

She opened the back door and Hannah bounded in, searching for the stranger she knew was there. Quentin held out his hand and the tail began to wag the dog.

"You remember me, girl?" Quentin bent down to pet her. "I think she remembers me." He appeared pleased.

"She's a pretty smart dog."

Quentin gave Hannah a final scratch behind her ears. "Well, I guess we should be going."

The restaurant was only ten minutes away, but it seemed to Athen that she'd been trapped in his car for hours. The ride was marked mostly by silence, Quentin making some effort at small talk to which she gave brief responses. Once they were seated at their table, however, the conversation flowed more easily, and before too long, her nerves calmed enough for her to respond in full sentences.

"Don't order any of the starred dishes unless you like really hot, spicy food," Quentin cautioned.

"I'm okay with a little spicy, but I'm not familiar with the menu. Maybe you could recommend something that's not too heavily seasoned. I'm afraid I haven't eaten a lot of Asian cuisine."

"You might like the Thai beef salad. It's a favorite of mine, and I've heard good things about the kitchen here, so it's worth a try."

"I'll try that." She folded the menu.

After their orders had been taken by a doll-like

woman wearing a brightly colored, heavily embroidered dress, Quentin told her, "My dad used to travel regularly to the Far East on business. Thailand, Japan, India—those were his usual stops. I accompanied him on a number of trips. He loved sampling local foods and always sought out the restaurants that served the most authentic foods wherever we went. I learned to love some pretty exotic things as a result."

"What did you father do?"

"He ran the family business. Actually, it was my mother's family's business." He leaned back from the table as the waitress placed a dish of shrimp lanced with long wooden spikes on the table. "Here, try these with a little peanut sauce. I think you'll like them."

"What kind of a business?" She bit into a shrimp, which she'd hesitantly dipped into the small bowl. "Mmm. You were right. This is yummy."

"Well, my mother's father bought several small businesses that he thought had potential back in the fifties, when everything could be bought dirt cheap. As those businesses did well, he bought others: real estate, hotel chains, manufacturing plants, you name it. He was not a man to put all his eggs in the same basket. Over the years, he had accumulated quite extensive and diversified holdings."

"And your father worked for him?"

"Worked with him, actually. My uncle Stephen, my mother's only brother, worked for the company with the understanding that one day he'd take over from his father. Unfortunately, my uncle hated it. After a couple of years of trying, he wanted out. My grandfather realized that his son would never follow in his footsteps, so he turned to my father."

"Your father liked it?"

"Dad loved it. He thrived on the stress, the travel, the long hours, all the wheeling and dealing."

"And you?" She speared a piece of beef with her fork, having passed on the chopsticks, which she noted he handled adeptly.

"Not so much. I was into it for a while." He looked down at his plate, as if concentrating on what to eat next. "Being the only son, I was expected to take the reins someday, but I guess I wasn't cut out for it any more than my uncle was. For my father's sake, I did try to find something about it that I liked, but running a large conglomerate like that was not my thing. My mother realized early on that it was not going to happen for me, so she was more than willing to let me move on after my father's death."

"So did she sell the company?"

"No, she appointed a board to oversee the entire conglomerate. Each company is self-contained, and each reports to the board on a quarterly basis. The only stipulation Mom made when I resigned was that I stay on the board and attend all the quarterly meetings. Other than that, I could do as I pleased."

"How long did you work there?"

"I stayed for a couple of years, but after my mom married Hughes, and with Cynthia gone, there seemed to be little reason to stay in St. Louis. It seemed like the right time to move on. It's important to me that Timmy have a good relationship with his grandmother, and it seemed like a good time for me to try my hand at something I wanted to do."

"And that would be . . . ?"

"I'd been hoping I'd find some time to write," he confided.

"Well, you're certainly doing that."

"Journalism, reporting . . . not exactly what I'd had in mind. That was Brenda's idea to keep me off the streets and keep me from getting lazy." He smiled. "From the first time I read about the Underground Railroad, I've been fascinated by the stories. I guess the concept of a whole network of people putting their lives on the line for strangers simply because it was the right thing to do appealed to the idealist in me. The first time I came out here to visit my mother, Brenda took me on a tour of the city and pointed out a few homes that had been part of the Underground, and she introduced me to Ms. Evelyn, and I was hooked. It was love at first sight." He grinned. "You know she grew up on the Hill, right? That she's the city's unofficial historian? She's agreed to work with me on a book I'm researching on the subject. She told me that as a child she spent hours listening to the stories that were told by the old folks about their experiences as they fled north. Some were firsthand accounts, others were stories passed down by her grandparents. I've been meeting with her once a week, and she's retelling all those tales for me to record. Once I complete the book, I'm going to give the tapes to the library so that none of it will be lost. I'll play some of the tapes for you sometime if you're interested," he offered.

"I'd like that, thank you."

The waitress refilled their cups with more of the aromatic tea, and then sent another tiny woman to clear the table.

"Ms. Evelyn isn't like anyone else I've ever met," Athen said. "She's involved in every aspect of this community, from running literacy classes in the housing project to singing in the church choir. She runs a taxi service all the way to Elizabeth twice a week to the medical center for senior citizens who need their prescriptions filled and young mothers from downtown whose babies need medical care. She's been doing this sort of thing for as long as I can remember."

Athen set her cup down on the table and held her hand up, signaling "No thank you" to the overly attentive waitress who rushed to refill it.

"I've known Ms. Evelyn since I was a child. She worked actively for my father when he campaigned, and John knew her well because he always bought plants from her. She's a one-woman redevelopment task force."

"You've heard about her latest project, right?"

"Her latest project?" Athen raised an eyebrow. "What's she up to now?"

"She quietly tracked down the owners of several vacant adjacent lots on Third Street and conned them into entering long-term leases with the UCC. She's planned an enormous community garden so people from the housing project can grow their own vegetables and flowers and fruits."

"Those lots that border on Schuyler?" Athen asked. "The ones that have been used as dumps for the past twenty years?"

"Yes, those." Quentin nodded. "She's enlisted volunteers from each of the churches to haul out the debris. She's also gotten someone she does business with at her nursery to donate topsoil and talked him into delivering free of charge when she's ready for it. She even talked one of her suppliers into donating some fruit trees."

"Where did you hear all this?" she asked curiously. How had it escaped the City Hall pipeline?

"From Ms. Evelyn. I stopped to see her this afternoon, and she told me she was looking for more volunteers to clean the lots next weekend and, by the way, did I know how to operate a backhoe?"

"Do you?" she asked.

"I can learn. There's no saying no to that lady. She showed me the sketch she made for the garden. It's amazing. She even has plans for an old-fashioned town green with a bandstand right in the middle." He smiled at the waitress as she delivered the check on a red enamel tray.

"Thank you for dinner, Quentin," Athen said. "I'd forgotten how enjoyable adult dinner conversation can be."

"Well, there's no lack of adult conversation at my mother's." He counted out several bills and left them on the tray. "But this certainly beats a replay of Hughes's golf game any day. I'm looking forward to doing this again."

"If we're ever childless on the same night again."

"Maybe we can arrange to be." He held her hand as they walked to the car.

Two blocks from her house, he slowed for a red light and, noting her silence, asked, "A penny for them."

"I was just thinking how nice it was that you kept your word. Do you realize you didn't mention City Hall one time?"

"That was the deal." The light changed and he made the turn onto Harper Avenue. "I have to admit I had to bite my tongue several times to keep from asking how you got rid of Edie and how you wound up with that character who sits outside your door. Interesting accent she has, by the way."

"Hey, I'll have you know that accent is one hundred percent pure Jersey City."

"Where'd you find her?"

"She had been working in the Personnel Department. As far as Edie is concerned, let's just say I arranged for her transfer."

"Why Veronica?" He pulled to the curb to park in front of her house.

Athen hesitated. In tipping her off to Rossi's little arrangement with Mary Jo Dolan, Veronica had presented Athen with the only weapon she had against Dan. As much as she was beginning to like Quentin, he was still a reporter, and she still wasn't sure how much she could trust him.

There was one way to find out.

"Quentin, if I told you something in complete confidence, would you promise that you would never use it? You'd never print it?" She turned to look him full in the face, watching his expression. "And that you'd never repeat it to anyone?"

"Of course," he replied without hesitation.

"Even if it was something that would make a truly great story? Could you still keep your word?"

"You mean the type of story that would make your average reporter salivate?"

"Exactly." She was testing him, and she suspected that he knew it.

"If it was told to me in confidence, then yes, I would keep my word."

Athen took a deep breath and told him how she had met Veronica, how Veronica had blown the whistle on Dan and Mary Jo.

"Whoa, are you serious?" He leaned forward. "Dan had an underage mistress, had her paid by the city for four years even though she didn't work, even gave her a city car?"

The light in his eyes flooded her with concern. "Quentin, you promised . . ."

"Didn't I tell you this guy was a crook? Good lord, Athen, you could bring this guy down in a flash with this."

"No, Quentin, I can't," she said quietly.

"What do you mean, you can't? Athen, this is precisely the type of thing that could . . ."

She shook her head slowly. "I can't. I can threaten Dan with it, I can hold it over his head, but I will not publicly use it. Of course, Dan doesn't know that."

"You've lost me." He held his hands palms up in bewilderment. "I can't think of one reason why you would sit on something like that."

"Mary Jo's father ran off about ten years ago, just left town and never came back. For years, her mother held down three jobs to keep her family together. She has five children, Quentin. Mary Jo looks like the only bad apple in the bunch." Athen's voice was a faint whisper. "Mrs. Dolan cleaned houses and cooked for the rectory at St. Michael's. She cleaned offices at night. Last year, she was diagnosed with cancer and hasn't been able to work. The woman is under incredible stress, yet every week she volunteers at her church's soup kitchen—maybe for only an hour or two, but she's there every week. She's a very good woman, a very good woman who's struggling just to stay alive. She doesn't know about Mary Jo and Dan. Finding out would probably kill her."

"Who told you all this?"

"Apparently everyone in Woodside Heights knows the story. It isn't a secret."

"Where does Mrs. Dolan think Mary Jo got her car?"

"Mary Jo told her she won it in a raffle."

"And that's why you won't use this, to protect her mother?" he asked incredulously.

"It's certainly not to protect Mary Jo or Dan."

"Even though this news could rid the city of Dan Rossi?"

"There has to be another way. I will not stoop to that level. My father always said that nothing good can be gained by deliberately hurting someone else. It's a tawdry story, and I'm not going to go after Dan over Theresa Dolan. I'll find a way to get to him, but it won't be by causing that kind of pain to a dying woman."

"You think she doesn't know about her daughter?"

"It's my understanding that she does not. Diana knows her. She told me that Mrs. Dolan thinks the sun rises and sets on her baby girl."

"But this could send Dan to prison. If Mary Jo was only seventeen when they began the affair . . ."

She waved him off.

"There are only two people who can speak to that. Do you really think either Mary Jo or Dan is going to admit the truth? We'd end up with a scandal that's based on a story that can't be proven, and at the same time, a good woman is destroyed." She shook her head. "Not on my watch."

He reached across the console and took her hand, threading his fingers through hers.

"You are quite a woman, Athena Moran."

She shrugged and went on. "You asked why Veronica's my new right hand. She is the only person in City Hall that I can completely trust."

"It must have been hard for you, knowing that every move you made was being watched."

"For a long time, I didn't know. Ignorance was bliss." She smiled. "But it's not so bad now. Veronica keeps her ear to the ground. It's amazing how much she hears from the other women in City Hall. And don't let her appearance fool you. Underneath all that hair and behind the makeup is a very bright young woman. She is funny and straightforward and honest, and she's a real breath of fresh air."

"And she is one hundred percent loyal to you," he observed.

"Yes. I believe she is."

"Well, then, not to be outdone by Veronica, I guess I will have to prove myself just as loyal." He leaned over and whispered in her ear, "Your secret is safe with me. I will keep my promise."

"Thank you, Quentin."

His face was so close she could see, even in the dark, the tiny laugh lines around his mouth. If she just turned her head, just the slightest bit . . .

"You're welcome." He drew her closer and very gently kissed her on the mouth. Before she could react, he'd opened his door and was moving around the front of the car. He opened the passenger door and reached a hand in to her. She took it, and side by side they strolled up the flagstone path to her door.

She was debating whether or not to invite him in when he said, "Thanks for spending the evening with me. After all that's happened over the past few months, I'm really glad that we're starting over. And thank you for trusting me. It means a lot to me."

Before she could reply, he leaned over and took her face in both hands and kissed her again. This time there was no gentle brush of his lips on hers, but a real kiss, one that set her head spinning and caused her breath to catch in her throat.

"I've been wanting to do that since the first time I saw you, Fourth of July last year," he told her.

Athen's shaking fingers dropped her keys, and they clattered on the concrete steps. Amused, he bent to pick them up and held them out to her. She found the door key and turned it in the lock.

"Thanks for dinner," she managed to say.

He smiled and planted one light kiss on the top of her head, then swung the door open for her.

"I'll be in touch." He walked backward for two or three steps before turning toward the street and heading to his car.

She watched through the curtains as he drove away, the headlights hazy under the streetlamp's glow. She sat on the sofa in the darkened living room, grateful to have the house to herself. The evening had left her with a lot to think about.

She touched her fingers to her lips where Quentin's mouth had been, acknowledging that she was more attracted to him than she wanted to be. She was glad that they'd put their animosity behind them, but wasn't sure she should have told him about Mary Jo. It had been so easy to confide in him. Would she later regret it? Would his journalist's desire for a story be stronger than his loyalty to a promise? Would he knowingly take from her the only weapon she had to hold over Dan's head? Or would he prove to be a man of his word?

Quentin aside, there was this news of Ms. Evelyn's latest project. Athen couldn't help but wonder what the woman was up to, and if it somehow tied into the creative plan Diana still insisted Ms. Evelyn would come up with to garner support for the shelter. Then again, Ms. Evelyn might have given up on that entirely. Maybe she'd decided to put all her energy into the community garden, which would require no approval from Council.

Athen raised her fingers to her lips again, and wondered when, or if, he would call her, and tried to remem-

ber just how long it had been since she had waited for a
man to call.

QUENTIN WASN'T SURE WHETHER THE buzz in his head was
due to the company he'd kept for the past few hours or
the bombshell Athen had dropped in his lap. He'd dated
his share of beautiful women in his day, but he couldn't
remember any of them being remotely like the one he'd
just kissed good night.

For one thing, she was a woman he could have a
conversation with. Not small talk, not flirty talk, not self-
centered "enough about you, let's talk about me" talk that
he'd had to endure on more occasions than he liked to recall. Athen had seemed genuinely interested in the book
he was writing, though he suspected that interest might
have been influenced by Ms. Evelyn's connection to the
subject matter. Still, there were no awkward pauses when
he'd had to work to keep things going, and he appreciated
that. What guy liked to be mentally sorting through a list
of possible conversation starters when all he wanted was a
nice dinner and some easy talk with a woman he was interested in?

And he was definitely interested in Athen.

Yeah, the conversation had flowed easily, and he
came away with the feeling of only having scratched the
surface where she was concerned. But that was all right,
too. He wasn't in any hurry, and he had the feeling that
she was more comfortable taking her time getting to
know him, too.

That he'd misread her right from the start had been
his mistake. He cringed with embarrassment every time
he thought back to the way he'd treated her. It had taken
him awhile, but he'd finally had to admit to himself that

his initial response had been to hold Athen up to Cynthia and compare. Athen doted on her daughter, was involved in Callie's life in ways that Cynthia never had been involved in Tim's, even when he was a baby. Cynthia had gone back to work after their child's birth before her maternity leave had ended because she was afraid she'd miss something—a plum assignment, an opportunity that might not come again. When Quentin first met Athen, she was a stay-at-home mom, and after Cynthia's abandonment of Timmy, Quentin had been impressed by Athen's devotion to Callie. Then she'd let that creep Rossi talk her into running for mayor, and his image of her as a sort of modern-day Madonna was shattered, and that was where the trouble had started.

God, he'd acted like an ass.

Except for Cynthia, he'd never been so wrong about a woman in his life. Athen really was the sweet woman he'd first thought her to be. He knew he was lucky that she'd been willing to give him a second chance.

Still, he wasn't unaware of the conflict between her job and his interest in her, and tonight he'd made a conscious effort to keep an even balance. He'd promised not to bring up anything to do with City Hall and he'd kept to that. Not that it had been easy. There were several times when he'd almost slipped but he'd managed to keep his word. Until, of course, she brought up that whole Mary Jo Dolan thing.

Mentally, he'd been writing the first paragraph of that story all night. But he wouldn't, under any circumstances, betray Athen's trust. He had the feeling that she was testing him, dropping a scandal like that in his lap after making him promise not to touch it. As juicy a story as this was, it was going to be a test of his willpower.

Quentin cursed Dan Rossi under his breath. The man was a crook and should go to prison. Surely if they dug deeply enough they'd find proof that Dan had been dallying with Mary Jo while she was still underage. As much as he was sure that even Athen would like to see Rossi fry, he knew she refused to use the information she had because of the pain it would cause an innocent party.

Surely no one would be happier to see Dan Rossi go away than Athen. Who else in her position would pass up an opportunity like that because it went against her personal code of ethics?

Who acts like that?

Well, since she wasn't going to go public with the Mary Jo Dolan story, she was just going to have to find another way to topple the giant. It would give Quentin great pleasure to help her in any way he could. For one thing, it bothered him that Rossi had taken advantage of an innocent person and used her to maintain his grip on the city. Athen hadn't deserved to be treated that way by someone she trusted, and it pissed off Quentin every time he thought about how Rossi had duped her. All the time Athen had thought she was doing something good, Rossi was just using her so that he could get his office back in two years.

Yeah, finding a way to bring down Rossi would be sweet.

The fact that it would probably win him major points with Athen would be the icing. He'd really enjoyed kissing her, and had every intention of kissing her again at the very first opportunity.

Still, it was going to drive him crazy to have this great story—his mind had written the second paragraph and was well into the third—that he couldn't use. He'd have to take comfort in the belief that a man like Rossi had more than one dirty secret in his background. If he couldn't use the one he had, he'd just have to find another.

That would be fine, too, as long as in the end Dan Rossi got what he deserved. Quentin drove through the gates of his mother's home thinking how good it would feel to help Athen deliver the blow that would bring the man to his knees.

⚜ 19 ⚜

"Mom!" Callie made a face. "Mr. Forbes is on the phone."

Athen took the receiver and tried to talk, feed Hannah, and make dinner at the same time. The call was brief and to the point.

"Why's he calling you?" Callie asked suspiciously after Athen hung up.

"I guess because we're friends," Athen replied.

"You have to be friends with him just because he brought flowers when you were sick?" Callie's hands rode high on her hips as she interrogated her mother.

"No, Callie, we're friends because we . . . well, I guess because we like each other." Athen avoided her daughter's eyes. "We had dinner together last night."

"You had dinner with Timmy Forbes's *father*?" Callie asked incredulously. "Mom, how could you?"

"Callie, Quentin Forbes is a very nice man."

"You didn't used to think he was so nice," Callie jabbed.

"Yes, that is true. I didn't used to like him."

"But now you do?" The statement, delivered flatly, sounded to Athen's ears like an accusation.

"Yes, I do."

"Is he the same Quentin Forbes who used to work for the newspaper? The one who embarrassed and humiliated you?" Callie asked pointedly. "That's what you told Aunt Meg, right?"

"Yes." Athen tried to ignore Callie's sarcasm. "And he still works for the newspaper."

"How do you know he won't embarrass you again?"

"Well, I guess I don't know for sure, Callie, but sometimes you just have to give people a chance." She set the pan of moussaka on the table.

They ate in silence. Athen knew how sensitive Callie was as far as her father's memory was concerned. Did Callie think she was being unfaithful to John because she'd shared the company of another man?

"Grandpa used to make this better," Callie muttered.

Before Athen could think of a way to approach the subject of her dating, Callie asked, "Are you planning on seeing him again?"

"He asked me if I'd be at the spring concert at school on Wednesday night," Athen told her. "I said I would be."

"If he asks you out again, will you go?"

"Yes. I will."

"Oh, God." Callie pushed her plate away and left the room, moaning loudly, "My mother is dating the butthead's father. I hope this doesn't get around school."

FOR THE FIRST TIME SINCE she took office, Athen found herself looking forward to the Wednesday morning press conference, knowing Quentin would be there.

"How do I look?" she asked Veronica before she set out for the large conference room.

"You look great." Veronica seemed puzzled. Athen never asked about her appearance. "You always look great, Mrs. M."

"Thanks." Athen took a deep breath and headed for the elevator.

She smoothed the collar as she stepped off the elevator and walked into the room where the press conferences were held. Quentin was there, in his usual spot in the front row, when she entered. She had some difficulty sticking to her agenda, knowing he was there. She cleared her throat and reminded herself to focus.

There were a few announcements that day, so the question-and-answer session was uncommonly brief. Quentin hadn't asked any questions, though she was pretty sure the reporter two rows behind him had identified herself as being on the *Woodside Herald* staff.

He caught up with her in the hallway.

"Will I see you tonight at school?"

"Yes." She nodded.

"Can I pick up you?"

Recalling Callie's horror at her mother's having had dinner with him, Athen thought it best to pass on the ride.

"No thank you, I may have to rush from work. I have a meeting at four that might run a little late."

"Then I guess I'll see you there."

She tried to act surprised when she found him waiting for her in the school lobby.

"Want to sit with me?" he asked.

"Sure." Callie would be onstage and would be none the wiser.

The band performance was an exercise in discipline for the audience, which tried desperately to refrain from open laughter at the inharmonious renditions of several tunes that neither Athen nor Quentin could identify. They finished up with a version of "Yesterday" that no one who'd ever heard the original would have recognized. The auditorium filled with cheers of gratitude when the instrumental nightmare concluded.

"God, that was bad." Quentin shook his head. "I'd say Timmy needs a few more lessons on that trumpet."

"They're just kids." Athen stifled a giggle. "They'll get better as they get older."

"Lord, I hope so." He moved his leg so that it rested against hers. "We have, what, seven or eight more years of concerts to endure?"

The choral group was much better, though it appeared that some of the younger members got off track a time or two and sang from the wrong page.

Athen couldn't keep from watching Quentin out of the corner of one eye. *Keep your feet on the ground,* she cautioned herself. *You both have jobs to do, and children to raise.*

But he is so handsome—she sighed softly—*with those little lines that crinkle around his eyes when he smiles, and shoulders big enough to stand on. . . .*

"It can't go on too much longer." Quentin squeezed her hand, forcing her thoughts back to the auditorium and the performance.

"It does make me wonder what they were doing, all those days Callie stayed after school for rehearsals."

Then, yes! The finale, with a beaming Mr. Halterman bowing at center stage to the audience.

The smiling parents were invited to the reception room to share refreshments while they waited for their offspring. Athen and Quentin were standing somewhat apart from the others, deep in conversation, when Callie and a few of her friends joined them. Callie rolled her eyes when she recognized her mother's companion.

"Well, that was some show," Quentin told her as she approached.

"It stunk and you know it," she said flippantly.

"Callie!" Athen protested.

"Would it make you feel better if I said that you were terrible?" Quentin asked matter-of-factly, unruffled by her rudeness.

Her efforts to get a rise out of Quentin having failed, Callie shrugged her indifference and addressed her mother impatiently. "Can we go home now?"

"In a minute." Athen was becoming more and more annoyed with her daughter's ill manners. "Why don't you get some punch?" It was a command and not a suggestion.

"Yech. School punch. How appealing," muttered Callie as she walked off to get a cup.

QUENTIN, I'M SO SORRY."

"Don't worry about it." He smiled good-naturedly. "I suspect that Callie's a good kid, but it looks like I bring out the worst in her. But it's perfectly understandable. Timmy was the same way the first time I went out with someone after his mother left. He got over it. Callie will, too."

"I hope so." Athen watched her daughter, who was sharing some whispered secret with her girlfriends.

Timmy joined his father, and Athen couldn't help comparing his courteous greeting to Callie's curt one.

Maybe Quentin is right, Athen thought. *Maybe it's just because he's the first man I've gone out with since John died.*

"Mom, I have a science test tomorrow." Callie pointedly ignored the boy's presence. "Can we please go?"

"Yes, Callie, we can go." Athen sighed.

"We're leaving too," Quentin said. "We'll walk out with you."

Callie rolled her eyes to the heavens for the second time in just under ten minutes.

"Do you have a science test tomorrow too?" Athen asked Timmy as they walked through the parking lot. "Aren't you in Callie's class?"

Before he could answer, Callie snapped, "No, he is not. He's in the brainy section."

"I thought you were in the top section." Athen fell in step with her daughter as they approached their car.

"I'm in the smart section," Callie told her with great exasperation. "But Timmy's *super*smart. He takes classes with the upper grades."

"Not for everything." Timmy sounded defensive. "I only take math and science with them. Everything else I take with you, so if I'm a brain, what's that make you?"

Callie ignored him and leaned against the car door, waiting for her mother to open it.

"How about dinner Friday night?" Quentin whispered. "You think she'll let you out?" He nodded in Callie's direction with more good humor than she had any right to expect, considering her daughter's behavior.

"Let me get back to you on that," Athen replied and opened the car door.

Quentin waved good-bye to Callie, who stood with her arms folded across her chest.

"Callie, you really embarrassed me," Athen told her the minute the car doors were closed.

"Well, you embarrassed me, too," Callie grumbled.

"How did I embarrass you? Was I rude to your friends? Did I insult anyone?"

"You did not have to go off in a corner with Mr. Forbes," Callie snapped.

"We were not off in a corner." Athen negotiated the turn onto the main road.

"You're my mother." Callie struggled with her temper. "You know how I feel about Timmy."

"Callie, what is wrong with Timmy? He's nice, he's polite, he's . . ."

"Oh, please." Callie groaned dramatically.

"Then what is it?"

"Timmy is the smartest kid in the entire school. He's the best at every sport. He gets to ride horses every day 'cause his grandmother owns a lot of them. And he's rich." Callie ticked off the litany of Timmy Forbes's offenses.

"Sounds like jealousy to me." Athen turned into their driveway and came to a stop.

"I am not jealous!" Callie was out of the car even before Athen turned off the ignition. "He is the perfect kid, Mom. He never gets anything wrong on tests, he never swears."

"Do you?" Athen interjected.

"Do I get things wrong on tests or do I swear?" Callie turned the outside light on over the back door so that Athen could find the keyhole. "Sometimes I do both."

Athen pushed open the door, and Hannah, aroused from sleep, barked as she ventured into the kitchen to investigate.

"Mom, Timmy doesn't talk to anyone or go out of his way to be friends with any of the other kids," Callie told her.

"How can you make friends with people who make fun of you?" Athen tossed her purse halfway across the room to the counter. "And has it occurred to you or your friends that maybe Timmy is shy? It isn't easy coming into a new school in the middle of the year, when everyone already knows everyone else. And he's had a hard time these last few years, Callie. His mother left them."

"Left them?" Callie's head shot up from her book bag where she had been searching for her science notes. "What do you mean, she left them?"

"She left them for a job. She lives in Europe now, and she never comes back," Athen told her softly. "And I'd appreciate it if you kept that to yourself."

"At least his mother is still alive," Callie retorted. "At least maybe he'll be able to see her again someday."

"Do you think that makes him feel better, when maybe he needs her now?"

"You're only taking his side because you like his father," Callie whined.

"I'm taking his side because I think he's a nice kid who is lonely and who's had to deal with a great loss in his life, a loss that is every bit as big and every bit as real as yours. Maybe worse, because your father did not choose to die, but his mother chose to leave." Athen leaned upon the counter. "I don't think you are being fair to him, and that makes me sad. I don't think he deserves the treatment he's gotten, and I'm ashamed to know that you are a party to it, Calliope Moran."

Callie dropped her eyes, picked up her book bag, and stomped off to the sanctuary of her room.

❧20❧

"Well, there are six different movies playing here to-night." Quentin took Athen's elbow as they entered the multiscreen theater on Friday night. "Do you have a preference?

"No." She shook her head. "You choose."

She stood slightly to the side while he bought the tickets.

"I hope *Silver Mornings* is to your liking." He ushered her through the glass doors. "It's gotten excellent reviews."

"I haven't heard anything about it, good or bad, but I'm sure it will be fine." She took his arm to keep from getting lost in the crowded lobby.

They took seats midway down the aisle as the lights began to dim. The previews of coming attractions began to roll and Quentin decided to go for popcorn. He returned just as the feature was about to begin. He handed her a cup of syrupy soda and placed the enormous box of popcorn between them. The rippling piano notes of the theme song faded as the scene opened onto a moonlit beach, where a woman paced anxiously in the sand, rubbing her hands together in obvious distress. The camera moved in on the woman until the unmistakable, flawless face of Dallas MacGregor filled the entire screen. Athen choked and Quentin patted her on the back.

"You okay?" he whispered. "Got popcorn stuck in your throat?"

Athen nodded dumbly and sank into her seat. She squirmed uncomfortably through the movie, to the extent that Quentin, assuming her view was obstructed, asked her if she'd like to sit somewhere else.

Yes, she wanted to reply. *The lobby would do nicely.*

She endured what she considered to be sheer torture. As always, the camera was devoted to Dallas, never showing her at a bad angle, if indeed there was such a thing. It lingered on her face so that every expression was viewed up close and personal on the wide screen. Quentin put his arm around her and she was tempted to bury her face in his shoulder to blot out the lavender eyes, the pouting smile, the perfect skin of her late husband's first love.

An hour and a half later, they emerged, holding hands, Athen grateful that the film had finally ended.

"Great movie," he commented as they walked to the car.

"Umm-hmm," she replied from between painfully clenched jaws.

"Where would you like to have dinner?"

"I don't care." She shrugged.

"Let's try Scotties across the street." He led and she followed quietly.

After they placed their orders for sandwiches, Quentin noted, "You didn't seem to enjoy the movie very much."

When she did not reply, he peered across the table, tilting his head to make eye contact with her. "What is it? Were you bored?"

"Let's just say that Dallas MacGregor is not my favorite actress." She glanced away, pretending to watch the antics of a group of teenagers, two of whom had shaved heads, and another, purple hair.

"I think she's terrific," he told her. "I thought she was great in this film. And she's certainly one of the most beautiful . . ."

"Quentin." Athen couldn't hold it in any longer. "John was in love with her."

"Yeah, well, so are ninety-nine percent of the men in the country." He shrugged. "Including yours truly. So what?"

"No, Quentin, I mean that they were in love with *each other*," she said meaningfully.

"John actually knew her?" Quentin's jaw dropped.

"They dated all through college."

"Wow. Your John must have been some guy to have had the two most beautiful women I ever saw in love with him."

"Very gallant, Mr. Forbes."

"Very true, Mrs. Moran," he told her pointedly. "You are every bit as lovely, every bit as fascinating, and certainly every bit as sexy as Dallas MacGregor. I tip my hat to John Moran, who, besides being a selfless hero, had impeccable taste—and apparently incredible luck—when it came to women."

Her fingertips tapped on the tabletop.

"Oh, come on, Athen, don't tell me you're jealous of her after all these years?"

"A few months ago, I found a box of letters she'd written to him, hidden in the back of John's closet."

"Recent letters?" Quentin's eyebrows rose. A married cop from some small city in northern New Jersey having an affair with one of the world's most glamorous film stars? Talk about a scoop.

"No. From years ago. Letters she had written after she'd graduated from college and moved to California."

"I don't understand the problem." He shrugged. "Especially if John had stopped seeing her before he started seeing you."

"I guess I just hadn't realized what she had meant to him." Athen unconsciously began to tear tiny pieces from one end of a paper napkin. "John never talked about her. I knew she'd been his girlfriend, of course, since I was best friends with his sister. But from the time we started dating, I don't remember him ever mentioning her name."

"Why should he have? It was obviously a closed subject by then."

"But he kept her letters all those years."

"Everyone keeps mementos of their past, Athen. And I would guess that he declined discussing her with you because she was, in fact, the past. You were his present and his future. Besides, only a totally insensitive man would have reminded his wife that his first love had been one of the most celebrated beauties of our generation. From all I've heard about John Moran, he was a pretty decent fellow."

"Yes, he was." She nodded.

"So why would John, who loved you, want you to harbor any doubts that you are as beautiful, as desirable, as she is, when he knew without question that you are?" His sincerity almost embarrassed her. "I suspect John simply put it behind him when it was over, and went on with his life and probably considered himself the luckiest man on the face of the earth when he married you. Which he was."

"Thank you," she said softly. "That's very sweet."

"Well, you should know that I am one hell of a sweet guy."

"I've said that very thing about you many times over the past few months."

"Now I thought we were going to let that dead dog lie?"

He grinned as the waitress passed by the table and handed him the check.

"Well, maybe it wasn't such a bad picture," she conceded as they strolled arm in arm to the car.

"And the acting was pretty damned good, wouldn't you say?"

"Yes," she replied. "I guess maybe it was."

When he stopped in her driveway, she hesitated only momentarily before asking, "Would you like to come in for a few minutes?"

"Sure." He nodded. "It's still fairly early."

Athen shushed Hannah, who met them at the door, her tail thumping loudly against the wall. Having decided that Quentin was her friend, Hannah made joyful noises as they attempted to get past her in the foyer.

Athen tossed her jacket onto the back of a chair and motioned Quentin to do the same before following her into the kitchen.

"What can I get you?" she asked. "Coffee, tea, Metaxa . . . ?"

"What was that last one?" He pulled a chair out from the table and sat down.

"Metaxa," she said with a smile. "It's Greek. Sort of wine blended with brandy."

"Sure. I'm game."

She went into the dining room and returned with a tall thin bottle and two small glasses.

"I used to keep this for my father. Would you like me to water yours down a bit? It's pretty strong, especially if you're not accustomed to it."

"I'll try it without."

She poured small amounts over ice, then added water

to one glass, explaining, "You might be game, but I can't drink it undiluted."

"Whoa." Quentin knocked back the first sip. "It's a bit heady, isn't it?"

Athen laughed and reached for his glass, but he waved her hand away, saying, "No, no. I've handled heartier stuff than this. I just didn't expect the bite."

She watched his face as he took another, more cautious sip.

"It has an interesting flavor. I get the brandy, but there is another note to it. I like it."

The muffled sound of the front door quietly closing sent Hannah to welcome Callie home from a birthday party. Athen wondered how Callie would react to finding Quentin Forbes alone with her mother.

A slight movement at the doorway caught Athen's eye. Callie stood with her hands on her hips, surveying the scene.

"Did you have a good time at the party, sweetie?"

"I guess it was okay." Callie appeared to be awaiting an explanation for their guest.

"Can you at least say hello to Mr. Forbes?" Athen tried not to glare at her daughter.

"Hello, Mr. Forbes," Callie replied flatly.

"Hi, Callie."

"We saw a really good movie tonight," Athen told her.

"You didn't tell me you were going to the movies."

"Well, I didn't know when you went to Julie's that I would be going out," Athen said without apology.

Callie remained at her post in the doorway.

"Well, I should be getting on home." Quentin stood up. "I've got an early date with Ms. Evelyn in the morning, and I don't want to keep her waiting."

254   MARIAH STEWART

"Ms. Evelyn?" Callie asked, her curiosity piqued. "You're going to see Ms. Evelyn tomorrow?"

"Yes," he replied casually. "I promised to be Ms. Evelyn's mule this weekend."

"What does that mean?" Callie kicked off her sneakers, intrigued in spite of herself.

"It means she has some heavy work to be done, and I offered to do it for her."

"What work?" Callie asked.

"She needs help cleaning up some vacant lots she wants to transform into a Garden of Eden."

"A real garden?" Curiosity trumped animosity.

"Oh, yeah," he assured her. "She's going to grow a little bit of everything: vegetables, flowers, even some fruits. She started a lot of the plants in her greenhouse."

"Who's the garden for?" Callie's stockinged feet padded into the room.

"It's for the people who live in the city who can't afford to buy a lot of fresh produce in the supermarket, or who don't have money to spare to buy a bunch of flowers to brighten up their home." Quentin became serious. "Some people don't know how to grow things, so Ms. Evelyn offered to teach them so they could learn to grow good foods for their families."

"Why did she ask *you* to help?"

"Well, actually, I volunteered," he told her.

"Why?" Callie pressed.

"Because we're friends, and she has a very big job to do, and friends help friends." He turned to Athen and said, "Maybe if you have a few hours to spare tomorrow, you can come down and give us a hand."

"I don't know how much help I'd be," Athen said with a laugh. "I never planted anything before last weekend."

"No, no, there will be no planting tomorrow," he explained. "We're going to spend the entire day just clearing the ground. It's overgrown with weeds, litter, trash. Right now, we're talking strictly dirty work. You game?"

"What time?" Callie asked before Athen could respond.

"Anytime," he told her. "We'll be there all day."

"Can we, Mom?" Callie begged.

"I guess we can drive down and see if there's anything we can do to help," Athen readily agreed.

"Let's get up real early. What time are you going, Mr. Forbes?" It was the first time Callie had spoken rather than spit his name.

"Probably around seven, but you don't have to go that early." Quentin made a point of addressing Callie rather than her mother. "There's some equipment that's being delivered—small tractors, some Dumpsters, stuff like that. But if you come around ten or so, I'll bet there'll be plenty for you to do."

"Thanks, Mr. Forbes." Her smiling face was evidence that he had gone from suspect to ally, all in the course of one brief conversation.

"Well, if we're all going to be working hard tomorrow, I guess it's time to say good night." He winked at Athen and headed for the front door, stopping to pick up his jacket from the chair.

"Mr. Forbes, will you tell Ms. Evelyn that I'm coming to help?" Callie had followed close behind him, climbing two steps up the stairwell to bring herself to his eye level.

"Of course. I'm sure she'll be delighted. I know you're a big favorite of hers."

"She told you that?" Callie bit her bottom lip to conceal her pleasure.

"On more than one occasion," he assured her.

"She's one of my favorite people, too," Callie said. "She always makes me feel good when I talk with her, and she never makes me feel like a pesky kid."

"Well, I think that's her way of showing her respect for a fellow gardener," he told her.

"Hmmm . . ." Callie considered this. Just as she turned to go up the steps to her room, she glanced at her mother, who was leaning against the kitchen doorjamb.

"Mom, the least you could do is walk Mr. Forbes to the door. . . ."

WHAT DO YOU THINK, MOM?" Callie asked over breakfast the next morning. "Jeans and sweatshirts?"

"Hmmm?" Athen glanced up from the newspaper. She'd been trying unsuccessfully for ten minutes to read the same article, her mind insisting on dragging her back to the night before, to long deep kisses in the darkened doorway that had rattled her to her soul and kept her riveted to the spot even after Quentin closed the door behind him.

"I said, maybe we should wear jeans and sweatshirts," Callie repeated. "It's a little chilly this morning."

"Maybe something a little lighter. It's supposed to warm up later."

"Okay." Callie poured herself a bowl of granola.

"Sounds like a good plan." Athen folded the paper and reached for her coffee. It seemed like a lifetime since she had been kissed that way. . . .

"This will be fun." Callie spooned yogurt on top of her cereal. "I wonder what Ms. Evelyn will want me to do. Mom, why are you grinning like that?"

"What?" Athen, shaken from her reverie, covered quickly. "Oh, I was just thinking about . . . about how nice it is to help a friend."

"I agree." Callie dug into her breakfast. "It was sure nice of Mr. Forbes to say we could help. Maybe he's not so bad, Mom. I mean, he was really pretty nice to me, even though I haven't been real nice to him. I'm going to run up and get dressed so I can take Hannah for a walk before we go."

Callie disappeared from the room in a flash, leaving Athen to shake her head. *Sometimes being a parent to a pre-adolescent child is like doing penance. One day, they're sullen and moody; the next day, they are responsible and resourceful. Then, suddenly, they are four years old again, dependent and demanding.*

"You are amazing," she'd whispered to Quentin the night before. "You totally turned her around in a flash. How did you know how to do that?"

"Kids like to be treated with respect and like to be recognized for their accomplishments," he'd said with a shrug. "Callie admires Ms. Evelyn and that admiration is returned. I thought it wouldn't hurt if I let her know."

"Callie hasn't treated you with much respect," Athen had reminded him.

"Sometimes kids need to know that you respect them first." He had started to nibble on her bottom lip, and if there had been further conversation after that, she couldn't recall what it had been about.

"Mom, you'd better get dressed." Callie breezed through the room, Hannah's leash over her shoulder, the dog bouncing and hopping merrily behind her. "Come on, girl. Mom, try to be ready when I get back, okay?"

"WOW!" EXCLAIMED CALLIE WHEN SHE and Athen approached their destination on foot. They'd parked almost three full blocks away due to the many cars that were parked along the street by the volunteers who had arrived before them. "Look at all the people!"

Scores of workers bustled about, filling the vacant lots. Some carried old tires and broken pieces of furniture to the Dumpsters that lined the Schuyler Avenue side. Some were carefully picking up broken bottles, while others were removing rocks so that the large lawn mowers could cut down the high grass. Along Third Street, other volunteers awaited the tractors that would turn over the hard, long-neglected ground into which another army of volunteers would work truckloads of topsoil and cow manure, the pungent aroma of which was just beginning to drift on a slight breeze.

"Hey, Ms. Evelyn!" Callie's face lit at the sight of the old woman in overalls and sunglasses who directed the activity.

"No, no, Joe, you have to finish clearing that side section before you can bring that mower in there." Ms. Evelyn pointed a long thin brown finger toward the back of the lot and addressed several people at the same time without missing a beat. "Now you, Thomas, go see Ms. Adeline for a bandage for that cut. I told you to watch out for broken glass. Callie, I heard you and your mother would be helping out today. I'm so happy that you came by to give us a hand."

"What would you like us to do?" Callie asked eagerly.

"Well, I see my good friend Timmy Forbes is still moving rocks over there by the back fence. I bet he'd appreciate your help," Ms. Evelyn suggested.

Athen closed her eyes and held her breath, awaiting Callie's protest.

"Sure." Callie drew heavy canvas work gloves from the back pocket of her jeans and took off without a backward glance at her startled mother.

Ms. Evelyn smiled and patted Athen's arm. "Let me see if I can find something suitable for our mayor to do."

"No, no." Athen shook her head. "I'm here as a friend, just like everyone else. I'll do whatever it is you need done now."

Ms. Evelyn surveyed the work in progress. "Why don't you join Georgia—she's the young lady in the green shirt over there. She and Mr. Tate are picking up bottles and other trash. There are recycling baskets for the glass right there by the sidewalk."

Athen picked up a basket and headed toward her assigned work crew, trying unsuccessfully to catch a glimpse of Quentin in the crowd. She introduced herself first to Mr. Tate, who looked to be in his eighties and who was hard of hearing, and then to Georgia, a slender, pretty young woman with skin the color of cocoa and eyes like chunks of coal who proved to be an amiable work companion. Georgia hummed and sang softly in a lovely lilting soprano as they carried out their chores. Athen found herself wishing she could carry a tune so that she could join in. At one point, a photographer from the *Woodside Herald* snapped a picture of Athen as she lifted a load of glass.

She glanced over her shoulder to locate her daughter in the ever-growing crowd of workers. As she scanned the throng, she found not only Callie standing next to Timmy, but Quentin as well. He was speaking to both children, and had the total attention of both. She smiled to herself as she watched him place a hand on his son's shoulder.

Far from being the wisecracking reporter she'd first met, he was now a man of strength and humor and a gentleness she hadn't expected. Not to mention that he'd awakened something inside her she'd assumed she'd never feel again.

"Well, I see you've met the boss." Riley Fallon exchanged a loving look with Athen's companion.

"Oh, you're Georgia's fiancé?" Athen was roused from her musings.

"Riley and I will be married in August." George beamed.

"Best wishes to you both." Athen smiled with genuine pleasure even as she sneaked a peek over Riley's shoulder. The children were back to work carrying rocks. Quentin was nowhere to be seen. "I wish you every happiness."

"Thank you, Athen," Riley said as a loud whistle pierced the din created by a hundred or so chattering voices.

"What was that?" Startled, Athen flinched.

"The signal for lunch break," Georgia told her.

"Gosh, it didn't occur to me to pack lunch." Athen thought aloud. "I'd better grab Callie and run out to pick something up. She's probably starving by now."

"That's all been taken care of," Georgia assured her. "When you work with Ms. Evelyn, you don't have to worry about going hungry. I'd better go see if I can lend a hand."

The young woman followed a path through the high grass to the sidewalk, where boxes were stacked high on tables covered with white cloths. The ladies of the AME Church of the Brethren were about to serve lunch.

"Ugh!" Athen studied her dirty hands, wondering how she could eat anything these fingers had touched. She waved to Callie as her daughter and Timmy approached her.

"Isn't this fun, Mom?" Callie's eyes sparkled.

"Let me see your hands," Athen demanded, and the child held out two blackened paws for inspection.

"Not to worry, Mom." Callie pointed to the line forming across the street.

She should have known Ms. Evelyn would think of everything. A hose hooked up to the faucet on the front of the row house across the street spewed water, and one of the AME ladies offered liquid soap in a large pump container. Rolls of paper towels were stacked in the back of a nearby station wagon and large trash cans stood by for the discards.

"Hey, this is great stuff," Callie exclaimed as she opened her box lunch. "Look, Mom, ham sandwiches, apples, brownies. Cool!"

They sat on the ground under a tree, surrounded by others seeking shade from the bright afternoon sun. Athen gratefully propped herself against the rough bark, happy to give her aching back a respite from bending over countless times to retrieve discarded bottles in the high grass. She popped open a can of soda and explored the contents of the white box.

"Hey, Timmy, over here!" Callie waved, then turned to her mother and pleaded, "Don't say it, Mom."

"Don't say what, Callie?" Athen suppressed a smile.

"Don't say, 'I told you he was a nice kid,' okay?" Callie whispered.

"Never occurred to me." Athen grinned as both dark-haired Forbeses approached.

"Hey, Timmy, I got brownies, did you?" Callie leaned over to open Timmy's box to peer inside.

"You look comfortable." Quentin smiled down at her. "Mind if I join you?"

"You're welcome to pull up a rock and join us, but the tree trunk is mine and I'm not sharing."

"A little out of shape, are we?" He plopped to the ground next to her.

"Pathetically so." She unwrapped a ham sandwich on what appeared to be a freshly baked biscuit. "I haven't bent over this much since Callie was a baby and made a game out of pitching toys from the high chair."

"Well, you know, some men find a woman covered in dry dust very sexy." He leaned closer to her, a glint in his eye. "I find those grimy smudges across your face irresistible. And those little pieces of dried leaves in your hair . . ."

"You're a sick man, Quentin Forbes." Her hands probed her hair until she found the foreign matter and pulled the crunchy brown leaves from the tangle of her long tresses.

"Well, would you look at Himself." Quentin sat up suddenly and motioned toward the center of the clearing, where Dan Rossi, Jim Wolmar, Harlan Justis, and Angelo Giamboni strode through the crowd like visiting royalty.

"What do you suppose he's up to?" Athen wondered aloud, her eyes narrowing as she watched her former mentor shake a hand here, pause to give a pat on the back there.

"Giving this effort his blessing." Quentin grinned and took a bite of his apple. "Creating a photo op at the same time. Look, there's the Channel Seven news van, just pulling up."

The mobile newsroom set up quickly, the street reporters and the camera crew seeking first Ms. Evelyn, then Dan Rossi, who seemed to be doing a lot of gesturing and smiling. Athen observed in silence from her place at the back of the clearing, hidden from the cameras by the sea of workers in whose midst she went unnoticed.

"What a charade," Quentin scoffed as Rossi prepared to take his leave minutes after the news van had departed.

"What good timing on his part," Athen noted.

"Good timing, my ass." Quentin laughed derisively. "You don't really think it was a coincidence that he just happened to arrive right before the cameras, do you?"

"Probably not. But to watch him, you'd think he was campaigning."

"Of course he's campaigning. A good politician never misses an opportunity to shake a few hands and make the people feel like he's one of them." Quentin paused. "Does that bother you?"

"Why would it bother me?" she snapped. "He knows the job is his to take back next year. It just seems a little . . . early, that's all."

"It's never too early, especially since there's bad blood between the two of you. I suspect he knows you're here, and he just wants to remind everyone that he's still around, too. There are a lot of votes out here today."

"So?" Athen gathered up the wrappers from her lunch and stuffed them into the box.

"So he's just letting them all know he's on their side."

"What side? There is no 'side' but his," she reminded him.

"Maybe," he muttered. "Maybe not . . ."

"Want me to take that, Mom?" Callie reached a hand out for Athen's empty lunch box. "I'll throw it in the trash can over there."

Callie and Timmy collected a stack of white cardboard containers from the adults sitting around them and headed for the trash receptacles that had been placed throughout the crowd.

"Guess it's time to get back to work." Quentin stood and offered a hand to Athen, who groaned as he pulled her up.

"What are you working on?" she asked. "I tried to find you earlier, but I didn't see you."

"I was helping Pat Greene and Reverend Davison with the tractors." He appeared pleased that she had admitted to looking for him. "And now I get to load cow manure onto wheelbarrows."

"Some guys have all the luck." She headed in the general direction of her workbasket, Quentin accompanying her as far as the end of the sidewalk.

"Well, now." Ms. Evelyn observed them with genuine pleasure, noting the casual manner in which Quentin's hand rested on Athen's shoulder. "Isn't this nice?"

If the morning had been long, the afternoon was endless. By four o'clock, however, the lots were devoid of debris, the weeds cut down, the ground plowed, and the new soil mixed with the old. Ms. Evelyn was delightedly tearful as she surveyed the acre and three-quarters of fertile ground. One by one, the work crews departed, Ms. Evelyn hugging each of her laborers and thanking every one for their efforts.

"Your father would be proud of you today," she told Callie. "You worked like a trooper." Callie beamed with pride at the compliment. "Ari would be, too." Ms. Evelyn took hold of Athen's hand. "God knows the man would have been right in the thick of things if he could."

"We'll be sure to tell him all about it," Athen assured her.

Quentin leaned over to place a kiss on the small woman's forehead. "Tomorrow morning, same time, same place?"

"Bless you, Quentin." She patted his arm. "You can start later tomorrow. After church would be fine."

"You mean there's more?" Athen asked in disbelief as they walked up Schuyler Avenue.

"Just for the carpentry crew." He laughed at the look of horror on her face. "We're going to build the bandstand I told you about. I told her I'd bring a hammer."

"Mommy, Timmy said I could come over and ride with him." Callie's delight at the prospect shone in her eyes. "Can I go? Please? I haven't gone riding in soooo long."

"Now?" Athen looked over the filthy urchin who stood before her. "I think you should go home and get cleaned up and have dinner."

"She can have dinner with us, Mrs. Moran," Timmy offered.

"That's a great idea." Quentin took hold of Athen's elbow. "Why don't you both plan on a ride, then stay and have dinner."

Athen groaned. "My knees are sore, my back is sore, and all I want is a long, hot bath. Sorry, guys, but a nice brisk ride is not on my agenda. And Callie is not fit for polite company until she gets a shower."

"Well, then, plan B. Why don't you go home, get cleaned up, and then drive out when you're ready? We can sit and relax while the kids have their ride, then we can all have dinner together." He lowered his voice. "Callie and Timmy are getting along great, and she hasn't snarled at me once all day. Things are looking up."

"All right," she agreed. "But I'll need at least an hour."

"Whenever." He unlocked his car and Timmy jumped in. "You remember where the house is, at the end of Pond Lane?"

"I do. We'll see you later." Athen nodded and steered Callie toward their car.

Dinner for the four of them would be interesting, Athen mused, but right now, nothing appealed more than the promise of a hot bubbly tub and clean clothes. The Forbeses would have to wait.

❧ 21 ❧

A then drove up the long lane leading to the Chapman mansion recalling the one and only other time she'd been there: the night of the rally where Dan had announced her candidacy. She inwardly shuddered at the memory of that evening. Looking back, it had been a nightmare from start to finish.

She parked at the side of the house, and she and Callie proceeded to the front door. Brenda Chapman responded to the bell, greeting them with much more warmth than she had the last time they met.

"Timmy's down in the barn," Brenda told Callie. "I'm glad to see you wore long pants to protect your legs. Have you ridden before?"

"I used to take lessons," Callie said as they proceeded through the long, wide hall. "But I had to stop last year."

"Well, let's see how much you remember." Brenda smiled at Athen as they passed through a banquet-sized dining room, then French doors that opened onto a wide veranda that spanned the length of the house.

"Lydia," Brenda addressed her stepmother, who was seated on a high-backed white wicker chair, looking for all the world like a duchess. "Athen and Callie are here."

Lydia Chapman welcomed them as if they had been the oldest and dearest of friends.

"Do sit with me, dear." She motioned for Athen to take the chair to her left. "Quentin tells me you're not up to riding this evening. Brenda, take Callie down to the stable and let her choose a horse, would you? And tell Quentin our guests are here." Turning to Athen with a charming smile, she added, "Quentin and Timothy went down to see a new foal."

"A foal!" Callie all but jumped for joy. "Can I see, too?"

"Of course." Brenda laughed. "Right this way, miss."

"Quentin tells me you and Callie worked very hard today," Lydia said as she pressed a button on the wall. "Wonderful project. If Hughes and I were younger and less arthritic, we'd have been working right alongside you. We're big believers in backing community efforts, but these days, we limit our contributions to monetary donations rather than physical labor."

"These community projects need financial backing, too," Athen noted.

Lydia turned to address the woman who appeared in the doorway, apparently in response to the push of the button. "Rose Ellen, do you think we might have some tea?" She placed a hand on Athen's arm and asked, "Or would you rather have coffee?"

"Tea would be fine, thank you," Athen replied.

"A small pot would be lovely, Rose Ellen. Thank you." When the woman left, Lydia told Athen, "Rose Ellen is my right hand. With a house this big, at my age, I just can't handle it all anymore. It's a blessing to have help."

"You have a beautiful home, Mrs. Chapman," Athen told her.

"Thank you, but please call me Lydia." She leaned back into her chair. "Hughes bought this place at auction years ago. Originally, it had been the home of a robber baron or some famous Mafia person, I forget which. In any event, Hughes spent years bringing it up to snuff. It needed everything because it had been vacant forever." She paused momentarily as Rose Ellen produced the requested tea. "Thank you, dear." Lydia smiled and continued. "We've had such fun buying antiques these past two years, though, of course, I had some of my own furnishings shipped out from St. Louis—family pieces, mostly. No point in leaving them in storage with this wonderful house waiting to be filled up."

Lydia seemed to possess the ability to speak indefinitely without pausing for breath. Athen's head was beginning to swim when she noticed Quentin's approach from across the vast lawn where, last Labor Day, tents had stood.

"Ah, there's my son now." Lydia beamed at the sight of him. "I can't tell you how delighted we are to have Quentin and Timmy here with us. They've had a bad time of it, what with Cynthia abandoning them like that." She made a "tsk-tsking" sound. "No one was more surprised than I was when she pulled up stakes with little more than a fare-thee-well and just left them. How any woman could walk away from such a good man and such a darling child, I'll never understand." A cloud crossed Lydia's face. "He's such a joy, my grandson—my only grandchild, you know. So like his father as a boy. Hello, darling, we were just talking about you."

"If I know you, you were talking and Athen was politely listening." He grinned, then said to Athen, "Feeling better now?"

"Much." She smiled and sipped her tea.

"Not too late for a ride." He perched on the railing that surrounded the veranda.

"You let her relax," Lydia instructed. "And besides, she's not dressed for riding. That blue-green color is wonderful on you, by the way, Athen. It's a lovely sweater. I've always loved those heather shades."

"Mother," Quentin interjected. "I think Hughes just pulled up."

"Oh? Perhaps I should dash down to tell him we've company for dinner." Lydia rose and bustled off into the house.

"My mother will talk you deaf, dumb, and blind if she likes you." Quentin laughed. "Obviously she likes you. She'll have you dizzy before the night is over."

"I don't think it's going to take that long." Athen shook her head, wondering what caused Lydia Chapman's apparent change of heart. The older woman's clear blue eyes, tranquil as a gentle sea today, had dismissed Athen with their frosty glare on their last meeting.

"Quick, let's walk down and watch the kids before she comes back." He held his hand out to her.

"Good idea." Athen placed the delicate porcelain teacup on the table and took his hand. Together they strolled down to the riding ring where Timmy and Callie were receiving some instructions from Brenda.

They hung over the fence for a while, quietly observing their respective offspring walk, trot, and canter at Brenda's command.

"Would you like to meet the newest member of the family?" he asked.

"Who's that?"

"Right this way." He took her hand and led her down the hill.

The air was warm and close inside the stable. He turned on a light, disturbing a sleepy fat cat who'd perched atop a bale of hay. The cat stretched long straight front legs, her eyes still closed.

"Here we are." He stood outside a double-wide stall and opened the gate. "Hey, Jassie, good girl. We came to see your baby."

He dug in his shirt pocket and retrieved a lump of sugar, which he offered to the chestnut mare.

"Athen, grab an apple out of that basket behind you and give it to Jassie so she'll know you're her friend." Quentin stroked the horse's muzzle with obvious fondness.

"A peace offering, is that it?"

"Right. No, no, don't hold it like that, she'll take your fingers along with the apple," he told her. "Hold your hand out flat with the apple on your palm. Like that, yes. That's the way."

Athen extended her hand and the horse leaned down to sniff at the offered treat. Large lips, soft as velvet, caressed her palm as the horse gently accepted the snack. Athen reached her hand up to the mare's head and ran her fingers along the white streak between Jassie's ears.

"She's lovely," Athen murmured.

"Do you ride?" he asked.

"Callie does"—Athen shook her head—"but I never have."

"Want to learn?" he offered.

"Someday maybe."

"Any time you want, I'll be happy to give you a lesson or two. Now," he told her, "step on in here and see who's hiding in the corner."

Athen peered behind him, where a tiny foal tottered on rail-thin legs.

"Oh, how precious," Athen whispered.

"Come here, Sophia," Quentin told the little one. "Come meet my friend."

"Sophia?"

"My mother named her." He coaxed the foal closer to him.

"I had an aunt named Sophia," Athen told him as she petted the little animal. "She was my mother's sister. I only met her one time."

"When was that?" He crossed the stall to reassure Jassie, who watched the stranger with wary eyes. Quentin's voice seemed to calm her, and Athen was permitted to continue to stroke the newborn.

"When my mother died, Aunt Sophia came." Her voice trailed off. "She and my father argued terribly. She blamed my father because my mother had polio. She blamed him because my mother died. She wanted to take my mother back to Greece to bury her."

"Did she?"

"No. My father believed her place was here, with us."

"Where is she buried?"

"How much time before dinner?" she asked.

"Probably an hour."

"Come on." She took his hand. "I'll show you."

SHE DIRECTED HIM TO DRIVE through the center of the park and out along the river.

"Go right," she told him. "Now here, through the gates of the cemetery and to the left, then follow the road back toward the river. Slow down." She peered past him, looking to the left. "Stop here." He did, and she got out of the car.

He followed, crossing over a ridge where a well-worn path led to the river. They passed a grove of trees beyond which was an embankment thirty feet above the riverbed. Amid the stone memorials was a statue of a woman who was seated on the ground holding a small girl in her arms.

Athen translated the inscription, which was written in Greek.

"'Melina Olympia Stavros. Rest in peace, beloved.'"

"The child is you, of course." He stepped closer to inspect the features.

Athen nodded. "My father's cousin sculpted this the year after she died. He knew my mother well, and was able to capture her delicacy quite nicely."

"She was beautiful," Quentin told her.

"Thank you, yes, she was." Athen stepped back to a small stone bench that stood nearby and sat upon it. "She was so tiny, so fragile. Her face could just about fit"—she held up one hand—"in the palm of your hand."

"How did she die?"

"She had polio when she was young. It left her legs crippled and her lungs very weak. She died of pneumonia."

He joined Athen on the bench and they sat quietly in the setting sun.

"When I was in high school, I walked out here in the afternoons. I'd sit and pretend I was talking to her while I did my homework."

"You walked all the way out here? It must be several miles."

"Two miles and seven-tenths." She nodded. "But I never minded. I always felt she was here waiting for me. My mother dying when I was so young changed my life. It took away my sense of . . ." She groped for words.

"Security . . . ?" he ventured.

"It went deeper than that." She shook her head slowly. "My father always tried to make me feel secure and safe, but I had lost the ability to believe that he would always be there for me. For a long time I had the feeling that he, too, could be taken from me, and I would have no one."

"And you wonder sometimes if Callie feels the same way?"

"Sometimes," she confessed. "But it's different for her. Callie was older when John died. I was five when I lost my mother. At least Callie was old enough to have had some understanding of what happened to John, and she has a wealth of memories that I didn't have."

Quentin eased her back to rest against him.

"When I found out about my father and Diana Bennett, I came up here and cried," she confessed. "I couldn't understand how my father could replace my mother, with her watching from up here."

"And now . . . ?"

"Now I'm beginning to see how Diana filled all those empty places inside him. I'm embarrassed that it took me so long to accept it."

The shadow of the stone woman settled over them as the sun sagged behind the trees. A cool breeze blew across the embankment, and Quentin caressed her arm to warm her.

"I guess we should get back." Athen stood, taking his hand and pulling him up with her. "Callie will wonder where we've gone. I just wanted to show you."

"Thank you for sharing her with me."

Athen glanced back at the statue, the features now in darkness.

"Which word is 'beloved'?" Quentin asked as they turned to go.

"*Agape mou.*" She pointed to the weathered wording. "It means 'my beloved.'"

He repeated the word to himself softly, as if to memorize it, as they walked back to the car.

DINNER WAS A RELATIVELY INFORMAL affair. Informal, because they dined on the veranda, but only relatively so because a staff of three served them.

Athen found Hughes Chapman affable and sweet. He obviously adored his loquacious wife, was indulgent of Brenda—his only child—and was totally captivated by Timmy.

"So, Athen." Hughes smiled pleasantly at her as the salad was being served. "What's that scoundrel Dan Rossi up to these days?"

Athen all but choked on her water.

"Hughes, dear, Quentin said we're not to talk about Athen's job, or politics, or any of the articles he's written on either topic." Lydia fixed her husband with a meaningful stare from the opposite end of the table.

"Well, then, that sort of narrows the field, doesn't it?" He chuckled. "Callie, Timmy tells us you're a crackerjack athlete."

Athen chose to listen rather than to participate in the conversation throughout dinner. From time to time she glanced across the table at Quentin, who ate quietly, an amused look on his face. At ten, when she could no longer keep her eyes propped open, Athen thanked her host and hostess, and promised Lydia she would, indeed, love to come again.

"Please bring Callie back next Saturday," Brenda pressed her. "She has the makings of a superb rider. Oh, I almost forgot. I want to get in touch with Meg. Would you happen to have her number with you?"

Athen scratched the number down on a piece of paper

and handed it over. She was curious as to why Brenda would want to contact Meg, but was too polite to ask. Quentin and Timmy walked them to the car.

"I'll talk to you soon," Quentin told her as he slammed her car door.

"Wake me when we get home." Callie yawned and Athen watched enviously as her daughter pushed the button to recline her seat.

Athen rolled down the window to let the cool night air flood the car and hoped to stay awake long enough to make the ten-minute drive to their home. She pulled in the driveway, woke Callie, and together they walked on wooden feet into their house.

"Carry me?" Callie plunked down on the steps, and Athen dimly noted that where once her daughter stretched from the first to the third steps, she now took up six.

"I'm not sure I can carry myself." Athen stepped over her. "So unless you want to wake up in the morning with a horrendous backache, I suggest you drag your little self to bed."

"Waaa . . ." Callie protested weakly before getting up. "It was a fun day, Mom. Thanks for taking me. And for letting me ride with Timmy." She yawned again. "We had fun. And Brenda is so neat. And Sunny—that was my horse—is the best horse I ever rode." She absently kissed in the direction of her mother's cheek before stumbling to the stairs. "Night, Mom."

"Sweet dreams, baby."

Athen followed her daughter to the second floor. She grabbed a nightshirt and barely had it pulled over head before all but crashing face forward onto the bed. Blurred images drifted behind her closed eyes as she fell asleep. Baskets of discarded bottles faded into mountains of rock, which gave way to a parade with Callie and Timmy on horseback and Quentin on a backhoe. Georgia Davison's hauntingly lovely voice drifted over the weeded lot through which the parade marched. Ms. Evelyn smiled with pride and triumph as she reviewed the marchers from a huge pile of mulch. Watching over all, from her place high on the ridge over the city, Athen's mother tapped her feet in time to the music.

Faces spun around and around, borne on the confused winds of a twister that blew through her semiconsciousness. She started awake momentarily and, dizzy with fatigue, stretched stiff arms and legs as she sought a comfortable spot on the pillow. She opened her eyes, remembering how it had felt to rest against Quentin earlier that evening as they sat overlooking the river. His body had been hard as a rock and yet as comforting as a featherbed. For the first time in her life, she fell asleep wishing she was wrapped in the arms of a man who was not her late husband.

"WE HAD A LOVELY TIME this evening, dear." Lydia caught Quentin's arm as he and Timmy started back to the gatehouse. "Athen is a lovely woman, and her daughter is just delightful."

"Thanks, Mom. Tim and I had a good time, too. Thanks for inviting them." Quentin ruffled his son's hair. "It's always more fun to have a friend to share things with, right, Tim?"

Timmy nodded sleepily and leaned into his father's chest.

"We have another early morning." Quentin leaned over and kissed his mother on the cheek. "Thanks again for dinner, Mom."

"You're most welcome, son. I'll see you tomorrow?"

"At some point, I'm sure you will." Quentin closed the door behind him and, with one arm over Timmy's shoulder, walked back to the gatehouse.

"The sky's real clear," Timmy noticed. "Look at all the stars."

Quentin stopped and looked up. "Do you remember the name of that constellation? The big one, straight overhead?"

"The Big Dipper." Timmy yawned.

"That's right." Quentin nodded.

Before his father could quiz him on another cluster of stars, Tim asked, "How early do we have to get up tomorrow?"

"Not as early. You can sleep in."

"Good. I'm beat, Dad."

Quentin smiled and stuck his hand in his pocket for the front-door key. "I imagine you are. You worked hard today and you played hard tonight."

"Now I'm going to sleep hard," Tim told him.

The door unlocked and pushed open, Tim waved good night to his father and went straight for the stairs.

"I'll see you in the morning, Tim," Quentin called after him. Tim merely nodded, taking the steps two at a time and disappearing into the dark of the second-floor landing. Seconds later, Quentin heard Tim's bedroom door open, then close.

He couldn't remember the last time his son had taken himself to bed with such dispatch. *He must really be exhausted,* Quentin mused. *He didn't even ask to stay up and watch some TV with me.*

The hall clock chimed ten thirty and Quentin went into the kitchen and opened the refrigerator. He took out a beer and popped the top, then opened the back door and stepped out onto the deck. He leaned over the rail and took a long drink from the can. His back hurt and he'd pulled a muscle in his shoulder lifting a bucket of concrete chunks that weighed a hell of a lot more than it had looked. He knew his time would be better spent in the whirlpool upstairs than down here on the deck, alone in the dark. But the day had been a whirlwind of activity and he felt as if he were almost on some sort of sensory overload. There'd been all the people and the bustling around this morning and afternoon, though the evening hours had made up for it.

He liked having Athen here, in his family's home, liked the feeling of sharing her with his mother and Hughes and Brenda, liked sharing them with Athen and Callie. It had felt like family. It had felt right.

It had been a long time since he'd felt that connection, and he wanted to hold on to it, savor it, for as long as possible.

He found himself envying John Moran for the woman he'd married, the child he'd fathered. While he certainly didn't envy his untimely death, Quentin couldn't help but respect the man. He'd had this wonderful family, a beautiful wife, a terrific kid, yet he'd put it all on the line—taken a bullet—for the sake of a child he'd never seen before, and he'd lost it all. For a moment, Quentin almost wished he'd known John. He probably would have liked him. Everyone else seemed to have. He'd been a real hero, all right.

And boy-howdy, the man sure had the golden touch when it came to women. Quentin shook his head. Dallas MacGregor—*Dallas Freaking MacGregor!* for crying out loud!—had been his college sweetheart. She left him—brokenhearted, no doubt, what man wouldn't have been?—and he rebounded with Athen Moran. Damn. The guy might have died young, but, man, oh, man, John Moran had *lived*.

Not that I'd trade places with him, Quentin thought, *and not that the man had wanted to leave it all so soon, but I have to admire him.*

Quentin raised his beer can to toast the departed hero.

"Here's to you, John Moran. You must have been one hell of a guy." He took a few sips. "I'm sorry for you that you came to such an end. It wasn't fair. You deserved better, and so did she. All that being said, I'm not sorry I met her."

Quentin finished the beer, went back inside, and locked the door. He crumpled the can and tossed it into the recyling bin, turned off all the downstairs lights, and went upstairs to bed.

🌾 22 🌾

"So, is my room ready yet?" Meg's cheery voice sang through the phone.

"I'm working on it." Athen silently resolved to do exactly that this week. "Are you planning on a trip home soon?"

"Sooner than I'd planned," Meg announced in a rush of excitement. "Athen, the most incredible thing happened. Brenda Chapman called me at nine this morning. You're never going to believe this, but it seems Hughes Chapman just purchased a cable TV station and he's looking for a news anchor."

"Seriously?" Athen bit her lip in gleeful anticipation.

Brenda certainly had wasted little time between last night and this morning.

"Totally. Brenda asked me to send her some tapes by overnight delivery. If they like what they see, they'll want me to come out to talk to them ASAP. Is this the craziest thing ever?"

"Meg, that would be wonderful." Athen all but danced at the prospect.

"You know, Brenda and I spoke briefly at the Chapmans' dinner party last year—the one Buddy took me to—but I never dreamed that our very casual conversation would lead to something like this. And speaking of Buddy, what's this Brenda's telling me? What is going on between the two of you?"

"I'm not sure that I know." Athen hesitated.

"Brenda tells me you're pretty tight. Why the change of heart?"

"It's a long story."

"One you'll relate in detail the very second I step off the plane. Assuming that I make the cut. I told you that Buddy had eyes for you, didn't I?"

"Yes, Meg, you did." Athen laughed at the memory.

"Well, he's a darling man and I think you could be very happy together."

"I think you're being a bit premature, since I've only seen him socially a few times," Athen said levelly. *But yes, he is darling, and I am happy when I'm with him.*

"But you really like him, don't you?"

"Yes." Athen sighed. "I do, but . . ."

"Good. I'm glad, if for no other reason than to remind you that you have a whole life ahead of you. I'm glad you're seeing someone, and I'm particularly happy that it's Quentin. He's still quite a catch."

"I'm not so sure I want to catch him or anyone else, but I will admit that I enjoy the time I spend with him."

"You make me crazy. What more could you possibly want? He's bright and funny, and you may not have noticed, but he's pretty hot."

"Can it, Meg." Athen laughed. "We'll talk about it when you get out here."

"Hopefully, that will be very soon. You'll know the minute I know," Meg promised. "Give my love to Callie."

"Will do."

What fun it would be to have Meg here, Athen mused as she washed the lunch dishes. *And I will call someone to come in and finish that wallpapering. What was the name of the man who did all that work for Mrs. Kelly earlier this year? Parker? Pepper?*

She dried her hands and went through the Yellow Pages. Here we go . . . Parsons. Norman Parsons. She entered the number and hit send. Mr. Parsons answered, and after listening to her description of what she needed, he agreed to come over on Tuesday evening.

She gathered up the Sunday paper and took it to the back porch. She was more than a little surprised to see her picture, bold as life, gracing the front page.

> *Woodside Heights mayor Athena Moran was one*
> *of the many enthusiastic workers at yesterday's kickoff*
> *of the UCC's new community garden. Story on page 3.*

Page 3 highlighted a series of photos: Ms. Evelyn waving a tractor onto the lot; a group of workers leaning on their shovels; Reverend Davison greeting several volunteers.

"Hey, Mom." Callie poked her head out the door. "I'm going across the street to Carolann's for a while, okay?"

"Sure." Athen nodded, absorbed in the text of the article.

She scanned the paper, then folded it over, making mental notes of several articles she'd read in depth later, but she was still tired from yesterday's exertion. Impulse led her up the steps and into the attic, across creaking floorboards to the alcove that overlooked the side yard.

The sheet that covered the easel was gray with dust. She carefully removed it, dropped it onto the floor in a heap, and studied the canvas with a critical eye. Turning on the lights, she leaned closer. The tall spikes of the pale pink flowers rose against a background of pale blue. White roses twined around a half-finished arbor. In the foreground, a branch of magnolia bent to frame the garden beyond the arbor. The painting, intended as a gift for John, had remained incomplete for over a year.

Athen stared at the canvas, wondering if the image of the garden that had been destroyed by the storm remained vivid enough in her memory to finish what she had started. *What a wonderful present for Callie if I could finish it*, she thought.

She gathered the tools she would need. Some of her paints had dried and would need to be replaced, but there was enough to begin. At first, the brush felt awkward in her hand, but soon she was lost in the colors, carefully shading here and adding light there. When her stomach reminded her that she had not eaten in hours, she looked at her watch and was surprised to find that the afternoon had passed without notice. Callie would be looking for dinner before too long.

She stepped back to assess her work. *Not bad*, she thought. *I've done better, but after a long hiatus, this is pretty good.*

She gathered her brushes to clean them and realized she was humming. How good it had felt to shape color into form again. Proving to herself that she could still bring a canvas to life unexpectedly filled her with peace. She was starting to feel whole again.

She cleaned her brushes and changed her paint-spattered shirt. She went downstairs and sat on the sofa, then leaned back against the cushions. *Perhaps just a short nap*, she thought as she pulled a light afghan up to her chin.

It was after six when she was awakened by the ringing telephone. Dumbly following the shrill sound to its source, she stumbled into the kitchen and lifted the receiver.

"Did I wake you?" Quentin asked. "You sound as if you're half asleep."

"There's a reason for that." She yawned mightily.

"We need to build up your stamina," he admonished with a chuckle.

"Did you get Ms. Evelyn's bandstand finished?"

"Yes, we did," he told her, static from his cell cutting him off briefly. "Of course, we had a lot of expert assistance. Mr. Rossi showed up, hammer in hand, smiling for the cameras so that tomorrow's paper can show him participating in manlier-than-thou work. No sir, no sissy stuff like filling baskets with broken glass for macho Dan."

Quentin added, almost as an aside, "He invited me to interview him."

"What?"

"You heard me."

"Why would he do that?" she wondered aloud.

"If you'll open the front door, I'll come in and tell you all about it in person."

She peered out the side window. His car was at the curb.

He was dirty and sweaty and, if possible, even more adorable than usual. The maroon baseball cap sat on his head, dark locks of hair stuck to his forehead with perspiration, and his Mets T-shirt bore the same smears of grime as his arms and face.

"So what's Rossi up to?" She opened the door, and wished she had the nerve to put her arms around him, maybe kiss that little smudge that ran across his upper lip. She'd never been the one to make the first move. She'd never known how.

"Beats me, but I thought it was really interesting that he sought me out," he said with a grin. "I'm going to meet him at his club for dinner. Curious, yes?"

"Curiouser and curiouser." She led him by the hand into the living room and in the general direction of the sofa.

"Uh-uh." He shook his head as she approached the sofa. "I'm too grimy to sit on your furniture. I just wanted to stop and see how your aching back is doing."

"Much better, thank you." She smiled as he leaned back against the wall and drew her to him.

"Perhaps a quick massage." He ran his hands up and down her back, kneading her muscles with his strong fingers.

"Ouch." She winced and he softened his touch. "We had fun last night, Callie and I."

"So did we." He watched her face as his fingers made their way more slowly from her neck to her waist and back again. "Mom made me promise to bring you back. And, of course, Timmy and Callie have made plans for next Saturday to ride."

"Well, I certainly don't want her to impose." His proximity made her dizzy.

"Tim loved the company, and Brenda enjoyed working with her." He rubbed her shoulder blades gently.

"Brenda called Meg this morning, did you know?" Maybe if she could keep a conversation going she could regain control of her breathing.

"I knew she was going to." He paused before asking, "What do you think of the idea?"

"Of Meg working here? Are you kidding?"

"That's what I thought, too." He tipped her face and kissed her. His lips were warm and soft and drew her deeper and deeper toward a place she thought she'd never find again. Forgotten emotions surged through her, and she felt the fingers of one hand move as if on their own to his face, and then upward slowly, winding their way through his damp curls.

The sound of the back door slamming caused them both to jump.

"Callie," Athen told him.

"Mom?" Callie called out from the kitchen as if on cue.

"In here, sweetie." Athen raised an eyebrow and reluctantly disengaged herself from his arms.

"Oh, hi, Mr. Forbes." Callie seemed glad to see him. "Did you work with Ms. Evelyn again today?"

"Yes, I did." He nodded, one hand still resting in the middle of Athen's back. "And you'll be happy to know we got the bandstand constructed. Maybe next summer we'll be able to go down there and hear some concerts."

"That would be cool." Callie draped herself over the back of the sofa and made no attempt to leave.

"I think I'd better get going. I'm supposed to meet Dan at seven, which doesn't give me much time to clean up."

"Give me a call later and let me know how the interview went," Athen said as she walked him to the door.

"I will, if I get in early," he told her. "See you, Callie," he called into the living room.

"See you, Mr. Forbes." Callie came into the foyer and stood next to her mother. Quentin saluted them both before heading to his car.

❧❧❧❧❧

RUNNING LATE THE NEXT MORNING after a sleepless night, Athen grabbed the paper from the front steps on her way to the car. Her first glimpse at page 1 came at her desk, and she spewed half a mouthful of coffee onto the headline.

ROSSI BLASTS MORAN

Below that, in only slightly smaller print:

Calls present mayor "the only political error I ever made."

White knuckles grasped the edges of the paper to hold it in front of her disbelieving eyes as she read:

> In an exclusive interview with the Woodside Herald, former mayor Dante Rossi said that he had committed a major "error in judgment" in backing political novice and current mayor Athena Moran for office.
> "Athen Moran is a lovely woman, and she means well, I'm sure," Rossi said, "but the fact is that she hasn't a clue about running this city, except maybe to run it into the ground by trying to give away parcels of valuable land that should be used to increase tax revenues, not add to the burden our citizens are already shouldering."

On and on it went for almost half the page.

"That son of a bitch," Athen sputtered. "When I get my hands on Quentin Forbes, I will kill him!"

Infuriated with herself for having let her guard down,

for believing he could be anything other than what he had proven himself to be in the past, Athen paced her office floor, fuming. She was too angry to realize that he had not broken his promise. His article contained no reference to Mary Jo Dolan.

"Mrs. Moran." Veronica's voice sounded through the intercom. "Mr. Forbes is on line seventeen."

"Tell him I'm not in." She seethed. "Not today, not any day. If he has something to say to me, he can address it at the next press conference."

"Excuse me, Mrs. M." Veronica teetered in on high-heeled red shoes that matched the color of her dress. "I don't think I heard . . ."

"You heard, all right." Athen's eyes blazed. "You tell that son of a bitch I have nothing to say to him."

Veronica calmly picked up the receiver on Athen's desk and announced in a slightly nasalized monotone, "Sorry, Mr. Forbes, but Her Honor is supremely pissed off and doesn't want to talk to you."

She covered the mouthpiece with her hand and asked, "How was that, Mrs. M.?"

Athen stared at her, and Veronica turned her attention back to the call. "What did you say, Mr. Forbes? Okay, hold on." She covered the receiver again and said, "Mrs. M., he said it's really important that he . . ."

"Not now, not ever." Athen launched into a string of bilingual curses.

"No go, Mr. Forbes," Veronica told him. "I'll give her the message, but I can tell ya, she's really steamed. It's not a good sign when she starts cursing in Greek."

"Hang up the damned phone!"

"Sorry," Veronica sang and hung up. She turned to Athen and asked, "What'd he do, if I'm not overstepping?"

Athen pointed to the newspaper, which now lay in a crumpled ball on the floor. Veronica picked it up, smoothed it out, scanned it, then whistled long and low.

"Wow," she said. "Rossi's got it in for you, all right. What an ass. But don't worry, Mrs. Moran, it's obvious he's just trying to make you look bad 'cause you pissed him off."

Veronica headed for the door, thinking a cup of tea might calm the boss down. She got as far as the hall, then she turned back to Athen and said, "I can see you wanting to lynch Rossi for saying all those things about you, but why're you mad at Mr. Forbes?"

"He wrote the article." Athen stated the obvious through highly clenched jaws.

A look of mild confusion passed over the young woman's face. "But . . . isn't that his job?"

"Out," whispered Athen, clinging to the very last shred of her patience. "And close the door."

Athen remained holed up in her office all day, taking no calls and accepting no visitors. Veronica brought her some lunch, which she could not eat, and when she left a half hour early, Veronica told her, "He called seven times, Mrs. Moran."

"I don't want to hear about it." Athen plugged her ears with her fingers.

"I promised him I'd tell you."

"And you have. Good night, Veronica."

It did nothing to improve her state of mind to walk into her kitchen and find him waiting there, calmly talking to Callie.

"Hi, Mom." Callie brightened as her mother came through the door.

"What are you doing here?" she asked coldly.

"I would like to talk to you," he replied.

"I don't have anything to say to you." She walked past him into the hallway.

"Fine. I'll talk and you listen." The newspaper containing the offending article was tucked under one arm.

"Guess now's a good time to take Hannah for a walk." Callie glanced from one to the other uneasily. "Come on, Hannah."

"You really have a lot of nerve, coming into my house." She spat out the words.

"Look, Athen, I can understand that you're angry that Rossi's come out swinging, but . . ."

"I didn't expect you to help him."

"What's that supposed to mean?" He grabbed her arm as she tried to breeze past him. "Athen, I didn't put words in his mouth."

"You promised me you'd never come after me in print again."

"Athen, I promised I'd be fair to you, which as a journalist I should be. But I could never agree to not report the truth, or not report what someone else says about you. Particularly when that someone else is Dan Rossi."

She went back into the kitchen and ran cold water in the sink. She filled a glass and took a long deep drink.

"I want you out of my house." The tears welled up and she fought to keep them from rolling down her face.

"Athen, do you honestly believe I'd deliberately write something with the intent of hurting you?" he asked softly.

"You gave him a forum to openly criticize me."

"So what you're saying is that I should have used everything except the negative things he said about you?" He leaned back against the counter and crossed his arms. "Do you really expect me to censor what gets printed so that only the nice things that people say about you get into the paper?"

She glared at him, but did not respond.

"Athen, I'm a reporter," he sighed, "not your personal press secretary. If you can't respect that . . ."

"You could have at least warned me it was going to be so . . . ugly."

"It was very late when I got home last night. I tried to call you this morning to give you a heads-up, but you didn't pick up your cell. What would you expect him to say about you, given the circumstances? For Christ's sake, Athen, if you'd read the article all the way through, you'd have seen that he's using you as an excuse to run again. 'I feel honor bound to take the city back from the misguided few who would create a fiscal nightmare.' That's a story, Athen. The fact that I wanted to put the SOB's lights out because of what he said has nothing to do with the fact that I have a responsibility to report what he says, as he says it. I can't pretty it up because of our relationship."

"Well, you won't have to worry about that anymore," she said quietly.

"What's that supposed to mean?" He eyed her cautiously.

"You said it best, Quentin. Fool me once, shame on . . ."

"Athen, please . . ."

"I'd like you to leave now." She avoided his eyes.

"You know, I thought I could pull this off. I really thought I could have a personal relationship with you and still maintain a professional one. Do my job, be objective, but still see you." He shook his head sadly. "Guess not, huh?"

They stared glumly at each other, the silence widening the distance between them.

Finally, he shook his head. "I'm sorrier than you know,"

he told her before tossing the paper onto the counter and walking out the back door.

Athen was still standing near the sink, the glass of water in her hand, when Callie came back into the house.

"You're not happy with Mr. Forbes right now, are you, Mom?" Callie seemed to choose her words carefully.

"No, Callie, I'm not." Athen turned her back on her daughter and emptied the water glass into the sink.

"Does this mean I can't ride with Timmy on Saturday?" Callie asked wistfully.

"Of course not," Athen assured her. "This has nothing to do with you and Timmy."

"Good." She sighed with relief. "Brenda said she'd teach me how to jump."

QUENTIN DROVE AIMLESSLY AROUND WOODSIDE Heights trying to understand what had just happened. Could Athen really believe that he'd written that story to embarrass and hurt her? Was she serious?

On the one hand, it pissed him off royally to think that she would think so little of him that she'd believe he'd deliberately try to hurt her. On the other, it pissed him off that she didn't understand the difference between him quoting Rossi and him saying those ridiculous things about her himself. Apparently, she didn't. Apparently, Athen believed those hurtful remarks came out of Quentin's mouth instead of Rossi's. Apparently, she found it easier to believe that he'd used her to get the scoop on every other reporter on all things related to City Hall.

He blew out a long breath and tried to put it all into perspective.

Okay, he could understand her being upset at seeing all those nasty remarks printed under his byline. And he should have tried harder to get in touch with her before the paper was delivered this morning. He'd give her that much. But, Christ Almighty, did she honestly think he cared so little for her that he'd want to hurt her? Did she think a byline on a good story was more important to him than she was?

He'd thought they'd gotten past that sort of thing, that they'd been moving toward a real relationship. His head was about to explode. What didn't she understand, and how could he explain it to her?

Every time he thought about the look on her face when she walked into her kitchen, the look in her eyes when she told him to leave, he felt sick.

He found himself at Ms. Evelyn's up on the Hill, so he parked at the edge of her drive and turned off his headlights. He sat and stared at the lights from the city below and waited for the red haze of anger to fade. When it finally did, he had to face the unhappy truth that this sort of thing had been inevitable. This was all his fault. There was no way he should have continued to cover the City Hall beat once he'd started to get involved with Athen. Sooner or later, there was going to be a conflict between her and his job. He'd known it was only a matter of time, but he'd told himself he could deal with it.

Yeah, well, he'd dealt with it, all right.

If nothing else, at least now he could do his job, because the conflict no longer existed.

The thought gave him little consolation. He'd kept the job, but he'd lost the girl.

"It should have been the other way around," he murmured. "I never should have let it go this far. What the hell was I thinking?"

He'd been thinking that he couldn't give up Athen, and he couldn't quit the job. Hughes had hired him so that he'd have an income while he wrote his book. His stepfather had treated him the way he'd have treated his own son, if he'd had one. He had welcomed Quentin and Tim with open arms and had been delighted when Quentin accepted the job he'd offered. Walking out on Hughes while he was trying to get his new venture up and running would make him look like an ungrateful brat, and Quentin couldn't do that to Hughes or to his mother.

He turned on the car radio, but it seemed every song that came on was one of those "I lost my girl and now I want to die" numbers.

Finally, Quentin sighed. He couldn't undo what was done, and things couldn't have kept on going the way they had been. Something had to give, and it had. It killed him to know that he'd caused her pain. But if she was hurt by his reporting, it was bound to happen again. He couldn't put words in people's mouths. He had to honestly report what was said.

He calculated how many more months Athen had left on her term. Maybe after she left office they could start again. Maybe she'd give him another chance. Maybe by then she'd have thought it through. Maybe by then she'd be missing him as much as he knew he was going to miss her.

It was the only even remotely consoling thought he had, so he clung to it, all through the long drive home.

❧23❧

LIFE SUCKS announced the bumper sticker on the car that stopped in front of Athen's at the red light.

"Tell me about it," she muttered.

The congestion caused by cars fleeing the city at rush hour normally would not bother her. Tonight, the maze of vehicles, the pouring rain, the honking horns—all combined to exacerbate her already cranky mood that had started when the alarm went off that morning and only got worse as the day went on. Veronica wisely kept Athen's door closed, not willing to venture into the big office herself other than to deliver phone messages, which she quietly placed on her the desk. For the better part of the day, Athen sulked in solitude.

So this is how it feels, she reflected, *to go from windshield to bug.*

The pity party was in full swing. As far as she was concerned, everyone had let her down.

Ms. Evelyn had not pulled through. Rossi made her look like the village idiot. *Thanks for that, Quentin.*

Quentin. How could she have believed for one minute that she would ever be more than a potential story to him? How could she have trusted him?

But he didn't betray your trust, a tiny voice inside reminded her. Athen told the tiny voice to shut up.

At least Meg will be home soon and I'll have a sympathetic shoulder to cry on, she comforted herself as she rounded the corner onto her street.

A strange pickup truck was parked in her driveway. Curious, Athen stopped at the curb, parked, and approached the man who sat in the driver's seat.

NORMAN PARSONS. PAINT & PAPER read the sign on the truck.

"Mr. Parsons," she called to him. "Am I late?"

"No, actually, I'm a bit early." He was a very small man, half a head shorter than Athen, with the face of a gnome and white hair upon which sat a painter's cap. The cap and his pants were speckled with multicolored bits of confetti-like dots of paint.

"Come on inside." She motioned for him to follow her.

"I can see you need a lot done here." He glanced around the entry and into the living room. "Yep, I'd say your whole first floor could use a sprucin' up."

He followed the faded walls right up to the second-floor landing. "Yep, all the way up. How long's it been since you painted in here?"

Athen tried to remember when John had last tackled the job. "Maybe ten years."

"Yep, I'd say you're due." He nodded. "But I can't get to a job this big till maybe August. I'm booked solid through July."

"Well, actually, the painting isn't what I called you about. There's a bedroom upstairs that's partially papered that I'd like to have completed."

They went up the stairs and paused when the gnome in the painter's hat stopped to check the wood moldings. "This should all be redone, too."

"We'll put it on the list." She led him into the spare bedroom.

Mr. Parsons surveyed the job that had been interrupted by John's death. "Yep. Not a whole lot here to do. You got enough paper?"

Athen pointed to the bundle of pale yellow paper rolls. "My husband started this, but he didn't get to finish."

"Ah, what a shame that was." Mr. Parsons shook his head solemnly. "Met him a time or two. Had all the tools stolen off my truck once. Your husband responded to the call. Nice young fellow he was. A real shame."

"Yes. Thank you." Athen nodded, wondering how she'd tell Meg she'd be stuck in the room with the bunny paper again. "Is there any chance you could fit this in before August?"

"Well, it's a real small job, maybe half a day at the most. Having the table and all set up, some of the paper already cut, that'll all save a little time. Did you need this done anytime special?"

"My sister-in-law will be here for a visit within the next week or so. I was hoping to have it finished before she got here."

Mr. Parsons studied the project. How 'bout Thursday morning. That soon enough?"

"This Thursday? Really?"

He nodded. "Like I said, it's a small job."

"That would be perfect, but I thought you were booked up?"

"This job is nothing, won't take any time at all. The big jobs get booked in blocks of time, but I can this fit in. I can probably do this myself. Seven thirty too early for you?"

"Not at all." *Yay! Bank error in my favor!*

"You really should think about doing the rest of the house before too long, Mrs. Moran," he said as they marched back down to the first floor. "Bright, pretty lady like you should not be living in such drab rooms."

"I've been thinking about repainting, but I haven't gotten around to it." She led him to the front door, her spirits raised. "Maybe while you're here for the papering, you can work up an estimate for the rest of it."

"I'd be glad to." He waved as he went to his truck. "I'll be around early on Thursday."

The phone rang once and Callie answered it in the kitchen. Judging by Callie's shriek of laughter, it was one of her friends. Athen went upstairs and changed into shorts and a light sweater. She had to do something about dinner, but had no inclination to cook.

"Callie, want to go for pizza?" She strolled into the kitchen.

"Wait, hold on, Tim." Callie put her hand over the phone. "What, Mom?"

"Pizza?" She frowned. *Timmy. I had to encourage her to befriend him.*

"Sure. Just a minute. Go on, Timmy . . ." Callie giggled.

Athen sighed, and went out onto the back porch. She sat on the top step with Hannah, and waited for her daughter to finish her conversation with the enemy's spawn.

MR. PARSONS DID, INDEED, FINISH the room on Thursday, and as it turned out, it wasn't a day too soon. When Athen returned home from work at six on Friday afternoon, she opened the back door to let Hannah out and found Meg camped on the back porch.

"For heaven's sake, what are you doing out there?" A delighted Athen hugged the new arrival.

"I forgot my keys." Meg grimaced.

"How long have you been here?"

"The cab dropped me off about forty minutes ago." Meg lifted her suitcase and carried it into the kitchen. "I thought Callie would be home."

"Ordinarily, she would be, but she has a big softball game tomorrow, so they had an extra practice this afternoon. I take it you're here at Brenda's request?"

"She called me at the station yesterday." Meg's eyes glowed. "She loved my tapes. She showed them to her father, and he loved them, too, so they wanted to meet with me as soon as humanly possible. Needless to say, I could not get out of Tulsa fast enough."

"When are you going to meet with them?" Athen put water on for tea.

"I'm meeting with Brenda tomorrow morning at her office. She said that you and Callie would be out to the house in the afternoon because Callie will be riding, so I'll go out with you and I'll talk to Hughes then, providing, of course, that I pass the test with Brenda. Great, huh? You get to schmooze with a hot guy, Callie gets a riding lesson, and hopefully, I'll get a job offer. Win. Win. Win."

"Well, two out of three ain't bad." Athen opened the cupboard and removed two cream-colored mugs.

"What does that mean? Two out of three . . . ?"

"Callie will be riding, and you will be interviewing, but I will not be schmoozing—or anything else—with the aforementioned hot guy."

"What?" Meg dropped her purse on a chair. "The last I heard, this was a promising romance. What the hell happened between then and now?"

"This happened." Athen pulled the previous day's newspaper from beneath a stack of papers on the floor near the back door and handed it to Meg. Meg sat and read through it, occasionally uttering a curse on Rossi's head.

"He is one nasty SOB." Meg read a particularly odious phrase aloud.

"Can you believe he did that to me?" Athen gritted her teeth. "And I trusted him, Meg."

"How many times did I tell you that Rossi was not to be trusted? I'm sorry you had to learn the hard way that . . ."

"I'm not talking about Rossi." Athen cut her off. "I'm talking about Quentin."

"What about Quentin?" Meg stared at her blankly.

"What do you mean, 'What about Quentin'? He wrote that garbage."

"It has his byline, but he didn't say all that crap about you. Dan Rossi did." Meg pointed out the obvious. "What's the problem?"

"The problem is that a man I was starting to care about and trust . . ."

"Whoa, girl. You stop right there." Meg held up a hand. "Are you telling me that you think that because you had something going with Quentin he should not have gone ahead with this story? Is that what this is all about?"

"Meg, Quentin promised me he'd be fair to me . . ."

"And from what I'm reading, he has. There's no editorializing here." Meg picked up the paper and waved it. "Don't you understand that this article has nothing to do with Quentin?"

"It has everything to do with him. He wrote the article." Where was the sympathetic shoulder of her best friend?

"Hello? Reporter? Doesn't make up stuff, just reports

the facts?" Meg sat back in her seat. "That's why they call us—duh—*reporters*."

"Very funny." Athen was clearly not amused.

Meg scanned the article again, shaking her head. "I just don't believe this."

"I didn't believe it either."

"It's your attitude I don't believe." Meg's eyes began to smolder the way they always did when her ire was roused. "Look, Athen, I don't know how else to say this, but your expectations are way out of line. You have no right to think that because you're cozy with the press . . ."

"He promised he wouldn't hurt me," Athen protested.

"And he hasn't," Meg nearly shouted. "Dan Rossi has. Can't you tell the difference?"

"You sound just like Quentin!" Athen glared at Meg.

"I should hope so." Meg glared back.

"I thought he cared about me," Athen tried to explain.

"I'm sure he does care about you, and I'm sure this"— Meg grabbed the paper—"has nothing to do with the way he feels."

"It hurt that he wrote those things about me." Why was she having such a hard time explaining herself? Why was she suddenly feeling like a child?

"Then develop some thicker skin." Meg poured herself another cup of tea. "If you take this type of thing personally, you and I could have some real problems. If I get this job—which I hope very much to do— there may be times when the news doesn't put you in a particularly favorable light. Are you going to expect me or the station I work for to only report on the positive and ignore the negative? Because if you do, the next year is going to be a very, very long, uncomfortable one for both of us."

Athen slumped deeper into her chair.

"And we need to get one thing clear right here and now," Meg told her bluntly. "Don't ever expect me to compromise myself for you the way you expected Quentin to. It won't happen. If I am hired to do a job, I'm going to do it. Same as Quentin."

They sat in stony silence, staring at each other.

"Are you angry with me?" Meg asked quietly.

"No," whispered Athen. "I guess I expected you to take my side and yell, '*Yes, damn it! Quentin's a bastard!*' But I'm not really angry with you."

"I am—now and always—on your side." Meg sighed. "You're one of the most important people in my life, Athen. I love you and I'm very sorry you feel wounded. But you're wrong this time, and I can't lie and tell you I think Quentin is a cad for not refusing to quote what Dan had to say. What you need to understand is that he had no choice. That's his job, and I'd be willing to bet he wasn't particularly happy about doing it."

Fingers tapping on the table, Athen stared into her cup of cold tea.

"And here's something else you probably don't want to hear: you owe Quentin a very big apology, regardless of how you feel about him." She paused. "How *do* you feel about him?"

Athen shook her head to indicate she didn't know. She was having trouble separating her emotions, and wasn't too sure of anything at that moment.

"Yay! Aunt Meg!" Callie flew through the door and engulfed Meg in a bear hug.

"The Woodside Slugger has arrived." Meg laughed and hugged her back. "Big game tomorrow, so I hear."

"Will you come?" Callie pleaded.

"Wouldn't miss it," her aunt assured her.

"Come on, Aunt Meg." Callie grabbed the flight bag with one hand and Meg's arm with the other, and pulled her toward the door. "We have a surprise for you upstairs. You coming, Mom?"

"In a minute." Athen tried to force a smile at her exuberant offspring.

"You think about what I said," Meg whispered as Callie dragged her from the room.

Mr. Parsons had done a fine job on the wallpaper, but unfortunately, the bed in which Meg was to sleep was still in pieces in the attic. After dinner, Athen folded up the worktable, and she and Meg carried it and the ladder to the garage. Then they carried the bed's components down to the second floor and assembled it. By ten o'clock, a guest room had emerged.

"This is wonderful, Athen," Meg said with a smile. "My own room. Temporarily, of course."

"For as long as you need it."

"Thanks." Meg held out a hand to her. "Am I forgiven?"

"There's nothing to forgive." Athen took Meg's hand. "But you're right. I behaved like a bratty child. I just don't know what to do about it now."

"Well, the shortest distance between two points is still a straight line." Meg sat down on the edge of the freshly made bed. "Why don't you just call him?"

"I don't know what I'd say." Athen leaned against the doorway.

"How 'bout, 'Quentin, I'm sorry. I'm a blockhead and I was wrong'?"

"I think I'll have to work up to it."

"Well, don't take too long." Meg unzipped her suitcase and searched for a nightgown and her toothbrush.

"I'm sure you're not the only woman in Woodside Heights who knows a hottie when she sees one."

"HERE, CALLIE, GIVE ME THAT." Meg reached for the picnic basket that Callie had packed with God only knew what.

"Thanks, Aunt Meg." Callie straightened her base-ball cap and grabbed her glove and cleats. "Mom, are you ready? I want to stop and see Grampa before the game."

"I know, Callie." Athen bent down to tie her sneakers. "I will be just one minute. What's the picnic basket for?"

"Oh, see, I thought since you and Aunt Meg would be at the game, you could have lunch together." Callie closed the door behind them as they headed out.

"That's very thoughtful, Callie." Athen rubbed a hand across her daughter's back. "Thank you, sweetie."

"Judging from the weight of the basket, I'd say you could probably feed the entire team." Meg laughed.

"Well, there are a few extra sandwiches and stuff," Callie explained. "I'll probably get hungry, too."

"HEY, LOOK!" CALLIE ALL BUT jumped from the car as Athen parked in the Woodside Manor lot. "Ms. Bennett's on the porch with Grampa."

Diana waved as Callie flew up the slight incline, and turned Ari's wheelchair so he could watch his granddaughter's approach. She folded the newspaper she'd been reading to him, and pulled three more chairs over to accommodate his visitors. They laughed and chatted for almost half an hour.

"Mom, it's almost ten," Callie noted with alarm. "I have to be on the field in fifteen minutes."

"Then we'd better get you there." Athen leaned over to kiss her father and told him, "Your granddaughter is the designated slugger, Papa. You should see her hit that ball."

"I, for one, can't wait." Meg stood up and stretched. "And since I remembered my camera this trip, we'll have lots of pictures to show you, Mr. Stavros."

"Ms. Bennett." Callie stood before Diana's chair. "Would you like to come to my game, too?"

"Why, I'd be delighted." A broad grin spread over Diana's face. "Thank you so much for inviting me."

Callie gave her directions to the field and instructed her not to have lunch, "'Cause I packed lots of stuff."

"YOU AND DIANA SEEM TO be getting along well these days," Meg noted as they carried the basket around the playing field, looking for a spot to set up their picnic.

"We are. I was so wrong about her, Meg. She is so devoted to my father." Athen stopped behind the fence that ran the length of the first-base line and dropped the blanket.

"That's obvious." Meg anchored one end of the blanket with the picnic basket. "What the hell could that child have stuffed in here? This damned thing weighs a ton."

"Let's take a peek." Athen lifted the lid and began to laugh. "Take a guess, how many sandwiches."

"Six?"

"Try eight, and an equal number of water bottles packed in plastic bags filled with ice. I guess that accounts for the weight."

They settled down on the blanket, Meg popping up every few minutes to snap a picture of her niece. Diana joined them within the hour.

"Have I missed much?" she asked as she sat between them on the blanket.

"Not by a long shot." Athen opened the basket and rattled off the contents. "Let's see. Peanut butter and grape jelly. Peanut butter and something red. Raspberry? Cherry? Hard to tell—let's just call it red stuff. Peanut butter and maybe peach or apricot."

"I'll have one with the red stuff, and a bottle of water." Meg peered into the basket. "What else has she got in there?"

"Doritos. Grapes. A bag of little candy bars, and a couple of packs of sugarless gum."

"Girl wasn't taking any chances on not having enough snacks." Diana chuckled. "Pass over one of those sandwiches. The mystery jelly is fine.

"Athen, have you had an opportunity to speak with Ms. Evelyn?" Diana asked.

"Yes, I did." Athen frowned. "But there's no sign of life there."

"What do you mean?"

"She didn't seem to have any ideas at all."

"Be patient." Diana reached into the basket for a bottle of water. "She'll come up with something."

"I don't know, Diana." Athen unwrapped her sandwich. "I'm not certain that she hasn't given up on the shelter and just put all her energy into the community garden."

"Not a chance," assured Diana. "If you ask me, that garden is just part of some master plan. Besides, it's not in her nature to give up."

"Well, she certainly didn't offer much encouragement." Athen dabbed at the glob of jelly that had plunked onto the front of her shirt.

"What did you expect her to say?" chided Diana good-naturedly. "'No problem, Athen. I'll just talk to Riley Fallon and influence him to change his vote'?"

"I guess I thought she'd be—I don't know—maybe more forthcoming," Athen admitted.

"'These things must be done delicately.'" Diana effectively mimicked the Wicked Witch of the West from *The Wizard of Oz*. "But don't worry, she'll come up with exactly the right approach at the right time, trust me. And when she does, you will be struck dumb by her ingenuity. I've seen her do some pretty amazing things over the years."

Callie came up to bat, and Athen stood near the fence to cheer her on. On the third pitch she hit a double, and her mother and Diana jumped up and down, yelling, while Meg whistled between two fingers. Two batters later Callie rounded third base toward home, and after crossing the plate to score the run that put her team ahead, she raised a fist and pumped her arm in the air in the general direction of her mother.

"But I sure wish I had a handle on what he's up to," Diana was saying to Meg when Athen rejoined them.

"Did you see that kid run?" Athen was out of breath from yelling. "What who's up to?"

"Diana was filling me in on Rossi's curious attachment to those vacant houses on Fourth Street." Meg tossed the bag of Doritos across the blanket to Athen. "She thinks whatever it is, it's something Dan has been sitting on for the last three or four years."

Meg picked through the grapes. "Do you think Callie thought to wash these? The last few tasted a bit gritty."

Athen laughed and picked up the bag of grapes and took them to the water fountain to wash them off. She returned just as Meg asked Diana, "So you think something Ari saw while he was speaking with you that morning was the catalyst for his stroke?"

"I'm certain of it," Diana said, nodding empathically. "I think that whatever it was, Ari had words with Dan over it. Here's the thing: Dan rushed to the hospital practically within minutes of Ari's admission. He waited there all night, as if he had to know what condition he was in and couldn't wait for the reports."

"So he goes to the hospital and waits, and finds out that the fates have intervened by sealing Ari's lips, so to speak." Meg was obviously intrigued.

"Throw me one of those little Snickers bars, will you, Athen?" Diana held up her right hand and caught the candy bar.

"What could Ari have seen?" Meg wondered aloud. "Something through the window?"

"Impossible." Diana shook her head. "The only window in Ari's office was at the opposite side of the room. The phone didn't reach."

"Something out in the hall, then, or something outside his door," Meg suggested.

"No. Ari had put the phone down and closed the door when we first started talking," Diana told them.

"Something he said before the phone call?" suggested Athen.

"I don't think so." Diana unwrapped the candy and took a bite. "We were talking about something else when, out of the blue, he said, 'I see he's gone too far this time.'"

"If he couldn't see out the window, and he couldn't see out into the hallway, what the hell could have be been looking at?" Meg scratched her head. "A memo? A letter, maybe?"

"The newspaper," whispered Athen.

Diana's head shot up. "Of course. It was the first thing he did every day, the first thing everyone in City Hall did every day."

"What was the date of your father's first stroke, Athen? Do you remember?"

"Late September, early October . . ."

"October 9, 2006," Diana said quietly.

"My interview with Brenda is at her office at the *Herald* at two," Meg told them. "Maybe if there's enough time after the interview, I can go through the paper's archives, see what's on the microfiche for that day."

"Get copies of anything that so much as mentions Dan Rossi's name," Diana suggested.

"Hey, Callie's up again." Athen went to the fence.

The three women shouted encouragement, and Callie responded by slamming a long ball into right field. The runners on second and third both scored, ending the game in favor of the Woodside Heights Girls Club. The jubilant winners lined up for the traditional handshake with the opposition, after which they threw their hats into the air and jumped up and down hugging each other. Meg was in their midst, snapping one photo after another.

"You guys save me any food?" The business of winning the game having been tended to, Callie plunged into the open picnic basket with both hands.

"Maybe you could eat that in the car on the way home." Meg tapped her on the head. "I have an interview in exactly one hour and thirty-five minutes, and I'm not showing up in jeans and sneakers."

AT FOUR THIRTY, MEG CALLED Athen's cell from the office of the *Woodside Herald*.

"Did you find anything?" Athen asked immediately.

"First you have to ask how my interview went," Meg instructed.

"Of course." Athen smiled, knowing there wasn't a snowball's chance that Meg had not wowed Brenda. "How did your interview go?"

"It was great," Meg told her confidently. "Brenda Chapman is one very savvy young woman. Forget the fact that she's the daughter of the man who owns the paper and this new cable channel. This gal can hold her own with anyone. We hit it off famously. Now you can ask me if I found something."

"Did you . . . ?"

"I don't know," she replied slowly.

"What do you mean, you don't know? You either found something or you didn't." Athen frowned.

"The only thing that seemed to relate to Rossi is a photograph that was taken at some fund-raiser, and I did get a copy of it. Rossi's in it, and there are a few other people in the photo, but I don't know who they are."

"Chances are I won't either," Athen said, frowning, "but maybe Diana will."

"We'll have to show her. Meanwhile, tell Callie I'll pick her up in fifteen minutes. That will give me just enough time to get to the Chapmans' for my meeting. Are you sure you don't need your car for the rest of the day?"

"Positive."

"Apparently, you haven't changed your mind about not going."

"Why would I go?"

Meg blew in long enough to hand Athen an envelope and to tell Callie to hurry up. They flew out the front door in a flurry, promising to be back around six thirty or shortly thereafter.

Athen sat at the kitchen table and opened the envelope. She held up the photocopy of the picture, and slid on her glasses to scrutinize the black-and-white image. A tuxedoed Dan Rossi gripped the arm of a tall white-haired man. Both men were smiling broadly for the camera. Immediately to the left of the duo and slightly in the background stood a third man who Athen thought looked vaguely familiar. The caption referred to a fund-raising event—"Woodside Heights mayor Dan Rossi greets contributors at weekend fund-raiser"—but gave no clue as to the identity of either of the other men in the picture.

She stared at the picture, but it was futile. She'd never seen the one man before, but wasn't sure if she'd ever seen the other. She put the picture on the refrigerator door with a magnet, and went outside to water her plants. She walked back into the kitchen just in time to answer the phone.

The Chapmans had invited Meg and Callie for dinner. Athen, too, of course, if she'd care to join them. Meg would drive back to pick her up, to which Athen snapped, "What are you thinking?"

"Would you be upset if we stayed? Callie's still riding. God, but she's good, Athen. Is there anything that child can't do well? Hughes and Brenda and I were just discussing the format for the proposed show. She's moving to the new network as manager. They have some really innovative ideas."

"Of course you should stay." Athen bit her lip. "I don't mind at all. I'll see you when you get back."

"Traitors," she mumbled after she hung up the phone.

Athen made herself busy cleaning the kitchen, grumbling the entire time. It did not take her long to realize that the person she was most annoyed with was Athen Moran. If she had called Quentin and apologized the way she should have, she wouldn't be home alone, she reminded herself.

She changed into sweatpants and took her bike out

of the garage. Maybe a little ride would lift her spirits. She pedaled out along the river road to the cemetery and pulled some errant weeds from the base of her mother's memorial. Hands on her hips, she stood at the top of the ridge overlooking the river and inhaled deeply. Scanning the view, she noted that from where she stood the back of the barn on the Chapman estate was visible.

"Geez." She shook her head. Even here she could not be rid of him. She rode home like one being pursued.

Callie and Meg are probably sitting at one of those lovely wicker tables on the veranda at this very minute, she thought. *They're enjoying a beautifully prepared dinner while I'm scrounging in a near empty refrigerator, deliberating between leftover pizza and yesterday's tuna salad.*

She flipped a coin. The tuna won.

Was Quentin having dinner with them? Maybe he had a date that night with someone, maybe one of those other ladies Meg alluded to who knew a prize when they saw one. Maybe he'd taken her to that little Thai restaurant. Athen could almost see him, urging his faceless companion to try the shrimp with spicy peanut sauce.

Hannah scratched at the back door and Athen let her in. She sat down on the hard kitchen floor and leaned back against the wall, the dog gazing up at her in adoration as she plunked her huge head in Athen's lap. She was still sitting there in total misery when Callie and Meg returned home shortly after eleven.

"Sorry we're so late," Meg apologized, "but . . ."

"It's okay," Athen assured her. "I took a long bike ride, and then Hannah and I just hung out for a while."

"Are you okay, Mom?" Callie asked.

"I'm fine, sweetie."

"Why are you sitting on the kitchen floor?"

"I just sat down to pet Hannah and was too tired to get up."

"Oh, okay. I'm going to bed, Mom." Callie stooped to kiss the top of her head. "I'm pooped."

Meg leaned back against the sink and sighed. "It went great, Athen. Chapman really seems to like me. He wants me to meet with one of their candidates for news producer to see what I think of her. Can you imagine? He wants my opinion."

"I take it they offered you the job?" Athen smiled.

"There are some details that need to be worked out, but yes," Meg said, a look of amazement on her face. "As she's walking us to the car after dinner, Brenda says, 'Dad and I both feel there's no need to look for anyone else for our lead anchor. We'd like you to think about when you could start. We'd like you to work with us as we get this thing rolling. And no pressure, but the sooner the better.'"

"Meg, that's wonderful." Athen got off the floor and hugged her.

"I can't wait to go back to Tulsa and stick this in Cal Robbins's smug face." Her eyes narrowed. "He has been jerking around with my contract the past two months."

"When does it expire?"

"October first," Meg said with a grin, "after which time I will belong to CCN—that's Chapman Cable Network—body and soul."

"Will he make you work through September?" Athen inquired.

"Probably not," Meg told her. "Cal really doesn't like me any more than I like him. I think he'll be just as happy to see me leave as I will be to go."

"How was dinner?" Athen asked casually.

"Wonderful. Man, what a cook they have. And what

a lifestyle: cocktails on the veranda, dinner in that lovely dining room."

"The big one?" Athen pressed.

Meg nodded. "The one with the enormous Waterford chandelier and the Degas on the wall."

"Were there a lot of people there?" The Chapmans' dining room was cavernous, not suited, Athen thought, for a small gathering.

"A larger group than I would have expected, considering we were supposed to be conducting a job interview," Meg noted. "The formality of the house aside, I got the impression that the Chapmans are pretty loose at home. There was some cousin of Lydia's there from St. Louis, with her husband and four children. And Lydia's daughter, Caitlin."

"Lydia's daughter?" Athen's eyebrows rose. Quentin had never mentioned a sister.

"She's wrapping up her residency at a hospital in Chicago." Lowering herself wearily into a chair, Meg kicked off her shoes. "Caitlin is quite a gal. She wants to work in an inner-city hospital or clinic, working with low-income families. With their money, she could probably build her own damned hospital. Did you know that Lydia Chapman's father founded Bradford International? And that she controls the trusts? We are talking major Yankee dollars here."

"Bradford International?" Athen's eyes widened. Had Quentin really given up a major position with the well-known corporation? "*The* . . ."

"Yeah. *The* Bradford International. Majorly huge dollars there."

"What's Caitlin like?" Athen wondered aloud.

"She's the image of her mother, except that she's a strawberry blonde, and taller." Meg studied her sister-in-law's face carefully. "Aren't you going to ask if Quentin was there?"

"No."

"Of course you were." Meg laughed. "Stop acting like you're not interested."

"Okay, was he?"

"Yes, he was." Meg lifted her legs onto the chair next to the one in which she sat.

Looking for something to distract herself, Athen picked up Hannah's water bowl, rinsed it out in the sink, and refilled it.

"Athen, I love you dearly, you know that, but you're a fool," Meg said levelly. When Athen started to protest, Meg said, "No, don't interrupt me. Quentin Forbes is one mighty miserable guy, though not, perhaps, any more miserable than you are. If you do not straighten this out, you will regret it for the rest of your life, and deservedly so."

"I know," Athen replied softly.

"You know?" Meg sat up straight in the chair and wrapped her feet around the lower rungs. "Then what are you going to do about it?"

"I guess I'll have to call him," she said.

"Don't 'guess,' Athen, do it." Meg reached down and scooped up her discarded shoes. "I suggest you start rehearsing what you're going to say. Get it down, then get it over with." She yawned widely. "God, I'm tired."

"Let's lock up, then." Athen bolted the back door and turned off the light over the sink. "Come on, Meg, we can talk more tomorrow."

Meg dragged herself up the steps, Athen following thoughtfully behind, mentally searching for an opening line.

❧24❧

"Damn! I overslept!" Meg blew into the kitchen at ten the next morning. "Brenda said she'd pick me up at eleven."

"Calm down." Athen shoved a mug of coffee in Meg's general direction. "You still have an hour."

"An hour to shower and find something to wear. I only brought the suit I wore yesterday. What was I thinking? I can't show up in the same thing." Meg tried to untangle her hair with her fingers. "And anyway, the skirt's wrinkled."

"I'll iron the skirt while you're in the shower, and you can borrow a top from me." Athen stuck the mug into her hands and pointed her in the general direction of the stairs. "Go take your shower. I'll find something for you to wear."

Forty-five minutes later, Meg was trying on shoes pulled from Athen's closet.

Meg admired the brown heels. "It's amazing when you consider that as tall as you are, and as short as I am, we wear the same size. Of course, what looks like a tiny delicate foot at the end of your long leg looks like a tugboat on me. It's the Moran curse, you know. Big feet and short stubby legs."

"Your legs are not stubby." Athen laughed. "You're petite."

"A marketing term for short and stubby," insisted Meg as she draped a belt around her hips.

"Blouse the front of the shirt a little," Athen suggested. "That's better."

She peered out the window at the sound of tires crunching in the driveway.

"Brenda's here," she told Meg. "And you look terrific. Go knock 'em dead."

"Thanks, Athen, for everything." Meg gave her sister-in-law a quick hug. "For the blouse, the ironing job, the shoes, the belt, the earrings." Meg sang off the list of borrowed items as she ran down the steps.

Athen collected the empty coffee mugs and took them to the kitchen. On the counter lay the reprinted newspaper photo Meg had given her the day before. As much as she'd stared at the picture, she could not come up with the name of the man in the background. If she had ever known his identity, it was gone from her memory bank now. After searching unsuccessfully for the phone book, she lifted the receiver and called information.

"I'd like the number for Diana Bennett on Rosedale, please."

THE HOUSE AT 417 ROSEDALE Avenue looked exactly like a house that Diana Bennett would live in. Small and compact, little more than a cottage built in the 1920s, it had charm and beauty and an air of romance about it. From the rose-covered arbor that framed the neat front door to the airy and light interior, it had Diana's name all over it.

The entire first floor was white, providing a simple background for Diana's collection of beautifully painted pottery.

"They're all American pieces." Diana volunteered

after Athen admired the pastel vases that paraded across the deep windowsills. "Grueby, Van Briggle, Weller—I'm partial to the Weller since I grew up in Zanesville, Ohio, where it was made, and my mother was a painter there. From time to time I've been able to find some pieces with her initials on the bottom where she signed her work."

Diana lifted a tall pale green vase adorned with white flowers and held it, base up, to show Athen the letters scratched in the bottom, but Athen's eyes were glued to the photograph that stood importantly at the center of the small stone mantel. Ari and Diana beamed—*glowed*—in full living color, Ari handsome as an aging movie hero, Diana soft and beautiful in a champagne-colored lace dress.

"What a beautiful picture." Athen quickly masked her embarrassment at having been caught gaping.

"That was taken two weeks before Ari's stroke," Diana told her.

Athen was unable to take her eyes from it. "You both look so happy."

"We were."

Athen swallowed hard. "I guess now is a good time to apologize to you for . . . for . . ."

"For thinking I was just a good time for a lonely old man?" Diana smiled gently.

"I don't know if I'd put it that way." Athen squirmed uncomfortably.

"Sure you would," Diana jabbed with more good humor and grace than Athen thought she could have mustered under the circumstances. "At least, once upon a time, you might have. But you don't owe me an apology, Athen. Neither Ari nor I gave you any reason to think otherwise."

"All those years, I should have made things easier for him, and for you. I should have included you in our holidays."

"Don't be so hard on yourself." Diana patted her hand. "I probably wouldn't have come anyway."

"You wouldn't?" Athen had never considered this possibility.

Diana sat on the ottoman in front of the oversized, overstuffed chair and shook her head.

"We'd made such a happy little world for ourselves here, I never wanted to share him. So on Christmas, he'd spend the day with you and John, and come home to me, and we'd have our own holiday together." Diana wiped a slow tear from her face and looked around the room. "The only truly happy birthdays, the only really merry Christmases I've ever had have been here, with Ari. This is the only place I've ever felt safe."

"Safe?" Athen asked cautiously.

Diana went into the kitchen and returned with a box of pale green tissues.

"I have the feeling I might need these," she said as she sat again. "I suppose the simplest way to explain is to say that I went from being an abused child to being an abused wife. I married Donald Bennett right out of high school. I thought he'd take me far away, and he did. He'd gotten a job with a pharmaceutical company about eight miles from here and went to graduate school at night. I got a job as a clerk in the finance department at City Hall. One of the girls in the office invited me to a campaign workers' meeting one night. Sam Tarbottom was running for mayor that year, do you remember?"

Athen shook her head. "Not really."

"Well, I had nothing else to do. Donald would be at

school. We'd made no friends, and I guess I was lonely, so I went. Ari was one of the organizers of Sam's campaign. I thought he was so wonderful. So European and suave and handsome."

Diana laughed, just a hint of blush rising to her cheeks. "Everyone was so nice to me. It was the first time in years I felt that I had a place to go, a place where I had friends. I didn't care who the candidate was. I'd have gone every week, just for the companionship, you know? Just to feel that I belonged somewhere."

Athen silently nodded. She too had felt isolated once.

"And so I went back, every week. I knew Donald would have a fit if he knew, he was so jealous, but I didn't care. For those few hours, I could be like everybody else, out for an evening with friends. We'd laugh and talk and drink beer. Once your father brought bottles of Metaxa and Tarbottom got drunk as a skunk." She laughed at the memory. "But mostly it was stuffing envelopes and laughing. That's what I remember most about those nights. Then one night I got back a little late and Donald was already at the apartment."

Her tongue flicking across her lips nervously. "He was not happy. I paid for my night out with two black eyes and a couple of broken ribs."

Athen was stunned at the thought of anyone striking this gentle soul.

"Of course, I had to call in sick the next day, and the next, until the bruising subsided a bit. And I had to plaster makeup on my face before I could appear in public. I didn't dare attend the next week's meeting, or the next few. But three weeks later, when Donald had exams, I went back. Carol Parker—she was my friend in the office— I know she knew, but she never asked. She promised she'd get me home early, but her car broke down. And Donald was waiting for me again. I decided maybe I didn't need friends after all."

She paused and blew her nose.

"The following week, when we were moving the finance offices from the second floor to the third, we all had to stay late, to move our own areas. Ari helped us to pack our desks. He kept looking at my face, and I knew he wanted to ask, but he never did. He carried my boxes for me." Diana's voice was almost a whisper. "Donald came to the office looking for me. He thought we were alone, since everyone else had gone upstairs. I'd gone back to get my jacket. Your father came in just as Donald was winding up for the second punch."

"Oh, my God, Diana," Athen whispered in horror.

"Ari all but put him through the file cabinets. He picked up the phone and told Donald if he wasn't out of the city in thirty minutes, he'd have him arrested for assault and battery." Diana's eyes began to glow softly. "Donald left, and Ari took me home with him, and he cried as he put ice on my face. By the next morning he'd arranged for surveillance of my apartment in case Donald decided to call his bluff, and he got me a lawyer to start working on my divorce. He was my hero, Athen. No one had ever defended me before."

"I always wondered why someone so young and beautiful . . ."

". . . fell in love with a man old enough to be my father? Ari is the only person who ever really loved me, the only one who ever really believed in me. My life began that night, and I thank God every day for having brought him to me. He's given me the only happiness I've ever known."

"But even now, when he's . . ." Athen bit her tongue.

"You need to understand this: I will love that man with my whole heart—in sickness and in health—until the day I die. No one could ever mean to me what he does. He taught me how to laugh, and how to love, and how to believe in myself. He talked me into going to college, and later he convinced me to get my CPA. He is the one and only love of my life, Athen. He's my real-life knight in shining armor."

Diana passed the tissue box to a sniffing Athen across the small space formed by their parallel knees.

"So," Diana said, "now you know. And maybe you understand why I had no interest in sharing him, with you or anyone else. He's all I have. I admit that I did want to be your friend. Especially after Ari's stroke, and when John died, I wanted to be there for you. Ari would have wanted me to."

"I'm sorry we didn't talk sooner. It must have been so hard for you when Dad was in the hospital and only John and I were allowed in his room for those first few days."

"Sharing the waiting room with Dan Rossi was the worst part," Diana said grimly. "He sat there praying for Ari to die while I was praying for him to live."

"You really think he hoped that Dad would . . ."

"If you'd seen the look on Dan's face . . ." Diana shivered. "Yes, I really do believe he was hoping your father would not survive." She smiled wryly. "I guess paralyzed and unable to speak was his second choice."

"Bastard."

"Amen," Diana agreed.

Athen covered her face with her hands. "I can't believe I let that man talk me into helping him get another term."

"It isn't your fault," Diana assured her. "Dan is a very good liar."

Athen suddenly remembered why she was there in the first place. "Speaking of Dan, maybe you can help me with something."

"What's that?"

Athen opened her purse and took the paper out, folding the creases flat onto her lap. "Meg found this photo on microfiche at the newspaper yesterday. This man, the one in the background, looks slightly familiar but I can't place him."

Diana leaned over for a better look. "Phillip Harper. He was a real-estate attorney from around New Brunswick."

"Was?"

"He retired last year. I heard he moved to Florida or Arizona, someplace warm. He was a real heavy hitter. He had a lot of money, and I think he thought of political contributions as an investment. I didn't know him well, but I met him a few times."

Diana studied the details of the picture silently. "We were at this party, your dad and I."

"You were?"

"It was at Wynn and Ellen Thomas's house in Saddlebrook. I remember every detail of that night. It was quite the society bash. Tickets were a thousand dollars a head. Everything was perfect—the caterer, the band. We danced until I could barely stand up. The ballroom was decorated to look like a Hawaiian grotto, complete with waterfalls, and there were flowers absolutely everywhere."

"Do you recognize the other man, the one in front with Dan?"

"I don't think so. I'm pretty sure I knew everyone there that night. These events draw the same people every time. State pols. County people. Only the wealthiest contributors and the candidates. This was the last big fund-raiser before the election, as I recall. But I don't think I remember this man." Diana shook her head. "I wish I did. Especially if this was what Ari was looking at that morning."

"Meg said she scanned the paper from end to end and found nothing that related to Rossi but this."

Diana handed the picture to Athen. "Maybe the key lies with the mystery man. I wish I knew who he was."

"So do I." Athen folded the paper and tucked it into her bag. "I wonder if my dad knows."

"I'm sure he does." Diana nodded. "But then again, if Ari could speak, we'd know the whole story, wouldn't we?"

WHAT A DIFFERENCE A YEAR *makes,* Athen mused as she dressed for the Memorial Day outing. *This time last year I was praying for gale-force winds. Today, I can't get there fast enough.*

She'd tried for the past week to make the call she knew she had to make, but each time she lifted the receiver, she'd returned it to its cradle without making the call. After torturing herself for days, she decided to wait until the press conference on Wednesday. The plan was to nab Quentin on the way out of the room and nonchalantly ask him to stop at her office before he left the building. That plan was scrapped when he blew out of the room as soon as the last question was asked and answered.

There was always plan B.

Chances were that he, along with just about every other living soul in Woodside Heights, would be at the picnic today. Well, Athen was ready for him. She'd corner him and give him her best, her most sincere apology. With any luck, maybe by tonight she'd back in his arms again.

There was no need this year for Callie to urge her mother to hurry. Athen was downstairs and dressed before Callie was awake.

"You look nice, Mom," Callie said as they got into the car. "I like that outfit on you."

It had been chosen carefully, black and gold checked Capri pants, a pale gold cotton pullover, black sandals, a chunky gold bracelet, and a gold scarf to tie back her hair. The picnic be damned: she was dressed for an impromptu dinner invitation, with maybe a stop afterward at the park to feed the ducks. Ever hopeful, her words of apology well rehearsed, Athen headed off for the day's events with Callie.

Diana had insisted on accompanying them. "Dan will be attempting to hold court as he has for the past sixteen years," she'd told Athen. "We're going to be there to remind him that he's just another ex-employee, just like all the other old-timers."

"What do you mean, remind him . . . ?"

"Just follow my lead," she told Athen.

Callie sighed as they waited for Diana when they stopped to pick her up. "I just love Diana's little house, don't you, Mom?"

Diana waved from the front window, locked the door, and walked briskly to the car.

"I've been meaning to ask," Diana said while en route to the park, "have you spoken with Meg since she left on Monday?"

"She called last night. Everyone at the station out there is buzzing about her new job. And of course, she can't wait."

"When will she start?"

"Officially, she goes on Chapman's payroll October first, though the station won't kick off until December. Of course, Brenda wants her here as soon as the station in Tulsa will release her from her contract." Athen pulled into the already filled parking lot at the park.

Callie went off in search of her friends, and Diana and Athen walked toward the gathering under the trees.

"Now stay close, Athen," Diana instructed. "Because today I'm going to teach you something you should have learned from your father."

"What's that?"

"How to work a crowd."

Athen marveled at how fluidly Diana floated through the throng, never matching the wrong name to the wrong face. Dressed all in white—a white cotton dress with a full skirt, a wide-brimmed white hat, white sandals—she could have been the hostess at a garden party.

"Mrs. Amory!" Diana took the hand of a plump woman who was headed for the food table and turned to Athen. "Athen, of course you know Mrs. Amory. She worked side by side with me every time your father ran for Council." She turned back to Mrs. Amory. "Oh, and wasn't that first election night one to remember? Did you ever see such rain? And how is your daughter? Did I hear she's engaged . . . ?"

Next it was, "Mrs. Simpson." Diana bent to place a kiss on the face of an elderly woman perched on the edge of picnic bench. "What a coincidence! I was just telling the mayor about that pothole at the end of your street. Athen, Mrs. Simpson is the lady I was telling you about. The most dreadful pothole . . . perhaps someone from Streets could go out tomorrow and take a look?"

"David Gilmartin." Diana hugged a thin, bald man. "I was devastated to hear about your wife. What a loss to us all. Athen, David's wife passed away in March."

And on it went until Athen whispered in her ear, "What in God's name are you doing? And when can we stop and sit down for a minute?"

"A cold drink would be wonderful, yes, thank you. Athen? Something cold?" Diana scooped up two cans of ice-cold soda from a huge cooler. "You are doing what the mayor is supposed to be doing at things like this, and we don't stop till it's over," she said out of the corner of her mouth as she handed one of the cans to Athen and popped open the lid of the one in her hand. "Before this day is over, you will have shaken every adult hand, kissed every baby, and said something endearing to every child in attendance."

"That's what you do when you're campaigning," Athen grumbled and searched the throng for the only person she was interested in talking to. "Which I am not."

Diana nodded in the direction of the small crowd that had gathered around the former mayor. "Dan certainly is."

"He can do whatever he wants." Athen made a face. "And he doesn't need to campaign. The job is his."

"Now, Athen, didn't your daddy ever tell you there's no such thing as a sure thing?" Diana turned to the couple approaching them from the left. "Ann . . . Mike. How good to see you again."

Athen scanned the crowd for a tall, dark-haired man with broad shoulders and a killer smile. She found him over by the ball field where the children were being divided into teams.

"Excuse me, Diana. Jim, Nancy, it was wonderful to see you," she echoed Diana's smooth tones in making a graceful exit. "My daughter is in the softball game, and I don't dare miss a play."

She took a deep breath and headed across the field, rehearsing what she'd say to him. With each step, her heart pounded a little louder. She came up behind him and fixed a smile on her face. She touched his arm and he turned around, obviously surprised that she had approached him.

"I thought that was you." She smiled at him as calmly as possible. "How are you?"

"I'm fine."

"Is there a score?" she asked.

"Not yet."

The awkward silence was her cue.

"Quentin." She took a deep breath. "I want to apologize to you. I had no right to interfere with the way you do your job. And I do understand that that's what you were doing when you wrote the Rossi story. I realize now that my expectations were out of line."

"Do you?" he asked, not looking at her.

"Yes, I do." She tried to sound as contrite as she could.

"Did Meg have anything to do with your change of heart?" He seemed to be looking at her from the corner of one eye, but the dark glasses made it tough to know for sure.

"We discussed it," she acknowledged, "and she told me I was dead wrong. Which I was. My feelings were hurt and I guess it was difficult for me to look beyond that at first."

"Athen, I would never intentionally hurt you," he said softly.

"I know that." She smiled, relaxing. The worst was over. "You were right, of course. If Rossi says something, you have to print it. Especially if it's about me. Whether I like it or not."

"I'm glad that you understand." He looked down at her, his eyes shielded by the dark glasses. "I'm very sorry that something I did upset you. But I can't promise that it will never happen again."

"I understand." She nodded. "You do what you have to do."

She waited for him to say something else, and when he did not, she took a small side step to better study his profile. There was no smile on his face, no banter forthcoming. No hand reached out for hers. Quentin looked distracted at best, uncomfortable at worst.

He turned to her stiffly. "Thank you for the apology. It means a lot to me to know that you understand that it's not personal."

She smiled her biggest smile, happy that it was behind them. Now they could pick up where they'd left off.

"Well, then," he said awkwardly. "I guess I'll see you next week at the press conference."

He nodded to her as if she were a casual acquaintance. She watched, dumbstruck, as he abruptly strode off across the field in the direction of the parking lot without a backward glance. Her cheeks flushed with embarrassment at his apparent disinterest, her mind numb in the wake of his sudden dismissal.

Her disbelieving eyes followed the maroon cap as it wound through the rows of cars, her stunned heart clanging dully on the macadam as it dragged behind him, all the way across the parking lot.

The night Callie left for Florida, Athen rambled aimlessly from one room of the house to the next, unable to shake the anxiety that had engulfed her when her daughter's plane became a shining silver dot that, seconds later, was devoured in one gulp by a monstrous cloud. Her only child having disappeared into the sky, beyond her control, beyond her reach, Athen somberly returned to the empty house, second-guessing her decision to allow Callie to fly—alone—to spend the last two weeks of summer vacation with the elder Morans. John's parents had every right to expect Callie to make the trip, Athen reminded herself, and of course she agreed. They hadn't seen her since John's funeral. They needed the connection with her, needed to see how like their son she had become. Athen simply had not anticipated the degree of angst she would experience as she watched a buoyant Callie, primed for adventure and savoring her independence, disappear into the unknown on the arm of the flight attendant who'd promised to take good care of her.

Vulnerability, thy name is Parenthood.

Athen fed Hannah and tried to stop pacing, tried not to watch the clock. Callie was to call the second she arrived at her grandparents'. The flight should take little more than an hour, and it had been almost that long.

She should be there by now. Why hasn't she called?

Athen had checked the charge on the cell phone she'd gotten Callie for the trip. The knot inside Athen grew and twisted until the phone shook her out of a mild frenzy shortly after seven.

The plane had been on time. Grandma and Grandpop were at the gate waiting for her. They were going to stop for dinner on the way back from the airport. The flight had been completely uneventful, everything was fine. They were taking her to Disney World tomorrow, and, "Oh, don't forget, I want my room to be *blue* blue, not *pale* blue."

Relieved that her daughter had been safely delivered by US Airways into the waiting arms of her grandparents, Athen could relax. Callie was going to have a whale of a good time. John's parents would guard her with their lives, spoil her rotten, show her off to all their friends, devote every waking minute to her every whim, photograph every move she made, and send her home with a whole new wardrobe to start school.

Athen ate a light supper, then took her coffee outside to accompany Hannah on an evening stroll around the backyard. The garden was almost spent now, the end of summer closing in. A few flowers remained in bloom, some pale lavender phlox that contrasted nicely against the brooding dark monkshood, and some roses, deep red climbers, their fragrance still heady this late in the season. The side garden, given over to annuals, was still happily ablaze with the sharp hues of the zinnias Callie had planted from seed. Delicate cosmos, pink and white, swayed gracefully on tall stems, their feathery leaves neatly framing the birdbath, the base of which was encircled with red impatiens. Athen bent over to remove a weed, careful not to shake its seeds back into the flower bed.

She wandered around to the front of the house, where a single yellow daylily, bright as the July sun, stubbornly continued to bloom in defiance of the calendar.

Hemerocallis. She smiled to herself as she repeated the name aloud, fondly touching the golden petals as she passed by. She had made a point to learn the names of all the flowers she and Callie had chosen, and was pleased that she remembered them all. Knowing their names had made them hers. *Knowledge is indeed power,* she mused.

Returning to the back of the house, she sat on the porch steps and drained a few drops of cold coffee from the cup that dangled from the fingers of one hand. The setting sun draped a pinky glow behind the trees and the warm evening air was thick with the scent of sweet autumn clematis. She leaned against the step behind her and inhaled deeply, thinking it might be good for her, after all, to have some time to herself. Meg always said that everyone should live alone for a while. Athen never had. Now, for two short weeks, she would have time to think about things she'd been avoiding, to do things she'd been putting off.

First thing tomorrow morning she would go to the paint store, and with luck, she'd find a blue to match the one Callie had her heart set on. She was going to put her house in order, a prelude, she hoped, to putting her life in order.

Hannah thumped into a huge half-moon at her feet, and Athen leaned down to scratch behind her ears.

"Miss your playmate, do you? I miss her, too," Athen confided. "But we are going to be very busy while Callie's gone."

She made a list of things she wanted to do. Clean the attic—that would be a weekend project. Not think about Quentin, or who he's seeing now, or how she missed him more than she'd expected. How her hand still shook slightly when he entered the conference room on Wednesdays, how she still harbored a faint hope that one day, when she'd least expect it, he'd hang around after everyone else had left instead of bolting from the room the minute the press conference ended.

Face it, she told herself sternly, *that is a closed chapter.*

For whatever reason, Quentin wanted nothing more to do with her, and that was a fact she would have to live with, and it was her own damned fault. She'd come through worse times. She'd get through this.

"Come on, Hannah." She stood up and stretched. "Let's go inside and put some of this free time to good use."

"NO, I DON'T THINK THAT'S quite the shade she had in mind." Athen leaned across the counter, sorting through the pile of colored strips spread before her by the young man in the paint store. "More like this one." She nudged the chip from its place in the pile.

"That's sort of strong for a little girl's room," the young man noted.

"She's a strong little girl, and that's what she wants."

The salesman retrieved a can of the blue and set it upon the counter. "Anything else I can get you?"

"Well, I need something for my hallway. I've been thinking maybe something in this cream color, with maybe a bit more gold in it."

He pointed to a sample that had been hidden toward the back of the pack, and she smiled. "Yes, that color. That's exactly it. And now something for my bedroom—a green. No that's too yellow. I want something soft. More sage. Yes, that one right there. . . ."

She purchased rollers and brushes and drop cloths, and wrote a check while Ed loaded up her car. When Mr. Parsons told her he wouldn't have time to do her painting until October, Athen decided to do it herself. She wanted the entire house repainted before Callie started school at the beginning of September. The new school year always seemed like a time of new beginnings to Athen, and so she was determined to start the new season with a newly redecorated house.

On her way out of the paint store, a display of stencils caught her eye, and she stopped to inspect them. She'd never stenciled before, but she liked the look and felt confident she could figure it out. She bought three—a grapevine, an ivy, and a rose border—along with the requisite brushes and jars of paints. Painting the inside of the house was going to be a huge undertaking, but it would give focus to her days with Callie gone for two weeks. Maybe she'd take a few days off herself, she thought, and finish it all before Callie got home.

She strolled leisurely across Harmond Avenue to her car, which she'd parked at a meter on the street. A sign in the window of the fabric shop two storefronts from the car caught her eye. She hesitated only briefly before redirecting her steps to the small shop.

"Your sign says you make slipcovers," she said to the young woman behind the counter.

"Yes, m'am, we do." The clerk barely looked up from her paperwork.

"Great." Athen smiled. "Here's what I want. . . ."

By the time she left, she'd selected fabric to recover the living room furniture as well as the dining room chairs, and she'd made an appointment for the measurements to be taken. She whistled as she walked back to her car. Over the past twenty-four hours, she'd not only come to terms with herself, but had laid the groundwork for revitalizing her home. What else needed to be done?

What else indeed? She paused in front of the pink stucco storefront closest to her car. She stood for a very long moment, pondering the possibilities. Having made up her mind, she placed the stencils in the trunk of the car and slipped a few more quarters into the meter.

"May I help you?" the perky receptionist asked.

"Do you take walk-ins?" Athen inquired.

"Sure thing. Did you have anything particular in mind?"

With her right hand, Athen reached to the back of her head and gathered her hair into a stream that cascaded almost to her waist.

"Shoulder length, I think," she replied.

"Are you sure?" The receptionist raised both eyebrows.

"Absolutely," Athen replied confidently.

"Have a seat." The young woman motioned to a row of chairs near the window. "I'll see who's free."

She started to walk to the back of the room, then paused. "You know, there's this program that makes wigs for young cancer victims out of donated hair."

"Locks of Love." Athen nodded. "I've read about it."

"Our salon participates. Would you consider . . . ?"

"Absolutely." Athen ran her hand the length of her hair. "I'd say we have the makings of several wigs right here."

"OH, MY GOD!" CALLIE DID a double-take at the woman who reached out for her when she got off the plane. "Mom! Your hair!"

"Like it?" Athen hugged her daughter, grateful to have her home again.

"I . . . I don't know." Callie's expression was somewhere between horror and admiration. "I mean, you look beautiful. But it's so different. Why did you do that?"

"It was time for a change."

"Do you like it?" Callie was still staring at her mother.

"Very much." Athen nodded.

"It sure is different."

"I admit I didn't recognize myself the first few days, and it took me a while to get over the shock." Athen laughed. "But I'm used to it now and wonder why I didn't do it sooner. And you'll be glad to know that my hair was donated to make wigs for children who are undergoing treatment for cancer. The program is called Locks of Love. So my hair is worth much more off my head than it was on it."

"That sounds like a good thing." That quickly, Callie was reconciled to Athen's new look.

Her mother's hair was not the only thing that had undergone a drastic change while Callie was in Florida.

"Well, what do you think?" Athen asked after Callie had gone from room to room and back again.

"Everything's changed," Callie said slowly. "I went away for two weeks and now everything's changed."

"Do you like it?"

"It's all so pretty, but it doesn't look at all like our house anymore." She sat down on the sofa. "This sofa doesn't go with the room now. And neither do the chairs."

"The new slipcovers will be done in about two more weeks," Athen told her.

Callie nodded and looked around, taking it all in.

"Did Mr. Parsons do all this?"

"No. He didn't have time." Athen smiled with satisfaction. "I did it."

"The stenciling, too?" Callie's eyes widened, following the tendrils of ivy that wound from the front hall through the living room.

"Yes. That, too." Athen beamed.

"Was it hard?"

"Harder than I thought it would be." Athen spared her daughter the details of her frustration the first day she wrestled with the stencils, all of which had three or four parts to the designs. It had driven her crazy until she had gotten a feel for it.

Callie's eyes rested on the watercolor that hung over the mantel.

"Did you paint that, too?" She pointed to the painting with its splashes of color depicting a summer garden as seen through a garden gate.

"It's one I started a long time ago, but never completed." Athen slid into a chair, wondering if perhaps she should have been a little less zealous in her drive to refashion their surroundings. "I found it in the attic, and after I finished it I decided to bring it down here."

"Where are Dad's pictures?" Callie asked uncertainly.

"In your room. I thought you might like to have them."

Callie nodded without comment.

"Are you all right?"

"It's just that everything's so different." Callie frowned.

"Change is not necessarily bad, Callie," Athen told her quietly. "As a matter of fact, it can be very good. Nothing can, or should, always stay the same. The house looked tired and gloomy, and I felt tired and gloomy living here. I wanted a pretty and bright house for us to live in. I felt that it was time for me to change the way I look, too. Do you understand?"

"I think so." She looked around the room again. "It is very pretty, Mom. So's your haircut. Did you do my room too? Is it blue?"

"Of course." Athen laughed. "*Blue* blue. Not *pale* blue. Go take a look."

Callie shot up the steps and Athen held her breath.

"Wow!" exclaimed Callie. "Wow!"

Athen smiled when Callie leaned over the second-floor railing and called down to her, "It rocks, Mom. It's just the color I had in my head. Everything looks great. It's like getting a new house without moving. Boy, oh, boy, will Aunt Meg be surprised!" Her voice trailed off as she went off to inspect her mother's room.

Leaning back against the chair, Athen relaxed. Callie would adjust to her new surroundings just as Athen had become accustomed to her own new look. Putting a bit more of the past behind somehow made the future seem a little closer. She could not foresee what it would bring, but she knew with certainty that whatever it was, she was ready for it.

LATE SUMMER EASED INTO A glorious autumn, followed, inevitably, by the first touches of frost. Athen and Callie spent a long weekend cleaning up the flower beds and preparing them for winter. They cut back the perennials and mulched the beds and treated themselves to a night out for pizza and a movie after they completed their work.

Dan Rossi lay low throughout September and early October, much to Athen's relief. She wanted nothing more than to serve out her term and step aside, leaving Dan to his devices. The voters who reelected him would only get what they deserved. The city seemed unusually quiet, and she began to wonder if the UCC had abandoned its efforts to obtain their shelter or if perhaps they were considering alternative sites.

She was musing over this thought one morning when Veronica stepped into her office to announce that Ms. Evelyn would like a minute of her time.

Athen greeted Ms. Evelyn warmly. "I was just thinking about you."

"It was time to check on those fruit trees we planted last summer up in the green." She motioned toward the window, beyond which once ugly, empty lots had been transformed into havens of beauty and abundance. "And I thought first I'd stop and see you and deliver my invitation in person."

"Invitation?" Athen asked, her curiosity piqued.

"Well, now, Athen, you know that fall has always been the time to celebrate the harvest, and this year we have much to be thankful for. We fed dozens of families with the produce from our garden. The ladies of the churches gathered what was left over and showed some of the young women from the housing project how to put up green beans and tomatoes. My, what a time we had." She chuckled. "There are families who'll have food this winter who last year had less, and there's plenty put aside for the kitchens where we feed the hungry." Her voice softened, and she told Athen, "It was the first time many of those young women had an opportunity to give to those less fortunate than they. Being poor themselves, they didn't realize that there were others who had even less. We all learned a little something from working together."

As always, Ms. Evelyn's generous spirit and true love of humanity humbled Athen.

"I thought we should celebrate our good fortune in some special way," Ms. Evelyn continued in her slow, precise voice. "That perhaps we as a city should unite to give thanks for the harvest we have been able to share. I was thinking a community day of prayer would be fitting, a day when the churches could unite in a common service of worship, perhaps to be held at the green. It seems right to give thanks in the midst of God's bounty, don't you think?"

"It's a wonderful idea, Ms. Evelyn," Athen readily agreed.

"It occurred to me that you, as mayor, as well as one who had volunteered her time to help with the project, might like to be a guest at the service." Ms. Evelyn looked at Athen from across the big desk. Something seemed to play behind her eyes, giving Athen just a hint of speculation as to what, besides prayer, Ms. Evelyn might have in mind.

"I'm honored that you thought to include me," Athen told her sincerely, "and I would be delighted to attend."

"Wonderful." Ms. Evelyn smiled. "Two p.m., the Sunday after next. Pray the weather holds. It so often turns cool at the end of October."

She rose to leave and Athen walked her to the door.

"Do bring Callie," Ms. Evelyn reminded her before she walked to the elevator and waved.

Something is afoot, Athen reflected as she opened the drapes to give full view to the lush green spot just three blocks from City Hall. The autumn sun danced off the trees that grew along the perimeter of Ms. Evelyn's garden, the russets of the oaks and the yellows of the maples forming a brilliant outline along the back border. Athen thought back to the day she spent there early in the summer. It had been the best weekend she'd had in a very long time.

She tried her damnedest not to think about Quentin. She still could not look at him without feeling confused. He'd set in motion feelings she believed she'd never feel again, and then quietly walked away. He was gracious to her at the weekly press conferences, yet avoided speaking to her outside the conference room, other than once to mumble "great haircut" as he passed by. He avoided making eye contact with her, yet she could feel his eyes on her from the moment he entered the room until his speedy exit. There were times when she wished she could grab him by the collar, shake him silly, and yell, "What is wrong with you?"

But, of course, she never would, so they continued to meet once each week within the confines of a public press conference.

Secretly, their mutual professional and forced politeness drove her crazy. She wondered what he felt, what he was thinking as he watched her from his seat in the first row. This Quentin was new to her and she could not read him at all. He looked the same but the fire he'd once displayed was gone. He had even, on several occasions, uncharacteristically passed on opportunities to grill her on one topic or another, choosing instead to defer to another *Herald* reporter, and his news stories lacked his old spice. She wished he would talk to her, if only as a friend. She still missed him, even after all these months. His presence in her life felt much like an unfinished sonnet. She wished that someday they would have the chance to write the last verse.

"THESE ARE PERILOUS TIMES, FRIENDS, and we are in the midst of a perilous journey." The Reverend Davison's voice boomed across the immense crowd that gathered for the UCC's Community Day of Prayer. "Mankind stands on the brink of the destruction of the spirit. Only by coming together in a common cause can we triumph over the forces of despair. The path before us is clear, sisters and brothers. We can, as a community, set in motion the means to care for those among us who, through no fault of their own, need a hand to help them along."

Athen bit her bottom lip and arched her foot inside her shoe, trying to distract herself so that she would not openly grin.

Ms. Evelyn was, in fact, a genius.

She had personally visited every member of the city's clergy to invite them to attend this event, and as a result, every church and synagogue in Woodside Heights was represented on the dais. As mayor, Athen had been seated in the first row. Next to her sat Riley Fallon and his new bride, Georgia, the Reverend Davison's daughter. Clearly, the seating arrangement had been deliberate. As the Reverend Davison launched into his plea for community support of the UCC's efforts on behalf of the homeless, he was backed on the platform by the mayor, a member of City Council, and every religious leader in the city.

Brilliant, Ms. Evelyn. Simply brilliant.

". . . and so we ask you to support us as we strive to do His work, to feed the hungry in our midst, to shelter the homeless, to clothe those whom the bitter winds of the coming winter would chill."

Looking out across the sea of faces, black and white, Hispanic and Asian, Greek and Italian, Irish and Polish, Athen knew that the battle would be won. Hundreds of people jammed the garden and spilled onto the adjacent street and sidewalk. She glanced sideways at Ms. Evelyn, seated at the end of the row, marveling that the spirit of this one small woman had proven to be greater than the forces of power that had opposed her for so long.

Athen's eyes scanned the crowd for Dan Rossi, wondering what thoughts were going through his mind. She had not seen him arrive, but she knew he would be there. To have avoided the event would have been a political error he would never have made. The press had built the Day of Prayer into a happening that no one of standing within the community would have missed. Athen would bet her last dollar that before the day was over, Dan would have arranged to have his picture taken with Ms. Evelyn.

". . . and just as our hard work has resulted in this beautiful garden wherein we now gather, so can we banish the blight from this city. Let us pray . . ."

As the closing prayer commenced, the clouds that had hidden the sun all afternoon shifted, allowing the warming light to cover the crowd. Athen suppressed a giggle. Only Ms. Evelyn could have arranged for so dramatic a touch to end the ceremonies.

Walking through the dispersing crowd, Athen realized that Callie was no longer at her side. Peering around, she saw her daughter walking toward the sidewalk with Diana. She headed in that direction, but found her way blocked by a solid form dressed in khaki pants and a brown tweed jacket.

"Hello, Athen."

"Hello, Quentin."

"Quite a gathering Ms. Evelyn put together," he said.

"I doubt anyone else could have pulled it off." She hoped he could not hear her sudden, erratic heartbeat.

"I guess she'll get her shelter built," he continued.

"I'd bet on it."

They'd been walking slowly, small steps through

the maze of people, neither paying attention to which way they were going. She realized they'd headed back to the garden, away from the sidewalk and Callie. Athen stopped, and so did he.

"Brenda tells me Meg will be home next week," he said.

"Yes. Tuesday." Her capacity for small talk had almost been reached. What was the point?

"Callie is doing exceptionally well with her riding, did Brenda tell you?" He still avoided her eyes.

"Yes, she did. It's really wonderful of Brenda to pick her up on Saturdays and bring her home."

"It's not out of her way, and both Callie and Timmy really have a great time. They've become best friends, almost like sister and brother. You should come out to watch some afternoon. You're always welcome."

A tense silence began to build and she struggled with a response. The old Athen would have let it go.

The new Athen decided that she'd been polite long enough.

"I don't feel welcome, Quentin. For some reason that I don't quite understand, I seem to make you extremely uncomfortable. I can accept the fact that you don't have any interest in dating me. But we're both grown-ups, and given the fact that our children are such close friends, I can't understand why we can't be friends as well. This polite but distant attitude of yours is very annoying. Could we forget about everything else and just be friends?"

For the briefest of moments he permitted his eyes to meet hers before looking away. In those few seconds she saw a flash of longing so defined that her knees all but shook.

"I'm afraid it isn't quite that simple, Athen," he said softly.

"Quentin . . ." She laid a hand on his arm just as Callie grabbed her from behind.

"I've been looking all over for you, Mom." Callie tugged on Athen's sleeve. "Oh, hi, Mr. Forbes."

"Hello, Callie."

"Can we go, please?" pleaded Callie. "I'm starving and I have a math test to study for."

"I was just going to look for you." Athen told her. She turned to Quentin. "It was good to see you. I'm sorry if I . . ."

"You have nothing to be sorry about." He cut her off. "It was good to see you, too, Athen."

"I don't understand you, Quentin," she said bluntly.

"I'm hoping someday you will."

"You make me crazy," she told him from between clenched jaws.

"Good," he whispered. "That's the best news I've had in a long time." He squeezed her elbow before turning and walking away.

IT HAD NOT TAKEN A political genius to figure out that at the following week's Council meeting, a motion would be made to lease the houses on Fourth Street to the UCC. Although Wolmar and Giamboni voted against it, George Konstantos voted with Riley Fallon to hand the properties over. Athen cast the deciding vote, and the deed was done.

"This is your first victory since taking office. How do you think the opposition will react?" she was asked at the press conference that afternoon.

"First of all, I do not see it as a victory for anyone other than the people who have worked so hard and so long for this," she said. "People like Ms. Evelyn Wallace, the Reverend Davison, and the other leaders of the UCC. It is their victory, not mine. And as far as the opposition is concerned, I would hope that Councilmen Wolmar and Giamboni would respect the wishes of the people of

Woodside Heights. Though it's beyond my comprehension why anyone would oppose such a worthy project, especially since it has the backing of the people in the community."

"And Dan Rossi?' A voice from the middle of the first row asked pointedly.

"Dan Rossi does not sit on Council, Mr. Forbes," she reminded him.

"It is my understanding that after the first of the year, Mr. Rossi will announce that he will run in the primary," he continued. "Since he has been an outspoken opponent of a shelter at that location, do you foresee any problems in getting the project off the ground before you leave office?"

"Do you mean will the shelter be open before my term expires?"

Quentin nodded.

"I have another year in office, Mr. Forbes. I cannot imagine that it would take a year to complete this." She tapped her foot in agitation. "The fact that last month's amendment moved the primary to May does not affect this project. I fully expect the shelter to be open well before next November."

"Then you are conceding that you will not run against former Mayor Rossi in the primary?" Dave Higgins from one of the local network affiliates asked her, as the TV camera lights flashed sharply.

"I never intended to seek reelection, Mr. Higgins," she told him bluntly.

"But if the shelter was delayed," he persisted, "or in jeopardy between now and May, would you consider . . ."

"The shelter will not be delayed in any way." She cut him off, seeing the line of questioning beginning to drift to waters she had no interest in treading. "There are plans in place to move this forward as quickly as possible. Perhaps Councilman Fallon would be good enough to fill you in on the timetable."

Quentin hung back at the end of the conference, and edged toward her. "Congratulations, Athen."

She had watched him out of the corner of one eye, wondering if today he would elect not to make his usual dash for the door. She was pleased to see that he was slowly gathering his things, seeming to time himself so that they would be heading for the door at the same time.

"Congratulate Riley. Or better still, Ms. Evelyn. She's the one who made this happen."

"You cast the deciding vote," he reminded her.

"I was happy to do it, I assure you."

"Do you really think Dan will let this happen?" They moved into the hallway.

"I can't see how he can stop it," she told him confidently. "What could he possibly do?"

"It just isn't in his nature to back off graciously." His leather binder began to slip forward from his grasp. She reached out and caught it before it could fall. Their fingers touched, and they stood frozen for a moment, politics and old hurts briefly forgotten. A current passed from one to the other and back again.

For a moment she forgot that she was the elected mayor of the city and that she was in the middle of a hallway at City Hall jammed with reporters. Their fingers instinctively entwined, and neither made an effort to disengage from this small, unexpected connection. When she met his eyes, he did not avert his gaze as had become his habit.

"Excuse me, Mrs. Moran." The photographer from the *Woodside Herald* approached her from behind. Quentin juggled his binder up under his arm and the spell was broken, their fingers sliding apart. "We'd like a picture with you and Councilmen Fallon and Konstantos."

Athen turned to the camera, smiling as she stood between the two councilmen. When she turned back, Quentin was gone.

❦26❦

"Good Lord, Meg, the only thing I've ever worn that was cut this low was a nightgown."

Athen stood in the dressing room of the upscale boutique Meg had dragged her to, and tugged at the front of the gown the saleswoman had brought her.

"Leave it alone." Meg slapped at Athen's fingers. "You're throwing off the lines of the dress."

Meg stood back to assess the fit. "It's perfect, Thena. Gorgeous. The color is perfect. The dress is perfect. Oh, and with your mother's garnet necklace . . ."

"I don't know, Meg." Athen shook her head uncertainly. "It shows a lot of skin."

"Yes, it does. But it shows it so well."

"Would you wear this in public?"

"If I were tall and built like you? In a heartbeat. I hate to sound corny, but you do, in fact, look like a Greek goddess."

Athen anxiously studied her reflection in the dressing-room mirror. The dress was beautiful, she admitted. The softest shade of red wine velvet, it had wide shoulder

straps and just skimmed her body all the way to the floor.
Melina's garnets *would* be spectacular. Athen looked back
at Meg, still undecided.

"I'm not used to being this dressed up."

"Look, this will be a very fancy party. Hughes has
invited everyone he knows to this bash to celebrate the
kickoff of his newest venture. People from the entertain-
ment world, businesspeople, politicians from every state,"
Meg reminded her. "Everyone will be dressed up. You
want to look spectacular, and in that dress you do."

"Which dress have you decided on?" Athen asked her.

"I think the cream lace over satin number."

"Go put it on and let me see." Athen shoved Meg
through the dressing-room door.

Athen reached behind her to pull the zipper down
and caught her reflection in the mirror, then turned and
looked at herself from all directions. The dress was more
beguiling than overtly sexy, she decided. Maybe she
should throw caution to the wind and go for it.

"What the hell." She shrugged and hung the dress on
its padded hanger.

When the saleswoman peeked back into the dressing
room, Athen handed her the dress, and said, "I'll take it."

"FOR PITY'S SAKE, ATHEN, GET that finger out of your mouth
and stop biting your nails. You'll ruin your manicure." Meg
stretched to fasten the wide gold strand of garnets around
Athen's neck.

"I'm nervous."

"Get over it." Meg popped earrings into her own
lobes and checked the mirror to make sure they were
straight. "Maybe I shouldn't wear these, they always turn
around. What do you think?"

"I like the pearls better." Athen handed Meg the box holding the pearl earrings.

"You're right." Meg slipped the gold earrings out and replaced them. "They look better with my hair back. Will you please get that glum look off your face?"

"What if he ignores me?" Athen tapped her fingers on the dresser top.

"How could he ignore you?" Meg shook her head, exasperated. "You look spectacular. If I could look like you for just one week of my life, I'd die a happy woman. Now come on. If we leave now, we can make an entrance."

"Oh, God, Meg." Athen rolled her eyes to the ceiling and Meg laughed.

"Leave the dress alone," Meg commanded as she pushed Athen toward the step. "That dress is precisely the reason God invented cleavage. Now, put on your wrap and walk your little butt downstairs. The car will be here any second. You just sit back and compose yourself. I have a feeling this will be a night to remember."

THE CHAPMAN MANSION WAS DECKED from top to bottom for the holidays. White Christmas lights illuminated every tree lining the drive and defined each window and doorway of the immense house. The illusion was, Meg noted dryly, of a crystal palace, plucked from the pages of a children's fairy tale and dropped into the upper regions of northern New Jersey.

After their driver assisted them from the vehicle, Meg snagged Athen's elbow and steered her to the front door.

"Smile pretty," Meg ordered, "and be prepared to have a wonderful time."

The entrance hall, festooned with trees trimmed in burgundy velvet and gold lamé, was mobbed with partygoers who, like Meg and Athen, had just arrived and were awed by the grandeur of the holiday decorations. Thick green garlands, draped with huge bunches of dried hydrangea and gold mesh ribbon, wound lavishly up the wide staircase. Gold lights wound through the garlands and burgundy ribbons festooned the chandeliers. The effect was stunning.

The throng of guests drifted in the direction of the music beckoning from the ballroom. Uniformed waiters offered delectable goodies from silver trays and served champagne in pretty flutes. Couples took to the dance floor and swayed to the music played by a band from New York generally reserved for society bashes. Athen and Meg were looking for their host and hostess just as Lydia came up behind them and placed a bejeweled hand on each of their shoulders.

"How lovely you both look. We're so glad you could join us." Lydia wore a green satin gown, chosen, no doubt, to set off the incredible emeralds at her neck and her ears. "Hughes, darling, look who's here."

"Ah, ladies, how delightful to see you." He kissed them each on the cheek. Turning to the good-looking blond-haired man beside him, he said, "Jeff, have you met Athena Moran, our mayor? And Meg Moran, the leading lady of our new cable network. Ladies, Senator Thompson . . ."

"It's Jeff Thompson. Mrs. Moran, I've certainly heard about you. Threw a curve or two at Dan Rossi, I hear." He chuckled and turned to Meg. "And, of course, I recognize you, Ms. Moran. I haven't missed a broadcast since you went on the air a few weeks ago. I was just telling Hughes and Lydia, you're a delight to watch. You're the right balance of intelligence and humor and beauty. That's an irresistible combination in my book. Hughes was a genius to hire you, as I just finished telling him."

"Why, thank you, Senator." Meg was actually blushing for the first time Athen could ever recall.

"Jeff," he reminded her, signaling for a black-tied waiter. "Champagne, ladies?"

Meg's eyes sparkled as the well-known bachelor senator proposed a toast to the success of the Chapman Cable Network. Athen took a step or two backward, trying to ease out of the picture while at the same time scanning the room for Quentin.

"Athen Moran?" A tall, lanky man with light brown hair touched her elbow.

"Yes?"

"Christopher Moore. The state attorney general's office? We met a few months back at the *New Jersey Today* conference."

"Oh, yes, of course. How are you?" She smiled, having no recollection of ever having seen his face before.

"Fine. Fine." His Adam's apple bobbed up and down along with his head. "I must say you look absolutely stunning this evening."

"My thoughts exactly." Quentin appeared out of nowhere and offered her another glass of champagne.

"Thank you both for the compliments." She shook her head to decline the drink.

The band began to plan a soft, slow ballad, and Athen watched as couple after couple headed for the dance floor. Quentin looked about to speak, but Christopher Moore beat him to it.

"Dance, Athen?" Before she could respond, Christopher steered her to the center of the room. "Excuse us, Quentin," he said over his shoulder.

Christopher was an accomplished dancer, and Athen tried her best to keep up with him. The song ended and another began and then yet another. She begged off the fourth, having long since run out of small talk.

"How about a cool drink?" Christopher suggested.

"A club soda or something along those lines would be fine," she told him, surreptitiously scanning the room for Meg and the senator, for Quentin, for anyone else she knew, but they were nowhere to be seen.

Christopher returned bearing a crystal goblet filled with shaved ice and wafer-thin slices of lime.

"Pellegrino okay?" He handed her the glass.

"Just right. Thanks." She drank thirstily.

"Would you like to make a stop at the buffet?" he asked, obviously charmed by her company. "Everything looks delicious."

"In a bit." She suddenly felt closed in by the crowd. "I think I'd like to wander and ogle the decorations."

"Great idea. This house is really something, isn't it? Let's see what's in here." He led the way through a wooden door with an arched top. A huge mantel dominated the room, and a fire burned brightly. They stopped to chat with several small groups gathered around it. Christopher seemed to know just about everyone there.

Moments later, they resumed their tour. Strolling into the dining room, he whispered, "I see Dr. Logan is here with his latest wife. Let's see, is she number five or number six? I've lost count."

"Seriously?" Athen's eyes widened. "Five or six *wives*?"

"That I know of, anyway. There, the couple right there in front of the punch bowl."

"You mean the thin man with the white mustache . . . ?"

". . . and the bad toupé, yes. You're too polite to say it."

"His *latest wife*, you said?" Athen tried not to stare.

Dr. Logan, short, tanned, and clearly well into his sixties, was overshadowed by the tall, shapely bleached blonde hanging adoringly on his arm. She wore shiny red stiletto heels and a red and silver beaded dress that barely covered her on either end, the skirt as short as hot pants and the top as revealing as a bikini. *And Meg thought I had cleavage*, Athen mused.

"This one is Mindy, if I'm not mistaken. The others, in no particular order, were, let's see, Candy, Lisa, Cherie, Samantha, and Tiffany. That's six. And they all looked exactly the same. As soon as they hit thirty, he dumps them and finds another look-alike."

"That's crazy."

"But true. What do you think, this one has maybe, what, six more years?"

"I don't know. She seems awfully young." She frowned as a vision of Dan Rossi with the very young Mary Jo Dolan flashed suddenly before her eyes.

Christopher's eyebrows wiggled up and down. "Just think of all the alimony. But then again, he can afford it. He has a lively practice and inherited a bundle from an uncle. Let's take a peek at the room across the hall."

They followed several other guests who also could not resist taking a tour of the Christmas wonderland. Athen paused momentarily to permit another couple to exit the room and Christopher grabbed her arm playfully.

"Why, Athen, you've stopped right under the mistletoe." He grinned meaningfully.

Good lord, was he going to kiss her?

"Ah, Athen, there you are. I believe this is our dance." Quentin's hand slid onto the small of her back. "Excuse us, Chris."

"Why did you do that? I was having a good time," she protested as he led her by the hand through the entrance hall to the ballroom.

Ignoring her question, he took her in his arms and hummed along pleasantly with the band before asking, "Would you have let him?"

"Would I have let who what?"

"Would you have let Moore kiss you?" His breath was warm against her ear and neck.

"How do you know he was going to kiss me?"

"It was written all over his face," Quentin said. "Not that I blame him, of course. However, dragging you from one room to the next, from the dining room to the library, to the drawing room, looking for the mistletoe . . . well, I thought that was a bit obvious."

"He wasn't dragging me," she protested, then laughed. "Quentin Forbes, you were following us."

"Every step of the way," he admitted.

"Why?"

"You think I'd let you disappear into the night with a womanizer like Christopher Moore? Especially after Brenda had the florist tack mistletoe up here and there?"

The music stopped and several of the dancers in the crowd applauded enthusiastically.

"And what if I had, Quentin? I haven't seen you beating much of a path to my door lately. As a matter of fact, every time I see you, you take great pains to run in the opposite direction. Don't deny it, you've been doing it for months."

"I don't deny it," he said, embracing her as the music began again. "Have I told you how beautiful you are tonight?"

"Yes." She was beginning to steam and wanted no

more of his flattery. "Quentin, I have had enough of this. I don't understand you. First you're my friend, then you turn on me and make my life just one long run through Hades. Then you like me again and you take me out and we get along splendidly. I didn't imagine that, did I? I mean, I thought we were . . ."

"Splendidly is exactly right," he readily agreed. "You didn't imagine anything."

"Then the next thing I know, you take off like a bat out of hell every time I get within five feet of you."

"Ten feet," he muttered. "I tried to keep it to about ten feet. And you left out the part where you wouldn't speak to me, remember? You were pissed off because I . . ."

"I remember exactly why I was pissed off, and I apologized to you. I thought you'd accepted my apology."

"I did."

"But you've still ignored me for the past few months."

"I was cordial when we ran into each other," he protested.

She'd grown weary of his playful quips. "I never figured you as one to play games, but I feel you've been playing one with me."

He was silent, holding her close and slowly rubbing her cheek with his. When the song ended he took her by the hand and led her to the small morning room off the kitchen. He turned on a light and bent down to stoke the fire before placing another log on it.

She leaned back against the table in the middle of the room, her arms folded across her chest. He turned to her, walked slowly to where she stood, and ran his hands slowly up and down her arms, staring deeply into her eyes. He kissed her mouth and her chin, her cheeks, her neck, and her shoulder before moving back to her mouth again.

"Stop it." She wanted an answer, even while her knees buckled and her heart pounded and she wanted him to keep on kissing her. "I want an answer."

"I thought things would be easier if we put our relationship on hold for a while."

"Easier for whom?"

"Both of us. Okay, yes, easier for me, mostly. Look, when I did that interview with Rossi, even though I wanted to put his crooked little face through the wall, I had to be objective." He paused and sat next to her on the table, taking her hand. "When the interview ran, you were so hurt—not because Rossi said unflattering things about you, but because *I* wrote the story. You thought I cared about you—and I did, very much—but that I hurt you anyway for the sake of a story."

"Quentin, I told you, I understood. At least, after I thought it through I did. It's all right. I thought we'd put this behind us."

"It's never going to be behind us, not as long as I remain on that beat—it's going to happen again and again."

"If it's any consolation, it didn't hurt so much after the first time."

"The article I did on Wolmar, when he called you an inexperienced embarrassment to the city . . ."

"I had to consider the source. They weren't your words, they were his. Anyway, I am inexperienced, though if I've embarrassed anyone from time to time, it's mostly been me."

"And the one where I quoted Rossi as saying that the city will be lucky if it doesn't go into bankruptcy between now and next November?"

"Rolled right off my back," she said with a shrug.

"How 'bout the one where Rossi . . ."

"Quentin, this is silly. Yes, I lost my head after that first article, but since then, I've come to understand that it's your job and that what you think and what you report are not necessarily the same thing. I thought I made that clear to you. At least I tried to."

"I figured once Rossi wins the primary, he'll forget you're alive. So I thought if I backed off for a few months, it would be easier for both of us. Then maybe we could pick up where we left off."

"Did it help? Backing off?"

"God, no." He ran his fingers through his hair. "It was a pretty stupid idea, if I do say so myself. I was so busy looking at you, I missed half of what you said at every press conference. Lucky for the *Herald*, we have another reporter assigned to cover the city."

"I noticed that. What's up with that?"

"I asked Hughes to bring on someone else for that desk. Look, I had to make a choice. If you and I kept seeing each other, as long as you were in office and I was working for the paper, there was going to be a conflict. I tried to convince myself that I could be objective, but, well, you saw how that worked out."

"That was my fault, not yours."

"It doesn't really matter who was at fault. The point is that my reporting on the city created conflict between us. But if I quit back then, I'd have been letting Hughes down. With Brenda leaving the paper to work at CCN, I didn't feel I could walk out on him at the same time."

"If you felt that strongly, why didn't you ask Brenda to assign you to another desk?"

"Every desk was already covered. I couldn't bump someone else out of their job just because I wanted it."

"So what you're saying is, it was easier to dump me."

"I did not dump you," he protested. "I merely put you on hold."

"Call it what you like. It still hurt." She crossed her arms over her chest. "And I don't see where anything has been resolved. I'm still mayor. You're still working at the paper."

"Not anymore."

She tilted her head to one side, not sure she understood.

"I resigned this morning."

"You . . ."

He nodded.

"But I thought you said you couldn't quit on Hughes . . ."

"Three months ago, I couldn't have done it. Hughes didn't offer me a job at the *Herald* just because there was an opening at City Hall. He wanted to bring me into his family, wanted me to feel part of it since he'd married my mother, and he wanted to offer me a means of making a living while I worked on my book. I owe him, Athen. I couldn't just walk out on him when he had no one there to pick up the slack."

"But Brenda's still at CCN. That hasn't changed."

"Hughes and I had a very long and very honest chat a few weeks ago. The end result was that he offered to hire someone else to cover the city. The agreement was that I'd stay until the new reporter had her feet on the ground, then I could leave if I still wanted to. We already had someone on staff who'd been going to the press conferences with me. She's a natural. She'll do a great job."

"Wait a minute, you gave up your job . . . ?"

He nodded.

"That's huge, Quentin."

"It is."

"I don't understand why you didn't bother to have this conversation with me before."

"What would you have said if I had?"

"I've already said it. I understood the position you were in. If you have to write something negative, then write it. If I deserve to be criticized, say so. If not, I'll have to defend myself."

"The part you don't understand is that I could not continue to fall in love you while at the same time, on any given day, something I would have to print would hurt you."

"I just said, I was all right with . . ." She arched her eyebrows. "Were you? Falling in love with me?"

"A little bit more every day since I met you." He leaned closer until they were forehead to forehead.

"Want to try again?"

"I think that's supposed to be my line." He kissed her nose and nibbled on her bottom lip.

"That was your line last time." She drew him closer, reaching up to kiss him, feeling their bodies mold together through the soft velvet of her gown.

"Quentin." The door swung open and Brenda rushed in. "Quentin . . ."

He reluctantly disengaged his lips and looked over his shoulder at his stepsister.

"I just got a call from downtown. There's a fire."

"Where?" Athen asked.

"Fourth Street," Brenda said meaningfully.

"Fourth Street . . . ?" Athen repeated, then understanding fully what Brenda was telling them, cried, "Oh, my God, no . . ."

"Come on, Athen." Quentin grabbed her hand and led her from the room. "Brenda, see if you can find Athen's wrap and meet me at the front door. I'll get a car and drive around."

❦ 27 ❦

The orange flames that filled the sky above Woodside Heights were visible from the end of the Chapmans' drive. Quentin took the winding curves on two wheels, yet neither Brenda nor Athen appeared to notice.

Fourth Street was blocked off at Schuyler Avenue and a uniformed police officer directed them to turn left, away from the fire. Athen rolled down her window and called to him.

"Officer, it's Mayor Moran. I need to get through."

"Oh, sorry." He walked to the passenger side of the car. "I didn't see you."

"How bad is it?" she asked anxiously.

"About as bad as anything I've ever seen." He leaned into the car slightly. "They got trucks up there from every company in the city and every surrounding town, but it's not doing much good."

"How close can we get?" Quentin asked impatiently.

"The city's fire marshal doesn't want any cars up there, on account of all the pumpers. Plus, there's the danger of the buildings collapsing, so he doesn't want anyone to go through. But you could probably drive a block or two more, then park and walk as far as they'll let you."

Quentin was off in a shot, turning briskly at the next corner and pulling into the last empty spot closest to the blockade.

"How fast can you move on those shoes?" He gesturing toward Athen's feet as he put the car in park.

Ignoring him, she opened the door and ran in the direction of the three houses that were engulfed in flame. The fire marshal met her a block from the conflagration and refused to let her go any farther.

"Any one of those walls could go at any moment, Athen. I can't let you get any closer. I'm worried enough about the men, without having to worry about you, too," he said. "We're trying our damnedest to keep it from spreading to the other side of the street, but it's touch and go. We've already evacuated two blocks in every direction and sent folks to their relatives or to their churches to wait it out."

Quentin and Brenda caught up with her moments later. They stood in silence, watching the conflagration, until Athen finally exploded.

Athen spit the words from between clenched teeth. "He will not get away with this. That son of a bitch."

"You don't think that Dan Rossi . . ." Quentin began, but she cut him off.

"Oh, yes, I do think. And I will not let him get away with this."

"Athen, before you start making accusations . . ."

"Convince me that somehow this is a coincidence." She turned wild eyes upon him.

Quentin watched the fire burn out of control, watched the façade of the first house crumble, sending red-hot bricks blazing in a shower to the street below. The heat and smoke surrounded them even at this distance and they were forced to pull back to the end of the block.

They watched in helpless disbelief as the second,

then the third house fell, shaking the ground beneath their feet and filling the night with smoke and thunder.

Quentin shook his head. "You're right. This can't be a coincidence."

Frozen to one spot, they stayed until there was nothing left to burn but the rubble. Then, stunned, Athen followed Quentin back to the car. Brenda caught up with the photographer from the *Woodside Herald* and was interviewing the city's fire marshal as they passed. She waved to them, indicating that she'd get a ride home.

"I can't believe this happened," Athen repeated over and over on the drive to her house. "I never would have believed that even Dan Rossi would stoop this low."

Quentin parked behind Athen's car in the driveway and together they went inside. Even Hannah's exuberant welcome could not break through Athen's daze. She went directly to the kitchen and opened the back door for the dog without saying a word. She stood at the sink, staring out into the dark, then suddenly grabbed a glass from the counter, turned, and pitched it against the opposite wall. Glass flew across the room and rained down upon the floor. When she reached for another glass, Quentin grabbed her arm.

"I understand the sentiment, but it isn't going to help."

"How could he do this to Ms. Evelyn? To all the people who have worked so hard?"

"You should know by now that Rossi doesn't have a conscience, and isn't going to be put off by you or anyone else from getting what he wants. And he wants his job back."

"He knows the job is his for the asking. He knows I have no intention of running again. He didn't have to set those houses on fire to make his point." Athen shook

her head. "Uh-uh. This is about more than just Dan
Rossi wanting his job back. This is about those properties. Why does he want to keep them in the city's hands
so badly?"

"Good question." Quentin paused thoughtfully for a
very long moment. "It's the question the *Herald* should be
asking. Just what is it that Dan wants so badly that he'd
risk setting an entire neighborhood on fire to get it?"

SOMETIME AROUND SIX THE NEXT morning, Athen fell asleep
on the living room sofa. Quentin sat at the kitchen table,
replaying the recording of his interview with Dan Rossi,
hoping to find something that would lead to an answer.
A weary Meg, her lovely cream satin and lace gown
wrinkled and limp, arrived home around eight thirty,
accompanied by the senator. Quentin went into the hall
when he heard them come in, and placed a finger to his
lips when Meg poked her head into the living room. Meg
nodded and tiptoed into the kitchen.

Athen roused slowly from her sleep shortly thereafter.
She sat up and sniffed.

"I smell coffee."

"In here," Meg said from the kitchen doorway.

"What time is it?" Athen stifled a yawn.

"A little before nine." Quentin came into the room
carrying a mug. "Cream, half a sweetener." He handed her
the mug.

"It wasn't a dream, was it?"

"No, sweetheart," he replied. "It wasn't a dream."

She sighed deeply and leaned back against the sofa,
unconsciously combing her hair with her fingers.

"As much as it kills me to say this, I guess that's it.
He's won."

"Only if you let him." Quentin's jacket, which earlier he'd removed and draped over her, slid off her shoulders. He reached over and pulled it up to cover her.

"What's that supposed to mean? Like there's something I can do to stop him?" She laughed bitterly. "No one can stop him. He's proven his point."

"All he's proven is that he knows where to go to find someone who'll torch a building for him." Quentin sat next to her.

"What would you call what happened last night?"

"A setback. One you could use to your advantage."

"Setback? The shelter went up in smoke." Athen reminded him.

"Only those buildings went up in smoke."

"Those buildings were the shelter," she pointed out.

"Then look for another site."

"There isn't another site," she snapped.

"Then find a way to use the one you have."

"You aren't making any sense."

"Athen, for starters, there are grants you can apply for from the government for this type of thing. All you need to do is track them down and apply."

Meg came into the room, her shoes long discarded and her hair hanging in disarray. "I'm so sorry, Athen. I know what this meant to you."

"It's not me I'm concerned about. It's all the people who needed that space to live in. Where will they go this winter? Riley told me on Thursday that the renovations would have been completed by the middle of January, the first of February at the very latest. Now there's nothing."

"Come on in the kitchen." Meg put an arm around her shoulders.

Athen glanced at Meg's bare feet. "I broke a glass. I need to get the broom and get the glass off the floor so that you don't step in it."

"Done," Quentin told her. "Hannah wanted in and I didn't want her to get glass in her paws."

"Thank you. I don't usually lose my temper like that."

"Understandable."

They followed the aroma of freshly brewed coffee. Athen was surprised to find Jeff Thompson at the kitchen table, his tie hanging from his open collar, the first few studs of his tuxedo shirt undone.

"My condolences, Athen." He pulled a chair out for her. "Meg's been filling me in on recent history with those properties. You will, of course, request a full investigation."

"Immediately." She reached for the fresh cup of coffee Meg offered. "I want the county fire marshal and the state fire marshal in on this now."

"How far up does Rossi's influence stretch?" Meg asked.

"I guess we'll find out soon enough, but I've heard he has friends in very high places."

Quentin stirred cream into his cup thoughtfully. "Jeff, isn't there money available at the federal level for projects of this sort?"

"You mean like community development grants, inner-city renovations, that sort of thing?"

Quentin nodded.

"There are some programs, sure," Jeff replied. "I'm not certain of the requirements, but I have a friend with the agency. I can give him a call first thing tomorrow morning, if you'd like."

"Would you do that?" Meg asked.

"Would it put you forever in my debt?"

"Absolutely."

"Consider it done," the senator assured her.

"That would be wonderful, Jeff." Athen managed a smile. "I'd really appreciate any help you could give me."

"Well, I have to admit that knowing the background of the situation, then listening to Rossi's sorrowful little dissertation last night about what a shame it all was . . ." Meg began.

"What you talking about?" Athen's head shot up sharply. "Where did you see Dan?"

"He was at the scene when we arrived," Meg told her.

"I didn't see him. Where were you?"

"I was on the City Hall side of the block," Meg replied. "Where were you?"

"We came down Schuyler." Athen plunked her cup down loudly onto the tabletop. "I can't believe he had the nerve to show up there."

"Complete with crocodile tears and words of the most heartfelt condolences for the UCC." Meg leaned back in her chair. "I even got him on tape."

"What?!" Athen fairly shrieked.

"I called the station from Jeff's car," Meg explained. "I requested a camera crew ASAP. They were there on the corner, setting up, by the time I arrived. I had no idea that Rossi was going to come along." She peered over her shoulder at the clock on the wall. "They'll probably run the tape around nine. We can catch his little performance in the living room in about five minutes. Come on, let's tune in so that we don't miss a minute of it."

"I can barely wait." Athen bit her bottom lip, her anger rising again. "That son of a bitch."

Quentin placed his empty cup on the counter. As he passed the refrigerator door, he paused, then leaned closer to inspect something held by a magnet.

"Athen," he asked, a look of puzzlement on his face, "what is this?"

"What? Oh, that." She waved a hand to dismiss its immediate importance. "Meg found that picture in the *Herald* archives. We were looking to see what had appeared in the paper the day my father had his stroke. I was trying to find out who the man standing next to Dan was but couldn't. It's a long story, Quentin."

She got up from the table, coffee in hand, to move into the living room.

"Paul Schraeder." Quentin was still focused on the photograph.

"What did you say?" She paused in the doorway.

"It's Paul Schraeder."

"This man? The man next to Dan?" She pointed at the picture.

Quentin nodded.

"You know him?" she asked in disbelief.

"He was corporate counsel for Rest America about five years ago."

"Rest America? What's that?" Athen was suddenly all ears.

"It's a company that owns several hotel chains, some franchise restaurants, that sort of thing," he explained.

"How do you know all this? How do you know him?"

"Rest America is owned by Bradford International."

"Your mother's company," she stated flatly.

"May I borrow this?" Quentin held the picture up and she nodded.

"What would he be doing with Dan Rossi?" she wondered aloud.

"That's a very good question." He folded the paper and tucked it into his pocket. "Now, let's go see if we can catch Dan's little performance on the morning news."

MEG AND QUENTIN BOTH SPENT most of Sunday interviewing the parties central to the issue. Ms. Evelyn, the Reverend Davison, Riley Fallon, and Edward Snipe, who as the head cook at the nearby UCC soup kitchen, spoke of the somber demeanor of those who had filed in for breakfast that morning. Face after face, each stunned by the unexpected turn of events, was photographed to appear either live on Meg's evening broadcast or in print in the next day's *Herald*.

Athen spent the afternoon in her office meeting with Ms. Evelyn and several others to commiserate. She tried unsuccessfully on several occasions to reach the state fire marshal. She did manage to get through to the county marshal, Ted Boyd, but despite assurances that a thorough investigation was being conducted, she held little hope that any conclusive evidence would be forthcoming after Ms. Evelyn pointed out that Boyd was a longtime supporter of Dan Rossi.

She was still trying to find a way around that, when Quentin called from his cell shortly before five to tell her he'd swing by her house around six thirty to pick her up. Understanding how busy they'd all been that day, Lydia had had dinner prepared for everyone. Athen arrived home shortly before Quentin did, and he waited patiently while she roused Callie, who, suffering from sleep deprivation following Carolann's slumber party the night before, had crashed on the sofa.

Although still festively bedecked, the Chapman house seemed somehow more somber, the events of the past eighteen hours overshadowing the holiday spirit of the previous night. Dinner was postponed in order that they might watch the seven o'clock rebroadcast of Meg's coverage of the fire.

"This is Meg Moran for Chapman Cable News." Meg appeared on the larger-than-life screen in the Chapmans' den, dressed in her lace gown. "I'm reporting from Woodside Heights at the scene of one of the worst fires in this northern New Jersey city's history. The buildings burning behind me had only recently been leased to the United Council of Churches, a grassroots organization that was formed to help the unemployed and homeless of Woodside Heights. I'm here with former mayor, Dante Rossi. Mr. Rossi, it's my understanding that you have been an outspoken opponent of this project since its inception."

"Now don't you think for one minute that this"—he waved his hand behind them toward the burning buildings—"gives me any pleasure. It saddens me more than I can tell you to see a portion of this city I've loved and served for twenty years go up in flames." He dabbed at his tear-filled eyes, pausing for effect. "As far as the shelter was concerned, that issue had been decided by a majority of the City Council. But I would like to remind you, Miss Moran, of two things. One, I was in opposition to using these old properties to shelter any of our citizens because I feared exactly what you see here tonight. I feared a loss of life, and God knows how many lives we would have lost had anyone been in these buildings when the fire broke out. And two, I have felt all along that taken in its entirety, the whole area could—make that *should*—be used to generate badly needed income for the city. I still believe that. Now, why don't you go on home," he said, his eyes narrowed to shining little beads and focused on Meg, "and ask that sister-in-law of yours what she intends to do now that she has several acres of empty ground on her hands."

"Mr. Rossi refers to the fact that Athena Moran, my

late brother's widow, is currently the mayor of Woodside Heights." Meg remained cool and professional, not missing a beat in spite of her certain embarrassment.

"Ouch!" Brenda, seated on the edge of the sofa, winced.

"Ouch indeed." Meg nodded grimly.

"You handled it very well, dear." Lydia patted her arm.

"That won't happen again, I assure you, Mr. Chapman," Meg told him apologetically. "Rossi was there when I arrived and there wasn't anyone else to do the interview. I didn't want us to lose the opportunity. And I did send someone else to interview Athen."

"You go with what you've got," he told her. "No apologies necessary."

"Hey, there's Mom." Callie brightened as Athen appeared on the screen.

". . . and of course, everyone's still in shock," Athen was telling Jennifer Gables, who'd been sent by Meg to cover this part of the story. "I'm grateful that no residents were injured, and I commend the firemen who did such an outstanding job in alerting the residents nearby and getting everyone to safety. I've had a report of several firemen who were overcome by smoke, but other than that, I'd say we were extremely fortunate."

"Is arson a possibility?" Jennifer stepped closer to Athen as the camera zoomed in.

Of course it's arson, you nitwit, Athen had wanted to scream. Cautioned, however, about what she said publicly, she appeared to pause thoughtfully before responding. "I think it's a bit premature to speculate. We'll have to wait to see what the fire marshal finds."

"Do you have any plans now for the use of that area?" Jennifer asked.

"The ashes are still smoldering, Ms. Gables." Athen

shrugged wearily. "No one's had time to consider where to go from here. We will, over time, look at several options."

"Good job, Thena." Meg leaned over and patted her on the back.

"You have no idea how hard it was for me not to have grabbed that microphone and spoken my mind," Athen said.

"Well, just keep biting your tongue," Brenda pointed out. "And, Meg, I'd suggest that you continue to have Jennifer cover this from here on out. I understand that you were on the scene, and I admire how well you handled things under the circumstances. But it should not happen again. We must avoid the appearance of a conflict of interest through this. And I'm thinking you might want to keep someone else on the paper's City Hall beat, Dad."

"I see the news hasn't caught up with you yet," Quentin told her. "I've already passed that torch. Which is just as well, since I'll be leaving for St. Louis tomorrow."

"What for, dear?" Lydia asked, noting Rose Ellen's signal that dinner was ready to be served.

"I thought I'd pay a visit to the Bradford home office and see what was going on out there."

"Well, the board meeting isn't until the end of January, dear." Lydia motioned everyone toward the dining room.

"I know, Mom." Quentin took her arm. "But I thought I'd check on a few things before the meeting, so I could be better prepared this year."

"Really, Quentin?" Lydia beamed as he first seated her, then took his place next to Athen at the table. "You've no idea how pleased I am that you're finally taking an interest."

"Oh, I'm certainly interested."

"Well, dear, you know that this being the holiday season, there won't be a full staff in the office next week.

I understand that a lot of the employees save some of their vacation days to take off this time of the year."

"That's all right." He smiled. "I think I'd just as soon poke around a little on my own."

"Well, then, I'll call Stafford's office in the morning and make sure that he and his staff give you full access to everything." Looking very pleased, Lydia took a sip of wine.

"Don't bother, Mom. I don't want anyone to make a fuss. I'll just pop in when I get there and see what I can find. . . ."

"JEFF SAID THAT YOU SHOULD form an agency within the city to deal with HUD," Meg told Athen on Tuesday evening as she reheated the dinner she had missed earlier. "He spoke to a friend of his who told him that if you had some sort of redevelopment authority, things would move more quickly."

"Hmmmm." Athen thought it over. "I'll talk to Riley and George about it in the morning and I'll ask one of them to propose it to Council. Jim and Harlan will vote against it, so I'll have to be the deciding vote, but we can get that through." She rubbed the space between her eyes. "We'll need someone really strong to head this up. I'll see if Ms. Evelyn would be interested. If not she, then perhaps the Reverend Davison."

"She'd be perfect, but he's a great backup if you need one," Meg agreed. "Jeff said you could expect a call from someone at HUD this week."

The timer on the microwave alerted Meg that her leftovers were ready. She opened the door and removed her dinner. "Isn't Jeff an ace?"

"An ace," Athen agreed.

"Speaking of aces, what's up with Quentin?"

"He called from St. Louis right before you came in." Athen plunked down in a chair and fiddled with the small centerpiece Callie had made for the kitchen table. Dried holly berries fell and ran the length of the table, small red balls that bounced onto the floor. Had she read somewhere that holly berries were poisonous? She bent to retrieve them before Hannah did.

"So what did he say?" Meg sat opposite her.

"Stafford Banks, who heads Bradford International, is in London with his family until the second week of January. As Lydia suspected, there's only a skeleton crew in St. Louis this week, which is certainly to Quentin's advantage. He can pull any records he wants without anyone asking too many questions."

"How lucky can you get? But just think, if you'd cleaned off the refrigerator door, as I'd been harping at you to do, we'd never have a lead on this."

"We don't know that we have a lead on anything," Athen reminded her. "But Quentin seems to think that somehow this Paul Schraeder may be a player in whatever it is that Rossi planned to do on Fourth Street."

"What do you think?" Meg twirled strands of spaghetti around her fork.

"I think it's terribly curious that someone in Schraeder's position would show up at a fund-raiser for a politician in a small New Jersey city. If that is the photograph my father was looking at that morning, Dad must have known or suspected who Schraeder was and why he was there. And whatever it was, it sent his blood pressure into overdrive."

"So it must have been something really serious." Meg put down her fork. "Considering that your father suffered a catastrophic stroke."

Athen nodded. "Serious? I'm thinking illegal, and I'm willing to bet that my father knew exactly what Dan was up to . . ."

❧ 28 ❧

I guess you're wondering what, if anything, I learned while I was in St. Louis." Quentin tucked his cell under his chin as he made his way to the baggage carousel.

"You're back!" Athen smiled. She'd missed Quentin while he was away, and now that he was back, she was dying to hear what he'd found out.

"I'm just leaving the airport," he told her. "How about I meet you at your house in about an hour? I don't want to have this discussion while you're on a City Hall line. You just never know if someone else might be listening."

"Good point. I'll be home by four."

"I'll see you then." He paused. "I missed you."

"What a coincidence," she replied. "I missed you, too."

Athen tucked the day's mail into her briefcase and swung her bag over her shoulder. She stepped out of her office and stopped at Veronica's desk.

"I'm leaving a little early today," Athen told her.

"Sure, Mrs. M." Veronica nodded, her up-do bobbing in time with the music from her iPod. "Anything you need me to do while you're gone?"

"Just the usual. Call my cell if anything happens that you think I need to know about, or if anyone calls that you think I need to speak with."

"Will do." Veronica held up the memo Athen had given her earlier. "I meant to ask you if you wanted me to include this part that you have scribbled in the margin, about Ms. Evelyn?"

Athen looked over Veronica's shoulder to the notes she'd made about the proposed redevelopment authority. "Let's hold up on that part right now."

"You got it." Veronica returned to typing.

"I'M GLAD YOU'RE BACK," ATHEN opened the door to let Quentin in.

"I'm glad to be back." He closed the front door with his foot, and put his arms around her. "First things first."

He drew her to him and kissed her, his arms encircling her and holding her close. "Mmmm," he murmured. "You feel good."

"So do you." She leaned back to look into his eyes. "I'm glad you're here."

"So am I." He kissed her again, then with an arm over her shoulder led her into the living room. "But I know you have questions."

"Do you have answers?" She sat on the sofa and pulled him down with her.

"I believe I do." He took off his jacket and placed it on the back of the sofa. "Let's start with the fact that Paul Schraeder is now the CEO of Clover Inns."

"The motel chain?"

Quentin nodded. "Rumor has it that he's set his sights on downtown Woodside Heights for a convention center and luxury hotel."

"A luxury hotel?" She almost choked on her words. "In downtown Woodside Heights? Who would want to stay in a hotel in the midst of all that urban blight?"

"Apparently, the plan is to dispose of the blight and start with a blank slate. Once the hotel chain has a foothold in Woodside Heights, Schraeder would offer to purchase the other homes in the immediate area."

"But those homes aren't worth very much, so I doubt the neighbors would sell," she told him. "They wouldn't get enough for their houses to be able to afford to go anywhere else."

"Ah, but that's where having a friend in local government comes in handy. Someone who could put pressure on the residents to move. There are all sorts of methods."

"What methods?" Athen frowned. "Either you can afford to move or you can't."

"Well, for instance, two years ago in Georgia, Clover Inns was building a hotel and wanted to buy up a block on the opposite side of the street for a park. The residents didn't want to sell. So Clover Inns got the local pols to pass an ordinance that extended the construction hours in the evening and permitted the work to begin earlier in the morning. After months of listening to the racket well into the night and again at the break of dawn the next day, one by one, the residents gave up their property to Clover Inns."

"How could they get the city to do that?"

"Crossing the appropriate palms with the appropriate amount of silver usually works."

"How did you find out about all this?"

"I called Pat Conte, Schraeder's successor at Rest America," he explained, "and asked him what was new, what was on the drawing board, that sort of thing. He said we're getting some stiff competition from Clover Inns now that Schraeder is there. Word has it that Schraeder has plans to get a strong foothold in the East, to try to es-

tablish his chain beyond their traditional Southern holdings, and that he has some very promising sites outside of
New York City, in northern New Jersey and Connecticut."

"Do tell."

"The location outside Greenwich is in the bag, but
apparently there's a bit of a snafu in the New Jersey site.
However, Schraeder apparently is confident that issue will
be resolved before the middle of next year."

"Assuming that the parcel of land he wants is on
Fourth Street. . . ."

"There's no question in my mind on that point."

"Why would he want to build such a complex in
Woodside Heights?"

"It's actually a good location. It's close enough to get
in and out of New York City in a short amount of time,
and land is comparatively inexpensive. It's not a bad idea,
from a strictly business standpoint."

"So what's the deal with Rossi?"

"I'm thinking that Schraeder offered Rossi cash to
secure the properties for him. Probably paid him off,
so much cash when he agreed to help Schraeder, with
a bigger bundle when Clover Inns took title. It's not
the first time Paul has engaged in underhanded deals.
Conte tells me the reason Schraeder and Rest America
parted company was over some scheme he'd cooked up
that was borderline illegal. Conte found out about it by
accident, but when he confronted Schraeder, Paul told
him that's the way business was done these days. Conte
threatened to go to the board with it, and Schraeder
walked out."

"So Schraeder could have paid Dan to obtain the
properties for the city so that he could in turn sell them to
Clover Inns and pocket a kickback." Athen nodded.

"I'm sure Dan is thinking of it as a 'finder's fee,'" Quentin said dryly.

"This all makes sense. While Dan was mayor, the city confiscated those properties for nonpayment of taxes. Two elderly brothers owned them, as I recall."

"Two elderly brothers who are in an assisted-living facility in Arizona. They are elderly, but they are not senile."

"How do you know that?"

"I checked the tax records, then had Brenda follow up with Social Security to track them down. I flew out to Arizona on Thursday to meet with them. Neither of them had any recollection of having received any notice of sale. They're under the impression that they still own those houses."

"Well, if Dan had the city confiscate those properties three years ago, why didn't he sell them to Schraeder back then?"

"Because the Greenwich deal came through faster than Schraeder had anticipated. I suspect he paid Dan a little bonus to sit on the Fourth Street site until the company had the cash flow to proceed in Woodside Heights."

"I'm not sure I understand how Dan could have had the city take title to the houses."

"Think for a minute. If the owners never received the tax bills—maybe the bills weren't even sent—the taxes weren't paid, and the city swooped in to take them over."

"Wouldn't the city have to post a notice? Like when a property goes to sheriff's sale?"

"With the owners out of state, they wouldn't have seen any notice that the city posted."

"Bastard." Athen growled. "I wish I could nail Dan for taking that money. And if that's how the city obtained those properties, I want to get him for that, too."

"Well, short of a signed confession, there's no way to prove any of this. Schraeder's not likely to admit that he's paid local authorities in exchange for their coopera-tion any more than Dan's going to admit he accepted the bribe or that he cheated the owners out of those houses," Quentin reminded her. "But there's no doubt in my mind that Schraeder promised Dan a bundle to sit on those lots for him. There's no other explanation for Dan's resolve to keep control of them."

"I wonder if my father knew," she murmured. "I won-der if that's why he hit the ceiling when he saw the pic-ture in the paper."

"Athen, what if maybe Schraeder approached Ari first?"

"You mean, he offered my father a bribe . . . ?"

"It's very possible," he continued. "Look, from what I've heard, before he had his stroke, your father was a very influential man. Some would say more influential than Rossi, back then. Schraeder might have made a mistake in judgment, offered to make a deal with your dad, then, when he was slapped down, went to Rossi."

"That would certainly explain Dan's actions after my father had his stroke, and it explains why it was so impor-tant that Dan be able to run again. If he was no longer mayor, he'd be of no use to Schraeder." Athen nodded thoughtfully. "But how much of this matters if we can't prove it? Dan will run again and he'll be elected. He'll get those leases back from the UCC—after all, how useful are those vacant lots to them?"

"Maybe they'll plan to build something there," Quen-tin suggested.

Athen shook her head. "They'll never get the building permits. Dan will be able to block those. No, he'll offer to buy them back, and the city will sell the property to

Clover Inns. Dan will make a tidy sum on the deal, and no one will be the wiser. But, as you said, this is all conjecture. Without any proof, he's going to get away with it."

Athen got up and began to pace, her arms folded over her chest.

"God, the whole thing makes me so damned mad." Her anger continued to rise. "What I wouldn't do to trip him up now."

"How far would you go?" Quentin asked quietly.

"As far as I had to." She leaned over the back of the sofa behind him and draped her arms around his neck and rested her chin on top of his head. "Unfortunately, without Schraeder admitting that he offered the bribe . . ."

". . . which will never happen," he interjected.

"There doesn't seem to be any way to beat him. Dan's sure to win."

"Well, as long as he runs unopposed, he's a sure thing." Quentin reached up to stroke her arm.

"I can't think of anyone who could defeat him," she murmured. "Except maybe Ms. Evelyn, and she's mentioned several times she has no interest in ever running for office. She likes to stay behind the scenes and do her own thing. And so far, she's been pretty damned effective in getting things done. Maybe she'd change her mind if she knew about Schraeder. Diana might have some ideas, though. I'll run it all past her."

"Have you thought about taking him on yourself?"

"Are you nuts?" She laughed out loud. "Me, go head to head with him and his machine?" She shook her head. "I can't beat him."

"I'm not so sure about that."

"I am." She shook her head. "I have no interest in putting myself or my daughter through that."

"So you'll just concede defeat and let him continue to rape and pillage the city?"

"I can't stop him, Quentin. Maybe someone else can, but it isn't going to be me."

"There is no one else who . . ."

"Can we change the subject, please? I don't want to run against him. He'll cut me to shreds. I've had enough. As far as I'm concerned, the matter is closed."

He sighed with apparent defeat. "All right, then. How about we talk about our New Year's Eve plans?"

"Do we have plans for New Year's Eve?"

"Yes, we do," he told her.

"Where are we going?"

"It's going to be a surprise."

"What are we going to do when we get there?"

"That's a surprise, too."

"Really? Will I like it?"

"You'll love it."

"How will I know what to wear, if I don't know where we're going or what we're going to do?" Athen frowned. "How will I know what to take?"

"Pack warm clothes, enough for two days." He reached around and pulled her over the back of the sofa and onto his lap. "I'll pick you up tomorrow afternoon around four."

"Whoa, wait a minute. Two days? Are you forgetting about Callie?"

"Callie has plans of her own."

"Oh, really? And what might they be?"

"While we are . . . at the place where we're going and doing what we're doing, Callie and Tim will be with my mother and Hughes in New York City, where they will see shows and take in the sights and have a wonderful time before they have to go back to school at the end of their holiday break. While they're there, they'll hook up with my sister, Caitlin, and have a ball. Cait is a barrel of fun, when she's not working, which she all too often is. I know I should have asked you first, before I allowed Mom to make her plans, but I really wanted to surprise you with a little vacation. And Meg thought it would be all right. If you don't want her to go, though . . ."

"What, and incur Callie's wrath for making her miss what is sure to be a grand time? It's very nice of your mother to include Callie in the plans." She paused. "Was this your idea or your mother's?"

"A little of both," he admitted. "Mom mentioned she was going to meet up with Cait in the city and asked if she could take Timmy. When I told her what I was planning, we both agreed that Callie might be a fifth wheel if she came along with us. Besides, she'll have more fun with Tim and my mom and Caitlin than she would with us."

"All right. Callie can go with your mother and Tim, and I'll go with you on the condition that there is no more talk of elections or Dan Rossi or me running for anything until we get back from . . . wherever it is that we're going."

"Agreed."

"Great." She grinned. "When do we leave?"

"SO WHEN DO I FIND out where we're going?" Athen snapped on her seat belt.

"When we get there." He grinned and started the engine.

"When will we get there?"

He turned on the radio and searched for a contemporary station. "In about an hour, hour and a half. Just sit back, relax, listen to the music." He backed out of her driveway and, two blocks down, followed the signs for the Garden State Parkway.

"We've got two days to ourselves and a couple of bottles of champagne. The kids are being taken care of, so what's not to love?" He reached over and took one of her hands.

"It sounds very romantic."

"It will be, I promise."

"You told me to pack all warm clothes." She thought of her suitcase packed with heavy woolen sweaters, socks, and a pair of long underwear.

"You're going to need them." He nodded.

"So what's your definition of romantic?"

He pondered the question for a moment. "Having a sense of the moment."

She sat back and thought about that. "Carpe diem, eh?"

Quentin laughed. "More or less."

The conversation was light for the first forty minutes, until Athen announced, "I swore I wasn't going to do this until we were on our way home, but I had a long talk with Diana last night. I told her everything about Paul Schraeder. She said she was going to talk to my dad about it first thing this morning."

"And . . . ?"

"And she called right before you came to pick me up. She said we were right about Schraeder offering my dad a bribe."

"How does she communicate with him if he doesn't speak?"

"She asks him questions and he responds by blinking. You know, one blink for yes, two for no. Once she knew about Schraeder, she knew what to ask. He confirmed that Schraeder approached him and offered him a very large amount of money to help him get his hands on the entire block of Fourth Street. Of course, my dad turned him down. When Dad saw the picture of Schraeder and Rossi in the paper, he figured out what had happened. He went to Dan's office and told Rossi that he was blowing the whistle on him."

"And then your father had the stroke that silenced him."

"I'll bet Dan couldn't believe his luck when he heard that Dad was taken to the hospital." She crossed her arms and stared out the window at the passing scenery without really seeing it. "I can't believe how I let him play me. I really did believe that he and my dad had been close friends. When Dad was in the hospital, Dan came to the house several times, and he was so kind to me and to Callie. Then when John died, he made such a big deal out of John being this big hero . . ."

"John was a hero, Athen," Quentin reminded her. "Dan didn't make that up."

"I know that. But looking back, I can see how Dan used John's death to keep himself in the press, to appear to be the kindly uncle. Just as he used my father's stroke to win votes from my dad's district." She shivered. "It makes me sick to my stomach to know that I fell for it. That I let him use first my father, then John, and later me, all for his own politic ends."

"I thought we weren't going to use the *p* word."

"I know, I know." She blew out an exasperated breath. "I'm feeling guilty because now that I know what a crook Rossi is, I'm pissed at myself for letting him use me to make it possible for him to run again."

"Did you ever figure out why he didn't ask Wolmar or Justis to run instead of you?"

"Sure. He knew that if either of them got into office, they wouldn't be so quick to leave. He knew he could manipulate me in ways he could never manipulate them." She looked across the console. "They know him for the weaselly little rat that he is. I can't believe how naïve I was."

"Don't beat yourself up over it. At least not until after the New Year."

At some point he'd gotten off the parkway, and they were headed south on Route 9.

"We're going to the beach?" She raised her eyebrows.

"To a private little place overlooking the ocean."

"I love the beach!" she exclaimed. Dark thoughts of Dan Rossi and her feelings of guilt at having let him use her faded away when she rolled down the window and breathed in the salt air. "I can smell the ocean."

"That would be the marsh there on your right," he teased.

"How close are we?"

"A few more blocks."

"Did you rent a cottage or something?" she asked.

"Or something." Quentin smiled.

The "or something" was a large, rambling weathered house that overlooked the Atlantic. A stream of smoke drifted from the chimney, and lights burned invitingly inside.

"Quentin, it's breathtaking," she exclaimed as they climbed the steps to the deck overlooking the sea.

"I knew you'd love it." He dropped the overnight bags he'd carried from the car and draped an arm over her shoulder to share the view with her.

The beach was deserted save for a foraging gull whose call was all but lost in the sound of the pounding surf. The air was crisp and cold and smelled of salt and the dunes below the deck.

"It's wonderful. Perfect," she told him. "Thank you for bringing me here. It's been forever since I've been to the beach. I can't think of a better place to ring in the New Year."

"Let's go inside and see what Mrs. Emmons has cooked up for us."

"Mrs. Emmons?" Athen ducked inside the door he held open for her.

"She's the housekeeper," Quentin explained. "I called her from St. Louis and asked her to freshen things up and prepare one of her wonderful dinners for us."

"Wait a minute. Whose place is this?"

"My mom's. Well, hers and Hughes's."

"They have a housekeeper who lives here all year round?" Athen inquired. "By herself?"

"She and her husband live a few blocks inland. She takes care of the house, and her husband takes care of the grounds and the boats, that sort of thing. Ah, there she is." He smiled as a pudgy woman with salt-and-pepper hair and a pleasant round face toddled into the kitchen.

"Hello, Quentin," she greeted him.

"This is my friend, Athena Moran." He made the introduction. "She'll be staying with us for a few days."

"Nice to meet you," the woman told Athen. "I hope you like seafood."

"I do," Athen assured her.

"Good. Dinner will be in about an hour or so. Now, Quentin, if you wouldn't mind." She smiled good-naturedly. "Out of my kitchen so I can work."

"I'll give you the downstairs tour." He took Athen by the hand and led her from the kitchen through a butler's pantry and into a wide front hall.

"This is not exactly my idea of a cottage." Athen looked up at the high ceiling.

"You were the one who used that term, not me. Come this way. There should be a fire and . . . ah, yes. There it is."

The stone fireplace dominated the enormous living room that was comfortably furnished with deep-cushioned sofas and chairs. In one corner stood an evergreen. Several cardboard boxes were piled off to the side.

"So, what's with the bare-naked tree?" she asked.

"It's waiting for us." He sat on the edge of a large hassock and patted the space next to him. "Sit down, and let's see what we have here."

He reached for one of the boxes and opened the lid as she sat. They both peered inside, and he smiled with genuine pleasure.

"These will be just fine. Perfect. What do you think?"

"They're seashells," she said, slightly puzzled.

"Of every variety and size and color." He grinned like a small child. "Just exactly what I wanted."

"Wanted for what?" She reached for another box and opened it. More shells.

Mrs. Emmons came into the room carrying a tray with mugs of mulled wine, a huge bowl of popcorn, and an equally large bowl of cranberries. She set the tray on a table.

"Oh, yum." Athen smiled. "I love popcorn."

"That should keep you busy for a while," the woman said cheerfully. She paused on her way out of the room to ask, "Would you like dinner in the dining room or would you prefer a table in here?"

He nodded to the windowed alcove opposite the tree. "How about over there?"

"Fine," she replied and disappeared once again.

"Now, as you can see, our tree has yet to be properly dressed for the season," he told Athen. "And a tree by the ocean should be decorated with . . ."

". . . shells," she said.

"Exactly. The Emmonses' son owns a concession on the boardwalk in Ocean City. Of course, this being the dead of winter, he doesn't have too much business right now. I asked Mrs. E to get some of his shells, and Mr. E drilled holes in them. Where's that little bag with the tree hooks? Ah, there, on the table . . ."

He stood up and reached a hand to pull her along and carried a box of shells to the tree. He speared a shell with a hook from the bag and handed it to her. "As the guest of honor, you should hang the first one."

She studied the tree for a moment and placed the first shell, a pearly oyster that glistened with luminescence in the firelight, near the top.

"Beautiful," she sighed. "Now you."

They worked side by side, taking turns hanging shell after shell, until all the boxes were empty. Then they sat on the floor and strung popcorn and cranberries on long sturdy threads until Mrs. Emmons appeared to set up for dinner.

They ate Caesar salad and grilled swordfish marinated in wine and vegetables sliced into slivers barely wider than the hooks they'd used to hang the shells upon the tree. They drank wine at the little table that overlooked the ocean. For dessert, there were bowls of raspberries and cream laced with Grand Marnier, petits fours, and a pot of freshly brewed coffee. Athen felt she'd been transported magically from the life she had known to some distant place that was strange and yet somehow comfortably familiar at the same time.

Languid with food and wine, Athen tried to beg off when Quentin tossed her parka at her. "Let's take a little walk on the beach while Mrs. E cleans up."

The night air was sharply cold and fragrant with the sea, the black sky ablaze with a thousand stars. The wind kicked up off the ocean as they walked hand in hand across the dark beach, from the dune down to the surf, where the breaking waves crashed and kicked up a salty mist. Athen tilted her head back and filled her lungs, taking in as much of the night and the sea as she could.

"This is the most perfect night ever." She wrapped her arms around him and kissed the tip of his chin. "Thank you for bringing me here. I can't remember when I felt this much at peace."

"You're most welcome." He kissed her mouth, then stood back to look down into her eyes. "Do you want to go back?"

"Not right now," she replied. "Why? Do I look bored?"

"No, but your lips are like ice."

"So are yours." She laughed. "Cold lips, warm heart, right?"

"Actually, I think it's 'cold hands, warm heart.'"

"Well, whatever. My hands are cold, too. Pretty much everything is cold out here tonight." She stopped just above the waterline and tilted her head, listening. "Did you hear that? What was that?"

"Something out there, in the ocean. A fish jumping out of the water, maybe."

"Land sharks?"

"Not in winter. The water's too cold up this far north."

"Did you ever see one?"

"Only on one of those *Best of Saturday Night Live* videos," he said, and she laughed out loud.

They strolled back to the house and Athen sat on the back steps. She unlaced her low rubber boots and shook out the sand, making a small pile on the concrete walk.

The house was quiet, warm, and cozy when they went inside. Mrs. Emmons had laid several more logs on the fire, and left a carafe of wine and two crystal goblets before she went home for the evening.

"I really like this room." Athen sank to the floor in front of the fire and gazed around at the simple but comfortable furniture. Overstuffed chairs and sofas, all in peach and dark green on cream, florals and plaids and stripes, stacks of cushions and casual appointments were an invitation to sit and stay.

"We don't seem to use this room much in the summer." Quentin tossed a pillow onto the floor next to her and sat, leaning back on one elbow. "Unfortunately, no one comes down much in the winter except for Timmy and me, which is a shame, since it's so comfortable and warm. Hey, we forgot something."

"What?"

"We forgot the star." He pointed to the bare branch at the top of the tree. "Now, let's see, where did I put that?"

"You brought a star for the tree?" She lay back and rolled over on her stomach to watch him.

"Here it is." He opened a small bag and held it out to her. "Would you like to put it on the tree?"

"You do it." She leaned up on her elbows to watch as he placed the object on the tree's uppermost branch.

"Why, it's a starfish."

"Sure." He joined her on the floor and lay next to her in front of the fire. "What else would we put up there?"

"Quentin, it's perfect." She sighed happily.

"I'm glad you like it. I wanted to do something that

was just for us, something that just you and I could share. You know, we both bring a lot from the past with us. I wanted us to make memories that were only ours."

He leaned down to kiss her and she pulled him to her with a fervor that surprised them both.

Quentin raised his mouth from her neck, and picked little bits of fuzz from her sweater off his lips.

"You told me to dress warmly." She laughed, then sat up and grasped the bottom of her sweater, as if to pull it over her head. A soft blush rose to tint her cheeks as she looked into his eyes.

"That first big step always seems to be the hardest, doesn't it?" He smiled gently, sensing her hesitancy, stroking the side of her face with his fingertips. "I guess only you can decide if you want to take that step, and see where it leads us."

His quiet assurance gave her confidence, and she pulled the sweater over her head and lay back against his arm.

"*Agape mou*," he whispered. "Did I say that right?"

She nodded that he had.

"I've been rolling that word around in my head since the night you showed me the statue of your mother, waiting for the right time. I would have waited forever if I'd had to, just to be with you now."

He caressed her gently, whispering her name over and over, leading her slowly and patiently onward toward a place where they could make memories that only they would share. His hands were warm on her skin, his mouth hungry, and heat spread through her like wildfire. The pounding of her heart was so loud she was certain he could hear it when he pressed his mouth to her breast. She arched her back and closed her eyes and let herself drift on the moment. Everything faded away except Quentin.

Under his hands, her control began to slip away, and she let it go without a second thought. Her need for him consumed her, and she gave in to it, urging him inside her, falling into the rhythm and letting it guide her along to completion. Later, half asleep, she stirred in his arms, and knew she was exactly where she was meant to be.

"COME ON, SLEEPYHEAD." HE NUDGED her from a most peaceful sleep. "Wake up."

"Why?" She tried to turn over but he refused to let her bury herself in the pillow.

"Because you have the opportunity to watch the sun rise over the ocean on not only a new day, but a new year." He kissed her ear. "So get up and come outside."

"Outside?" she grumbled. "It's eighteen degrees and I'm wrapped in a blanket and you want to go outside?"

"Here." He handed her a pair of flannel pajamas and a heavy woolen robe. "These are Cait's. I'm sure she won't mind if you borrow them."

She grumbled even as she pulled the flannel over her legs and arms and wrapped herself in the robe. She followed him through the French doors opening onto the front deck. He flung a heavy blanket over the cushions of a settee and pulled her down to sit next to him.

"Better?" He pulled the ends of the blanket around her shivering form.

"A little." She snuggled next to him and fixed her eyes on the horizon as the first stray shards of light broke through the morning sky. As the minutes passed, the light spread slowly over the dark ocean, turning the brackish water into glowing greenish gray and gold beneath the mist.

"Oh, that's beautiful. Thank you for making me get up to see this."

The sky continued to unfold and the first morning of the new year spread out around them. All too soon the show ended as daylight reached the shore.

"What a lovely thing to share with me."

"It was my pleasure." He pulled her closer to snuggle. "So, did you make any New Year's resolutions?"

"A few."

"Care to share?" His fingers toyed with a strand of her hair.

"Not to make the same dumb mistakes I made last year and the year before." She shivered. "If I'd known then what I know now . . ."

"Do you regret it?" he asked. "Running for mayor?"

She paused, thinking back over the past year, all she'd done and all she'd learned. Down below, on the beach, the waves rolled onto the shore leaving a line of foam, and for a moment, she seemed mesmerized by the ocean's easy rhythm.

"I'm sorry I let Dan use me," she said finally. "I'm sorry that I will have to give the office back to him. But the truth is, I'm not the same person I was before I saw him for what he really is, before I saw the faces of the people he was hurting, and before Ms. Evelyn showed me what people could do when they work together. And besides, the woman I was before I took this job would never . . ." She paused and bit her lip.

"Would never what?" he asked quietly.

". . . would never be here with you," she said simply.

"If I have Rossi to thank for bringing you into my life, I'll give the devil his due," he whispered and drew her closer. "I've spent so many nights wondering what it would be like to wake up with you. What it would be like to share my days with you and to fall asleep next to you so that I could wake up again the next morning and find you there again. You've been in my head since the first time I saw you at the footraces in the park on the Fourth of July. Remember?"

She nodded. "You were standing so close to me, it took my breath away."

He stood and lifted her in one movement. "Next summer, I promise you, we will make love in the moonlight at least once every weekend."

"Well, since I can't wait that long, we're just going to have to make do with what we have, moonlight or no . . ."

🐾 29 🐾

"So," Meg prodded, her eyes twinkling.

"So, what?" Athen dragged her overnight bag into the hallway and left it by the bottom of the stairs.

"So how was it?"

"It was heaven." Athen sat on the step, her chin in her hand.

"Oh my." Meg laughed and plunked herself down on the next step up. "This does sound serious."

"It was wonderful. Two days of walking on the beach and lying by the fire . . ." Athen closed her eyes, as if remembering.

"Did you behave yourself?"

"No, I did not." Her eyes still closed, Athen rested against Meg's knees.

"I'm so glad." Meg sighed.

"Glad about what?" Callie skipped into the hall and sat down at her mother's feet.

"Glad that your mom had a good time," Meg replied.

"Did you?" Callie turned to her mother.

"I did. It was great," Athen assured her. "And you? How was New York?"

"Great," parroted Callie, leaning back against her mother's legs, much as her mother rested against Meg's. "We stayed at the Warwick Hotel, Mom. The Beatles used to stay there. I shared a room with Timmy's aunt Caitlin. She's a doctor in Chicago and she met us at the hotel. We saw a show at Radio City Music Hall and skated at Rockefeller Center and had room service breakfasts and ate at restaurants two times a day. Caitlin is really neat. She's Mr. Forbes's sister and she talks real fast. We ordered ice cream from room service last night and stayed up late to watch a spooky movie, and she asked a lot of questions about you."

"Like what?"

"Like what you do, that kind of stuff." Callie shrugged it off.

"What did you tell her?"

"I told her you had a job, that your job was to make sure that things were done right in Woodside Heights because you were the mayor," recited Callie. "And that this year I taught you how to plant flowers and we had a big garden and that you were a fast learner."

"Thank you, Callie." Athen rubbed her daughter's shoulders and wondered how the information had been received by Quentin's curious sister.

"Did I say something wrong?" Callie turned her earnest little face to her mother.

"Of course not." Athen kissed the top of Callie's head.

"Good." Callie grinned. "Can we go food shopping now? We have no snacks."

MY JOB IS TO MAKE sure that things are done right in *Woodside Heights,* Athen mused after she had turned off her bedroom light later that night. *Out of the mouths of babes. And to that end, I will ask Ms. Evelyn to meet me for lunch tomorrow.*

She turned over and stretched her hand out to the emptiness on the other side of the bed. She closed her eyes and wished she could open them and find herself back in the house overlooking the ocean, where the bed had never been empty and the world had not extended beyond the one she and Quentin made for each other. For just a few short days, the hours had been filled with love and warmth and a kind of peace she'd forgotten existed.

That first big step had not been so difficult after all. Now she looked forward to the rest of the journey.

"PAPA, THERE'S SOMEONE I WANT you to meet." Athen knelt before her father, her eyes sparkling, her hand holding on to Quentin's. "Papa, this is Quentin Forbes."

"Mr. Stavros." Quentin pulled a stool up to the wheelchair. "I have heard so much about you from Athen. I am honored to meet you."

"Quentin and I have been seeing a lot of each other, Papa. I wanted you to know him, and I want him to know you."

Ari's eyes softened as they went from Athen's face to Quentin's and back to rest on his daughter.

They made small talk for a few minutes, Athen reading a short story Callie had written in school for which she'd won an award. When she'd finished, Quentin suggested she take a walk down to the pond.

"I'd like a few minutes with your father, if you don't mind," he told her.

"All right." She was curious, but didn't press him. Instead, she kissed her father on the cheek and wandered off by herself.

Almost a half hour passed before Quentin joined her on the bench overlooking the pond.

"What on earth were you talking about all this time?" she asked, not happy at having been left out of the conversation for so long.

"Guy stuff." He shrugged and zipped up his jacket. "They just brought your dad lunch, or I'd still be there. It's getting nippy. How 'bout I drive you back to work before we both freeze our butts off?"

"Oh, fine." She needed no coaxing toward the warm car. "When it's your butt that's at risk, we get to leave. When it's my butt . . ."

"I'll be more than happy to warm it for you." He grinned and rubbed her bottom briskly.

"Quentin!" She laughed while trying to protest. "What if someone sees you?"

"'Mayor mauled by newsman.'" He opened her car door. "'Film at eleven' . . ."

"You're so lucky, Mrs. Moran." Veronica sighed and watched Quentin walk from Athen's office to the elevator. "I swear if my Salvatore was not the natural hunk that he is . . ."

Athen peered over the rims of her glasses, thinking how amused Quentin would be to have been compared to that "natural hunk" who was the apex of Veronica's young life.

"You want me to put this over here, by the sofa?" Veronica was carrying a tray to prepare for Athen's lunch with Ms. Evelyn. "Mr. Forbes isn't staying? You said to order three of everything."

"Ms. Bennett will here, too," Athen told her.

Thinking perhaps the occasion called for a little more political savvy than she herself possessed, Athen had, as an afterthought, called Diana to discuss her plan. As suspected, Diana agreed that Ms. Evelyn would be a perfect opponent for the Rossi forces, and had volunteered to help convince Ms. Evelyn of the fact.

"As much as I hate to see him run unopposed," Ms. Evelyn said later, after Athen had outlined her plan, "if Dan is going to build that hotel complex he announced in his press conference yesterday, he'll at least be bringing jobs into the city. I can't even offer the voters that much. The very idea of building a luxury hotel while folks are sleeping in doorways." She shook her head. "It makes me see red just to think about all those city blocks being used for some damned fool hotel instead of what the city really needs."

"What's that, Ms. Evelyn?" Diana asked.

"Well, the shelter aside, let's start with the fact that this city has no true medical center, no emergency facilities." The old woman jabbed an index finger in the air for emphasis. "And we need a community center, with a job training center and a place where folks can learn basic skills. There are folks in Woodside Heights who cannot read or do basic math. Let's do things that could help people learn to help themselves."

"I love your ideas, Ms. Evelyn, and you're exactly right. That's exactly what the city needs, but I doubt any of those things were part of the deal the Dan made with Schraeder," Diana said softly. "But the UCC does still hold the leases on the property. You could refuse to turn them back to the city."

"And be accused of blocking the jobs that would result from the development of that area?" Ms. Evelyn raised an eyebrow. "I don't think so, Diana. Tempted though I'd be, at least some folks would be working. I just don't see the point in opposing him without having anything better to offer the city."

"AND SHE'S RIGHT," A GLUM Athen told Quentin over dinner that evening. "Ms. Evelyn may be the best person to beat Rossi one on one, but he's holding all the cards. Some jobs are better than no jobs."

"What if she had something else to offer as a better choice?" Quentin asked thoughtfully.

"Something like what?" Athen frowned.

"Like the medical center, for example."

"Right, 'cause, you know, they grow on trees. Do you have any idea what that would cost?"

"Roughly." He smiled at the waitress who served their salads. "What happened at your meeting with the federal grant people?"

"Not encouraging." She shook her head. "We'd have to hire someone just to fill out the forms and complete the applications. It would be so far down the road, Rossi would have his hotel built and operational before we could even get the preliminary paperwork done."

"Hmmm . . ." He dug into his salad, lost in thought.

"What are you thinking?" she asked after he'd sat wordlessly for several minutes.

"Oh, just that if there ever was someone whose dreams should come true, it's Ms. Evelyn."

"Well, unless we can find her a fairy godmother within the next few weeks, it won't matter." Athen picked at her salad.

"A fairy godmother . . ." he repeated, his mouth sliding into a slow grin. "Yes. Exactly. A fairy godmother . . ."

ON VALENTINE'S DAY MORNING, QUENTIN showed up at her office bearing not the expected bouquet of roses or a satin encased box of chocolates, but a long cardboard tube tied with a big red bow.

"Happy Valentine's Day, sweetheart," he whispered.

"What is it?" Athen stood to examine the cylinder.

"Open it and find out."

She tugged at the rolled-up papers inside the tube, casting mystified glances in his direction. Finally, she withdrew the contents and opened them flat across the surface of her desk.

"Oh, my God!" she exclaimed when she realized what she'd unrolled. "Oh, my God . . ."

"It's something, isn't it?" He grinned.

"How did you ever get this done so quickly?" she gasped.

"Actually, I didn't. These were the plans for the medical center Caitlin wanted to build outside of Chicago, but the deal on the site she wanted fell through. So I called her and asked her if she'd consider moving her operation to Woodside Heights."

"How could she afford to do this?"

"With a generous donation from the Bradford Foundation." He rubbed her back, and found her shoulders were trembling.

"The Bradford Foundation," she repeated blankly.

"Mom controls the discretionary funds."

"Do you think she would . . . ?" Athen could barely get the words out.

"She already has," he told her, obviously pleased with himself.

"Oh, Quentin . . ." The full import of his words dawned on her. "Oh, Quentin, I truly love you . . ."

"Well, if I'd known this was what it would take to pry those words of out of you, I'd have called Caitlin sooner."

"You are unbelievable!" She all but danced gleefully into his arms. "Quentin, do you know what this means?"

"Yes." He kissed her soundly. "It means Evelyn Wallace will be the next mayor of Woodside Heights."

BY THE END OF MARCH, the campaign turned into a hotly contested race. Ms. Evelyn, to Dan Rossi's utter amazement, had found a plan that spoke to the voters in a way that he could not. Though still favored in the polls, Dan's margin was clearly eroding. Athen worked tirelessly with her candidate, vowing to do whatever was necessary to ensure a victory for the tiny woman who would save the city from itself.

Beginning to feel that a win might be possible after all, Athen spent a long weekend with Quentin at the beach house, the first time they'd been alone for more than a few hours in weeks. They walked on the beach and made love in front of the fire, and savored every minute of their forty-eight-hour respite. When they returned to Woodside Heights, they were refreshed and renewed, ready to resume the battle.

A sobbing Callie met them in the driveway.

"Mommy . . . Mommy," she choked.

"Oh, God, Callie." Athen jumped from the car and grabbed her daughter. "What's happened?"

"Mommy, Ms. Evelyn . . ." The weeping child flung herself onto her mother.

Meg rounded the side of the house.

"She had a heart attack." Meg answered the unspoken question.

"Oh, no. . . ." Athen collapsed backward onto Quentin's car, holding Callie's shaking form. "Oh, no. . . ."

"When?" Quentin asked.

"About two hours ago," Meg told them. "Riley just called from the hospital. She's hanging in there, at least for now, but apparently it doesn't look good."

"Can we go see her?" Callie sobbed.

"Not until she's stable, sweetie." Athen rubbed Callie's back.

"She's in ICU, honey," Meg told Callie. "They don't let kids under sixteen into that unit."

"What's ICU?" Callie turned and asked.

"It's the part of the hospital where they treat people who are really sick and try to make them better," Meg explained.

"But you could go, right?" Callie looked up at her mother. "You could go and see how she is and tell her . . ." Her lips began to tremble.

"Yes, we can do that." Athen looked over her daughter's head to Quentin. "We could go to the hospital and see if we can get any information."

"Will you let me know if she's all right?" Callie asked.

"Of course. You stay here with Aunt Meg, and we'll call you as soon as we know something."

Callie backed away from the car, and Quentin and Athen got back in. He drove slowly from the driveway and down to the first block, where he made a left, then took off like a rocket.

They were directed to the third-floor waiting room, where they found the Reverend Davison and Riley and Georgia Fallon. The minister had just finished leading a prayer when Quentin and Athen arrived.

"We just heard," Athen told them. "How is Ms. Evelyn doing?"

"She's holding her own right now, and that's a good sign," Riley replied. "Her daughter is in with her now. I expect as soon as she gets an update, she'll let us know."

Athen and Quentin took seats across from the others, and they all sat wrapped in their own thoughts. Quentin offered to get coffee from the cafeteria for everyone, and Riley went along with him. They had just returned and passed around the Styrofoam cups when the door to the waiting room opened and Dan Rossi came in.

"Where is Ms. Evelyn's daughter?" he asked without bothering to greet anyone in the room.

"She's in with her mother," the Reverend Davison told him.

"Has there been any word yet on Ms. Evelyn's condition?" Rossi asked with the greatest concern.

"She's coming around," the minister told him.

"Good, good." Dan nodded. "Glad to hear it."

Athen met Quentin's eyes over the top of her coffee cup.

He's such a phony jerk, she thought, and Quentin nodded as if he could read her mind.

Dan stood by the door, his hands clasped in front of him, his demeanor somber as befitted the occasion, but no one in the room doubted that his reason for being there had nothing to do with concern for the woman's health. His gaze locked on Athen's, and she saw from across the room how his eyes gleamed.

Twenty minutes later, Lily, Ms. Evelyn's daughter, came in to thank them for being there.

"Mom knows you're all here, and she said to tell you that she appreciates it and that she's going to be just fine. She's going to have to take it easy for a time, but she's going to be all right," she told them. "Unfortunately, she's going to have to give up a number of things that are most dear to her heart." She turned to Athen. "She asked me to tell you that she's so very sorry, but she's going to have to drop out of this race she's in."

"Of course she does." Athen took the woman's hands. "You tell her that the only thing we want is for her to make a full recovery. Her health is more important than anything else. We can find another candidate, but we could never replace her. You tell her that as soon as she's feeling up to it, Callie and I want to come in and visit for a while with her."

"I'll do that, Athen." Lily squeezed Athen's hands and turned to give a hug to Georgia.

Diana's description of how Dan had fled to the hospital when he'd heard Ari had suffered a stroke came suddenly to mind, and Athen knew instinctively that Dan had worn the same malevolent look of triumph then that he wore now. How fortunate for Dan that fate appeared to have intervened not once, but twice, sparing him from engaging in a final fight.

Not this time, Athen told him wordlessly as she lifted her chin defiantly, her eyes narrowing as she met his. They stared at each other openly, he silently issuing a challenge, she accepting it.

"I can't let him win, Quentin," Athen said after they left the hospital.

"No, you can't."

"And there isn't anyone else who could step in this late in the race—at least I can't think of anyone."

"There isn't anyone but you," he readily agreed. "But you do understand that Dan will come after you with everything he has, that it will be as ugly as it can get between now and the May primary?"

"I know."

"I almost wish I could cover this one," he told her.

"But you can't."

"No, but after that scene in the hospital, when I saw that Dan could not make you blink, I knew what you had to do. And I figured there might be a different job for me."

"What's that?"

"Well, you're going to need a good press secretary. Whatever I have is at your disposal—time, energy, money. Whatever you need to beat this bastard."

"I might not win, Quentin," she reminded him.

"Win or lose, we're in this together."

"Thank you."

"You don't have to thank me. We're a team, you and I. For better or for worse, right?"

"Right." She nodded.

Her life had come full circle as, one by one, she found the bits and pieces of herself that had been scattered when John died. Somehow, she'd found the strength to put those pieces back together again. In Quentin, she found all the love and joy she could ever hope for. She regained her self-confidence and found self-respect when she defied Dan.

There was great comfort in knowing that there was nothing Rossi could take from her now except her job.

"Now get on the phone and get Diana over here," Quentin was saying. "We have a lot of work to do."

Diana was an excellent choice for campaign manager. She had been with Ari through all his campaigns, and knew all the old stalwarts and all the new blood. Night after night, they worked into the wee hours, planning their strategy and making up lists of the ward leaders and committee people they would be calling on. Athen would announce her decision to run the following Wednesday, and they had many weeks' worth of work to accomplish in a very few days.

True to his word, Quentin worked around the clock on the literature and posters they'd plaster all over the city. Posters bearing the replica of the new medical center, the shelter, and the community center asked the residents to "Keep the dream alive."

Full-page ads in the local papers carried Athen's promise that the vision of a new Woodside Heights offered by Evelyn Wallace was still within reach, that her work would be carried on as a testament to her commitment. Ms. Evelyn had promised her help as soon as she was able. She'd drafted letters to the editors of all the local papers, asking the residents who'd supported her to offer that support to Athen.

Dan swiftly retaliated, dismissing Athen as no more than an opportunist who "quickly moved in to declare her candidacy before Ms. Evelyn had settled into her hospital bed, one who'd fight to hold on to her office even if it meant taking advantage of the misfortune that had befallen a woman she'd called friend."

"Think," he crooned to the TV cameras, "what a hotel, a convention center would mean to the city, of the revenue it would bring in. Think how the city could grow and prosper once the center of town had been cleared of the blighted neighborhoods."

At his rallies, he'd address wildly supporting crowds.

"Put Dan Rossi back in office, and Dan Rossi will put Woodside Heights back to work!"

"Dan Rossi means he'll put Woodside Heights back to work for him," Athen had responded. "Ask him where he was when all those jobs were leaving Woodside Heights."

"Ask Athen Moran what she's done for this city in the past two years," Rossi taunted.

"Ask Rossi what he accomplished in the previous eight," she replied calmly, then added, "I think getting a commitment from the Bradford Foundation to fund not only a badly needed medical center but a true community center and the shelter envisioned by Evelyn Wallace is a pretty big accomplishment. Not only jobs for the city, but doctors. A trauma center. Neonatal and pediatric specialists . . ."

"She's a novice," Rossi sputtered upon hearing Athen's remark. "An amateur. The hardworking taxpayers of Woodside Heights want to see this city soar, want to see this city become a mecca here in the northernmost part of the state."

"If that's what the citizens of this city truly want, that's what they'll vote for on Election Day," Athen told the reporter from the *Herald*. "They will choose. All this harping from Mr. Rossi is a smoke screen. For eight years he sat back in his chair and smoked his big cigars and watched this city fall apart. For the first time, someone is offering Woodside Heights a choice, and the choice is greater than him or me. It's an opportunity to decide the direction in which this city will grow. Until the first Tuesday in May, no one will know for certain what that choice will be. We'll all just have to wait, and we'll find out together."

"MORE WINE, MAYOR MORAN?" THE waiter offered solicitously.

"No thank you." She shook her head. "Quentin, don't you think this is odd? The entire room is deserted."

Athen surveyed their surroundings, clearly puzzled. They were, as she observed, the only diners in the small, elegantly appointed side room of Étienne's, the lavish restaurant that just months ago had opened in a lovely old mansion on a hill that overlooked the city. "Where do you suppose everyone is?"

"Probably at the polls doing their civic duty." He shrugged nonchalantly. "Besides, this is a Tuesday night, and the night of the hottest election this city has ever seen. I'm sure people will begin to filter in later."

"Maybe we ought to get back." She shifted nervously in her seat. "Maybe we ought to check the returns."

"Sweetheart, the polls don't close for another hour." He entwined his fingers with hers. "Just sit back and relax a little. We've plenty of time."

"I didn't expect to be this nervous," she confided. "I never thought a day could be as long as this one has been."

"Well, it's almost over and we'll know soon enough," he reminded her. "I think I'd like some coffee. How about you?" He signaled for the waiter.

"Quentin, I have had about ten cups past my limit." She sighed. "I'm positively wired."

"Two decafs," Quentin told the waiter.

"Quentin, I feel like I should be back at headquarters, waiting with everyone else."

"Nonsense." He moved his chair closer to hers and massaged one of her tired shoulders with his right hand. "It's going to be a long evening, and after the past few months, I think you've earned the right to relax and have a peaceful hour or two."

He leaned back as the waiter placed their cups on the table, then moved Athen's cup slightly to the side and placed a large goblet filled with raspberries and whipped cream before her.

She frowned. "I didn't order dessert."

"Étienne made it special for you, madame." The waiter beamed.

Athen managed a smile. After the waiter left the room, she told Quentin, "If I eat another bite, I'll be sick."

She passed the goblet to him. He passed it back.

"Of course you won't be sick." He smiled. "Eat your dessert. Raspberries are good for you. Superfoods, and all that. I read about it in a health magazine."

"Quentin, I don't want . . ." She protested as he lifted the spoon to her mouth. "Oh, honestly, Quentin . . ."

"Athen, you don't want to offend Étienne," He leaned forward. "He's the best chef in town."

"Oh, all right, I'll eat some of it." She shrugged. "But you have to finish it."

"Sure."

He watched closely as she dipped her spoon into the frothy cloud of whipped cream, playing with it, unconsciously raising small peaks here and there.

"You know, it's funny." She put the spoon down on the plate beneath the goblet. "The last election was just an exercise. I hadn't the faintest idea what was going on, nor did I really much care, and I won so easily. Of course, that time I was unopposed and had Rossi's backing. This time, when it means something, when there's really something at stake, it's so difficult. I want so badly to win, Quentin. Not just to beat Dan, but for Ms. Evelyn."

"She's very proud of you, just as I am," he said. "Everyone who loves you is proud of you. Not just for taking on Dan, but for the way you've conducted yourself all through this. And Dan should thank you for not throwing Mary Jo Dolan in his face."

"You know I couldn't do that."

"Weren't you even tempted, just a tiny bit?" he teased.

"Maybe a little," she conceded. "But that would make me just as bad as he is."

"You are an amazing woman." He leaned over and kissed her ear. "Now, finish that little confection and let's get going."

"Quentin, I feel like a whale," she moaned.

"Well, you haven't been eating regularly these past few weeks. At least polish off the whipped cream." He held out the spoon.

"I can see you won't be satisfied until I explode." She grimaced, taking the spoon. "Maybe if I just move it around a bit it will look as if I've eaten more than . . ."

She stopped in midsentence, her attention on the bowl of the spoon, her mouth half opened in surprise.

"May I clean that up a bit for you?" he asked softly.

Her eyes filled with tears as they moved from the spoon to his face.

She passed the spoon to him and he dipped it into his water glass, then retrieved the sparkling ring from the bottom of the glass and dried the diamond with his napkin.

"I guess having gone this far, I should go the whole nine yards." He smiled and pushed back his chair.

Her eyes never left his face, even when he dropped before her on one knee.

"Athena Stavros Moran, will you marry me?"

Still stunned and speechless, Athen sat wide-eyed, barely blinking.

He cleared his throat.

"Athen, this is no time to go mute," he told her in a mock stage whisper. "This is supposed to be a big moment."

She nodded her head slowly.

"Was that an affirmative yes, you know it's a big moment, or yes, you will marry me?' His rested an elbow on his raised knee, his eyes twinkling.

"Both." Her voice came out in a squeak. She cleared her throat and repeated, "Both."

He took her hands in his and slipped the ring on her finger. She hardly seemed to notice.

"Don't you want to see it? It's almost three karats, Athen—at least look at the damned thing," he said with a laugh.

"It's gorgeous." She leaned over to hold his face in her hands, and he kissed the trail of tears that streaked down her face. "Are you sure you want to do this? If I get elected, things could be pretty hectic."

"Nothing could be more hectic than the last few weeks have been, and yes, I'm sure I want to marry you. I've never been more certain of anything in my life. I love you more than I thought it could be possible to love anyone. Your future is my future. Whatever happens tonight, we'll celebrate together or we'll lick our wounds together. Whatever the future brings, we'll deal with it together."

She leaned over and kissed him again, the election forgotten for a few long moments. Finally, she tugged at his lapels.

"You can get up now." She laughed when she realized he was still kneeling on the carpeted floor.

"So, do you have any thoughts on when you might like to tie the knot?" He moved his chair close to hers and draped an arm around her shoulders.

"I always wanted to be a June bride," she said wistfully.

"June it is."

"That's barely a month away." Her eyes widened at the thought.

"Then I suggest we enlist my mother," he said. "She's a whiz at putting together big parties."

"What do you think the kids will say?" she wondered aloud.

"Guess there's only one way to find out." Quentin signaled for the waiter to bring their check. "By the way, you're thirty-seven votes behind with three more precincts to be counted."

"How do you now that?" Her jaw dropped.

"Diana's been texting me all night, and I've been checking every time you turned your head."

QUENTIN PULLED INTO THE DRIVE at the carriage house on the Chapman estate that had been converted into Athen's campaign headquarters and turned off the car lights. They sat in the dark for a few moments, savoring the last few minutes of calm they'd have for the next few days. He ran his fingers lightly through her hair, and she rested her back against his shoulder.

"Ready?" he asked.

"Quentin, I just want you to know that, whatever the final outcome is, I will never be able to thank you for everything you've done. I don't mean just the material you wrote or the money you raised. You always made me feel that this was as important to you as it was to me. That you believed in me."

"I do." He kissed the side of her face. "Now and always. Win or lose."

"Let's go see which it is." She took a deep breath and unfastened her seat belt, then opened her door.

They could hear the shouts before they reached the door. Mayhem greeted them as they walked into the carriage house and her jubilant supporters welcomed her wildly. The tally from the final precincts had just been announced.

Athena Moran had defeated Dan Rossi by one thousand fifty-three votes.

❧30❧

A then leaned on the top railing of the deck and watched the gulls sway in graceful circles above a serene blue sea. The morning sun danced a dazzling ballet of endless, glittering arabesques across the water for as far as the eye could see. She shaded her eyes with one hand to cut the glare and watched an osprey dive for a meal. The warming sand lay before her seductively, and she was unable to resist its lure.

Kicking off her sandals, she set off across the beach, startling a red-winged blackbird that landed on the outstretched arm of a lone scrub pine at the top of the dune. The bird took off in an agitated flurry, one short dark feather spiraling down to rest on the sand. Athen picked it up as she passed and followed the wooden boardwalk toward the shore.

She ventured a hesitant toe into the white froth of water left behind by a gentle wave. The sand at the waterline was still cold, the early summer sun not quite strong enough to have warmed the sea, and she stepped backward, her feet seeking a dry, warm spot where the low tide had not reached. A glint in the sand caught her eye. She reached down and picked it up. The sunlight radiated off the bright green piece of sea glass, and she cleaned it off so that it glowed like an emerald. She turned it over and over in her hand to study it before slipping it into the pocket of her shorts. Small bits of well-polished quartz, pink and yellow, went into her pocket as well. On her way back to the house, she kicked up the sand to reveal a cream-colored shell lined with pale pink that lay next to a small, perfect scallop shell. She added both treasures to her bulging pocket.

Halfway up the beach she plunked herself down in the sand and leaned back on her elbows, squinting as she glanced up first one side of the beach and then the other, not seeing a soul on either end. She dug her toes beneath the sand and hung her head back, her face lifted to the sky, savoring the moment's solitude and the joy of being exactly who and where she was.

There is something so primitive about being on a deserted beach, she mused, *something peaceful in lying alone on the sand with the cry of the gulls and the soft lapping of the ocean the only sounds.*

"There you are." Quentin followed the path of narrow boards. From her vantage point, he took the form of a giant striding across the sand.

"Come join me." She patted the space next to her. "Pull up some beach and sit down."

He lowered himself to the sand, waving a fat white envelope to taunt her.

"Guess what I have?" he teased smugly.

"Wedding pictures?"

"The ones Brenda took. She just emailed them to me and I printed them off." He pulled a stack of photos from the envelope and she reached for them. "Uh-uh. Not with those sandy hands. I will hold them and we can both look, but you may not touch."

"Stop teasing, Quentin, I can't wait to see." She leaned

over his shoulder. "Oh, look, your mother looks positively flustered."

"That must have been right before the wedding, when she discovered that the florist had placed the topiaries at the wrong end of the garden."

"Like anyone would have noticed. But, oh, look how beautiful everything was." She sighed as he held up the next picture.

The Chapmans' grounds had been transformed into a bower of roses for the wedding on the previous Saturday. Lydia had insisted that only a rose garden would do for the marriage of her only son, and it had taken several florists to bring her vision of clouds of roses to life. "Was there ever a more beautiful wedding?"

"Never. It was spectacular," he agreed.

"Look at my father." She leaned closer for a better look. Ari sat proudly in his wheelchair, Diana behind him, smiling happily, her hands resting on his shoulders. "Wasn't he handsome? And wasn't Diana beautiful? I'll have to have that one enlarged and framed for both of them. And Callie—oh, my, how serious you both look, Quentin. What were you talking about?"

"Callie was informing me in the gentlest possible terms that while she was in fact delighted that I was marrying her mother, I had better not be harboring any thoughts of becoming her father, because she already had one, thank you very much, even if he was dead."

"Leave it to Callie." Athen grimaced slightly. "What did you say?"

"I told her that I have great respect for her father, and I am very much aware of how close they were, and that I would never try to step into his place, but that I would always be there for her if she ever needed me."

"We should have spent more time talking to the kids about what this will mean," she thought aloud.

"I think we handled it well, before the wedding. You can't anticipate every possible scenario, but we'll handle things as situations arise."

"I guess Timmy must feel the same way." She hugged her knees. "I mean about me not being his mother."

"I don't think it's quite the same," he told her. "I don't know that he has many glowing memories of Cynthia. Timmy might like to be mothered just a little."

He shuffled through the pack of photos, Athen peering over his shoulder. Meg—a beautiful maid of honor in pale rose silk. Veronica on mile-high spikes— dyed baby blue to match her dress, natch, her hair piled skyward and freshly lacquered for the occasion—clinging to the arm of her husband, the stalwart Sal, who, all muscle, was almost as wide as he was tall. Brenda, in a yellow silk sheath, with her man of the hour, a film producer from California. Caitlin Forbes, in a green raw silk suit, her hair short and casual, her arms around her brother. Athen met her for the first time the week before the wedding, and they sat for hours talking like old friends.

"I will never forget the way you looked when you came through the doors onto the veranda." Quentin held a picture of his bride as she walked from the shadow of the house into the sunlight, stunning in a simple ankle-length dress of deep champagne lace. "I have never been so touched by a single moment as I was when I looked up and saw you walking toward me."

He seemed to struggle for a second, collecting the right words.

"It seemed right then and there that I knew what it

felt like to be reborn. That after all the pain of the past few years there was something so wonderful waiting for me." He rubbed the side of his face against hers, his voice all but a whisper. "I would have endured a thousand heartaches to have had that one moment when I knew I'd be spending the rest of my life with you."

Athen's eyes filled with tears and she sniffed quietly. She swallowed hard in hopes of gaining control of her voice.

"I feel exactly the same way. When John died, I really thought my life was over. That there would never be another truly happy moment, or a day when I would ever be filled with the sheer joy of being alive. I honestly believed that my only purpose on this earth was to raise my daughter, that there would never be a reason to laugh or feel pain or watch a sunset. No joy, no wonder, not even real pain—nothing to make me feel alive, just a dull ache inside me from the minute I opened my eyes in the morning until I closed them again at night."

"And then along came Dan Rossi," he whispered in her ear.

"How can you mention that man's name at a time like this?" She glared indignantly.

"Because he was the devil who prodded you back into the world," Quentin reminded her. "As much as I hate to admit it, it was Dan who coaxed you into taking that first step."

"I'll give him that much, the scoundrel." She leaned back against him. "It all seems so long ago now. I look back on those first days in City Hall and it seems like another lifetime."

"It was. And we have yet another lifetime to discover together."

"Funny how it worked out, isn't it?" she asked, drawing circles in the sand with one finger. "You coming east when you did to take the job with Hughes's paper, me being in City Hall . . ."

"Everything that happened before was leading me here." He kissed her. "To this moment, to this place."

He studied the circles she had drawn, then kissed the top of her head and stood up. She watched him walk across the sand. He was looking down, as if searching for something. He picked up a large clamshell, then began drawing something in the sand about ten feet from where they sat. Amused, she stood to watch him, and then walked closer.

"Watch where you step," he told her. "You're standing on the *S*."

"What *S*?" She backed up and looked down at the markings on the sand.

"There you go." He stood back to admire his work, placing the shell in his pocket.

QUENTIN LOVES ATHEN

They both laughed, and she draped her arms around his neck.

"And I love you." She kissed him soundly on the mouth. "With all my heart."

"Ah, that's what's missing." He pulled the shell out of his pocket and leaned over, enclosing his message inside two swooping arches.

"What do you think?"

"I think it's perfect," she told him. "As perfect as this morning, as perfect as this week has been."

"And as perfect as the rest of the day will be. Let's go upstairs and open up those doors." He pointed to the French doors off their bedroom balcony. "And let the sun and sea air into our room and take an early siesta."

"What will Mrs. Emmons think?" She nudged him as they walked clumsily, their hips and shoulders gently colliding from time to time as their feet sunk into the sand.

"We're sending Mrs. Emmons to Manasquan to do some shopping and as many other errands as we can come up with."

"Good idea."

"I forgot the wedding pictures." He sprinted across the dunes to where he'd left the envelope on the sand.

Athen climbed the steps and stood at the railing, watching Quentin walk toward her, a smile of deep contentment on his face. They would have today and the rest of the week to enjoy each other before returning to Woodside Heights and its turmoil, before taking the first steps into the unknown waters of stepparenting and blending their families into one, before she would face the many problems of her city and the battles that still awaited her there.

For now, it was enough that they were here and alone, and that they had these days. Behind Quentin on the sand she could see the outline of the heart he had drawn. The message it held told her all she needed to know.